'Everything a reade̶ ̶ ̶ ̶ ̶ ̶ ̶ ̶ ̶ ̶ ̶ ̶ ̶sh for. It's brilliant. Read it!' *Ban̶ ̶ ̶ ̶ronicle (For Better, For Worse)*

'If you enjoy Cookson you will love this.' *Bradford Telegraph and Argus (Legacy of Shame)*

'Strong characters and a persuasive storyline make this a memorable tale.' *Coventry Evening Telegraph (Tina)*

'A stirring tale rich in heartache and warmth with an unquenchable zest for life.' *Northern Echo (Gift of Love)*

'An unforgettable story of love and heartache.' *Dundee Courier (Lost Dreams)*

'A rich and rewarding tale.' *Bolton Evening News (A Woman of Spirit)*

'Packed with atmosphere and strong characters. A good read.' *Newcastle Evening Chronicle (A Woman of Spirit).*

About the Author

Nora Kay was born in Northumberland but she and her husband lived for many years in Dundee. They now live in Aberdeen.

NORA KAY

Fall From Grace

coronet

CORONET BOOKS
Hodder & Stoughton

First published in Great Britain in 2002 by Hodder and Stoughton
First published in Great Britain in paperback in 2002
by Hodder and Stoughton
A division of Hodder Headline
A Coronet Paperback

2

A CIP catalogue record for this title is available
from the British Library

ISBN 978-0-340-81870-1

Typeset in Centaur by Palimpsest Book Production Limited,
Polmont, Stirlingshire
Printed and bound in Great Britain by
Clays Ltd, St Ives PLC

Hodder and Stoughton
A division of Hodder Headline
338 Euston Road
London NW1 3BH

For Bill and Raymond

Chapter One

It was the sound of the car stopping that made Felicity Morrison raise her head. Getting up from her knees she removed her gardening gloves, straightened her skirt and walked quickly down the drive. There was a surprised but welcoming smile on her face. Tim wasn't alone, he had brought someone home.

'Hello, dear.'

There was no answering smile. 'Felicity, give me a hand with these, will you?'

'Of course.'

The young man, a stranger to her, was taking cardboard boxes from the boot of the car. He looked up briefly, gave Felicity an uncertain smile, then carried on. When the boot was emptied and the boxes on the pavement, he looked to Tim as though for instructions.

'Take that lot up to the front door and leave them there. Then you had better get on your way,' he said curtly.

Felicity felt embarrassed. Surely there was no need

for that tone of voice. Giving Tim a questioning look which he ignored, she went ahead with two of the smaller boxes. The front door was wide open, it usually was when the day was sunny and warm, and after putting her load inside the vestibule she went back.

'My briefcase, take it with you,' Tim said handing it over. It was bulging with papers.

'Tim,' she began.

'Not now.' When the pavement was cleared he turned to his helper. 'Thanks,' he said.

The young man nodded but it was obvious he was uncomfortable and anxious to get away. The car door shut and a moment later the car moved off.

This was becoming more puzzling by the minute. 'Where is he going with your car?' Felicity asked.

Tim didn't answer and they walked in silence up to the front door, Felicity with Tim's briefcase and he with an armful of folders. The briefcase was heavy and Felicity was glad to put it down beside the boxes.

'Tim, what is going on?'

'You'll know soon enough,' her husband said grimly. 'Meantime I suggest you help me carry these to the foot of the stairs. They can remain there for the time being.'

In a short time they had the boxes neatly stacked.

'What now?' she said, straightening up and looking at him.

'Nothing more for you to do, but before I take these to my study I need a drink, a stiff drink, and I suggest you have one as well.'

If Felicity was uneasy before she was scared now.

'Stop this, Tim, and tell me what has happened. Tell me now, this minute,' she said her voice rising.

'Something has happened, you're right about that,' he said going along to the sitting-room. Felicity followed. Tim went straight to the drinks cabinet and taking out the whisky bottle poured himself a generous measure.

'What can I get you?'

'Nothing, thank you.'

'Sure?'

'Quite sure.' A cup of tea would have been very welcome but it would take too long to make.

'Then I suggest you sit down.'

She did. This was unbearable. Felicity swallowed nervously and clasped her hands together to stop them from shaking. With every passing moment she was becoming more fearful and angry too. It was cruel of Tim to do this – keeping her in suspense. Was it so awful that he was afraid to tell her? She shivered.

Tim took his whisky with him and sat down in the deep leather armchair. First he swallowed more of the amber liquid then put the glass down on the rosewood table close to a bowl filled with fresh flowers picked that morning from the garden.

'As from today,' he said slowly, 'I am out of a job.'

She stared at him. He had to be joking, though it didn't look or sound like it.

'You have to be joking.'

'I only wish I were.'

'Why are you home at this time of day and with

3

half the office with you?' She wasn't going to take him seriously.

'I've just told you. My employment with Paton & Noble ceases as from today.'

'Tim, none of this is making sense. You are a lawyer, a good one. Why would Paton & Noble want to terminate your employment?'

'Because, my dear, certain irregularities have come to light,' he said very quietly.

'That can't have anything to do with you.'

'I'm afraid it has.'

'No, Tim, I won't believe this.' Her eyes widened in shock. 'No, not you, you wouldn't.' She was shaking her head and pleading with her eyes, yet knowing from the look on his face that he wasn't going to deny it. 'Why? Just tell me why?' she said spreading her hands.

'What I did wasn't stealing, Felicity.'

'No? What would you call it then?'

'Borrowing. It goes on all the time.'

'I find that hard to believe.'

'Believe it or not as you wish but I can assure you it does. I was unlucky, things happened too quickly and I wasn't prepared.'

It was early afternoon and the bright June sunshine was streaming in the window making the crystal vase on top of the china cabinet sparkle. The day was warm and Felicity wore a thin cotton skirt in a floral pattern with a short-sleeved white blouse open at the neck. Her long, slim, bare legs were tanned to a golden brown and on her feet she wore an old pair of Scholl's sandals. The day hadn't suddenly turned cold but she had. Felicity wrapped her arms around herself and waited for her husband to go on. He was taking his time.

'I don't intend going into the details,' he said at last. 'Suffice it to say I needed a fairly large sum of money quickly.'

'How much? What does a large sum mean?'

He carried on as though she hadn't spoken. 'The money would have been' – he appeared to be searching for a word – 'returned if only things hadn't happened so quickly.'

She could guess what that meant. Felicity hadn't been married to a solicitor for twenty years without learning something. It did happen but never to a law firm like Paton & Noble.

'You were using a client's money,' she said accusingly.

'A temporary loan, Felicity, I keep telling you,' Tim said from between clenched teeth.

'There are other ways of getting a loan.'

'And paying through the nose. No thank you.'

'Better paying through the nose than losing your job I would have thought.'

'True, but I never expected this to happen. We are all wise after the event.'

Felicity moistened her lips. 'Did some poor old soul catch you out by passing away without giving you time to juggle with—' her voice broke and she put her hand to her mouth.

He shrugged, reached for the whisky and drained the glass. 'Something like that,' he said.

'Tim, I am trying very hard to keep calm but I am not making sense of this. What you haven't explained to me is why you should want a large sum of money.'

He sighed and remained silent.

'Tim, if you are in trouble I need to know about it.'

When he still remained silent she felt anger boiling up.

'This doesn't just concern you, it also concerns your wife and daughter.'

'I'm aware of that.'

She swallowed. 'Where has the money gone? What have you been doing? We enjoy a good standard of living but we don't live beyond our means.'

'Are you sure?'

'I am very sure.'

'You have your own car, a beautiful home and you and Joanna don't want for anything.'

The unfairness of it almost rendered her speechless.

'Tim, you have a very convenient memory. My car, since you brought that up, was bought to replace the old banger I had been driving for years and came out of the money Aunt Jean left me. And let me add that the little I earn from my illustrations keeps the car on the road.' She didn't add, not wanting him to know, that what was left went into her own bank account. There was something reassuring about having a few pounds in one's own name. It wouldn't go far but it gave her a little independence. A thought came to her. 'Your car—'

6

'That's gone.'

'I see.' She looked about her at the tastefully furnished room remembering the time and care spent on the house to have it looking as it now did. 'The house, will it have to go?'

'We can't stay here, we will have to move.'

Felicity took a deep, shaky breath. 'Maybe, Tim, you could get your job back . . .'

'Not a chance, not a hope in hell.'

'Don't give up so easily. Listen,' Felicity said urgently, 'you've worked very hard, long hours, ridiculously long hours and you've brought work home with you. All that should be—'

'Taken into consideration. I made that point myself and it didn't do me any good.'

'What you did was very wrong and it is small wonder that everybody is shocked and disappointed.'

'Don't preach, for God's sake.'

'I wasn't but it is better to face the truth.' She worried her lower lip. 'There has to be a way of you getting your job back.'

'There isn't.'

'You seem very sure.'

'I am.'

'Well, I'm not. I'm trying to be supportive, Tim, but it isn't easy when you are not being open.'

'I made a mistake, I'm paying for it, leave it at that.'

'We are paying for it,' she corrected him.

'If you want to be supportive then think about

7

getting yourself a job, a proper job I mean, not fiddling about with little drawings that nobody wants.'

Felicity felt outraged that her illustrations should be treated with such contempt but she kept her temper under control.

'I'll start looking at the jobs vacant columns in the newspaper. Who knows, they may actually have something I could apply for.'

He smiled. 'No need to take up that attitude, it was merely a suggestion but if you don't want to help out—'

'I do.' Her eyes filled.

'I'm sorry and I'm afraid I haven't told you everything.'

'What do you mean?'

'Paton & Noble are going to make a case of it.'

'A case of it,' Felicity repeated stupidly.

'A court case,' he said bitterly, 'I could go to jail.' Getting up abruptly he refilled his glass and she saw that his hand was shaking.

A look of horror crossed Felicity's face. 'No, Tim, she whispered, 'not that, please not that.'

'Better that you should be prepared.'

Until then Felicity had felt mostly anger and disbelief. It was seeing his hand shake that brought a rush of pity. Tim had been foolish, criminally foolish, but she was his wife. He would need her now as he never had before and he wouldn't find her wanting. She would stand by him.

'Tim,' she said softly, 'we'll get through this. And

don't worry too much about Joanna, she is a sensible girl—'

He looked up sharply. 'There is no need for Joanna to know anything.'

'I don't see how we can keep it from her.'

'She doesn't have to know *now* is what I meant.'

Their daughter, Joanna, was a first-year student at Edinburgh University and that was far enough away from her home in Hillhead, a village a few miles from Dundee, to make only the occasional visit to see her parents.

Felicity was smiling. 'No, you are absolutely right. This will all blow over. Heavens above, Ralph Knight wouldn't do that to you.'

'He has.'

'That would be to give you a fright and make sure the seriousness of the matter was brought home to you.'

'Don't be ridiculous.'

Why did he always manage to make her feel foolish?

'Ralph is a friend, a friend of both of us,' she said defensively.

'Past tense. Our so-called friend was at pains to explain that the matter is out of his hands.'

Another door closing.

'Have you been gambling, is that it?' Felicity shook her head vigorously and answered her own question. 'No, that can't be it. I've never known you to take any interest in gambling. Heavens! You don't even have a bet on the Derby.'

'Very true but for everything there is a first time, Felicity.' When lying, he told himself, it was safer to stay within the shadow of truth. She was off on the wrong track but in a sense it had been a gamble and he'd lost. Playing around with a client's money wasn't as easy as it had at first appeared.

So that was it, Tim had been gambling. It was hard to believe but he had admitted it himself. She watched him get up.

'I'm going up to my study and I would be grateful, Felicity, if I was not disturbed.'

'That's all right, Tim, I won't disturb you,' Felicity said quietly.

Sitting crouched in the chair, Felicity wished she had someone to confide in. A close relation, perhaps, but she had no one, no sister, no brother. Her father was a blurred memory of a kindly man who had sat her on his knees and told her stories and at other times had held her high up until she was squealing half in fright and half in excitement. Then the noise would have brought her mother through from the kitchen to scold him but she would be laughing. If only her mother were here now and she should have been, Felicity thought with the familiar ache. When it was only a slight discomfort she should have gone to see about it, not waited until she was in agony and it was too late to operate. From then on it had been downhill and in six weeks her darling mother was dead. That had been fourteen months ago yet the pain was still there, dulled but still very much there.

Felicity dragged herself back to the present and her worries. Tim made all the decisions, always had. She was seldom consulted about anything, her agreement taken for granted. Why hadn't she asserted herself before this and demanded her say? She could only answer that by saying it hadn't seemed to be important, not in the early days. Tim, clever Tim, would see to everything while she put all her energies into keeping the house the way it should be kept. That and seeing to her husband's needs as well as her daughter's and when necessary acting as the charming hostess.

She had been happy with her life and any spare time she had was spent working on her illustrations. Tim had always been slightly mocking about her funny little drawings as he called them but she didn't let that bother her. Any small success she had was kept to herself. Felicity had done well at art school and at one time had dreamed of success in the art world. That had all changed when tall, handsome Timothy Morrison had walked into her life. Her friends had envied her. Six years older than Felicity, Tim had qualified as a lawyer gaining distinction and great things were expected of him. She thought herself so very, very lucky. Tim was everything she could have asked and more. As well as his good looks he had great charm. Only later did the little flaws appear. He could be very selfish and he could be jealous. It would anger him if he thought her over-friendly with a colleague and accuse her of flirting. It would appear to be all right for him to flirt with a pretty secretary at the Christmas party or some other function. Felicity never felt threatened. It all ended when the party finished and it was time to go home.

Chapter Two

Tim went slowly upstairs and before going into his study went into their bedroom. The window was open and a light breeze was blowing the curtains. He took off his jacket and put it over the back of the basket chair. Then he loosened and removed his tie and undid the top button of his shirt. It was a relief to get the pressure away from his neck. Felicity, he knew, would give him a hand with the boxes if he asked but he wouldn't. It would mean more talk and he couldn't face any more of that. Better to bring the stuff upstairs now then he could close the study door and be alone.

It had been exhausting carrying the boxes upstairs. Tim wasn't used to manual work but he found the physical effort helped to keep his mind off his troubles. When the task was completed he shut himself in the study and sat down behind his desk. The clutter was now in front of him which offended his eye. In a while when he could face it, he would have to sort through the papers and decide what should be kept and what could safely be thrown away. Some of the files should have been left behind in the office and he would have to find some way of returning them. Given more time it wouldn't have happened. The speed of his departure, the unnecessary haste to get him off the premises, had been humiliating and deeply wounding.

Timothy Morrison groaned out loud and dropped his head in his hands. There was no escape from this nightmare. He only had to close his eyes and he was reliving the scene in Ralph Knight's office. They had always got on well, he and Ralph, and there had been a small hope that his lapse would cost him no more than a severe reprimand. The matter would be left for the senior partner to deal with in his own way.

That way became clear the moment Tim stepped into Ralph Knight's office and he saw his superior's expression. All hope of clemency faded. Worry was etched on the older man's face but so, too, was disgust.

'Ralph, believe me, I am desperately sorry.'

'Are you? I wonder. Sorry you have been found out would be nearer the truth,' Ralph Knight said harshly. A hand waved him to a seat. Tim sat down.

'I've been all kinds of a fool.'

'You've been a damned fool and a whole lot worse.'

Both men were dressed in the obligatory dark suit and white shirt and on their feet each wore well-polished, black leather shoes. Ralph Knight was a small stout man with bushy eyebrows and around the eyes he was heavily wrinkled.

Tim, sitting opposite, looked shaken and apprehensive. He should have known that Ralph would take a very serious view. He was, after all, an Elder and a pillar of the church. They were nearly always the most unforgiving, he thought sourly.

'Ralph, I can only repeat that I very much regret what has happened.'

'You used your position of trust for your own ends. I was about to say that you are no better than a common thief but in my book you are worse.'

Tim flushed. 'None of us is perfect,' he mumbled.

'True, but few of us stoop that low.'

'No second chance?'

'Did you expect one?'

He shrugged. 'I haven't spared myself as you know. I've worked very hard for Paton & Noble and I hoped, I still hope, that it would be taken into consideration.'

'You were well paid for the work you did.' He paused and Tim flinched at the cold contempt in the light blue eyes. 'Unless I am very much mistaken this shocking business is going to cost the firm a few clients. Our reputation will suffer and that, I may tell you, I find more distressing than anything else. As for you, Tim, I have absolutely no sympathy, none whatsoever, you knew what you were doing.' He paused and looked long and hard at the younger man. 'It will be up to the court to decide your punishment.'

Tim's handsome face turned a sickly white and his stomach clenched with fear. The threat had always been there but he hadn't believed, not for a single moment,

that they would take it that far. Not for his sake but
to protect the good name of Paton & Noble, that old
established and prestigious firm of solicitors.

'Why take it to court,' he said shakily, 'when that
can only damage the firm?'

'Too many people already know or suspect and that
in the long run could be more damaging. We have to
be seen to get rid of the bad apple.'

'For God's sake, one mistake. You wouldn't do
that – you couldn't do that to me?' He was almost
spluttering.

'It is out of my hands.'

'You are the senior partner, you make the decisions.'

'I do and as the senior partner I did my duty as
I saw it.'

Which meant, Tim thought despairingly, he hadn't
raised a finger to help.

'My sympathy goes out to your wife and daughter.
I am very sorry that Felicity and Joanna are to suffer.'
Ralph knew that Joanna was finishing her first year
at Edinburgh University and he just hoped that this
wouldn't jeopardise her chance of graduating. With a
need to end this here and now, Ralph got to his feet
and Tim felt obliged to do the same.

'You are finished here, Tim, and all that remains
for you to do is clear your desk and hand over your
car keys.'

'Surely – I mean, I need the car,' Tim said desperately.

'You don't, one of the clerks will drive you home.'

It was the final humiliation and Tim's face went a dull red. He couldn't fail to notice that rumours were circulating among the clerical staff, not a lot missed that bunch and now this would give substance to the rumours. As if that mattered – in a short time everybody would know. Tim almost stumbled from the room.

When he had gone, Ralph Knight sat down heavily and taking a folded white handkerchief from his pocket, mopped his brow. The whole, unpleasant business had taken its toll on him. Retirement had never looked more inviting. In all his years with Paton & Noble nothing like this had ever happened before. What, Ralph wondered, made a man do something like that. Was it greed or more likely in Tim's case, had he got himself into some kind of trouble? He shook his head in perplexity. Such a waste. Timothy Morrison had appeared to have everything going for him. He had a good brain, handsome looks and a tall, athletic figure. His ready smile and that ease of manner never failed to charm his female clients. What would those same ladies think of him when it all came out?

In marriage he had chosen well. Felicity was a lovely woman with thick, blue-black hair and wonderful eyes. There was a warmth about her smile and it was for everybody. Ralph Knight was happily married to Lily, had never strayed, never wanted to, but that didn't stop him from admiring a lovely woman. Joanna was very like her mother in appearance and from all accounts she was enjoying university and the freedom of living away from home. Too much freedom for our young wasn't such a good idea, he often thought. This was 1965, the middle of the swinging sixties they were calling it. Today's youngsters were pulling away, no longer willing to listen to the voice of experience. The 'we know what is best for you' ignored or ridiculed. Even the tinies were taking advantage. Children needed freedom to develop so said the experts and climbing on and over furniture was no longer frowned upon by young parents. Grandparents suffered in silence rather than risk being called old-fashioned. The price to pay if the visits were to continue.

Tim drew his hand across his tired eyes as though to rid himself of that scene with Ralph Knight. The wonderful career he had mapped out for himself was over. The dream of one day occupying the senior partner's chair, shattered and gone. This would all be lost too, he thought, looking about him. When he had declared his intention of making the best bedroom – the master bedroom had been the description in the house details – his study, Felicity had tried to talk him out of it but his mind was already made up. The size of room was just right and it had the added advantage of being square-shaped. Tim was picturing the handsome desk and leather chair which had once belonged to his father and used by his mother, positioned to get maximum light from the double window. The walls would lend themselves to sturdy fitted shelves for his many books and files. A bedroom on the other hand was merely for sleeping in and provided there was enough space and there was to take a double bed and the essential furniture, that was all that was required. Holmlea, the name given to the house by the previous owner, had five bedrooms, four since one was now a study. The guest room and Joanna's bedroom were similar in size and the smallest, which could only take a single bed, became a boxroom. Felicity had thought about making it her own, a place to work on her illustrations instead of making do with the kitchen table, but it had never come to anything.

Downstairs, Felicity couldn't settle to anything and kept wandering about the kitchen like someone in a daze. She was forever lifting things up then putting them down again. Her brain was working but kept jumping from one thing to another. What would they do now that Tim had lost his job? How would they manage? Where would they live? With no reference how would Tim get another job? Who would employ him? A voice dug up from long ago answered her question. She remembered Tim saying in happier times how a good lawyer need never be without a job. There were always those shady concerns willing to turn a blind eye to any wrongdoing. In return they had that person's considerable expertise to use as they wished. Tim's fall from grace needn't hold him back, not with his grasp of the law. Felicity went cold with dread. Would desperation make Tim go down that road? Her throat went dry and she crossed to the sink to fill the kettle, then stood watching as though that would help it come to the boil all the sooner. After she made the tea she wondered if she should take a cup up to Tim then decided against it. He might not thank her for it. Sitting down at the kitchen table she nursed the cup and began to take little sips from it.

This was the day she took the car and did her weekly shopping in Dundee. There was still time but she wouldn't do it. They would have to make do with what was in the house. The remains of the cold ham served with lettuce and tomato and fried potatoes would take very little time to prepare. The lettuce would be limp though the heart might not be too bad. How nice to pop out of the back door and pull a fresh one from the garden. She had wanted a small vegetable garden but Tim had not been in favour. He thought it would be untidy as well as unnecessary. Most of what was grown would be surplus to requirements and end up being given to neighbours or left to rot. Far better to buy what she needed.

At six thirty Felicity put out the place mats on the dining-room table and arranged the cutlery. At seven o'clock when the fried potatoes were turning a golden brown, she went to the foot of the stairs and shouted to Tim that the meal was ready. Maybe he hadn't heard her voice through the thickness of the study door and she went up. When she was halfway there the study door opened.

'I thought you hadn't heard me,' she said turning round and going down again. He grunted something.

Felicity served the meal and for the first few minutes there was silence apart from the ticking of the clock which seemed louder than usual. Neither of them finished what was on their plate.

'Nothing else for me, just coffee,' Tim said getting up.

'I'll bring it through to the sitting-room.' She cleared the dining-room table, put everything away in its place then collected the coffee pot from the kitchen and joined Tim. The cups and saucers were already on the small table with a small bowl of brown sugar and a jug of milk. They both preferred milk to cream.

'Thanks,' he said when she handed him a cup.

'Tim, we need to talk.'

'Yes, I suppose we do.'

She swallowed. 'How soon before the case—'

'Comes to court? Hard to tell. With some there is a long delay while others,' he shrugged, 'perhaps two or three months.'

'If it should be a hefty fine will your mother help?'

'Felicity, you don't seem to understand or you are refusing to do so. There is a strong possibility that I could go to prison.'

She raised scared eyes. 'No, Tim, it won't come to that.'

'I wish I could believe that.'

'Joanna, what is this going to do to her?' she whispered. 'How do we tell her?'

'We don't.'

'She will have to know some time.'

'Some time in the future. I told you all this before.'

'I know, but what if she finds out? There is bound to be talk.'

'Hereabout yes but she isn't likely to hear anything in Edinburgh.'

Felicity was shaking her head. 'The risk is there, I would rather she heard it from us.'

'So she shall when I consider the time is right. Why distress Joanna now? She can go on enjoying herself or is it that you would rather she was made miserable now?'

'Of course not.' Why did he always put her in the wrong or make it look as though she were?

Somehow Felicity got through the rest of the evening. Tim had returned to his study and she ironed two shirts and a blouse. The rest were damp enough to be left until the morning when she might feel more like doing them. She put the iron on its heel to cool and after folding the ironing board put it away in the cupboard under the stairs.

When eleven o'clock struck Tim came downstairs. Felicity thought he looked terrible but didn't say so. They each drank a cup of tea and ate a Rich Tea biscuit. When Tim suggested he should sleep in Joanna's bedroom Felicity merely nodded. Sleep wouldn't come easily but in separate rooms they could toss and turn without disturbing the other. If this was to go on for more than a night or two Felicity decided she would make up the bed in the guest room. Joanna might arrive unexpectedly and not take too kindly to finding that her room had been occupied. She would wonder why her parents had ceased to share a bedroom.

Felicity thought she should keep as much to routine as possible though there would be nothing to hurry for in the morning. She set the breakfast table with the blue and white china and put out a clean white napkin for Tim. That done she put the empty milk bottles on the back step ready for the milkman. Tim usually saw to the locking up but he must have forgotten. Felicity checked that both front and back doors were securely locked and all the downstairs windows shut. With that taken care of she climbed the stairs and went into the bedroom where she was to sleep alone. After undressing she slipped a nightdress over her head and got into bed. She lay on her own side of the bed and prayed that sleep would come quickly. It didn't and, throwing back the covers, she got out of bed and padded over to the window. Opening the curtains a few inches she pressed her forehead against the cold pane and gazed out at the night. All was still, not a thing moved. She shivered and wondered why it was that everything seemed so much worse at night. Was it the combination of darkness and silence? Closing the curtains she went back to bed. Sleep did eventually claim her but it was a disturbed sleep. In her dreams she could only watch as her husband was being led away, not handcuffed, he had been spared that indignity, but sandwiched between two burly policemen. The van with Tim in it sped away and she, still in her nightdress, waved to the departing vehicle.

When Felicity awoke she was bathed in sweat. Although far from rested she didn't want to stay in bed any longer. Better to be up and doing something, that was the trick, keep busy, keep occupied with no time to think. She dressed in the clothes she had worn the previous day and went down to prepare the breakfast. Only at the weekend did they have a cooked breakfast. During the week it was a small glass of orange juice and a cereal followed by tea and toast. When Tim appeared at his usual time he was shaved and dressed as he would have been going into the office. She didn't remark thinking it better not to.

'Might as well carry on the pretence for a while,' he smiled and Felicity marvelled that with this hanging over his head, he could still manage to look much as usual.

She put the toast rack on the table and Tim sat down. Taking the napkin from its ring – a ring with the initial T on it – he placed it over his knees. Lifting up the glass he drank the orange juice then began to help himself to cereal from the packet.

'Most of this is dross.'

'I know. Yesterday was my day for a big shopping. I must do it today.'

'You can't mean you are intending going into Dundee?'

'I do.'

'That's out of the question, Felicity. In case it has escaped your memory I have no car.'

She looked at him but said nothing. Instead she

spread her toast with home-made marmalade and waited to hear what more he had to say.

'I thought of going to Carnoustie and paying Mother a visit.'

'In that case I'll come with you. Carnoustie is quite good for shops.'

He shook his head. 'No, I don't think that would be a good idea.'

'What wouldn't be a good idea?'

'You coming to Carnoustie. Telling Mother about my troubles is something I would prefer to do on my own.'

She nodded. Felicity could understand that. 'Fair enough if that is what you want.' She paused. 'Any time of day will do for Carnoustie, Tim, and since you don't want me to accompany you I'll do my shopping this morning and you can have the car in the afternoon.'

'That doesn't suit me.'

'Why not?'

'Never mind why not. For heaven's sake, Felicity, don't be so disobliging. We do have a few local shops, why can't you shop there?'

'For the simple reason there is very little choice and you are not long in complaining if the food isn't to your satisfaction.' Felicity took a deep breath. This was out of character for her. She couldn't recall a time when she had stood up to Tim. When they were first married she had just accepted that her husband knew best and when she decided he didn't always know best it didn't seem worth arguing the point and having to put up with a husband in a difficult mood.

'I see you are determined to have your own way in this, so all right I'll go to Mother's immediately after lunch.'

Felicity was taken aback, she hadn't expected it to be that easy.

'We can have an early lunch,' she said not wanting to be thought of as disobliging.

'The fact is I must have my own transport and in the present circumstances we shall have to go back to being a one-car family. My suggestion, Felicity, is that we trade in yours for something bigger.'

Her mouth opened but no sound came and she closed it again.

'The future is so uncertain that we will have to go carefully. And I – we have to face it that I may be out of circulation for a while. If I am sent to—'

'Don't say it,' she said sharply.

'Not saying it isn't going to help.'

'I know that, Tim, but talking about it, about the possibility that you may have to go away, brings it nearer and I – I just don't know how I am going to cope.'

He made no attempt to comfort her, instead he gave his usual shrug and said, 'You'll have to. I'm pleading guilty, no point in doing anything else so I can expect—'

'How long?' she said fearfully.

'Anything from six months to two years. They might want to make an example of me which would mean the maximum. In a case like mine a lot depends on the mood of the judge.'

'How can you be so calm and matter-of-fact?'

'Would you rather I went to pieces? I'm anything but calm, but if that is how I look then fine. My best course of action is to show plenty of remorse for my sins and assure the learned gentleman that it was a loan which, but for circumstances, would have been repaid in full.'

'No, Tim, don't say that. It may be the truth but it doesn't sound good.'

He looked thoughtful then smiled. 'You could be right. Deep remorse will be best and leave it at that.'

'Don't you feel shame for what you did?'

'I regret what I did.'

'That doesn't answer my question.'

'Truthfully I don't feel shame, no one was losing out.'

'If you gambled the money how were you going to repay it? Oh, I see,' she said bitterly, 'another client would be owed money – it was just a question of moving it around and being clever.' She bit her lip and fell silent for a moment or two. 'Tim, I don't think I am accepting that the money did go on gambling.'

She thought he looked startled then scared. The laugh was forced.

'That imagination of yours is working overtime.'

'No, I don't think so. It doesn't ring true. I believe you are in some kind of serious trouble and you are afraid to tell me what it is.'

'This is too silly for words and not worth answering. We'll get back to what we were talking about. Trading your car in is by far the most sensible thing to do.'

'For you, not for me. Tim, this is one occasion when I am not giving in to you,' she said quietly and firmly. The nerve of him, she thought, it was his dishonesty that had got them into this mess and here he was making his selfish demands. She was going to hold firm and if she did feel some shame for making such an issue of it, it wasn't strong enough to make her change her mind. It had never been more important to hang on to what was hers. She likened the situation to a time when she was very small and in danger of losing a favourite toy to a much bigger child. Sheer determination to hang on to what was hers won the day. Determination and flying feet. Kicking was naughty and not to be tolerated and Felicity had been severely scolded. Yet later she had heard her mother positively bragging about the incident saying that it proved her daughter was not to be scared off by someone bigger and stronger. She had used her feet because there was nothing else. Funny how she should be remembering that now.

'I wouldn't have believed you could be so selfish, Felicity. What was all that about you going to stand by me?'

'Of course I am. There was never any question about that.'

'Then try to be reasonable. A car is a necessity for me but not for you. You don't really need one. Nice for you to have your own transport, I was all for it when things were normal but now they are not.' He paused. 'Shopping and meeting your friends for a natter is about all you do. If you asked I am sure one of your friends or a neighbour would take you shopping.'

'I have no intention of asking anyone.' She didn't add that very soon, or so she imagined, she would be hiding away rather than having to face their pitying looks. The thought of what might lie ahead made her feel sick inside. 'I haven't asked but do we have any money?'

'Very little and it wouldn't do for me to be seen splashing out on a new car. Different if it was just you trading yours in. However, since you are not going to help, Mother might.'

'I thought you didn't want that.'

'I don't but since my wife is going out of her way to be awkward I may have no choice.'

Felicity thought about her mother-in-law, she liked the woman. They got on well though she wouldn't have described their relationship as close. Maud Morrison had a fierce independence and Felicity admired her for it. Now that she had difficulty getting about and was becoming forgetful there had been a suggestion from Tim, backed by her doctor, that she should consider selling her house and going into one of the comfortable nursing homes springing up all over the country where she would be looked after. She was well able to pay.

Felicity had been there when Maud Morrison showed what she thought of that suggestion. She would leave her house, she said, when she was good and ready and that would be when she was in her box. There was no mention of a nursing home after that. A kindly, middle-aged woman was engaged to come in for two hours every morning except Sunday. She would be a replacement and an improvement on the previous woman who had taken on several cleaning jobs none of which was done in a satisfactory manner. The new cleaning lady was called Mrs Haggarty and she proved to be a good, conscientious worker who kept everything clean and tidy. She was also completely trustworthy as was shown by the coins and items of jewellery left lying about on various surfaces. She was also prepared to cook a meal or do shopping. The neighbours were helpful and took turns at going around in the evening to see that all was well with the old lady. Maud Morrison had much to be thankful for and knew it.

Felicity had always been slightly in awe of her mother-in-law and her brusque manner but not now. Failing health had brought out a gentler side. Felicity tried to go over to Carnoustie once a week timing her arrival for midday. She would bring with her food that would appeal to an elderly lady with a small appetite. While they ate they would exchange scraps of news but mostly they would talk about Joanna.

Chapter Three

Tim was extremely fond of his mother and it saddened him to see her becoming confused. Her memory was going and very little of what she was told would be retained. Yet strangely enough she could recall with amazing accuracy something that had taken place twenty or more years ago.

Maud Morrison had been a good-looking woman of medium height and blessed with an exceptionally quick mind. Just occasionally they would be reminded of that quick mind when she surprised them all with a particularly sharp response. Until recently Maud had kept up with all that was happening at home and in the wider world. Each morning, bar Sunday when she got *The Times* delivered, two quality newspapers came through the letterbox and landed on the coconut mat.

It was as much due to Maud as to her late husband that they were so comfortably off. Edward Morrison had been a skilled electrician but with no head for business. An easygoing man, he was a soft touch for a sob story and Maud could see all that they had worked for being lost. Before that could happen she stepped in and made the books and the running of the business her responsibility. Hard luck stories got short shrift from her and Maud saw to it that accounts were settled on time. As the workload increased they were able to take on more qualified electricians who, in turn, were training apprentices. Business flourished and when it was sold their bank balance was extremely healthy. Edward enjoyed only two years of retirement before collapsing and dying of a heart attack.

There never had been any question of Tim following in his father's footsteps and taking over the business. Maud and Edward had great hopes for their only son. The boy was bright and at school he was never far from the top of his class. Tim, they were agreed on this, would have a profession. Perhaps he could become a doctor of medicine or a lawyer. A doctor was ruled out when he was seen to turn pale at the sight of blood. A lawyer it would have to be and Tim went happily along with that.

Tim got into his wife's car and moved the seat back to accommodate his long legs. He was trying to be calm but every little while his stomach would bunch with fear when he thought of what might lie ahead. The dreadful possibility of a prison sentence could have been avoided if only he had gone to his mother in the first place and confessed. She would have been shocked, horrified even but the money would have been forthcoming. In any case it was money that was going to be his one day. Why hadn't he? That was easy enough to answer. He couldn't bear to see her disappointment. She had always been so proud of him. Instead he had decided to be smart and borrow the money — borrow not steal. A client's money to be used to get him out of a difficult situation. No one need ever have been the wiser. A careless omission on his part had brought it to light and landed him in this god-awful mess. Paton & Noble had shown him no mercy, he thought bitterly. Promising to pay back in full what he had borrowed wasn't going to save him. They were determined to drag his good name through the mud.

He switched on the engine and the car moved off with his thoughts now on Felicity. Fancy her objecting to his suggestion that they trade her car in for something more to his liking. Not a new car, possibly a year-old one with not too much mileage on the clock. That would do him very well. He sighed. She was always a bit slow was Felicity, the dreamy sort, typical of arty types. All the same she had been alert enough when it was her car they were discussing. In the mirror he could see that Felicity had come out to close the garage doors and for a moment she looked at the departing car before turning away.

Once away from Hillhead, Tim made for the coast road passing through Broughty Ferry and Monifieth and then on to Carnoustie where he occasionally played a round of golf. He thought it unlikely he would play there again. At the far end of Carnoustie, Tim slowed down to take a sharp left turn and then another into a quiet cul-de-sac. Grange House was halfway down and set apart from its neighbours by the high neat clipped hedges. The gate was never closed and Tim drove straight in scattering gravel before coming to a stop at the front door. There was a large tub of flowers at either side giving a colourful display. He got out, shut the car door and went to stand on the step. To announce his arrival he rang the bell then opened the door. That the heavy outside door should be unlocked did not surprise him but the fact that the glass door was also unlocked had him frowning.

He found his mother in what she called the morning room. It was small and comfortable and the view from the window was of the drive up to the house and a strip of the front garden. The drawing-room was used about twice a year. Even with a huge fire it was never warm enough for Maud to sit in unless she was wearing a cardigan or had a shawl draped round her shoulders. At this moment she was sitting in her favourite chair at the window with her feet on an embroidered footstool. She turned her head when the door opened.

'Saw the car,' she said, 'and thought at first it was Felicity. Where is she?'

'Busy at home,' he answered and went over to brush his lips against the papery dry skin. 'Mother, do you know that both the outside door and the glass door were unlocked? Anyone could come in.'

'Nonsense, I'm here at the window and would see whoever it was. Let me remind you, Tim, that this is a respectable area, we don't get undesirables.'

He shook his head and smiled.

'Why isn't Felicity with you?' She sounded disappointed.

'I told you, Mother, she's busy. Actually I wanted to come alone because I thought it would be nice to have a chat, just the two of us.'

'Dear me! What's brought this on?' Maud said drily. 'Usually you've hardly time to sit yourself down. Since you appear to be staying I think we should have a cup of tea. Go and find Mrs What's-her-name, she'll make a pot of tea.'

'Mrs Haggarty, you mean?'

'Yes, nice woman but I can never remember her name.'

'She won't be here, she comes in the mornings and this is the afternoon.'

'Is it, are you sure? I must have had lunch though I don't remember. No matter, I'm not hungry.'

'I'll make you a cup if you want one.'

'Don't bother. What you can do is bring your chair nearer. Like everything else about me my hearing isn't what it should be.'

'Where is your hearing aid?'

'In the bedroom I think.'

'It won't do you much good there.'

'Oh, aren't we smart? If you must know the wretched thing whistles and I don't find it much of a help. I'm not all that deaf and if only folk would talk clearly and not mumble I would hear perfectly well.' She paused and gave a small cough to clear her throat.

'Tim, I could always read you like a book. Something is troubling you.'

'Yes, Mother, I'm afraid something is.'

'Serious?' There was a trace of the old sharpness.

'I've lost my job.'

She looked puzzled. 'Lost your job, you mean you are no longer with Paton & Noble?'

'That's right.'

'You've resigned?'

'No, I was told to clear my desk and go. That was yesterday.'

'You had words? Happens I suppose, clash of personalities. All the same, this couldn't have been just an ordinary disagreement?'

'No, it was a lot more than that.'

'You should have held on to your temper, losing your job was a big price to pay. Am I going to be told what this is all about?'

'It's rather complicated.'

'And I'm not up to it is what you are suggesting. You could be right. Maybe you should make that cup of tea,' Maud said wearily. Thinking for any length of time tired her and that was when she became confused. The past got mixed up with the present.

Tim felt both relieved and ashamed to know that very little of what he said would be retained. His disgrace needn't touch her. He got up and went through to the kitchen to make the tea. The house was much as it had been when he was a boy. It had been built at the end of the nineteenth century and was described then as a very desirable family house set in ideal surroundings. The rooms had high corniced ceilings and the panelled doors had brass knobs which were kept gleaming. The floor of the vestibule was covered in black and white tiles and along one wall on a deep shelf were plants with trailing greenery. The man who came to do the garden also looked after the indoor plants. The drawing-room was large and had two windows with floor-length deep blue velvet curtains. By today's standards it was over furnished but Maud liked things to remain as they were. Many of the pieces would be valuable but the overall effect was of a dull room seldom if ever used. There was a dining-room and a small sitting-room referred to as the morning room. A cloakroom with a toilet and wash-hand basin had been added a number of years ago and was the only major alteration that had been made to the house. It had been money well spent and Maud blessed the day when she and Edward had made the decision. The idea originated with Edward. He had thought that with advancing years it might be more convenient to have a toilet both upstairs and downstairs. Maud was reaping the benefit. Climbing the stairs was becoming increasingly difficult and though she did manage to go upstairs to bed and come down in the morning, that she was finding was quite enough exercise.

The upstairs had three bedrooms and a very large walk-in cupboard. The bathroom had cork tiles on the floor and the white bath had claw feet.

Tim made the tea and set the tray. Looking about

him he thought the kitchen needed to be gutted. Everything was old and shabby and as for that ancient cooking range it was a monstrosity.

'Mother, I had forgotten how awful the kitchen is,' he said pushing open the door with his shoulder.

'All in working order,' Maud said tartly. 'I'm not modernising at my time of life. Once the house is yours you can do what you like.'

This could be his opportunity. He would go carefully.

'Here you are, Mother, tea not too strong, you see I remembered the way you like it.'

'Thank you, dear. That's right, bring that table over and put it between us.'

He put the tray down on the table. 'Shall I be mother?' he smiled.

'Yes, you have a steadier hand. What were we talking about?' she said fretfully, 'I do wish I wasn't so forgetful.'

'You are not bad at all and forgetting occasionally at your age is excusable.'

'It is never excusable, Tim, and it is a damned nuisance.'

'Mother!'

'It makes me feel such a fool.' Her face creased into a smile. 'That was me using a bad word and when you did that what did I tell you?'

'That if I used it again I wouldn't go to heaven.'

'Such silly things we mothers say and I'm sure the Almighty wouldn't be too bothered. A swear word does seem to help to get the anger out. Stealing, taking what doesn't belong to us, that is different. I would find that difficult to forgive.'

For a moment Tim closed his eyes.

She noticed. 'Headache, dear?'

'No.' He moved to a more comfortable position in his chair. 'You said you wanted to know what we were talking about.'

'So I did.'

'We were talking about me losing my job.'

'Yes. Yes. I hadn't forgotten that bit. There was something else, wasn't there?'

'Only my remark about the state of the kitchen and you saying it would do you well enough and that I could do what I wanted with it once it was mine.'

'You would sell it I imagine. You and Felicity like where you are.'

'Yes, we do. Does the thought of that upset you?'

'Not in the least. There are some folk who would be sorry to see a house go out of the family but I am not one. There are things I can be sentimental about but not a house. Bricks and mortar is all it is after all.'

'You were always sensible.'

'Was I?' She was silent, seemingly deep in thought and when she did speak it was very slowly. 'This must be a worrying time for you. No money coming in and the bills to pay.'

'The price of my foolishness.'

'Yes, I would say you have been very foolish. Still

it has happened and we can't make a better of it. What would be sensible in the circumstances and what I propose doing is to let you have part of your inheritance now when it will be of most use.'

'That is very generous of you.'

She smiled. 'I like my creature comforts so rest assured that I shall make certain that there is plenty for my future needs.'

'I would always look after you, Mother.'

'Would you, son? Are you sure about that?'

Tim looked hurt. He was hurt.

'It's all right, dear, I am only teasing. And don't worry too much about losing your position with Paton & Noble, something will turn up, something always does. We all do silly things but losing your temper and walking out or whatever happened was stupid and not at all like you.'

'I know and I deeply regret what I did.'

'Would a genuine apology be enough for them?'

'No.'

Maud wiped the corners of her mouth with a dainty lace-edged handkerchief. 'What is Felicity saying about it?'

'Not much but it isn't always easy to know what Felicity is thinking.'

She looked at him sharply. 'Don't underestimate Felicity. She might be quiet but there is strength there. I like my daughter-in-law and I can tell you, Tim, that I was very glad and so was your father, that you didn't fall for some flighty piece.'

'Since you are being so generous, Mother, and believe me I am deeply grateful, would you mind if I used some of the money to buy myself a car, a good second-hand one would do very well for the moment?'

'The money is yours. Just remember if you get it now—'

'I won't get it later,' he laughed.

'Bear that in mind and now tell me about my granddaughter.'

'Joanna is fine and appears to be enjoying university life.'

'Enjoyment, that is all young people think about today. Tell her she is there to work.'

Tim laughed. 'You'll see her during the holidays so tell her yourself.'

Her eyes were closing and her head lolling to the side.

Tim got up to move the table back to the wall. Her eyes flickered open.

'Dear me, I'm having trouble keeping my eyes open.'

'You're tired.'

'A bit.'

'I'm sorry, I've exhausted you.'

'No, you haven't. I'm glad you came.'

'So am I,' he said. It would take a miracle to remove all his worries but at least his immediate financial problems were taken care of.

'Before you go take that tray through to the kitchen. Rinse out the cups to keep them from staining and

Mrs What's-her-name will do the washing-up when she comes.'

When he got back to the morning room her head was nodding.

'You would be more comfortable lying down on the sofa. Sitting that way will give you a crick in the neck.'

'And painful that could be. Help me over and bring an extra cushion – yes that one will do.'

He saw her settled and put a travelling rug over her legs. 'How is that?'

'Fine, dear, just fine, I'll have forty winks.'

'I'll go then, Mother and I'll lock the doors, I have my key.'

'No, don't do that. My neighbours wouldn't get in and they like to pop in now and again when Mrs—'

'What's-her-name isn't here.'

'Cheeky. Don't fuss, Tim, I'm perfectly safe, no one is going to run off with me.'

'No, just your valuables.'

Her eyes were closed and she didn't answer. For a few moments Tim stood looking down on her and then left quietly. He wasn't happy about leaving both doors unlocked but he could do no other if they were left that way for the neighbours. Just as long as his mother locked up at night and he rather thought she would.

Tim looked at his watch. He had told Felicity not to prepare a meal for him and to have her own. She had nodded but made no comment. Perhaps she thought he would have something with his mother and he would let her go on thinking that.

He left the cul-de-sac, turned the car and headed in the opposite direction to home.

Chapter Four

It was not very long after Tim had gone when the phone rang. Felicity, lost in thought, jumped at the sound and hurried to the hall to answer it.

'Hello.'

'Mum, it's me.'

'Joanna! This is a surprise.' Then a little fearfully, 'Nothing wrong is there?'

'Of course not, why should there be?' The impatience of youth was in her voice.

'It's just you don't usually phone at this time of day.'

'Well, here I am. Mum, I don't have much money so let me do most of the talking.'

'You usually do but I'll keep quiet.'

Tim had put his foot down when Joanna, on two occasions, had reversed the charges. That was perfectly acceptable in an emergency, he said, but for a chat it was definitely out.

'Tell me, have you and Dad anything arranged for Saturday?'

'This Saturday coming, you mean?'

'Yes, this Saturday.'

'No, we haven't.' Then she thought she ought to qualify that. 'I have nothing arranged and as far as I know neither has your father.'

'In that case will it be all right if I come home?'

'When has it been necessary to ask? This is your home.'

'I know. The thing is, Mum, I want to bring someone to meet you and Dad.'

'A boyfriend?'

'Got it in one.' Felicity could imagine her grinning. 'His name is Stuart Milton and he is a second-year law student. Dad will be pleased, they will have something to talk about.'

'Will you be staying overnight?'

'No, this is just for the day. Stuart has his own car and now that I know it is OK we'll arrive in time for lunch and get back to Edinburgh in the early evening.'

'That will be lovely.' Felicity was smiling. 'I take it this boyfriend of yours has a hearty appetite?'

'Eats like a horse though to look at him you wouldn't think so. He's just skin and bone. Hold on a sec, Mum, while I feed the brute, the phone I mean not Stuart. This thing gobbles up money.' The coins went in. 'One more thing and it is important so listen carefully. Stuart's parents have friends who have a farm in Provence – that's in France.'

'Yes, darling, I did know that.'

'Stuart absolutely loves it and spends most of his

holidays there. I think he was probably kidding but he told me that given the chance he would rather be a farmer than a lawyer.'

'Would he be given the chance?'

'No, I shouldn't think so. The Miltons have a family law firm and it is just expected that he will follow his father. He isn't struggling or anything, in fact he is doing rather well, but that wasn't what I was going to say. Mum, Stuart wants me to go with him to Provence and I had better tell you that it would be for most of the holidays,' she ended in a rush.

'Darling, can't we talk about this on Saturday when you come?'

There was what sounded like an exasperated sigh. 'Mum, the whole purpose of this phone call is to give you time to work on Dad. You know how stuffy he can be when he chooses.'

'No, I don't.'

'Yes, you do.'

'Then if he is it is only for your own good.'

'The times I've heard that one. Oh and I almost forgot and this could be helpful, tell Dad he won't have to dig into his pocket except for the fares, of course. We'll be earning our keep by helping on the farm.'

'You don't know the first thing about farming.'

'I can learn, can't I?'

'Yes, dear, of course you can.'

'You'll plead my case?'

'I'll do my best.' Felicity felt a flood of love and wished she could reach out and hug her daughter. 'Be sure and tell Stuart that he is very welcome and we look forward to meeting him when you come on Saturday.'

'Thanks, Mum. I love you. Now wasn't that neat just as the money was running—' The line went dead and Felicity, still with a smile on her face, put down the phone.

She didn't see Tim making any objections to the holiday in France. It could be that he would welcome it in the circumstances. Tim was very protective of Joanna, much too protective his daughter thought. He wouldn't have been happy about this boy and his daughter wandering about the country on their own and to be honest neither would she. In this day of greater freedom they would be considered old-fashioned parents. Tim wouldn't agree it was old-fashioned, rather that it was sensible. However, this was different, the two young people would be living on the farm with responsible adults in charge. It would be a wonderful experience for Joanna. Felicity closed her eyes for a moment. There were difficult times ahead for them all and Tim was probably right to keep the truth from Joanna for as long as possible. Was he clinging to the hope, just as she was, that somehow things would work out? Felicity accepted, she hadn't before but she did now, that Tim could never again work for Paton & Noble. What terrified her was the thought of Tim going to prison. He didn't deserve that. A lesser punishment would be enough, the loss of his job, wasn't that enough? Wrong though it was no one actually suffered for what he had done. Tim had her almost convinced that it was not stealing. The money was there and all he had done was make use of it in an emergency. What emergency? – but she wouldn't think about that now. Worse things were done and never came to light.

Her head began to ache, the aspirins only helped for a short time and she knew it was dangerous to take too many. The worst part of this nightmare was having no one to talk to. All this bottling up was making her ill. She felt she would go mad if she had to carry this burden alone. Her mother would have been such a help. She would have known how to handle it. In her quiet way she would have reasoned it out and then together they would have come to a decision as to what would be best. But there was no mother to run to and only one other person she could trust completely.

Rachel Reid and Felicity had been school friends and had remained in touch, seeing each other two or three times a year and phoning every four or five weeks. Rachel hadn't married though there was a man in her life. She seldom spoke about Terence other than to say there was no question of marriage and that the arrangement suited them both.

She was a tall, heavily built, good-looking woman with short cropped auburn hair, good skin and a spattering of freckles. Her manner was pleasant and businesslike though not with Felicity. When together they could giggle like schoolgirls. After leaving school Felicity had gone on to art college while Rachel enrolled for a business course. Rachel had no clear idea what she wanted to do other than that she did not want to work in an office. When someone suggested the hotel trade Rachel wasn't enthusiastic but decided to give it a try. To learn any trade properly one had to start at the bottom and work up. Rachel wasn't too proud to do that. She worked as a room maid followed by a spell as a waitress and then as a receptionist. After experience in several hotels, the last as manageress, Rachel decided the time had come to branch out on her own. The Cairn Hotel in Perth had come on the market. It had been poorly managed and was shabby and run down. What it did have in its favour was an excellent situation and Rachel could see the potential. She could also see the problems ahead. The Cairn Hotel required money to be spent on it, a lot of money. It also needed hard work and great quantities of optimism. Rachel had never been afraid of hard work and she had never been short of optimism. For her there was always a light at the end of the tunnel. All she had to do was persuade the bank manager to give her a loan, a substantial loan. That hadn't been too difficult, in fact it had been surprisingly easy. Rachel had several influential friends and that did help but what had impressed the bank manager most of all was her quiet confidence and her wide experience of the ups and downs of the hotel business. She wasn't the type to panic if there were a few temporary setbacks. The middle-aged, stout bank manager declared himself satisfied and authorised the loan. They shook hands.

A few years later the Cairn Hotel made its appearance in the *Good Hotel Guide*. It was enjoying a reputation for excellent service, a high standard of comfort and good food at reasonable prices. With its central position it attracted both the businessman and the holiday visitor.

Felicity sat down to make the call and in a short time it was answered.

'The Cairn Hotel, can I help you?' came the pleasant, rather sing-song voice.

'I would like to speak to Miss Reid if it is convenient,' Felicity said and prayed it was. The need to unburden, to share her worries, was greater than ever.

'I'll see. May I have your name, please?'

'Felicity Morrison.'

'Hold the line a moment.'

Felicity could hear voices in the background and then the phone was lifted and a slightly out-of-breath voice said, 'Felicity, how strange that you should phone just now. You were in my thoughts.'

'Was I?'

'You were. We haven't had a good gossip for ages.'

'I know and we must do something about that.'

'Felicity, is it my imagination or do I detect something in your voice? Is something the matter?'

Felicity's voice broke and she had been trying so hard to keep control.

'I'm so sorry, Rachel,' she sobbed, then gulped.

'Don't be. For heaven's sake, this is me, you don't have to apologise. Is it something to do with Joanna?'

'No, at least not directly.'

'Thank God for that. For one terrible moment I thought it might be. Is it Tim?' Rachel made a face, she hadn't much time for Timothy Morrison. She

thought him pompous and self-opinionated and not
the husband she would have chosen for Felicity. Felicity
was generous to a fault and Tim was selfish. Probably
spoilt from the cradle, she thought.

There was no love lost between Rachel and Tim
and when obliged to be in each other's company they
were coldly polite. Though he thought her bossy and
overbearing Tim did have a sneaking admiration for any
female who could make such a success of a business and
by her own efforts.

'Rachel, this is confidential and I can't tell you over
the phone,' she said unsteadily.

'It's all right, I understand. Take a deep breath then
we'll talk about Joanna.' That would give her a chance
to compose herself.

Felicity managed a laugh. 'You are so good for me,
just hearing your voice helps.'

'We are good for each other, now tell me the latest
on my godchild.'

'There is a boy friend, Stuart somebody or other.
Milton, that's it. Stuart Milton. He is a second-year law
student who apparently spends most of his vacations on
a farm in Provence.'

'Nice for some.'

'You've been there, I seem to recall.'

'Yes, a long time ago but I remember it as being
very beautiful.'

'Stuart wants Joanna to go with him and, of course,
she is dead keen.'

'Is that a problem?'

'No, not at all. I'm happy for her to go and, although Tim doesn't know yet, I don't see him raising any objections.'

'Now that I know all is well with my favourite teenager tell me what I can do to help you?'

'Probably nothing anyone can do.'

'Oh, come on. Terence once told me that I had a clear-eyed approach to the practicalities of life so I could well be of help.'

'I wouldn't talk about this with anyone but you. All I want, Rachel, is for you to listen to me and at the end give me your advice. I'm not sure I'll take it, in fact I'm not sure about anything. Oh, God, I sound pathetic.'

Rachel was worried. 'Shall I come to you?'

'No, I think it would be better for me to come to Perth. You have a hotel to run.'

'As I've said to you before a good hotel almost runs itself.'

'So you have and I don't believe you.' She paused. 'Can we make it Monday, please?'

'Fine by me, or would you rather it were sooner?'

'I think I had better make it Monday. I have Joanna and this boy coming on Saturday, only for the day so I have no spare room to prepare. Tomorrow I must go and see my mother-in-law. Poor soul, her mind is beginning to wander.'

'Monday it is. Come early, I mean as soon as you like after Tim leaves for the office.'

Felicity felt her stomach clench. Tim wouldn't be

going to the office. If only he were none of this would be necessary.

'Yes, I'll do that.'

'And you are not to worry. Promise?'

'I'll try.'

'Whatever it is we'll work something out between us. Nothing is ever as bad as you imagine.'

Felicity thought she might have agreed with that at one time. She didn't now. This was as bad as it could get. They said their goodbyes and Felicity put the phone down.

There was a slight lifting of her spirits and that must have been Rachel's matter-of-fact approach to all problems. She refused to let anything defeat her. On Monday she would tell her friend everything, hold nothing back. That would mean confessing, if that was the right word, that she and Tim were growing apart. There was no particular incident she could bring to mind, she supposed it had been very gradual. Other couples went through this and it didn't have to be serious. She and Tim would get back to what it had been. Once this was all behind them they could start again, not in Hillhead, they would have to get right away.

Felicity was becoming increasingly concerned when the hands of the clock moved to ten. Accidents could happen so easily when one's attention strayed and Tim had a lot on his mind. In fact, though he didn't show it, he must be worried sick. Of one thing she was all but sure, he couldn't have been with his mother all this time. The old lady tired easily and was nearly always in bed by eight o'clock. At half past ten, Felicity sighed with relief when she heard the car being driven into the garage. Would Tim close the garage doors? He didn't always do so and occasionally they were forgotten and left open all night. She listened and was relieved to hear the lock being shot into place.

For the past hour Felicity had tried to interest herself in a book. That should have been very easy since it was written by one of her favourite authors. Only it wasn't easy at all. She seemed to be incapable of concentrating and kept on reading the same paragraph again and again and still not taking in a word of it. When Tim came into the room she closed the book and placed it on the leather pouffe.

'Hello, dear,' she said with a smile. 'Can I get you anything or have you eaten?'

'I had something, thank you.'

'A cup of tea then?' She made to rise.

'Later perhaps.' Tim sat down in his usual chair then stretched out his long legs crossing them at the ankles. For a man he had surprisingly neat ankles. Felicity had often thought that. Like a thoroughbred, she had once told him and he had grinned, well pleased.

She was curious to know where he had been but she wouldn't ask him for the simple reason that he would most likely manage to avoid the question. Once she had found him out in a lie, but had never faced him with it. He had given the usual excuse of pressure of work when she knew he had left the office at his usual time.

His secretary had told her when she phoned. The only reason for the phone call was to find out if he was to be delayed since it was a meal that wouldn't improve with keeping. She had made a joke of it. Felicity wondered if his secretary had mentioned it to him in the morning. If so had he thought that his wife was checking up on him? It was one of those situations when one kept quiet rather than risk saying the wrong thing. Felicity had reluctantly come to the conclusion that Tim could twist the truth to suit himself. It meant she was silently questioning everything he said. Gambling could mean many things. Betting on the horses was the first to spring to mind but Felicity was dismissing that as highly improbable. Wasn't it more likely that Tim had got involved in some venture that had gone terribly wrong? It would have embarrassed and humiliated him to confess to her that he had misjudged and lost a great deal of money. Felicity felt saddened that it should be like that and that Tim hadn't been able to confide in her. We all make mistakes and he should have known she would be supportive.

'How did you find your mother?' Felicity asked quickly before he could hide behind the newspaper.

'Not bad at all, in fact I would have said she was amazingly alert.'

She was glad to see him put aside the newspaper and watched as he made an arc of his fingers. She smiled to herself, it was a habit her husband had when he had already made up his mind what he was going to say.

'She does have her good days,' Felicity said.

'Mmmm. Incidentally Mother wondered why you hadn't accompanied me.'

'I hope you told her I wanted to come but you preferred to be on your own.' Felicity was pretty sure he hadn't.

Tim shrugged which meant nothing. 'I said you would be paying her a visit quite soon.'

'Tomorrow. I had made up my mind to go tomorrow.'

He smiled a very satisfied smile. 'As usual my dear old mother has turned up trumps. Bless her, she is going to give me part of my inheritance now when my need is greatest and I didn't even have to ask.'

'That was both thoughtful and generous of your mother.'

'Yes, wasn't it?'

'You must have told her.'

'Well, of course I told her, I had to, hadn't I?'

'Yes, I know that. I just wondered how much you told her.'

His eyebrows shot up. 'Does it matter?'

'Yes, it does matter. Surely I should know so that I don't put my foot in it.'

'Ah, of course, point taken, you could very easily do that. For your information I told mother that it was entirely my own fault that I am no longer employed by Paton & Noble.'

'That must have distressed her.' Felicity knew how very proud the woman had been when her son went to work for such a prestigious law firm.

'It did upset her but not as much as it would have done had she been her old self. She wanted no details, said her brain didn't work at that level these days.'

'Do you really think that, Tim?'

He looked surprised. 'Why? Don't you?'

Felicity was silent for a few moments. 'I could be wrong,' she said slowly, 'but sometimes I get the feeling that she doesn't bother to listen if she thinks she would rather not know.'

He nodded thoughtfully. 'You could be right and she doesn't want to make the effort. As regards her memory, that is going.'

'She gets confused.'

'It is more than that. By morning she will only have a hazy recollection of what was said. Incidentally Mother was as anxious as I was to have everything in order and to sign the relevant papers.'

Felicity nodded and waited for him to go on. The newspaper was forgotten, it was obvious he had more to say.

'The mortgage payments will be taken care of.'

'Does that mean we don't have to sell?'

'No, it just means we don't have to rush into anything. And there is good news for you.'

'Oh?'

'I can now afford to buy myself a car though I'll make a good second-hand one do. You won't be inconvenienced.'

Felicity was angry and hurt. 'That is unfair of you, Tim. You know very well that I was prepared to share the car. What I objected to was your suggestion that I should trade in mine for something more to your liking.'

'It doesn't matter now.'

'Joanna phoned not long after you had gone.'

'What did she want?'

'She wants to come on Saturday and bring a friend with her.'

'This will be some boy she has got involved with?'

'Yes. Stuart Milton is the boy's name and he is a second-year law student.'

'Is this an overnight stay?'

'No. Stuart has his own car. They will arrive for lunch, Joanna said, and they would hope to be back in Edinburgh by early evening.' She paused. 'The real reason for the phone call and the coming visit is to get our permission for her to go on holiday with this boy. Apparently Stuart spends his holidays in Provence with friends of his parents.'

'Mmmm.'

'I was told to be sure and tell you that you wouldn't have to dig into your pocket, apart that is for the fares. They are to earn their keep by helping on the farm.'

'That should keep the pair of them out of mischief. Actually,' he said thoughtfully, 'it might work out rather well.'

'I thought that too.'

'We must be careful when they are here to give no hint of our troubles. That will be easier for me.'

'How do you arrive at that?'

'Because, my dear, I'll be with them for the meal, then make pressure of work my excuse to escape to my study only coming downstairs before they depart.'

'I'll manage,' Felicity said quietly. She was about to tell him that she had been speaking to Rachel on the phone and had arranged to go to Perth on Monday then changed her mind when he picked up the paper. Instead she went through to the kitchen to put the kettle on. It might be better to keep quiet. Tim wouldn't want her discussing their affairs with Rachel but just so long as he didn't know — it struck her then that she, too, was becoming secretive.

Chapter Five

There was very little change in the morning routine. Tim had his breakfast and left the house at his usual time carrying his briefcase. Felicity wondered what could be in it. She thought it would be very easy to believe these were normal times and dismiss the rest as a bad dream. Tim said he was doing it this way to save the neighbours remarking and Felicity having to come up with an explanation. The neighbours, she could have told him, were the least of her worries. She was friendly with them but not what you would have called close. Not like it used to be when Netta Gordon lived in the next house with her husband and two children. Netta had been a good friend and they had been there for each other. Felicity missed her neighbour when promotion took the family to Glasgow.

The new owners, a Mr and Mrs Howard, were very different. The husband, Felicity was to learn, had taken early retirement and they both enjoyed the outdoor life. He was a burly man with a ruddy complexion and his wife, who was a little taller, was of a sturdy build. Dressed in tweeds and wearing heavy footwear they would go for long walks in all kinds of weather. They were also keen golfers.

Felicity, anxious to be welcoming, had thought it better to wait until the removal van was leaving before going over. Her offer of tea or some other refreshment was politely but firmly refused as was her offer of help. They were well organised, the woman was quick to explain, she had prepared a picnic basket, the contents of which they would enjoy later. Much as the offer was appreciated they preferred to do everything themselves and in their own time. Her husband nodded several times to show that he was in total agreement. Felicity thought it was to discourage any hope of sociability that the woman added that she had always found it better to settle these things at the beginning in order to save any misunderstanding.

Felicity had listened to all this in silence. She had been taken aback to have her neighbourly act more or less thrown back in her face. When the woman waited for her to speak, Felicity had nodded, smiled, said she understood perfectly and left them to it. Tim and she had laughed about it in the evening. That had been four years ago and very little had changed in that time. Neither had been inside the other's house and when they did meet there was always a smile and some remark about the weather before going their separate ways.

Tim put down his napkin and Felicity picked it up,

folded it and pushed it through the napkin ring. It was crushed but would do another day.

'You did say you were going to Carnoustie,' he said getting up.

'Yes, I did. I thought late morning would be a good time to visit your mother unless, that is, you have urgent need of the car.'

'No, you can have it,' he said as though bestowing a favour. 'I'll take a walk to the garage and get myself a hired car for a day or two. That will let me look around and see what is on offer.'

'Good idea.' Felicity smiled and nodded as she began to clear the table. 'But before you go I need to have some idea about meals. What time do you want to eat?'

He frowned and ran his fingers through his hair. 'Impossible to say and that was something I meant to talk about.'

Felicity stopped the clearing up and sat down.

'The way things are I think we should make our own arrangements. If you are not around I can make something for myself. I'm not completely useless in the kitchen.'

'No, you're not.' He could cook something and leave a most awful mess for her to clear up.

'Better my way, don't you think, than having you rushing back and then feeling annoyed if I didn't turn up.'

She smiled at that. 'Tim, about me getting a job—'

'Not the same urgency for that but, all the same,

you would be better to try and fix up something. You are going to have plenty of time on your hands.'

'I'll start looking.'

'And I must get on my way.'

After he had gone Felicity washed and dried the dishes. Then she went upstairs to make the beds and give a quick tidy to the house. It deserved more but that was all it was going to get. A few days ago a film of dust on the furniture would have made her feel guilty whereas now she hardly noticed.

The weather was holding up and the day was warm enough for summer clothes. Felicity had a quick look in her wardrobe and decided to wear her pale yellow linen dress buttoned down the front. There was a matching jacket which would go on the back seat of the car in case the weather turned cooler. It could be warm in Hillhead and decidedly cooler on the coast.

The traffic was light with the morning rush over. The real influx of holidaymakers came during July and the beginning of August. Those who wanted to avoid the crowds and were in the fortunate position of being able to choose when to take their holidays, came in June. When she reached Carnoustie and Grange House, Felicity saw her mother-in-law at the window and gave her a wave.

'Felicity, how lovely to see you,' Maud said, receiving her daughter-in-law's kiss on the cheek. 'I was so hoping you would come.'

'And here I am,' Felicity smiled.

The woman's brow puckered and she looked annoyed with herself.

'There was something I wanted to talk about and, do you know, for the life of me I cannot think what it was. Never mind it will come back.'

'I'm guilty of that. I can go upstairs to the bedroom and completely forget what it was I wanted.'

'The difference is, my dear, that with you it is only absentmindedness or too many other things on your mind. With me it is plain forgetfulness which comes with old age. No, that is not true. There are others of my age who do not have that problem.'

Felicity bent down to pick up the newspaper from where it had fallen to the carpet. She tidied the pages, folded the newspaper neatly and put it down on a nearby chair.

'You've been reading the newspaper.' Felicity had never known what to call Tim's mother and like so many young wives had ended up not calling the woman anything. It was possible to do that, to carry on a conversation without using that person's name but it wasn't very satisfactory. These days folk were making greater use of Christian names. In hospitals nurses were addressing elderly patients by their first names believing it to be more friendly. Maud said it took away one's dignity. If a pink-faced junior nurse dared to address her that way she wouldn't do it again. She would be told icily that she was Mrs Morrison and to kindly remember that.

'Hardly that, my dear.' Maud's spectacles were on a

chain round her neck. 'It takes a clear mind to make sense of what is happening in the world. I do manage the headlines but most of it makes depressing reading. We live in difficult times, Felicity, but then I suppose we always have. The same problems face us all the time. Some folk have far too much and so many more haven't enough to live on. Enough of that, you didn't come here to get a lecture on the starving millions. It is getting near to lunch time but a coffee would be welcome I daresay.'

'Yes, it would. Shall I make it?'

'No, but you could go in search of Rita and ask her to prepare a pot of coffee and bring it through.'

'Rita?' Felicity said questioningly. And then the penny dropped. 'Oh, you mean Mrs Haggarty?'

'Yes, I mean Mrs Haggarty. You know it was quite dreadful I never could remember the woman's name and Tim said I couldn't go on calling her Mrs What's-her-name. Rita, I can remember that and the woman doesn't seem to mind me making use of her Christian name.'

'I'm sure she doesn't.'

Felicity got up and went along to the kitchen to find Mrs Haggarty already preparing the coffee.

'I saw you coming, Mrs Morrison, and since you are here I can ask if a biscuit would do or would you rather I cut a piece of gingerbread?'

'A biscuit will do nicely.'

'Leave the doors open if you will and I'll follow in a minute or two with the tray.'

Felicity got the coffee table in position and drew her own chair closer.

'Thank you, Rita, you anticipated our need. Take your own and would you like a quick glance through the newspaper?' said Maud.

'No, thank you, I keep that for night when I can get my feet up. You'll pour?' Mrs Haggarty said, looking at Felicity.

'Yes, I'll pour.'

The woman went away closing the door quietly behind her.

Maud took a few sips of her coffee, then carefully returned the cup to its saucer. She liked to be dressed and took a pride in her appearance. The light grey knitted suit had been dry-cleaned and she wore it with a darker grey blouse. Her thinning white hair was brushed back off her face but even so little patches of pink scalp could be seen. In her younger days her thick, brown wavy hair had been her crowning glory and a bit of its natural wave still remained.

'It was something to do with Tim and it is coming back to me now. Funny thing the memory, it can play tricks.' She looked thoughtful then nodded. 'Tim came to see me yesterday. Did you know?'

'Yes, I knew.'

'He said you were too busy to come, was that the way of it?'

'No, that wasn't the way of it. I wanted to come but—'

'Then why didn't you?' she interrupted.

66

'Because Tim made it perfectly clear that he wanted to see you on his own.'

'I can't think why. Husband and wife should not have secrets from each other. Edward and I didn't. Secret thoughts, now that is different. One has no control over one's thoughts but one needn't voice them. Here I am rambling on again.' She was silent for a few moments. 'I am worried about Tim, very worried and you must be too. He isn't resigning from Paton & Noble, he has been told to go.'

'Yes, it is all very – unfortunate.'

'Felicity, it is a lot more than that.'

'Yes.'

'I may be forgetful but I still have a brain that functions. When a solicitor is dismissed with such haste it usually means he has been guilty of misconduct or embezzlement. I can't believe my son could be guilty of either but I have to face facts. Is he in financial difficulties?'

'I know very little, Tim hasn't confided in me. I thought he might have told you more.'

'To be honest I was so shocked to learn that he was no longer with Paton & Noble—' she shook her head. 'I had such high hopes. In the years ahead I saw him as the senior partner. I'm just glad Edward didn't live to see this day.'

Felicity moistened her lips, she would have to go very carefully. It was right and proper that Tim should have to pay for his wrongdoing. What was wrong, as she saw it, was the severity of the punishment. The loss of his job should have been enough. It was monstrous to have the threat of a prison sentence hanging over his head although it was true that she wasn't in possession of all the facts. Tim hadn't been very forthcoming. He had told her only what he had considered necessary, in other words what she had to know.

Why did the innocent have to suffer? They had done no wrong yet at least three lives were affected, three lives broken for one man's mistake. In time she supposed she would learn to live with it just as Joanna would. Life had to go on. But for an old lady coming to the end of her life it was very different. She shouldn't have to end her days knowing that her much-loved son had brought disgrace on the family. Felicity vowed in those moments that she would do her utmost to hold back the truth. If that needed a white lie or two then so be it.

Felicity patted the brown-spotted hand. It was ringless since her fingers were too thin to keep on even her wedding ring.

'You are not to worry yourself about this. Tim made a mistake and he has been very stupid, he admits as much but no one has suffered, not outside his own family I mean.'

'Are you sure of that, my dear?'

'Yes, I am.' That part was true, Felicity thought. Tim had betrayed a trust and that for a lawyer was a crime but no client had suffered. The firm could bear the brunt, only that wouldn't be necessary. Tim was in a position to clear the debt. 'Try to understand I can't go into the details—'

'I don't wish to know them. In any case it would require a legal mind.'

'Perhaps.'

'Felicity, I just want my mind put at rest and you are the only one who can do that. If I insisted, Tim would answer my questions but I doubt if I would find the answers satisfactory.'

'That could be because he wants to spare you.'

The woman's faded eyes flashed with a trace of anger and two tiny spots of red appeared on her cheeks. 'If that were the case he wouldn't have got himself into this mess.'

Felicity smiled. 'I have to agree with that.' She paused not quite sure what she was going to say but knowing she had to say something. 'From what I gather I believe Tim made an unwise investment, maybe it involved a friend or someone he trusted—'

'And the whole thing went horribly wrong?' Maud nodded. 'Yes, Felicity, I think I could accept that. Money, a great deal of money, was required quickly and the temptation was there. Poor boy. Poor, stupid, stupid boy. Felicity, it was all so unnecessary,' Maud said brokenly, 'all I have is his as he well knows. No doubt I would have shown my shock and displeasure at his foolishness but the money was there for the asking and he must have known that.'

'Perhaps he was too ashamed to ask.'

'Very likely. Did Tim tell you that I am making over part of his inheritance so that he can have it now and free himself of this debt?'

'He did tell me and he is deeply grateful.'

'Paton & Noble have shown my son no mercy even though the debt will be repaid in full. I feel anger at their harshness. Tim has learnt his lesson and surely in the circumstances a severe reprimand would have been enough. They could be punishing themselves, a first-class lawyer is not easy to replace.'

'That's true.'

Maud sounded very wearied and her face was an unhealthy grey. 'We'll say no more about the matter. As for you Felicity,' she smiled tiredly, 'you are being quite wonderful and I only hope that Tim appreciates you. This must be such a disappointment and as for Joanna—'

'Joanna doesn't know, not yet,' Felicity said quickly.

'Is that wise? She is an intelligent young woman and not to tell her is to treat her like a child.'

'Tim thinks it best. I didn't agree to begin with but I do now. I was going to tell you that Joanna is coming on Saturday. She phoned to say she is bringing a boyfriend.'

Maud smiled. 'Not the best time to tell her.'

'No.'

'Tell me about the boy.'

'Not a lot I can tell you except to say his name is Stuart Milton and he is a second-year law student. Oh and he goes over to France for the holidays and has asked Joanna to accompany him.'

'Oh!'

'No, don't look like that,' Felicity laughed. 'They

the room or put on the bedside light and read a chapter of a book.

Though she was longing to see Joanna, Felicity couldn't help being nervous about the coming visit and it was constantly on her mind. She knew that she couldn't afford to drop her guard, not for a single moment. Joanna would be quick to notice any sign of worry and demand to know what was wrong. Mother and daughter were very close.

She kept making plans in her head, then changing them. Not the shopping, she must do that on Friday. She liked the Broughty Ferry shops. Like Carnoustie it had quality shops and boasted an excellent baker. With so many worries chasing about in her head Felicity couldn't even think about baking unless to make an almond tart, a favourite of Joanna's.

Felicity made an early start and when she got there Broughty Ferry was bustling with shoppers and holidaymakers. Some families were making for the beach laden with all the paraphernalia required for a day on the sands. Squealing children ran ahead with their buckets and spades every now and again turning round to show impatience with their slower moving parents. Felicity smiled to one particularly harassed looking woman then walked quickly towards the shops. She would make McCormack the butcher her first call. Like his father before him Archie McCormack was very discerning, taking only the best of meat to sell in the shop. Those who wanted cheaper cuts had to go elsewhere. He was a pleasant, red-faced man and it was said he was very good with the new and inexperienced housewife. Before she left the shop she would have been given instructions on how to cook the meat. Care and attention was needed but the end result was well worth the trouble. With a smile and a wink to those others in the shop he would tell the blushing young woman that the way to a man's heart was through his stomach.

Felicity left McCormack's with a pound of beef sausages and three thick pork chops, two for Tim and the other for herself. The main purchase was a leg of lamb for the Saturday lunch. The greengrocer was next and since they were to have Scotch broth she would need barley and a lot of vegetables. It was tasty and filling and would make a good starter. The young folk might like second helpings so she would use the big pot. Tim didn't care much for Scotch broth but he would take a little. Then they would have the roast leg of lamb. She would have it tender and succulent and serve it with mint sauce, roast and boiled potatoes and a selection of vegetables. The dessert would be almond tart with pouring custard and she would make two when she was about it. Joanna might like to take one back to Edinburgh and share it with her friends. Which would mean she would have to look for a suitable tin to hold it otherwise there was no saying in what state it would arrive.

Felicity had a feeling that this boyfriend was special. Something in Joanna's voice when she spoke his name gave her away. She wanted her parents to like this boy and the visit to be a success. There was no reason why it shouldn't be a success. The awful problems, and that was how Felicity saw them, would come later. She shook her head as though to get rid of her thoughts. She mustn't let herself think. She must keep herself occupied. One day at a time, look no further, was the only way she was going to cope.

Perhaps it was the sleep of exhaustion but Felicity slept soundly. When she awoke her mind was free from worry and she snuggled into the delicious warmth reluctant to leave it. Then with a startling suddenness it all came crowding back. Another day and with it the ever-worsening strain of trying to appear her normal self. Not just another day she reminded herself, today was to be a testing time.

Throwing back the covers, Felicity swung her legs over the side of the bed and went over to open the curtains. The window had been open an inch at the top and she opened it more to let in the fresh air. She saw by the puddles on the path that divided the back garden that there must have been a heavy shower overnight. The paving stones would dry up quite quickly, now that the sun was breaking through. The gardens were in need of a good soak and not many complained about the rain when it came during the night.

Felicity ate her breakfast of tea and toast. Tim could sleep on. Saturday was a non-working day so no pretence of leaving for the office was necessary. Her husband had come back last night with a hired car which was locked away in the garage and hers was in the drive close up against the garage door. They were both being so careful. Joanna, if she saw a different model, would want an explanation. She would remember that her father was not due a new car for another year. Of course an explanation would not have been difficult. It could have been a fault in his own car and a spare part not immediately available. The trouble was when it wasn't the truth one tended to overdo the explanation thereby arousing suspicions. Far better to say as little as possible.

Taking her dishes to the sink, Felicity suddenly remembered that there was no cereal, it had completely escaped her memory. A week ago and she would have been upset and full of apologies for her carelessness. Not now, Tim would just have to do without.

She went about the house opening the windows but not the one in the study. It remained shut. Tim would not have it open since the slightest breeze could disturb the papers on the desk. As he had told her, not once but several times, it was unnecessary. The windows in the office were never opened, no one would think of opening them. He had laughed and said he very much doubted if they could be budged.

Once the housework was done she would prepare the vegetables, a time-consuming task she always thought. Felicity considered herself a good cook and this was a simple meal well within her capabilities. Last week she wouldn't have given it a second thought. She would have gone about the task humming to herself and looking forward to seeing Joanna and meeting this new boyfriend. It was true she couldn't wait to see her darling daughter but she was so afraid. It took such willpower to keep her mind on what she was doing. To let it stray was to invite the panicky feeling. Joanna's father disgraced and sent to prison, how would Joanna cope with that? How would any daughter cope? And the boyfriend would he stand by her or fade out of the picture?

One thing was sure it would all have to come out. The newspaper would have a field day. It was sad but true that the public rushed to read of someone's downfall.

When Tim came downstairs for breakfast, Felicity was surprised to see him wearing his blue and gold dressing-gown. The dressing-gown had been a gift from his mother for his last birthday. Maud had given her son the money to buy himself something and he had gone alone to Draffens in Dundee and chosen an expensive silk dressing-gown. At the time he had said he would keep it to take on holiday or wear it for special occasions. Having his breakfast at the kitchen table hardly qualified, she thought, but still if he felt like wearing it then why not?

Another surprise came when Tim made no fuss about missing his cereal though she thought she detected a faint sigh. Felicity hadn't felt like apologising for her forgetfulness so she didn't. Instead she tried to concentrate her whole mind on what had to be done. It was strange but true that the simplest of tasks seemed to take twice as long to carry out when one was nervous or apprehensive and she was both. It wasn't going to be easy to act as though everything was normal when it was far from that. Yet that was what she must do. She felt her eyes filling with tears and was horrified and scared by her lack of self-control.

'Felicity?'

She jumped. 'For goodness sake, Tim, you gave me a fright.'

'Sorry.'

'It's all right.' She tried to smile. 'If you've finished I'll get the table cleared.' She made to collect the dishes.

'Leave them and try to calm yourself. You are a bag of nerves.'

'I am not, I'm perfectly all right.' She sniffed then used her handkerchief to blow her nose.

'That you most certainly are not. We are going through to the sitting-room, Felicity, and I am going to give you something to calm you.'

'I don't want anything.' But she made no protest when he led her through and guided her to a chair. She watched him go over to the drinks cabinet.

'Not whisky, Tim, I couldn't.'

'Don't worry, you are getting very little.' He took out a small sherry glass and smiled as he handed it to her. 'That amount would be lost in a whisky glass.'

After a moment's hesitation she raised the glass to her lips and drank a little. It made her shudder and she pulled a face. 'Must I finish it?'

'Yes.'

She took small sips until most of it was gone then she put the glass aside.

'Good girl. You'll find it will help.' Tim paused. 'I know what you are afraid of,' he said quietly.

'Do you?'

'Yes. You are afraid that you won't fool Joanna and that she'll suspect that something is wrong.'

'You have to admit it is more than possible. You know how quick she is.'

'Coming on her own that could be true but don't you see, Felicity, she will be completely taken up with this boy and she'll notice nothing because there will be nothing to notice unless you do something silly and give the show away.'

'No, Tim, I won't do that. The nerves were getting the better of me but I'm fine now.'

'Thanks to the whisky, told you, didn't I? That's the whisky doing its work.' He sounded pleased and relieved.

'You could be right, it must have helped.'

'Don't be acquiring a taste for it,' he said trying to make a joke.

'Not a chance, I find the taste revolting.' This might be a good time, she thought. 'Tim?'

'What?'

'Please, I don't want you to disappear to your study. This is hard enough for me and I shouldn't have to do it alone.' As she said it she felt a spurt of anger. No, she jolly well shouldn't be left on her own and Tim had had a nerve suggesting it in the first place.

'Very well, you'll have my support since you appear to need it.'

'Thank you.'

'Do you know what Mother said?'

She shook her head.

'She was quite serious when she said not to underestimate you, that the quiet kind, meaning you, very often have an inner strength.'

'I can only hope she is right.'

'That goes for me too.' It was true, his wife would need to be strong to face what was ahead. The worst was still to come.

Felicity's eyes went to the clock and she got up quickly. 'Look at the time.'

'For heaven's sake,' Tim said irritably, 'they won't need feeding the minute they come in the door.'

'No, but I must get on.'

Before she could move away he took hold of her hand and for a fleeting second she thought she caught an expression of absolute despair.

'Felicity, whatever happens in the future try not to think too badly of me.'

'I could never do that,' she said gently. She wondered what he could mean and felt a lump in her throat. 'We'll get through this, never fear.'

Had he been about to confide in her or confess to whatever he had done? If only he would it would help them both. This could be the time and perhaps all it needed was a little push. It was worth another try.

'Darling, I do wish you would trust me. I know you haven't told me everything and no matter how bad it is or how bad you think it is, a trouble shared is a trouble halved and more than anything I want to help you.'

He got up abruptly. 'Hadn't you better get on with whatever it is you have to do?'

It was like a slap in the face.

'Yes, as you say I had better get on.' She gave him a long cool look then turned her back on him.

The housework was done and the preparations for the meal well in hand when Tim came into the kitchen.

'That smells good.' He was his usual self again.

'Yes,' she said closing the oven door.

Tim was wearing brown cords, a cream shirt open at the neck and a cream and light brown V-necked sweater. Felicity thought he looked fresh and smart. She felt hot and sticky.

'I'll take the newspaper with me,' he said picking it up from the chair. 'If you need me for anything I'll be in the sitting-room.'

He didn't usually offer to assist and Felicity couldn't think of anything that required his attention. When they had visitors he was in charge of the drinks but Joanna and Stuart would not be offered anything. If they were thirsty Joanna could get them a soft drink from the fridge.

She was glad they were getting a nice day to come. The sun was shining and the sky was a clear blue. It was a day, she decided, for her pale green sleeveless dress. It had been a spur-of-the-moment buy several years ago and remained a favourite. Tim liked it and that had been important. When he first saw the dress he had nodded approvingly and remarked that the colour suited her and so did the style with its simple lines. Felicity had no conceit about her appearance but she did consider herself lucky that her measurements had hardly changed since her early twenties. The memory of that particular compliment from Tim had remained with her because after that they were few and far between. It saddened her to think that Tim no longer saw her as an attractive woman but merely as someone who was there to see to his needs, keep the house tidy and cook the meals.

It was shortly after twelve when they heard a car stopping at the gate. Tim hastily dropped the opened newspaper – she wished he wouldn't do that – and crossed to the window.

'That's them,' he said and went to open the door. Felicity took a few moments to pick up the paper, even up the pages and fold it. Tim hated it if anyone got to the paper before him but he didn't mind whoever followed having to tidy the pages after him. He wasn't the only man guilty of this, Felicity's father had been the same and no doubt there were many others.

When Felicity went outside, father and daughter were in a close embrace but on seeing her mother Joanna broke away and rushed over.

'Mum, hello, it's great to see you.' She was flushed and happy.

'Hello, darling,' Felicity said and held her daughter close, then she let her go when she saw the boy. He was standing a little apart and smiling.

'Stuart, come and meet the parents.'

The youth, tall and painfully thin, came forward. There were smiles and handshakes.

'How was the journey?' Tim asked.

'Pretty good, the roads weren't too busy.'

'What are you two doing all dressed up?' Joanna said in her outspoken way.

'I wouldn't say we were,' her father answered. 'You, I would say, must have looked out your oldest.' He was smiling as he said it.

It was true, Felicity thought, neither of them could be called smart. If they had dressed for comfort they had excelled. Stuart wore baggy flannels and a loose-fitting jumper that hung on him and accentuated his thinness. As for Joanna she wore the skirt she had been told to leave behind since it was so shabby. Felicity thought it not good enough for the jumble sale.

'Dad, nobody dresses up these days, except oldies I mean.'

'In my student days,' Tim said a little pompously, 'the girls took a pride in their appearance and so did the boys. Not the art school lot, they dressed to draw attention to themselves,' he said with a sly look to Felicity.

'Were you at art school, Mrs Morrison?'

'Yes, Stuart, but I was perfectly respectable. Had I not been, my mother would not have allowed me out of the house.'

They were all laughing when they went indoors.

'If you like I'll show you some of Mum's stuff.'

'Stuff indeed! Is that how you see my efforts?'

'I'd love to see them, Mrs Morrison.'

Felicity was smiling, she had been worrying needlessly. Tim was right as usual. Joanna had eyes only for this boy.

Tim took charge of Stuart. 'If you would like to freshen up, top of the stairs and first on the left.'

'Thanks.' He took the steps two at a time.

Felicity went through to the kitchen. She felt almost happy. It was lovely to have Joanna home and to meet Stuart. I like him, she thought. Nobody could call him handsome but he had a nice face, a good face. The grey eyes were clear and honest and about him was a warm friendliness.

Joanna had come in quietly to stand beside her.

'Well, what do you think? Do you like him?'

'Of course I like Stuart, he seems like a very nice boy, but remember I have just met him.'

'I know but first impressions are very important,' Joanna said seriously.

'In which case, dear, your boyfriend has come through with flying colours.'

'I've met his people,' she said softly.

'Have you? And are they as nice as their son?'

'No, and that isn't to say they are not nice. They are but a bit stiff.'

They heard Stuart on the stairs. 'I'm going up to the bathroom then I'll give you a hand.'

'No need, I have everything ready. You concentrate on looking after Stuart.'

She grinned. 'Thanks, Mum, you're the best.'

The dining-room table was set with a white damask

tablecloth and on each side plate was a stiffly starched napkin. Felicity put down a jug of water, then went through to the sitting-room.

'Lunch is about to be served if you would just go through.'

'Great! Stuart and I are starving.'

Very little was said during the soup course.

'This is really a winter soup for the cold days but I had a feeling—'

'Mrs Morrison, this is very, very good and I am not just saying that.' Stuart put down his spoon.

'Could you take a little more?'

'I could if you don't mind.'

'Stuart, if you hadn't wanted any I would have been disappointed.'

'What about you, Joanna?'

'Yes, please, but not a full plate.'

Tim shook his head before being asked.

'How is Gran?' Joanna asked.

'Much the same, Joanna,' Felicity said stopping on her way to the kitchen. 'I told her you were coming but it was only a flying visit so you wouldn't manage to see her this time.'

Joanna bit her lip. 'I meant to write but you know how it is?'

'No, I don't. What I do know is that there is always time to do what you want.'

'That's not fair.'

'Yes, it is, Joanna, your mother is right.'

'Do you write to your grandparents?'

'Can't, they are all dead. Come to think about it I'm extremely short of relatives.'

'That can be a blessing.'

'Tim!' Felicity protested.

'It's true. You can choose your friends but not your relations.'

'Mum, I promise I'll write to Gran.'

'Then see that you keep your promise.'

'Stuart will be off the notion of that second plate of soup if you don't get a move on.' Tim said with a smile to show he was joking.

'Sorry, but I'm on my way now.'

Felicity ladled soup into Stuart's plate and put a little into Joanna's.

'You must tell us about this holiday in Provence and now that we have met you, Stuart, we know that Joanna will be quite safe with you.'

Joanna looked outraged. 'Honestly, parents are the absolute limit. Anyone would think I was a child and not to be trusted.'

'No, we don't think that at all, dear.'

'You could have fooled me.'

'Joanna, if I had a sister I bet my parents would be the same.' He smiled to Felicity. 'I have been going to the farm for years, first on family holidays then on my own.'

'Satisfied?'

'Yes, Joanna, we are perfectly satisfied. It will be a lovely experience and from what I hear Provence is a very beautiful part of France.'

'My most favourite place, Mrs Morrison. I'm always reluctant to leave it.'

'You like the open-air life?'

'I do, Mr Morrison, and it agrees with me too.'

'If you are going into the legal profession a good part of your life will be spent indoors.'

'I know, it is quite a thought but I'll get used to it. Ours is a family law firm, Mr Morrison, and it was just expected that I would follow my father.'

'Are you an only son, Stuart?'

'No, I have a young brother. Nigel is fourteen and not in the least academic.'

'He's sport mad, isn't he?' Joanna laughed. 'He's fun,' she added.

'The despair of my parents. He's only happy when he is kicking a ball about.'

They had done justice to the lamb, enjoyed the almond tart, and Felicity was suggesting they went through to the sitting-room where she would serve coffee.

There was a general move.

'Mum, after the coffee I'll help you clear up.'

'No, you won't, there will be plenty of time to do that when you are on your way to Edinburgh.'

'Dad will give you a hand.'

'That will be the day.'

'Oh, I don't know, it has been known.'

Joanna jumped up. 'Nearly forgot, I was to show Stuart your sketches.'

'I'm sure it wouldn't have mattered if you did forget.'

'Not so, I want to see them. We have no artists in our family.'

Joanna raced upstairs. The folders were kept on a shelf in the hall cupboard. She took a quick glance in the top folder and decided it would do. Her mother wouldn't want her bringing down too many. She was very modest when it came to her hobby.

'Here we are,' she said waving the folder and then sitting down beside Stuart on the settee. She moved as close to Stuart as possible then opened the folder.

'Excuse me, I'll finish off the paper,' Tim said.

'These are terrific, absolutely first class,' Stuart said looking amazed. 'You made them sound as though they were nothing.'

'My mother is very modest.'

'She most certainly is.'

Joanna was looking with new eyes at her mother's drawings. 'My mother did very well at art school.'

'Their star student or pretty near it I should think.'

'Now! Now! Don't overdo it,' Felicity said and felt her colour rising. She wasn't used to such praise.

'You might have been famous, Mum, if you hadn't fallen for Dad.'

'But I did and I have no regrets.'

Joanna nodded. 'You didn't do too badly, you became the wife of a successful lawyer.'

Felicity caught her breath. 'Yes, that is what I became,' she managed to say. She was glad that Tim was behind his newspaper.

'I'm certainly impressed, I think they are terribly

clever. It seems such a shame to hide your talent, Mrs Morrison.'

Felicity felt a glow of pride. She needed this praise to give her confidence. Her small successes hadn't amounted to much but then she probably wasn't going about it the right way. Not that the small cheques weren't welcome, but if she could do better ...

They took a long time over coffee and there were no awkward silences. The day had been a success and when the time came to depart there was genuine regret at the parting.

'Don't forget the almond tart.'

'I won't.'

'I put it in a tin for safe keeping.'

'Thanks.'

Felicity turned to the boy who had got to his feet. 'Stuart, it has been lovely meeting you and we hope you both have a wonderful time in Provence.'

'We will and thank you for having me, Mrs Morrison. It has been great and you are a super cook.'

Tim was standing looking completely relaxed. 'With you being away from home you must miss your mother's cooking.'

Stuart shook his head. 'My mother doesn't do anything. Oh, gosh, she wouldn't have to hear me say that. What I meant was she doesn't do anything in the house. Mrs Allardyce, our housekeeper, does everything. She isn't a bad cook but nothing special. Mum is kept busy with all her meetings and goodness knows what else.'

Felicity wanted to say he would always be welcome but thought it better not to. The future for all of them was too uncertain.

'I'll come and look at this car of yours,' Tim said jovially.

'Please do, I only got her about six weeks ago,' he said proudly. 'My first one fell to bits, a complete write-off.'

'You mean it was involved in an accident?' Tim said frowning. He didn't want Joanna risking her life with a daredevil driver.

'No, touch wood, I haven't had a scrape.' He grinned. 'Don't know how many previous owners it had but they must have been a careless lot. My mother was ashamed to see it sitting outside the house and I have her to thank for persuading Dad to dip into his pocket and buy me something more roadworthy. He wasn't too keen, the careful lawyer you know. He believes that what you work for you appreciate and what you get easily you don't.'

'I would go along with that.'

'You lawyers stick together, don't you?'

Felicity saw a shadow cross Tim's face. 'Usually but not always,' he said quietly.

The two men went outside leaving Felicity and Joanna together.

'Mum, thanks for everything.'

'There is nothing to thank me for, dear. This is your home and I'm glad you brought Stuart.'

'He chatted quite the thing, didn't he?'

Felicity looked at her daughter. 'Why shouldn't he?'

'No reason at all except that when we were having a meal in his house he hardly opened his mouth and his brother left the table as soon as it was polite to do so.'

'Who did the talking or was it a silent meal?' Felicity smiled. Joanna was good at exaggerating.

'His parents talked about things in general and then Mr Milton asked me questions.'

'What kind of questions?'

'He wanted to know where Dad worked. When I told him he nodded as though I had passed.'

Felicity laughed outright. 'Joanna, you have a great imagination. The man had a perfect right to ask questions. This girl sitting at their table could be a future daughter-in-law.'

'Half a mo – there is nothing like that.'

'Maybe not but he wasn't to know that.'

Joanna grinned. 'He was favourably impressed that Dad was a lawyer with Paton & Noble. He knew of the firm. You can tell Dad if you like.' She broke off when her father appeared.

'Better be off, sweetheart, Stuart is ready and waiting.'

Joanna hugged them both then ran out with her parents following. Once they had waved the car out of sight there was that curiously empty feeling that follows a parting.

'It went well, I think,' Felicity said as they went indoors.

'Yes, it did. He is a nice enough lad.'

'Just nice enough?' she said disappointed. 'I liked him very much and it is very obvious they are happy together.'

'A couple of kids that's all they are. They will have this holiday in Provence then we'll see. They may well have had enough of each other by then.'

'I wouldn't call them kids but I agree it will be a testing time when they are to be so much in each other's company.'

'Mmmm.'

'Come on, Tim, make yourself useful. Carry the dishes through to the kitchen and maybe you could dry them.'

'Get me a tray and I'll help you clear the table but I'll leave you to do the rest.'

'You are not going to disappear to your study are you?'

'Yes.'

'I thought you would stay down here and we could talk.'

'What about?'

'Everything and nothing or we can sit in a companionable silence,' she said with a trace of sarcasm.

'No, I'm going up to my study to work.'

'What work? You can't have work to do.'

'That is where you are wrong. This is an opportunity for me to clear out what is no longer of use. I may be unemployed but I need to keep up-to-date.'

'Of course, I didn't think — and don't worry, something will turn up.'

'Nothing will unless I do something about it. There is no question of moving away, not as long as Mother needs me.'

'And after that?' she said looking at him steadily.

'We'll just have to wait and see. Mother is my main concern.'

'What about us, your wife and daughter?'

'Mother is old for heaven's sake.'

She hasn't always been old, Felicity said silently, but she has always come first with you. It shouldn't be that way but it is.

Chapter Seven

This had been a good spell of weather with the rain being kind and coming during the night. Tim was keeping strictly to routine and leaving the house at the same time. Before he set off he didn't ask Felicity her plans nor did he tell her his.

'That's me off, Felicity,' he called on his way out.

'Yes, all right, see you when you come,' she answered.

With her husband gone she could get ready. There was a small niggle of guilt but not big enough to really bother her. It was just a slightly uncomfortable feeling about keeping her own plans secret. Then Felicity shrugged and excused herself with the thought that Tim would not have been interested. The real truth was that she didn't want Tim to know she was going to Perth. He might guess that she was going to share her worries with her oldest and best friend.

Sitting before the dressing-table she put on her make-up. Felicity was sparing with it, a good skin didn't need much but a trace of lipstick brought the face to life. She must have read that somewhere. She took to wondering how long they could go on staying in Hillhead. It was a good place to live and it would be a wrench to leave but she wouldn't break her heart. She liked Angus and Perthshire. Perth would be an attractive place to live. It was a city and a county town rolled into one with much to offer. It was small wonder that visitors flocked to it. The locals were proud of their city's history and not without reason. Had it not been for the murder of the poet-king James I, Perth might so easily have been the capital of Scotland.

Felicity enjoyed driving and it was a pleasant run. After parking the car at the back of the Cairn Hotel she walked round to the front and went quickly up the three wide marble steps. The entrance hall was pleasing to the eye. It was spacious with fresh blooms in a large vase on the desk and green and gold carpeting covering the floor. For a moment or two Felicity stood still and looked about her, then she walked across to the glass case, it hadn't been there on her last visit. A card with gold lettering informed prospective buyers that the goods on display could be purchased at a nearby shop giving the name and address. Felicity studied what was there. There were small framed pictures of Perthshire beauty spots, several good quality leather purses and pocketbooks, crystal glasses in satin-lined boxes and cairngorm brooches nestling in their velvet boxes. Nothing was cheap and tawdry and though tartan was in evidence it was played down. This tendency to overdo it was a mistake. Too much of anything took away from its value.

Turning away, Felicity went over to the reception desk. The young woman had been writing but stopped what she was doing and looked up with a smile.

'Good morning.'

'Good morning.' Felicity smiled back. 'I'm Mrs Morrison and Miss Reid is expecting me.'

'Yes, she said so and I was to tell you to go straight to her own rooms.'

'Thank you.'

'You know the way?'

'Yes, I do.' Then she saw Rachel approaching.

'There you are, Felicity, I thought you would be arriving about now.' They touched cheeks.

Rachel wore a deep blue fine jersey suit and looked well. She turned back to address the girl at the desk.

'Have coffee brought to my room in about fifteen minutes, Marion. Will you see to that?'

'I will, Miss Reid,' she said already reaching for the phone as it rang.

'Marion, you may remember me telling you, took over from Rhona,' Rachel said as they moved away from the desk. 'She is very good. Rhona, if faced with anything out of the usual would get flustered. Marion doesn't and she has a very pleasant manner.'

'Yes, I thought that. Incidentally I've been looking at the show case. I like it and it will draw people over.'

'Something new I am trying. If it proves to be a

success I may consider having another, possibly on the opposite wall.'

They left the hall and walked along a corridor to the very far end. There was an annexe which had been added to the side of the hotel and Rachel decided to make it her living quarters. The accommodation consisted of a bigger than average sitting-room, a double bedroom, a room with a single bed, a small well-planned kitchen and a bathroom. The kitchen was seldom used except for breakfast. Rachel took all her other meals in the hotel dining-room where she had her own reserved table.

Rachel had good taste and avoided the cluttered look. If Felicity could find fault it would be because it was rather too sparsely furnished. Certainly the room was without frills, a little like its owner. There was nothing showy or flamboyant about Rachel. She was honest, straightforward and thoughtful. She would never willingly hurt anyone but neither would she deny them the truth. For those who found it difficult to face the truth it could be uncomfortable.

'I haven't had a chance to say but I do like what you are wearing.'

'Thank you. I felt it wasn't a summer dress day, there is quite a chill in that wind, and this is such a handy jacket. It goes with any of my skirts.'

'New?'

'Not really, I bought it in the spring.'

The bouclé jacket had been expensive. The cut was simple and allowed the fabric to speak for itself. In a myriad of colours with pink the most outstanding it would team with most colours. She heard all that from the shop assistant, sales talk but true in this case.

'It seems ages since we were together,' Rachel said once they were inside the sitting-room.

'It is ages.'

'Thank heaven for the phone I always say. If we had to depend on letters I for one would have fewer friends.' She paused. 'Let me have your jacket and do make yourself at home. You shouldn't have to be told that.'

When Rachel returned from hanging the jacket on a coat hanger on the back of the bedroom door, she brought her chair closer to Felicity then got two small tables and put one beside each chair.

'Ready for the coffee when it comes.'

'How is business?'

'Can't complain but never mind that. I thought of you on Saturday. How did it go?'

'It went splendidly.'

'And the boy, come on I'm dying to know what he is like. Joanna is my godchild and I need to hear all about this romance.'

Felicity laughed. 'Joanna would be embarrassed to hear you say that. She admits to me to him being special but for all that they are just good friends.'

'Is he nice?'

'I liked him, Rachel, I liked him very much.'

'Tall, dark and handsome?'

'No, he isn't handsome. Stuart is tall, thin as a rake with a narrow face and a sallow complexion. I liked his smile and he has strong, even white teeth.'

'Good teeth, I like that. In fact to me he sounds just fine. Give me an interesting face, one never gets tired of that. So many handsome men are impossibly vain and would bore you to death in no time. Ah, here comes the coffee,' she said getting up to answer the tap at the door.

'Thank you, Winnie, I'll just take it and you close the door.'

The girl went away quietly and Rachel put the tray on the sideboard. She poured the coffee, handed Felicity a cup and put the sugar and milk beside her as well as a plate of biscuits.

'We won't be interrupted unless something dreadful happens like the ceiling collapsing.'

'Heaven forbid.' Felicity took a drink of the coffee, then put the cup down on the saucer. 'That's good and the way I like it.'

'We aim to please.'

There was silence. Felicity was finding it difficult to begin.

'Take your time, we have all day if necessary,' she said gently.

'Tim has lost his job.'

'Oh.'

'He was told to clear his desk and go.'

'I find that hard to believe.'

'I did too, but it is true.'

'Had you an inkling that something was wrong or did it come as a shock?'

'A complete shock, Rachel. Someone, one of the clerks I suppose it was, drove him home with his belongings. It was a company car so that went too.'

'How awful.'

'Yes, it was and so unnecessary.' Felicity gulped and lifting the cup drank some of the coffee. Rachel waited.

'I didn't know what kind of trouble he had got himself into, I still don't know. He tried to tell me it was gambling debts but I can't accept that. He isn't the easist person to talk to and he is being very evasive. If I try to get at the truth he gets angry.'

Rachel nodded. 'I think I might be ahead of you, Felicity. Since the firm has dispensed with Tim's services and it would appear at short notice, I can only think that your husband has borrowed money to get him out of a difficulty. Something pretty pressing.'

'Spot on I would say.'

'Do I take it he has borrowed from a client?'

'Yes. Tim used the expression borrowed. Me, I call it stealing which is what it is.'

'No, Felicity, I don't go along with that. Stealing is taking something with no intention of replacing it. I'm guessing here but if the money was required in a hurry Tim might have been panicked into doing what he did.'

'I suppose you could be right but it makes little difference,' Felicity said wearily.

'May I ask you something?'

'Of course, that is why I am here, to talk it over.'

'Has the money been repaid?'

'It has or it shortly will be. Tim's mother came to the rescue. She is very comfortably off and Tim only had to ask.'

'Why didn't he?'

'Because, Rachel, my husband adores his mother, always has and always will. Her good opinion is very important.'

'She knows now?'

'She knows that Tim has lost his job,' Felicity said.

'And has probably guessed the reason for his dismissal.'

'I think so. She doesn't ask questions.'

'Because she believes she already knows the answers.'

Felicity nodded. 'Old people have their own way of coping. Hers is maybe to ignore what is too painful to accept.'

'You could be right.'

'Tim is to get part of his inheritance now.' Felicity raised her eyes and looked at Rachel.

'That should make a difference. With the money repaid and no one having suffered perhaps Paton & Noble will have second thoughts and re-instate Tim.'

Felicity shook her head slowly.

'A sharp reprimand should do. Tim isn't likely to reoffend.'

'It's too late, has been from the start. Paton & Noble

are taking it the whole way. They are going to make a case of it.'

'A court case?'

'Yes.'

Rachel looked very shocked. 'That seems excessive in the extreme.'

'He betrayed a trust and that is a very serious offence. It could mean a prison sentence.'

'Surely not.'

'Tim is resigned to it.' Felicity choked. 'He expects to go to prison and says all that he can hope for is a light sentence.'

'I never dreamt it was anything like this.'

'Now you know what I am going through. Bad though it is for me it is so much worse for Tim. He is the one facing a prison sentence.'

'He is the one who has sinned, you haven't.' She bit her lip. 'How much have you told Joanna?'

'Joanna knows nothing, nothing at all. To begin with, Rachel, I wasn't happy about keeping this from her, but now I agree with Tim. At some stage she will have to know but what is the point of making her miserable and unhappy before she need be.'

'It has to be a risk but on balance I think Tim is right. Poor child she is going to be devastated.'

'I try not to think that far ahead.'

'This holiday in Provence must seem like a god-send?'

'Yes and please God let her have a wonderful holiday is what I ask. No one can take that away from her.'

'When is the case likely to be heard or don't you know?'

'Tim thinks it could be late September or thereabout.'

'Joanna could still be out of the country?'

'It is a possibility.'

'Shall I ring for more coffee?'

'Not for me, thank you, I should be getting back.'

'What for? There is nothing hurrying you.'

'No, I suppose not. Maybe I'll do some shopping before I go home.'

'Late afternoon will do for that. We need to talk some more.'

'This is unfair of me putting my worries on to you.'

'That's what friends are for. I'm here for you and always remember that. Look on this as a bolthole if you like.'

'A very nice bolthole.'

'Should this go to court life could become difficult for you in Hillhead.'

'The gossip? Yes, I'm sure there will be plenty of that. The thought of that worried me to begin with but not any more. I could say it is the least of my worries.' She gave a twisted smile. 'No one is likely to say anything to my face and what is said behind my back won't harm me.'

'No one is going to think badly of you, Felicity.'

'Some will say I must have known what was going on.'

Rachel shook her head though she did think there could be some truth in that. There were those who would think a wife should know what her husband was doing especially when it concerned a large sum of money. 'Those with some sense won't think that. You will have their sympathy.'

'I don't want their sympathy. They can think what they like. As I said it is not all that important; you see, though I am friendly with my neighbours I am not close to any of them. The one I might have confided in moved away to Glasgow and the couple who bought the house keep themselves to themselves.'

'Fine,' Rachel said brusquely, 'we've got that out of the way. Now if you don't mind me asking how are you placed financially?'

'No immediate worries but I need to try and earn some money. Tim suggested that I should get myself a job.'

'With your talent that shouldn't be difficult. I take it you still do your illustrations?'

'In a very small way, I earn a little.'

'Then you aren't going about things in the right way.'

'I wouldn't know how to.'

'I'll ask Terence, he'll know.'

'How is Terence?' Felicity had met Rachel's friend on several occasions. She liked the big, broad-shouldered man who with his florid complexion could easily be taken for a farmer particularly as he favoured tweed suits. Perhaps he came from farming stock but according to Rachel, Terence Mitchell was a very astute businessman.

'Terence is always fine,' Rachel smiled. 'I'll sound him out and with his wide circle of friends he is bound to know someone who could be helpful. You leave that to me.'

'Thank you, I'm very grateful. Joanna showed Stuart some of my illustrations and he did seem to be impressed.'

'Of course he was. The lad recognises talent when he sees it. If I had been so gifted I would have made good use of it. Learn to believe in yourself, Felicity, that is halfway to success.'

'What would I do without you?'

'You would manage but since I am here let me help.'

'You already are. I'm so glad I have you, Rachel,' Felicity said unsteadily. 'I didn't realise it before but to have no one must be terrible. I do have friends who would be deeply hurt if they could hear me saying that, I mean that I only have you to turn to. They would want to help I do know that but I know too, they would be quite unable to keep it to themselves. The whispers would begin.' She smiled. 'The times I've heard: "Don't tell a soul I'm only telling you because I know it will go no further."'

'Very true.'

Chapter Eight

As soon as she entered the morning room of Grange House, Felicity saw the letter propped up on the mantelpiece beside the marble clock. It was from Joanna, she recognised the writing on the envelope and smiled, pleased that Joanna had kept her promise to write to her grandmother.

'Yes, that's right, Felicity, a letter from Joanna. Wasn't that thoughtful of her to write to me before going off to France with that boy?'

'I felt sure she would.' Felicity had hoped but she hadn't felt sure. The young could so easily forget their promises when other things clamoured for their attention.

'Before you sit down would you hand it to me, please?'

Felicity reached up for the letter and gave it to Maud.

'Thank you.' She put on her spectacles and drew out the pages but she didn't offer them to Felicity to read.

'The dear child sends her apologies for not coming to Carnoustie when she was at home but as she says here' – she tapped the page – 'there just wasn't the time.'

'That's true,' Felicity said hastily, 'the four of us had lunch, a very leisurely lunch, and then it seemed no time before we were waving them off.'

'Of course I was disappointed not to see Joanna and to meet the boy but I quite understand. When this holiday is over they will take the time and make an old lady happy,' she said scanning the letter for bits to read out. 'Ah, yes, this is the bit I was looking for, it is typical Joanna. "Life in Edinburgh is very hectic, there is loads to do and before you say it, Gran, I am working or doing enough anyway. You know the saying 'all work and no play makes Jack a dull boy' and you wouldn't want your granddaughter to be a dull girl, would you? I bet you weren't." Little monkey,' Maud smiled as she folded the pages and put them back in the envelope.

'Is that all – three pages to say that?' Felicity laughed.

'The rest is confidential and is between Joanna and me,' Maud said looking pleased with herself. 'The very old and the very young get along well which I daresay would surprise a great many people. It doesn't surprise me, I had this relationship with my own grandmother. You see we have the time to listen when parents don't.'

'That might be true of some parents,' Felicity protested.

'Most parents, Felicity, and let me say that I was as guilty as the rest. You don't believe me but I speak the truth. When it comes to their own precious child the parents want only the best but the best for whom? Who are we to say what someone should do? It is their life and no, don't interrupt,' she said putting up her hand, 'let me say what I have to. Tim's father and I made up our mind that our son should have a profession. We, not Tim, decided that he should study law. As it happened Tim didn't object and he seemed pleased enough to go along with our wishes.'

'It was probably what he wanted. Must have been when he passed his exams with flying colours.'

'He did do well and made his parents very proud.' Maud paused and she looked sad. 'Where does that leave us now?'

'I don't follow, what do you mean?'

'We got our lawyer in the family and now look at him.'

'Tim made a mistake – that doesn't mean he stops being a good lawyer.'

'Doesn't it?'

'One mistake.'

'One mistake perhaps, but don't make it sound trivial.'

'I didn't mean to.'

'Tim did something very, very wrong, he must have, Felicity, when it has cost him his job. There will be no reference and he will have to try and explain that away. I may not be as bright as I once was but neither am I stupid. It is sheer cowardice that I ask no questions. I don't want to know the answers because I believe, more than believe, I know they would distress me. I see the worry in your face and in my son's.'

'We are all worried, of course we are, Tim has to find himself a job but he will, I am confident about that. You are troubling yourself needlessly.'

'Am I?'

'Yes.'

'Thank you, I want to believe that.' She shook her head. 'I do feel in some part responsible.'

'You are in no way responsible and neither am I. Tim got himself into this mess and no one, least of all you, is to blame.'

'No blame is attached to you, Felicity. You married a solicitor whereas I encouraged Tim to become one. Without that encouragement I wonder what Tim would have chosen for himself?'

'More than likely the law,' Felicity smiled.

'Perhaps and then perhaps not. What I am trying to say and I am not making a very good job of it is that Tim should have been left to make his own decisions without feeling he had to please us.'

Felicity was shaking her head. 'I don't see it that way at all. Tim, like so many others might not have had a clue as to what he should study and you suggested something that he thought he would like. He was probably very relieved to have it settled for him.'

'You are such a kind soul. And now, my dear, we

have Joanna who doesn't know what she wants to do when she leaves university.'

'She is only saying that. When the time comes she will go on to teacher training college.'

'No, she won't, that is the last thing she wants to do,' Maud said firmly.

Felicity was frowning and looking puzzled. 'Is this all in the letter she wrote you?'

'No, she told me long ago, before she went off to university. She said her father wanted her to have a degree and since English was her best subject she should study that.'

'Sounds very reasonable to me.' Felicity had thought so at the time.

'Yes, to us it sounds very reasonable but don't you see, my dear, Joanna might want something very different but feels reluctant to tell you, since she believes you wouldn't approve.'

'What does she want to do?'

'I don't know, perhaps she isn't all that sure herself what she wants but the point I am trying to make is leave it to her. Let her choose. Do that and you'll have no regrets in the future.'

'What if she makes the wrong choice?'

'Then she will learn by her mistake.'

'No she won't, it will be too late.'

'I've done enough talking, I'm tired.'

'I'll make a cup of tea.'

'Thank you, dear, that would be very welcome. You aren't angry with me, are you?'

'Why should I be angry?'

'I have been very outspoken. The advantage of being old, and believe me there aren't many, is that one can be shockingly outspoken and forgiven because we are too old to be taken seriously.'

'I take you very seriously and I shall give careful thought to what you have said but first of all I'll make that cup of tea.'

The days were turning into weeks. Felicity both feared and dreaded what was ahead though a part of her wanted the time to fly so that it would be over and they could put it all behind them. Nothing, she felt, could be worse than this uncertainty. There were times when Felicity would look at her husband and try to imagine him in a prison cell and couldn't. If the worst came to the worst and he had a sentence to serve would he be put among hardened criminals or was there some method of segregation? She didn't know and it wasn't something one could ask. In any case who, among her friends, would know? She shivered. How many friends would they have after this?

Tim had been remarkable but now the strain was beginning to show and he was becoming ever more silent. They should have been able to draw comfort from one another but instead they were moving further apart. They continued to sleep in separate rooms and very little was said at the breakfast table. The routine was the same. Tim left the house at the usual time and seldom returned before early evening.

Where did he go? Where did he spend those hours? Twice a week he visited his mother, staying only a short time. Maud never remembered how long her son stayed. She kept nodding off and then was confused about the time. Not so Mrs Haggarty, she noticed and would mention to Felicity who had called and for how long they had stayed to keep the old lady company.

Felicity knew that since her husband set such store on routine he would expect his wife to do the same. But she didn't. She was going out of her way to avoid people she knew would want to stop and chat. She changed her hairdresser and was going further afield for her shopping. In the house she would let the phone ring until whoever was at the other end grew tired and rang off. Two phone calls she did answer were from friends concerned that they hadn't seen her around and wondering if she was well enough. Maud became her excuse. Her own health was fine she told them but Tim's mother was ill and required attention. Someone had to be with her. That was why they hadn't seen her, she was spending a lot of time in Carnoustie. How long it would go on for she had no idea but for the foreseeable future she was accepting no invitations and please would they spread the word?

Maybe it was because Felicity felt guilty making her mother-in-law the excuse but she began to spend more time with Maud. She would drive to Carnoustie every other afternoon. She never met Tim since his visits were made in the early part of the day. Mrs Haggarty's hours had increased, she had no ties, she said and would be available at any time.

Like her son but not for the same reason, Maud was becoming silent. Talking seemed to tire her more now but the silence was restful. Daughter-in-law and mother-in-law could sit together for long periods of time without a word being spoken. The old lady would sit gazing into the fire. Winter or summer there was always a fire. A good going fire in the coldest days and in the warmer days there would be a few pieces of coal burning at the bottom of the grate. Maud said a fire was cheerful and it was company whereas an empty grate was depressing. Occasionally Maud would reach out and pat her daughter-in-law's hand as though to thank her for just being there.

The silence was shattered. The phone began to ring and went on ringing while Felicity stood in the middle of the floor, her hands clenched deep inside the pockets of her flared skirt and debated with herself whether or not she should answer it. She wished that there was some way of telling if a call was important or not. If it was and she didn't answer it how would she ever forgive herself? The sudden urgency to reach the phone before it stopped ringing sent her flying across the room. With a shaking hand Felicity lifted the receiver.

'Hello,' she said quickly and sounding breathless.

'You do take your time to answer, Felicity. Have you

just got in or something? I was on the point of ringing off,' Rachel said.

'Sorry, I was upstairs,' Felicity lied. 'I was in the bathroom,' she added to account for the delay in answering.

'No matter, I'm glad I did catch you, since this happens to be a slack time with me.'

'I thought you never had those.'

'Once in a while I do and now before I say another word tell me how you are?'

'Me? I'm fine.'

'You don't sound it and I'm not easily fooled.'

'Think what you like but I'm telling you I'm fine.' Her head was beginning to ache and she was wishing now that she had let the phone ring. Why were folk so slow to take the hint? Couldn't they understand that all she wanted was to be left alone. Surely that wasn't too much to ask?

'You are far from fine, you are sick with worry.'

'I'm fine I tell you.' She was almost shouting.

'No, you are not.' In contrast Rachel's voice was steady and firm.

'Then why ask a stupid question when you know the answer?' Felicity closed her eyes, appalled at what she was doing. Here she was snapping at her best friend, perhaps in a short time her only friend. Who would want to know her when it all came out? 'I'm sorry, so sorry, Rachel,' she said wretchedly, 'I don't know what is coming over me.'

'Worrying is responsible for a lot and this, I gather,

has been a really bad day,' Rachel said sympathetically.

'I only have bad days and I know they can only get worse.'

'Thoughts like that are not going to help.'

'I know.'

'It could be that you are too much on your own.'

'Oh, no, it isn't that. I like being on my own, it is what I want. You see, Rachel, when I am in the house with the door shut I no longer have to act a part, I can let myself go. I can howl my head off if I want and I can do what I damned well like. And believe you me that makes a change.'

'What makes a change? You doing what you damned well like?' By now they were both laughing but in Felicity's laugh there was a hint of hysteria.

'Yes.' She paused. 'Just lately I've begun to feel like the invisible woman. Tim hardly opens his mouth. Granted my husband is worried to death but then so am I. I believe talking and sharing our worries would help, he doesn't agree. I hardly ever see him – God knows where he gets to – but he is treating our home like a B & B.'

'He could be trying to line up a job for himself.'

'I don't think so. What starting date would he give?'

'Sorry, that was stupid of me.'

'It's all right.'

'Try to take it easy, Felicity, you know, one day at a time.'

'I do try but it is all so hopeless. Tim won't talk to me and I've given up on him and, wait for it, when I am in Carnoustie,' she said hardly pausing for breath, 'I sit with my mother-in-law in near silence.'

'How is the old lady?'

'Going downhill, she is failing and her voice is getting weaker. But let me say that this is not an awkward silence.' Felicity was anxious to get that right.

'A companionable silence?'

'Yes, that about describes it. She is rather a wonderful old lady and though I am sure she has aches and pains you don't hear her complaining.'

'A lot of old people are like that. They don't want to be a nuisance and prefer to suffer in silence.'

'Rachel, sometimes she makes me want to weep, she is so touchingly grateful for my company.'

'What about Tim, is he a dutiful son?'

'Tim adores his mother, always has.'

'That doesn't answer my question.'

'As a matter of fact he is a dutiful son, Tim calls in regularly to see her.' She didn't know why but the question annoyed her.

'Glad to hear it. Not all families visit their aged parents but daughters on the whole are more thoughtful than sons. Enough about that, I wanted it all out of the way before—'

'Before what?' she asked at once apprehensive.

'Before I tell you my news.'

'Oh dear, nothing bad I hope?'

'Just listen will you? I have good news, in fact it could

be great news, it all depends on you. Those illustrations you sent on to me—'

'Oh, those, I had completely forgotten about them.'

'Sorry it has taken so long, but as Terence explained to me it was important to get them to the right person.'

'And now he has, is that what you are telling me?' Felicity tried and failed to get any enthusiasm into her voice.

'Yes, that is exactly what I am telling you. Terence has really put himself about.'

Felicity heard the thinly veiled annoyance in Rachel's voice and the disappointment and was immediately ashamed. What must Rachel think of her? She must get a grip on herself. Were her gloomy thoughts taking over? Could this be the first sign, a warning, that she was in danger of slipping into a depression if she wasn't careful? She was becoming alarmed. Felicity had never thought of herself as the type to sink into a depression but now she knew better. There was no type, it could happen to anyone. It would happen to her if she wasn't very careful.

'Rachel, forgive me, I'm not myself.'

'No, you are not and I am becoming concerned.'

'Don't be.' She gave a little laugh. 'The danger would be if I wasn't aware of it. I am and I'll watch myself. The last thing I can afford is to have a nervous breakdown.'

'That is not going to happen to you, do you hear?' she shouted, making Felicity take the phone away from her ear. 'You don't even talk about it. All that is happening is that you are going through a bad patch and you will get over it. I know you better than you know yourself. To my mind you have too much time to think, not enough to occupy you but that is all to change. There will be time for your Carnoustie visits but little else.'

'Why?'

'Because from now on your time is to be completely taken up.'

'Stop it, Rachel, I'm not in the mood.'

'Then get yourself in the mood and stop feeling so sorry for yourself.'

'Thank you very much,' she said huffily.

'Sorry, Felicity, but you needed someone to say that and now this is the good news. Your clever illustrations are causing quite a stir and an agent, Adam Silver by name, will be in touch with you very soon.'

'Rachel, I'm very sorry to sound so stupid but I am not making sense of this. What do I want with an agent? I'm not with you.'

'You can say that again. Concentrate, woman, and pull yourself together. I have it from Terence that this Adam Silver is very impressed with your work. As it happens there is a children's book coming out and in need of good illustrations. Yours appear to fit the bill or will when they tell you what they want. Let me spell it out. They want you to do the illustrations.'

'Me?'

'Yes, you. You will have to work closely with the author but your agent will sort that out.'

'My agent? You mean I've got one?'

'He will be offering his services and you would do well to accept pronto. Good agents are hard to come by and from all accounts this Adam Silver is one of the best.'

'Rachel, I don't know what to say,' she said unsteadily.

'You could start by saying that you are interested and pleased.'

'I am, I'm thrilled to bits but panicky too. What if after all this I don't produce what they want.'

'They are professionals, it will have been discussed, and it isn't often they make a mistake. Think yourself lucky, this could be your big break.'

'I'll do my very best, that I can promise.'

'You had better, my girl, this has to be a one hundred percent commitment. If Adam Silver is to take you on he won't be put off with excuses. You have to deliver on time and if that should mean burning the midnight oil then so be it. There will be a lot of people depending on you.'

'This is my big chance,' she said nervously.

'It could be. Make a success of it and there will be plenty to follow.'

'How do I begin to thank you?'

'By distancing yourself from Tim and his troubles. He has made it patently clear that he doesn't want you involved and you should accept that. Worry will stop you producing your best work and only your best will be good enough.'

'Yes, I understand that,' Felicity said quietly. 'Rest

assured I won't let anyone down and please tell Terence how grateful I am. He must have gone to a lot of trouble on my behalf.'

'He did.' Rachel saw no reason to play down her friend's efforts, he had worked jolly hard. 'Terence said to tell you that when you become well-known and successful, he will be taking some of the credit.'

'And so he should.' Felicity laughed, a carefree laugh. 'The minute I put down this phone I am going to get out my sketch pad. It is ages since I did anything and I am itching to get started.'

'All that talking and we haven't mentioned Joanna but I gather from my postcard that everything is sheer bliss. Apparently she is having a whale of a time and enjoying every moment.'

'They are supposed to be working for their keep,' Felicity laughed.

'Maybe they are and it is all enjoyment. The writing was very small and cramped and it took me a while to make it out. Not that I am complaining, I much prefer that to a few words scrawled over the postcard.'

'Yes. I have to say, Rachel, that my daughter is in my good books. She took the time and trouble to write a long, newsy letter to her grandmother and made one old lady very happy.'

'That was nice but then those two have always got on well.'

'Yes, they have. The very young and the very old seem to have a lot of time for each other. Rachel, before you ring off I have a confession to make.'

'Make it snappy then, I have a salesman waiting for me and showing signs of increasing impatience.'

'I wasn't going to answer the phone.'

'Why ever not?'

'Don't know. It's been that way with me for a while. The phone rings and I want to hide, the same when the doorbell goes. Crazy isn't it?'

Rachel thought it was deeply disturbing and not something to be taken lightly. 'You are beginning to worry me, Felicity, this is no joke. If it goes on you will have to seek professional help. You have been under a lot of stress and stronger folk than you and me have snapped.'

'Not you?'

'Don't be so sure.'

'I am very sure but not to worry. Not to worry about me I mean. I have been given a tonic which is doing me the world of good. The black cloud that has been following me around has gone or to be more accurate the big black cloud has gone. There will be other smaller ones, nothing surer but I'll cope. As you so rightly put it I was dwelling too much on my troubles because there was nothing else for me to do. The house is getting the minimum, I can't be bothered doing a proper clean though I must make an effort. Joanna is away and Tim doesn't need me.'

'Plenty of time for your little sketches.'

'Oh, yes, all day if necessary. Oh dear, I am just remembering that poor salesman. Do go and see to him and to make up for that long wait give him a big order.'

'Whether I need it or not?'

'Yes, the least you can do.'

'And you are too kind-hearted. As a businesswoman you would be a disaster. Cheerio for now and don't forget to keep me up-to-date.'

'I won't. Cheerio and many, many thanks.'

Felicity put the phone down. She was smiling hugely and then hugged herself. The excitement was making her quite light-headed and she went through to the sitting-room and sat down in one of the armchairs. Life was so strange. One could be in the throes of despair seeing no hope, no light at the end of the tunnel and then suddenly something wonderful and totally unexpected happens and life takes on a new meaning. The worries don't disappear but they become manageable.

Already there were fresh ideas in her head and she needed her sketch pad to get them down. Working at the kitchen table hadn't bothered her because it was only for short spells. But it was far from ideal, the kitchen table served so many purposes and it meant removing her working tools which was both a nuisance and time wasting.

The traitorous thought wouldn't be stilled and why should it? Surely she had a perfect right to the study and Tim's desk when or if he was to be away for some time. It seemed likely that she would be staying in Hillhead. Tim had made no mention of selling the house. Tim, she thought, could hardly object to her making use of the study. Even so she knew that she would make no mention of it. What he didn't know wouldn't upset him whereas if he were to forbid her to use his desk then she would feel guilty about doing so.

Should she share her exciting news with her husband? Better perhaps to wait until she had something definite to tell him. And that would be when this Adam Silver telephoned. She wondered what he would be like.

Chapter Nine

Had it been a dream? Felicity wondered as she opened her eyes and stared at the ceiling, then decided it hadn't. She hadn't dreamt it, it was real. Didn't dreams fade the moment one awoke and no matter how hard one tried to recapture them they proved elusive and drifted away. Rachel had telephoned with the wonderful news about her illustrations. It hadn't been her imagination. Only she must go carefully and not let herself get carried away. Had there been a letter, she wished there had been, she could have read and reread it whereas with a telephone conversation there was never total recall. Another thought. Had Rachel been so anxious to cheer up her friend that she had exaggerated the possibilities for success? That could be it. Felicity nodded her head as though to emphasise the point and make sure she took that into consideration. It was very important that she keep calm and not let herself get over-excited, then if nothing came of this the disappointment would not be so great.

Even so the bubble of excitement wouldn't go away and Felicity was humming to herself as she prepared the breakfast. Tim, looking smart but with dark shadows under his eyes, came into the kitchen and raised his eyebrows.

'You sound cheerful,' he muttered as he sat down and removed the napkin from its ring.

'I'm trying to be. Being miserable only makes everything worse. Tim, go easy on the milk, that is all there is. I had to throw away almost a pint. You left the bottle out last night instead of putting it back in the fridge and in this weather it doesn't keep.'

'Are you sure I was the culprit?' he said mildly.

'Yes, I am. It wasn't me and there are only two of us in the house.' The humming started again as she made the tea.

'Must you? What on earth has brought this on?' Tim said looking at her strangely.

'Brought what on?' She lifted the teapot stand and put it on the table then went back for the teapot.

'This sudden bout of cheerfulness and for no apparent reason.'

'Nothing really.' She sat down. 'Nothing brought it on. I woke up feeling happy so you never know, Tim, perhaps that means that something good is going to happen.'

'That would make a change.' He sighed.

'Tim, try to look on the bright side.'

'I can't if there isn't one.' He finished the cereal and put the dish to the side. 'What you have to remember,

Felicity, is that you don't have my worries.'

'That's true but I have plenty of my own. This doesn't just concern you.'

'I don't require to be reminded.'

'No, I don't suppose you do.' She was expecting and waiting for it and watched as he selected a piece of toast then slowly turned it over and frowned heavily. One side was pale brown, lightly toasted the way he liked it, the other was black or near enough to black. He didn't say a word just held it in front of her, black side up. Speech wasn't necessary.

'Not burnt, just well done and perfectly edible. As though to prove it, Felicity took an equally black piece, spread it with butter, added marmalade and bit into it. 'Nothing wrong with the toast. Give it a little scrape if you don't like the look of it.'

'I do not like the look of it, that is a burnt offering. When you are making toast you cannot afford to let your mind wander which is what you must have done. Why couldn't you have thrown it out and made more?'

'For the simple reason that was the last of the loaf. I knew there was just enough to do the breakfast and I would get a fresh one today.'

'You made no allowance—'

'Stop it, for goodness sake.' Then she began to laugh and kept on laughing until the tears were rolling down her cheeks.

'For God's sake, Felicity, what is the matter with you? I can't see anything to laugh at.'

She dried her eyes with a handkerchief and managed to control herself.

'You. Me. Us. That is what I find funny. Tim, do you realise that instead of our usual silent breakfast, we are actually carrying on a conversation. Not exactly scintillating stuff, I grant you, but it has got us talking and that has to be good.'

'Something has happened and you are keeping it from me,' Tim said suspiciously.

'Nothing has happened,' she said quietly but she was beginning to feel uncomfortable. She was keeping something from him. Should she tell him or give him an inkling? Felicity had almost decided to share her news then drew back. That might not be such a good idea. She didn't want her hopes shattered or herself ridiculed and he was capable of both. She wanted to hang on to her dream for as long as possible.

'Which makes your behaviour all the more peculiar. You know, if it wasn't so early in the morning I would say you had been drinking.'

'No fear of that though many women going through what I am going through might have been driven to the bottle.'

'Then I have to be thankful.' He wiped his mouth with his napkin. 'What are you doing with yourself today?' he surprised her by asking.

'Heavens above! I can't remember the last time you asked me that. Don't tell me you are interested?'

'I must be or I wouldn't be asking.'

She smiled. 'All right, Tim, I'll tell you my plans

for the day if you tell me where you go. You first,' she added.

He shrugged. 'Nowhere special,' he said getting to his feet.

Felicity thought she might be getting somewhere but, no, he wasn't going to give anything away. She was more puzzled than ever. Why all the secrecy? Why couldn't he say?

'Same here, I'm going nowhere special.'

'You are going out of your way to be awkward.'

'I could say the same about you.'

She saw by the set of his lips that she had annoyed him and in a perverse way that pleased her. Anything, even a bad-tempered exchange, and theirs hadn't been that, was preferable to being ignored. If he only knew she had spoken the truth and was doing nothing special. A bit of shopping in Dundee and she might treat herself to a light lunch before driving back. The remainder of the day would be spent at home waiting for the telephone to ring. Rachel had said this Adam Silver would be in touch very soon. What did that mean? The next day or the next week. Very soon had a different meaning for different people.

She heard his feet on the stairs, then he was calling to her from the hall.

'That's me away, Felicity.'

'All right, see you when you come.'

Once she heard the outside door closing, Felicity poured herself another cup of tea. Tim didn't always take the morning newspaper with him but this morning he had. Pity, she could have had a few minutes reading the headlines while she drank her tea. She took the last piece of toast from the toast rack, gave it a scrape then spread it with butter and a little marmalade. She ate it.

It was a change to feel energetic and she had the kitchen tidy and the housework done in record time. By ten o'clock she was dressed and ready to go out. Felicity wore her grey flannel suit that hadn't been out of the wardrobe since it had been dry cleaned. They asked about the stain at the cleaner but she had no idea what it was or indeed when it happened. It had been barely noticeable until she began rubbing away at the material and making it worse. Fortunately it had come out. Her red blouse went well with the grey as did her black patent shoes and matching handbag. Felicity felt smart for her visit to town.

She drove the car out then went back to close the garage doors. Once again behind the wheel she noticed that she was low on petrol and certainly hadn't enough for the return journey. She would have to fill up.

In the forecourt she switched off the engine and got out. A small, stout, elderly man came over.

'Good morning, Mrs Morrison, you're a stranger these days. I hope that doesn't mean you are taking your custom elsewhere.'

'As if I would.' She smiled. 'No, John, you haven't seen me recently because we have illness in the family and I've been kept busy.' Sorry, Maud, I'm making use of you again, Felicity said silently.

'Sorry to hear that.'

'My mother-in-law lives in Carnoustie and it is the going back and forward that takes up the time.'

'Ah, well, we've all to lend a hand when sickness strikes, it could be our turn next.' He shifted his position. 'I often tell the wife that given a choice I'd much rather the end came sudden. You know, drap deid, no warning.'

'John, that's a terrible thing to say.'

'I don't know. Granted it would come as a shock for those left but given time they would get over it. Better that than being a burden.'

She laughed. 'I prefer not to think about it.'

'Not a very cheery subject. Tell me about that lass of yours, is she doing well at university?'

'I don't know so much about the studying but she is enjoying the social life. At the moment she is on holiday in France.'

'France?' He made a whistling noise. 'My! My! The young folk today are lucky and they don't know it. All that foreign travel and they take it as their right. Me now, when I was a nipper the best we could do for a holiday was a week in Blairgowrie at the berry-picking. Hard work it was too and what we made was handed over to our mother for new clothes for when the school took up again.' He screwed the cap on, made sure it was tight, then wiped it and round about with a filthy rag. 'Looking back, it was a hard life but then we knew no other.'

'Perhaps it was a happier time, John. Folk had less but maybe they were more contented.'

'You could be right there. We made our own entertainment and there was plenty of laughter. That isn't to say there weren't tears and squabbles.'

'Like all families.'

A car had drawn up. 'No rest for the wicked, Mrs Morrison,' he said taking her money. 'Take care how you go, there are some idiots on the road.'

'I will.'

Felicity drove through the village and once out of it she increased her speed. Some time later when she reached the Perth Road she stopped in front of a row of shops and got out to do her shopping. It didn't take her long and since it was a pleasant day and she could do with a bit of exercise, Felicity put the shopping in the boot, locked the car and set off at a brisk pace. Leaving the Perth Road behind she walked along the Nethergate towards the High Street and the big stores. Window shopping was all she had in mind. The non-essentials were a luxury she could do without. Tim had reduced her housekeeping but not by very much. A bit of careful budgeting and she was managing very well even to putting a little aside. Without her mother-in-law's assistance it would have been a very different story.

After the walk Felicity began to feel peckish. Not a proper lunch she didn't want that. Coffee and sandwiches or failing that a plate of soup and a roll and butter. That had been a restaurant she had just passed. She turned round and went back then wished she hadn't. She was just inside when she saw him obviously waiting for a table. She tried to edge her way backwards but couldn't for the office workers arriving and hemming her in. And in any case it was too late, she had been seen. With a look of startled pleasure he was excusing himself and pushing his way out.

'Felicity, I am so pleased to see you,' Michael Lawson said taking both her hands in his.

Looking into that kind face, Felicity felt a rush of shame to think that she had tried to avoid him. Dear Michael, perhaps the only one of Tim's former colleagues she would truly miss.

'Michael, you shouldn't, you've lost your place.'

'No matter, I was having second thoughts anyway. I had no idea it would be this crowded, wrong time I suppose.' He took her arm. 'We'll find somewhere else less like a battlefield.'

She didn't want this. 'No, Michael, thank you, but no.'

'Why not, we both have to eat.'

'All I wanted was a quick snack before I headed for home.'

'Where did you leave the car?'

'Beside the shops in the Perth Road.'

'A good walk, you must have been feeling energetic.'

'I enjoyed it, I don't do enough walking.'

'Nor me, the car is too handy. Felicity?'

She looked at him.

'We have always been good friends, don't let us be awkward with each other.'

'With you perhaps I'm not.'

'Thank you.'

'I want to help.'

'No one can, Michael.'

'You are wrong there.'

'I'm not. You can't help Tim and his troubles are mine.'

'Even so. Look, we'll go across to the Royal Hotel. They will serve us coffee and sandwiches in the lounge and we can talk in comfort.'

He was very persistent and perhaps she should just accept.

'I feel guilty, you were going to have a proper lunch.'

'Sandwiches will do me very well.'

'Maybe I should warn you that I'm not the best of company.'

He smiled. 'We can cheer each other up.'

'Are you in need of cheering?'

'I'm divorcing Geraldine. Did Tim not tell you?'

He took her arm and they hurried across the busy road.

'No, he didn't,' she said when they were on the pavement, 'but Tim has very little to say to me. I'm sorry about you and Geraldine.'

'Don't be, it should have happened a long time ago.'

Felicity was inclined to agree as would most of the staff at Paton & Noble. Michael was forty-seven, two years older than Tim. He, too, was a solicitor and had joined the firm shortly after Tim. Felicity had always liked him and thought he was one of the nicest men she knew. He was tall and thin and inclined to be round-shouldered. For some men sitting at a desk for long periods of time did that. Tim was careful it didn't happen to him. She liked his courtly manner and his quiet good humour. At office functions they would often find themselves together. Tim liked to circulate, saying it was expected. Michael's wife, Geraldine, a pretty blonde with a silly giggle, deserted her husband at the first opportunity. She loved to flirt and was never short of a partner.

They were an ill-matched couple, Michael and Geraldine, and Felicity often wondered what had brought them together.

The premises of Paton & Noble wasn't very far from the centre of Dundee and this being lunch time it was quite possible that someone from the office would see them. Would that set the tongues wagging – someone seeing Tim Morrison's wife and Michael Lawson going into the Royal Hotel together? Undoubtedly it would. All offices liked a bit of gossip, the juicier the better, it made the working day pass more quickly and, needless to say, the story would gain a little extra in the telling.

In normal times, and for Felicity, normal could only mean when Tim had been a much respected solicitor with Paton & Noble, she and Michael could have come face-to-face in the street and greeted each other warmly. They would have spent a few minutes talking then gone their separate ways.

Felicity was discovering that nothing worked out as one expected. She should have been eating a sandwich and drinking coffee in a restaurant filled with office workers laughing and joking and seemingly without a care in the world. Not as she was doing entering a hotel in the company of a former colleague of Tim's. If he were to learn of it what would her husband have to say? Felicity surprised herself by finding that she didn't care. Perhaps she was beyond caring about anything.

There was a determined smile on her face when together they went into the hotel and up the broad carpeted stairs to the coffee lounge. From there came the murmur of voices and several heads turned to see who was coming in. When they saw a strange couple they turned away to continue their conversation.

Farmers had a distinctive look about them. Maybe it was their healthy, good-coloured skin and their liking for tweed suits – whatever it was Felicity suddenly remembered that this was farmers' day. A time when they congregated in the centre of Dundee to discuss farming affairs and exchange news. The wives came too and they made a day of it. It was a marvellous opportunity to do some leisurely shopping, have a coffee, do more shopping before winding up in one of the stores' restaurants for lunch.

The majority of the farmers gathered in a restaurant close to the City Square. Contrary to popular belief the restaurant was not anxious for their custom and would happily have seen them go elsewhere. They were well-known for over-staying their welcome and largely ignored pointed hints. As well as that they were noisy and shouted to make themselves heard thus discouraging others from eating there. The air was blue with cigarette smoke and the ash-trays full to overflowing. When they did eventually remove themselves the waitresses were quickly over to whip away the tablecloths with their coffee stains and put on fresh ones.

'Farmers' day,' she whispered to Michael.

'Yes, I rather envy them their life.'

'Why?'

'They seem happy and contented.'

'I thought they were always full of complaints. If it wasn't the weather it was something else.'

'One can complain and still be contented. They have no control over the weather but a good moan helps.' They were talking softly. 'In a very short time we are going to have the lounge to ourselves. Our farming friends are having a drink until called to the dining-room. Speaking of drinks what will you have, Felicity?'

'Nothing, Michael, I really don't want one.'

'I won't trouble either.'

'Oh, please, you have one.'

'I do like a drink in the evening but not in the middle of the day.'

She nodded.

'This has all been done up since I was last here, much needed too. If hotels can look tired this one did.'

'I like it, I give it full marks. So many places nowadays

go mad about colour, the more garish the better. Joanna would say and with some truth I suppose, that her mother is hopelessly old-fashioned.'

He shook his head. 'That you are not. Like you I don't go for bright colours, I prefer something more restful. And if I may say so, Felicity, you are looking very well.'

It wasn't so much the compliment rather the way he was looking at her that made her colour rise. 'Thank you,' she said dropping her eyes.

He could have said so much more. Michael would have spoken from the heart if he said that Felicity was beautiful in looks and in nature. He had loved her for a very long time. A love that must forever be a secret. Had she known of it Felicity would have been embarrassed. She had always been charming and friendly to him as she was to everyone. Michael Lawson was a friend and if he wanted to remain that he would have to take good care that she never found out his true feelings. She was very much in love with Tim and whatever the cost to her she would stand by her husband. Felicity was that kind of woman.

They were sitting in comfortable chairs beside a low, glass-topped table. Felicity had opened her jacket and placed her handbag at her feet when the waiter came over for their order. In a few moments another waiter arrived to tell the other occupants of the lounge that their table was ready. A few carried their own unfinished drinks with them and the others were put on a tray to be taken to the dining-room by the waiter.

In a short time the sandwiches and coffee arrived. The waiter poured the coffee into the two cups and set the coffee pot on the table.

'Will that be everything, sir?'

'Yes, thank you.'

'Doesn't that look tempting?' Felicity said. The sandwiches were dainty triangles and beautifully presented on an oval plate.

Michael smiled. 'It is the presentation that counts, isn't that what the food experts tell us?'

'It's true. Just to look at that makes me hungry whereas a doorstep of a sandwich would put me off.'

'Be thankful then that you are spared my efforts.'

Felicity took a sandwich and put it on her plate then she looked up quickly. 'How are you managing on your own?'

'Rather well I would say. Mrs Bremner, she's been our daily for a long time, is looking after me. She required no persuasion to stay on after Geraldine and Trudy left. Less work of course. The house is much too big for one person and before long I must look for a more suitable abode.'

'In roughly the same district?'

'That's what I am not sure about.' He paused to take a bite of his sandwich. 'Not much eating in these but they are good and we can order more. The reason I am not rushing to put it on the market is because I may not be here.'

'Not be here, what do you mean?' The thought that

he might not always be here and near to her depressed her. It was silly but she couldn't help it.

'Felicity, I think I need a change.'

'You would leave Paton & Noble?'

'I could do that very easily but there is nothing decided.'

'Don't be hasty, Michael, that could be very short-sighted. Ralph Knight can't have long to go before retirement.'

'That makes no difference to me, I'm not in line for that promotion.' He wondered if he should tell her and decided he should. 'Tim would have had an excellent chance of becoming the senior partner and he must have known that.'

'If he did he didn't tell me. You didn't mind? It didn't bother you?'

'Not a bit. I wouldn't have wanted the responsibility. I have never been particularly ambitious, what a confession, and it annoyed Geraldine. That doesn't mean to say I don't like my job. I do, I enjoy being a solicitor and I think I am a good one. You see, Felicity, a friend of mine in the Borders approached me before and I turned it down. His is a small practice, a country practice, which appeals to me. He gets plenty of work and wants me as a partner.'

'And you are giving it serious consideration?'

'Yes, I am. Geraldine would have had a fit at the mere suggestion. Much of the trouble between us you see stems from the fact that she sees me as a dull chap totally lacking in ambition. Probably she has got that right and if you are wondering how we ever came to get married I often wonder that myself. The attraction of opposites I suppose. The very things I found fascinating, like her gaiety and high spirits began to get on my nerves. As a young person they were acceptable but as a person approaching middle age they were not. Some of her antics could be embarrassing. We stayed together as long as we did for Trudy's sake.'

'How old is your daughter?'

'Thirteen. Trudy is very much a mother's girl which is hardly surprising. When I first qualified and for a time after, I worked all God's hours and by the time I got home the child was in bed and asleep. When she got a little older I did suggest that bedtime be postponed to allow me to get to know my daughter but that wouldn't do, it would have interfered with routine and be bad for the child. If we had been pulling together I'm sure we could have worked something out. As a father I suppose I've been a wash-out.'

'Nothing of the kind.'

'Thank you. Do eat up those sandwiches.'

'I am and enjoying them. What about coffee?'

'Yes, please.' She filled his cup and then her own.

'My wife and daughter will be all right. By a piece of luck the house next to her mother's was for sale and though it meant offering more that it was worth I felt it was money well spent. The three of them have always got on well together.'

'You'll miss your daughter.'

'Of course.'

'You'll see her regularly?' Felicity thought it would be so sad if father and daughter were to lose touch and that could happen all too easily. The girl's name had been mentioned in conversations but Felicity had never met her.

'I made sure of that and I have a feeling that when we are on our own we will get on much better. Children from broken homes don't have it easy but better the complete break, I think, than trying to pretend that all is well when it very obviously isn't. Children are not so easily taken in.'

She nodded. 'They can sense an atmosphere and poor mites they wonder if somehow they could be at fault. Anything that threatens their safe little world frightens them and they, too, learn to pretend.'

'All that you say is perfectly true.' He sighed. 'Whatever the outcome there is always pain.'

'Sadly it is a sign of the times, Michael, in our parents' day marriage whether it be happy or not, couples stayed together.'

'Life for some must have been unbearable.'

'Exactly and they could do nothing about it. Many would have wanted to make the break and couldn't. It takes money and a lot of courage to walk out and money in those days was in very short supply.'

He nodded.

'And let me add that mothers would rather suffer all kinds of abuse than have their family made to experience hardship.'

For a few minutes they gave their attention to the food.

'Tim and I, we don't talk, not the way we should,' Felicity said abruptly. Then wished she hadn't, there had been no need to say that.

'In the circumstances not all that surprising, Felicity, Tim must be going through agonies. Bad enough to know what he has coming to him—' He broke off when he saw her face.

'What do you mean – what he has coming to him? Is there something I don't know?'

'Tim said you knew,' he said slowly.

'He said there was a possibility that he could be – that he could be sent away but I thought he was only trying to prepare me in case it came to that.'

She saw the sympathy in his face. 'You think it will come to that?'

'Felicity, I think I have said too much already. Clearly I've upset you and that was the last thing I wanted to do.'

'No, it is better that I should know. I did know, I just couldn't face believing it,' she said quietly. Hearing it from you I can – I've got to believe it.' She swallowed painfully. 'Tim will go to prison for what he did.'

'I'm afraid it will be a custodial sentence. The court will come down very hard on a solicitor.'

'Will he be struck off?' Tim hadn't said and she hadn't thought to ask him.

He was looking more uncomfortable. 'I can't tell you that.'

'But you think it is very likely?'

'I'm afraid so.'

'Why should Tim suffer more than someone else? To me it is all so unfair. The money he so stupidly borrowed has been repaid. No one has suffered for what he did.'

'There I cannot agree with you, Felicity. No client suffered financially it is true, but Paton & Noble's reputation cannot fail to have been affected. Trust is something that is earned and if it is lost through the dishonesty of one of its solicitors it can take a long time to recover. That is hard for you to accept, Felicity, but that is the way of it. We could lose clients.'

'Yes, I suppose so,' she said wearily. She looked at her watch. 'Michael, I should be going now and you should be behind your desk.'

'Felicity, don't go, not just yet,' he said quickly.

'I should go, I'm depressing company.'

'You could never be that. Felicity, I have nothing but admiration for you. Tim, and I hope he knows it, is lucky to have such a loyal wife. I as good as told him—'

'You've spoken to Tim since all this – since all this happened?' Her eyes widened in shock.

'Didn't he tell you?' he said raising his eyebrows.

She shook her head.

'That does surprise me. I can't imagine why he wouldn't tell you. Several times we've had a drink together and when I offered to be there for you if you needed me he seemed both pleased and relieved.'

'That was kind of you, Michael,' Felicity said unsteadily.

'No, it isn't a kindness, it is something I want to do. My biggest worry is that you won't contact me, that you will struggle on alone.'

She smiled. It was very near to the truth.

'Give me your promise, Felicity, that you will take my offer of help seriously. In time of need we all need someone and I'm hoping that someone will be me.

She was touched. 'Then you have my promise.'

'A phone call away, that is all I'll be. So far we haven't mentioned Joanna.'

'Joanna is in France with her boyfriend. They are to be there for most of the vacation and before you ask let me tell you that Joanna knows nothing, absolutely nothing. She doesn't know her father has lost his job. Tim and I decided against telling her.'

He drew in his brows.

'At first I thought she should be told, then I agreed with Tim that there was no need to make her miserable until we had to.' When he still didn't speak she became angry. 'Tim was right, why spoil her holiday? Judging by Joanna's postcards they are having a wonderful time. Not on their own I may add, Stuart has family friends who have a farm in Provence and they are working to pay for their keep.'

'Good for them.'

'Don't you think we did the right thing?'

'It is not for me to say, Felicity.'

'It is if I am asking the question.'

'I'm not a gambler, Felicity, I don't tend to take chances. The girl could find out from another source.'

'Not when she is out of the country.'

'No, I agree it would be highly improbable that Joanna should hear anything.'

'Even so, you would prefer to be one hundred percent sure.'

'Yes. That apart, I think you are being unfair to your daughter. She has always struck me as being a very sensible young woman and she might resent being treated as a child who requires protection. It could be that she would have wanted to be with you.'

'Doing what?' she said harshly.

'Being supportive.'

'Tim would hate that.'

He smiled. 'Felicity, my opinion isn't important. Tim and you did what you thought best.'

'Yes and it is a bit late to have second thoughts.' Felicity made to get up. 'Michael, I think I needed to talk and you have been a good listener. And when you talked and I listened I learned something.' She smiled and he thought it a very brave smile.

Outside on the pavement in front of the hotel they shook hands.

'Goodbye, Michael, and thank you for everything.'

'Not goodbye, just au revoir, Felicity. A phone call, that is all the distance between us.'

They moved apart, then she called, 'Michael—'

He came back to stand beside her.

'I've decided not to mention to Tim that we had

coffee together. He didn't think to tell me that you two had a drink together and more important he didn't bother to give me your message.'

'I shan't mention it either.' He touched her arm then they walked away in opposite directions.

Chapter Ten

What a huge difference it made to feel really well rested. A good night's sleep did wonders, Felicity thought. It gave one the strength to face another day and the sense to keep things in perspective. Big worries one could do nothing about were better pushed to the back of one's mind though it needed a determined effort to keep them there. The secret, she was only just discovering, was to dwell on something good. Like the telephone call that might, just might, come today and brighten her life.

Felicity dressed quickly and went downstairs to prepare the breakfast. She caught herself humming a catchy little tune and stopped. Tim might have had a bad night and her humming would get on his nerves. Taking the orange juice from the fridge, she poured a glass for Tim. She wouldn't bother with one for herself. After returning the jug to its shelf, Felicity went to stand beside the cooker. The bread was under the grill and though tempted to do something rather than stand idle, she remained where she was until the bread was lightly toasted. The last thing Felicity wanted was a repeat of yesterday morning, though come to think about it she wasn't down to the last slice of bread so burning the toast would not have been a disaster. She could have popped the overdone slices in the waste bin and started again. The answer, of course, would be to invest in a new toaster. She tried to remember why they hadn't.

Felicity slotted the slices into the toast rack, brought the kettle back to the boil and made the tea. When the door opened and Tim came into the kitchen she looked up and smiled.

'Good morning, Tim, that was nice timing,' she said putting the lid on the teapot. 'You will be relieved to know that the toast is just as you would wish it.'

He frowned heavily and sat down at the table. 'If you are referring to yesterday morning, Felicity, and I gather you are, I do not recall making a fuss. The toast was burnt, no question about that and I merely pointed that out to you.' It was spoken in the precise, quiet voice of the trained solicitor talking to a client and a dim one at that.

'You did rather more than that but never mind,' she said brightly, 'some of us are not at our best first thing in the morning. Incidentally, Tim, why didn't we get a replacement for the toaster?'

'We found the grill made a better job.'

'So we did. One piece would be fine and the other hardly touched.'

Tim finished his orange juice and reached for the cereal packet.

'Is there plenty?'

He raised his eyebrows. 'I would think so since the packet is just started.'

'Of course, silly me.'

Felicity poured some cereal for herself. Tim liked his bowl three quarters filled then he drowned the flakes in milk. Felicity sliced a banana into hers. She had picked up the habit from Joanna who said it was a great source of energy. Maybe it was though she hadn't noticed any difference.

They ate in silence and when Tim put down his spoon she finished hers quickly and took the empty bowls over to the draining-board then came back to pour the tea.

'Thank you,' Tim said accepting a large breakfast cup.

Felicity wanted to talk. 'Did you sleep well?' she asked.

'Not too badly, I suppose. Did you?' he added as an afterthought.

'I did. I slept like a log, best sleep I've had in a long time,' Felicity said cheerfully.

'Mmmm.' He stirred his tea and drank some. Then perhaps to discourage any further conversation, Tim reached for the newspaper Felicity had collected from the doormat and dropped on to a nearby chair. She watched him prop up the paper between the milk jug and the bowl of sugar. Only very recently had he started to do this. Good table manners were important to Tim, they had been instilled at an early age and his parents had set him a good example. Maud's good-natured husband had not been given the same careful upbringing as his wife and she had determined to put that right. Gently but firmly he had been taken in hand. Many a time at the breakfast table Edward had longed to enjoy his second cup of tea with the newspaper turned to the sports page and stuck up in front of him. The teapot with its quilted cosy cover would have made a perfect resting place. But it was not to be. Bad habits were quickly picked up and copied by the young. Master Tim would grow up with the confidence that came with a good education and perfect manners. Their son would fit into any society.

Felicity considered herself well brought up but an occasional lapse wouldn't bother her. Tim was welcome to read at the breakfast table if he so wished. What his mother didn't know wouldn't hurt her. Felicity found herself wanting to protect her mother-in-law. She could imagine how saddened and distressed she would be to see the standards she had set beginning to slip.

She saw the quick glance Tim gave to the clock before he folded the newspaper and put it back on the chair. Then he got to his feet, pushed his chair under the table and left the kitchen to go upstairs. She heard him moving around as she set about clearing the breakfast table. In a short time he came back down. Tim didn't come into the kitchen but spoke through the half open door.

'Felicity, I'm just going.'

'All right. When shall I see you?'

'Don't know, I shouldn't be late though.'

'See you when you come.' It had become a habit to say that.

The door closed. Tim had gone to wherever he went and suddenly a wave of depression swept over her. In spite of her best efforts the fears and insecurities were crowding in on her. What did the future hold? It was like living in limbo. There was no working day, no yardstick, no timetable and most worrying of all she was no nearer to knowing what her husband did with himself. How he spent those hours. Could it be that he had a job of sorts he didn't want her to know about? Why was she kept in the dark? she thought despairingly. Why not confide in her? However difficult it was for him, surely the telling would be a relief. She sighed. Obviously not. Her thoughts jumped the way they often did these days. Wouldn't it be marvellous if she were to have some success with her illustrations? The money Tim's mother had made over to him would not last long if that was to be their only means of support. She desperately needed to earn money.

Felicity worried that what Tim was doing might be slightly shady and get him into more trouble. No, he wouldn't be as stupid as that. Michael hadn't known, she was almost sure. He and Tim had got on well as colleagues but not outside of business. Michael was a gentle, quiet man whom everybody trusted. They must have talked about something over that glass of beer but if in confidence Michael wouldn't have broken his word. She thought back to the time she and Michael had spent in the Royal Hotel and smiled. For a man who could be so gentle he was a tower of strength. To his credit he raised no false hopes. He was a lawyer and a lawyer dealt in facts. In his view Tim could expect a custodial sentence and all that was in doubt was the length of time he would serve. The judge, he had warned her, would not want to be seen to be lenient. This was a betrayal of trust and the sentence would have to act as a warning. Anyone tempted down that road would know what to expect.

Felicity had been standing at the sink staring out of the window for how long she didn't know. Long enough for the washing-up water to have gone cold. Outside the morning blazed with blue skies and her neighbour, an early riser, was busy cutting the dead heads off the roses. Everything was normal and yet nothing was. With a sigh she emptied the basin of the cold water and turning on the tap let it run until the water came hot. She added washing-up liquid and plunged her cold hands into the hot, soapy suds. With the dishes washed and left to dry, Felicity tidied the kitchen and was halfway upstairs to make the beds when the phone rang. Her heart gave a painful jolt and turning quickly she flew down the stairs, into the hall and grabbed the phone, fearful that whoever was at the other end might ring off before she reached it.

'Hello,' she said breathlessly.

'Good morning, would I be speaking to Mrs Felicity Morrison?' It was a man's voice, a pleasant voice.

'Yes, I'm Felicity Morrison.'

'This is Adam Silver, Mrs Morrison.'

'Oh, yes.' She couldn't think what else to say. Her heart was thumping so loudly that she thought he must hear it.

'I take it you were expecting a call from me?'

'Yes, I was, Mr Silver. Rachel, Miss Reid told me you would be getting in touch.'

'And here I am.' She could hear the laughter in his voice.

'There you are.' She was smiling foolishly.

'I have, beside me, some of your illustrations—'

'Do you like them?' she burst out, then closed her eyes in agony. She was much too anxious. Why had she interrupted to say such a stupid thing? What kind of impression was she making?

'I like them very much or I wouldn't be talking to you.' He paused. 'You must know they are good since you have already had your work accepted, or have I got my facts wrong?'

'No, you haven't.' She was shaking her head. 'I have been paid for some of my work but I am speaking only of a very small concern.'

'I see and quite rightly you want to aim higher?'

'It was suggested to me that I should try.'

'We have come to a point in our conversation when I should tell you that I am an agent and would be happy to represent you. I am good, Mrs Morrison, I make no apology for blowing my own trumpet. Work comes to me and only very rarely do I go seeking it. Your work was brought to my attention I may add.'

'You did say you wanted to represent me?' Felicity said nervously.

'If you are agreeable.'

'I should just say I am.'

He was laughing. 'Mrs Morrison, I think you and I are going to get along famously. There are things we need to discuss but we can go into that later unless—'

'No, later will suit me.'

'Good. We will deal with what is important or rather what you should know now. Cynthia Sutherland, a very talented author of children's books, is looking for an illustrator for her latest book. I took the opportunity of showing her your work and she was charmed with your delicate little drawings. She believes that you can produce what she wants.'

'What if I can't?' she said worriedly.

'Mrs Morrison, I didn't hear that.'

'Sorry.'

'My dear lady, of course you will produce what is required. Cynthia, I can tell you, is looking to team up with an illustrator as soon as possible. She and her previous illustrator have parted on amicable terms. Cynthia feels the need for a fresh approach and you could be the person she is looking for. Mrs Morrison, you are not to worry about anything, that is what I am paid to do, do your worrying for you.' He laughed. 'All your energies must go into your work.'

'I'll work hard, that I can promise.'

'I would expect no less. We do have a lot to talk

about, Mrs Morrison, and we should meet. Do you think you could make that very soon?'

'Yes, I can fall in with your plans. I'll have no trouble doing that. My husband is away all day and he will manage very well on his own.'

'What a splendid chap.'

She didn't say anything to that. 'My daughter, Joanna, is at university though at present she is on holiday in France.'

'You are making life very easy for me. What a very obliging lady you are.'

'May I ask where you are speaking from?'

'I am in Edinburgh. Give me a moment, Mrs Morrison, while I think what would be best.' There was a long pause. 'How about this? If I travel to Dundee I can kill two birds with one stone. Could we say Friday at ten thirty or thereabout?'

'You are talking about this coming Friday?'

'Yes, unless that is too soon for you?'

'Oh, no, that suits me fine. I wanted to be sure I had the right day.' She paused to take a shaky breath. 'I know Dundee quite well and do a lot of my shopping there.'

'Do you drive?'

'Yes, and I have my own car.'

'In that case could we possibly say Broughty Ferry instead of Dundee? When I am in your area I like to put up at the Parkside Hotel.'

'Make it Broughty Ferry and I won't require instructions, I know where the Parkside Hotel is.'

'You do, that is excellent. Parking is round the back as you probably know. Don't be rushing. I'll be working away in a little corner somewhere. When you arrive, Mrs Morrison, announce yourself to the receptionist and she will let me know.'

'I'll do that.'

'This is all very satisfactory and I think we have settled all that is necessary for the moment. I'll say goodbye, Mrs Morrison, and look forward to seeing you on Friday.'

'Goodbye, Mr Silver and thank you very much.' Felicity replaced the receiver and then stood still beside the phone and tried to recall all that had been said. Adam Silver actually wanted to be her agent. It seemed to be too good to be true and she hugged herself wishing there was someone in the house, someone who would be delighted for her. A husband should be proud of his wife's success and once he knew Tim might say so and congratulate her. Of course it was early days and there was no guarantee that other work would come her way. Only it had to look promising. Adam Silver would do his best for her. She wouldn't tell Tim just yet. A longing for her daughter swept over her. If Joanna knew she would be ecstatic. Had she been at home she would have waltzed her mother round the room. She could write the good news but that could pose a problem. Joanna, very naturally, would expect her father to know about her mother's success and would be amused to hear what Tim had to say since he had always been dismissive of her mother's talent. Once life had been so simple and now everything was so difficult and complicated. Her news would keep. Joanna would hear about it when she was back in this country and Tim – she would choose her time to tell her husband.

Rachel would hear her news and right away. Rachel who had made it all possible. How pleased she would be and they would laugh and joke. Only Rachel wasn't family. Michael wasn't family either but she would love for him to know. Should she phone him or would that be wrong? Was she being disloyal to Tim? Perhaps she was. Tim had seen nothing special in her delicate little drawings but he might look at them with different eyes if he was to hear they were in demand.

She was back to thinking of Michael. He hadn't agreed with Joanna being kept in ignorance about her father's troubles. In fact he had been alarmed that she might hear about them from another source. That was highly improbable but nothing was impossible. Joanna was in France far enough away one would have thought but Michael's unease was getting back to her and bringing on a nagging doubt. Was he right and were they treating Joanna like a child who needed protection. Felicity wasn't sure about anything any more. What she did wish was that the holiday was over and her daughter back home.

Feeling a little shaken at the direction her thoughts were taking, Felicity made herself a cup of tea and sat at the kitchen table nursing the cup and taking little sips. It was pointless dwelling on what couldn't be changed. No one could foresee the future and she and Tim had done what they thought best. Rachel, sensible Rachel, had agreed with them. Not wholeheartedly, but on balance she thought they had done the right thing, postponing the painful facts until the holiday was over.

Forget all that, she told herself. What she must do was concentrate on the work that had to be done and be able to deliver on time. All else must take a back seat and she must plan her days to give herself the maximum time. The visits to her mother-in-law would continue as before. Felicity didn't think of them as duty visits, she looked forward to them. The two women had grown closer over the years and were at ease with each other. Felicity knew that Maud tired easily especially if there was a lot of talking. The neighbours and friends who came about her shortened their visits when Felicity explained. They understood and had less to say. It was only occasionally that Maud mentioned her son's name, she was more interested in hearing about her granddaughter and was so touchingly grateful for the postcards that came regularly.

The house would not be neglected, Felicity promised herself, but there would be less polishing and no unnecessary jobs would be allowed to get in the way of her drawings. She would get her priorities right.

A glance at the clock told her that this would be a good time to phone Rachel. Her friend preferred personal calls in late morning when the early rush was over. Felicity picked up the phone and was very soon put through to Rachel.

'That was quick.'

'Comes of having a well-trained staff. You timed that beautifully if I may say so. Here I am sitting with my feet up and a cup of coffee to hand.'

'Somehow I don't see it.'

'Forget the feet up,' she laughed. 'And would I be right in thinking you sound very bouncy?'

'I don't know so much about the bouncy but I do feel marvellous and when last did I feel like that?'

'You haven't had much to feel marvellous about.'

'The troubles are there, they won't go away but I refuse to think about them at the moment. Rachel, I am over the moon. Your Mr Silver phoned.'

'A little less of my Adam Silver, I have never met the man.'

'No, neither you have, I had forgotten.'

'Does this mean it is all beginning to happen?'

'Yes, at least I think so.'

'Calm down and take a deep breath. Your voice is shaking.'

Felicity took time to take a deep breath. 'Cynthia Sutherland—'

'Who might she be when she is at home?'

'A very successful author of children's books.'

'Who is delighted with your cute little drawings and wants you to do the illustrations for her next book. Am I right?'

'Yes. That is if I can produce what she wants.'

'Which you will and with the greatest of ease.'

'No, I will have to work very hard and hope I come

up with what is wanted. Adam Silver sounded very nice on the phone.'

'I gather he is the agent?'

'Yes and he wants to represent me. Doesn't that sound impressive? Me, Felicity Morrison, having an agent.'

'I take it you have agreed?'

'Like a shot. Apparently he does everything, leaving me to get on with my work. As yet I know nothing about the financial arrangements but we will sort that out when we meet.'

'When is that?'

'Friday. We are meeting at the Parkside Hotel in Broughty Ferry. He favours it when he is in the area.'

'I don't have to tell you how pleased I am for you. You deserve a break. Many, many congratulations. Seriously, Felicity, this could be your big chance so whatever you do don't let anything get in the way. Clear your mind of your troubles.'

'Actually, Rachel, I am lucky there. When I am working on my sketches—'

'You are in a world of your own?'

'Sounds daft but that is about it.'

'Not daft at all. Total concentration is what it is.'

'You will tell Terence?'

'Of course and he will be so pleased.'

'I owe him such a lot.'

'He gave you a helping hand, that's all. We don't want to embarrass the man with too much praise.'

Rachel paused. 'What about Tim? What is he saying about his wife's change of fortune?'

'He doesn't know. Remember I only got the phone call this morning and you are the first to hear.'

'Thank you, I appreciate that. Felicity, you are going to tell Tim? You must, you can't not tell your husband.'

'I can very easily not tell my husband. Tim has never shown any interest in my drawings.'

'We can't all be artists.'

'No, but we can appreciate each other's talents and give an occasional word of encouragement.'

'I can't argue with that.'

'When I think the time is right I will tell Tim. Nothing is signed as yet and you can bet your bottom dollar that is the first question my husband will ask.'

'The poor man can't help himself. It is the result of all that training in legal affairs.'

'Why all of a sudden are you sticking up for Tim? You don't even like him.'

'Did it show that much?'

'To me it did.'

'True, he isn't one of my favourite people, but I have to feel sorry for him. I do believe I am a good judge of character and Tim is not dishonest by nature.

'No, he isn't.'

'Taking such a risk for one thing was out of character. It must have been something god-awful to make him do it.'

'So awful he can't talk about it to me?'

'Particularly you, perhaps.'

'Meaning I am not an understanding wife?' Felicity said stung to hear her best friend make the accusation.

'Meaning nothing of the kind. We don't want to hurt those we love.'

'If he loves me,' she said but too quietly for Rachel to hear. She raised her voice. 'It will have to come out some time.'

'Not necessarily. Tim will plead guilty won't he?'

'Yes.'

'In which case he won't have to say any more unless he wishes to. Most folk will have decided that it was a gambling debt that had to be honoured immediately. And it could still have been that, Felicity.'

'I no longer know what I think.' She laughed but without mirth. 'You are about the last person I would have expected to say something nice about Tim.'

'One can admire a person without liking him.'

'How strange you should say that.'

'Why strange?'

'I just think it is. You don't like each other yet here you are admitting to a sneaking admiration for Tim and he admires you for what you have accomplished.'

Felicity didn't see the face Rachel made. 'That makes me hopping mad. Because I am a woman I am not meant to accomplish much. Men – honestly, can't they be infuriating.'

'Are you all flushed and angry?'

'You bet I am.'

'He has a point.'

'What?'

'As you so often say yourself, women have to be that much better than men to succeed. Tim was not being patronising, the compliment was genuine.'

'Oh, well, maybe I was a little hasty.'

'And on that note I'll ring off.'

'Thanks for phoning and again congratulations,' Rachel said before putting down the phone.

Chapter Eleven

By Friday morning Felicity was nervously excited and two or three times she had been on the point of telling Tim her news but always at the last moment she held back. Better to wait, she thought, until she had something definite to show him, like a contract or something in writing.

It could have been that she was so taken up with her own affairs and the forthcoming meeting with Adam Silver that she hadn't noticed the change in her husband. The silences were longer and the dark shadows under his eyes more pronounced. Just now he had the newspaper propped up in its usual place between the milk jug and the sugar bowl but didn't appear to be reading it.

'Tim?'

He looked up quickly. 'What?'

'You look so tired as though you hadn't slept.'

'I didn't get much sleep.' He folded the newspaper and put it aside. 'I should break the news to you now, I think, no point in waiting.'

'What is it, Tim?'

'I suppose I was expecting it. The case is likely to come up shortly,' he said speaking with difficulty.

'Oh!' She hadn't been expecting that.

'Pencilled in for late September I am led to believe.'

Fear gripped her. 'That is only a few weeks away,' she said catching her breath.

'Yes.' He got up abruptly to look out of the kitchen window.

'Joanna should be home by then,' Felicity whispered.

'Poor kid, what a home-coming.'

'She isn't a kid, she isn't a child, Tim. We have treated her as though she were and I have a feeling we have made a mistake and will regret it.'

He came back to the table and sat down. 'A bit late to be having thoughts like that. You agreed with me that it should be kept from her for as long as possible.'

'I know that, I'm not denying it. I just think we were wrong but, as you say, it is a bit late now to be having these thoughts.'

He closed his eyes and banged his fist on the table. 'Why was I so bloody stupid?'

'We all do things we regret.'

'It was all so unnecessary. A bit more thought on my part and my daughter would have been spared all this.'

'Tim, it has happened, we can't make a better of that. Joanna will cope, I know she will, the young do, you know.' She wanted to comfort him, to put her arms around him but didn't think that would be welcomed and to be pushed aside was more than she could bear.

'Joanna won't cope, she will take it badly. I know my daughter.'

Did he think she didn't understand her daughter? 'She might surprise us. Tim, you are the one I am concerned about,' she said worriedly.

'No need to be. Believe it or not, Felicity, I was almost managing to convince myself that it would never happen, that the case would never get the length of court. I should have known better,' he said bitterly.

'I was praying for that too.'

'I wouldn't bank on prayers, they are seldom answered.'

Felicity sat silent. Whether it was a short custodial sentence or a long one, for Tim, for them all, it was a life sentence. There was no wiping the slate clean. The disgrace was forever there.

'In a way I am protected, I'll be locked up and out of it. It will be different for you and I am rather afraid that what is ahead could be unpleasant.'

'I'm not too worried about that. I'll try to remember what my mother used to say.'

'And what gem was that?' He tried to smile.

'That no one is given more than he or she can bear. She was talking about pain but pain comes in different ways. I like to believe that we get extra strength from somewhere.'

'While we are on the subject of mothers, mine is more and more living in a world of her own. I am selfish enough to be glad of that, it means my disgrace isn't likely to touch her.'

'Your mother is quite content.'

'She doesn't say much to me.'

'She doesn't say much at all. Your mother smiles as though her thoughts were pleasant. Talking tires her but she likes to have someone beside her.'

'When mother does have something to say it is usually to sing your praises and I am frequently reminded of the treasure I have in you.'

'You don't think that, do you?'

'Fishing for compliments?'

'No, I know better.' She gave a short laugh. 'To be talking together is something and I have the feeling that this must be leading up to something.'

'Yes, and my peace of mind depends on your answer.'

'I would want to be helpful.'

'Then give me your word. Please, Felicity.'

'Very well, you have my word.' Just as she gave that promise, Felicity realised her mistake. She had no idea what he was going to ask. 'I'm taking a chance, Tim, I don't know what I am letting myself in for.'

'Nothing that would harm you. Heavens, surely you didn't think—'

'No, of course not,' she said hastily, 'but I am curious.'

'Before I satisfy your curiosity let me say how glad and relieved I am that you will have Joanna with you.'

'Only until she goes back to Edinburgh.'

'There is nothing to stop her coming home at the weekends. You could meet her at the station or for that matter Joanna could catch a bus.'

'Aren't you forgetting something? There is the little matter of money for her fare.'

'I hadn't forgotten. We must sit down one evening soon and go into the financial situation. There should be sufficient for your needs and enough left over to take care of the fares from Edinburgh. You aren't extravagant and I know you will continue to be careful. And now for that promise you have given me.'

She looked at him and waited.

'I am not asking this, I am insisting on it.'

She allowed herself a small smile. That was more like the Tim she knew.

'You are not under any circumstances to be in court and that, needless to say, applies to Joanna as well.'

'Joanna perhaps but not me. Of course I'll be there. What kind of wife would I be if I didn't support my husband?'

She could see he was getting agitated. 'I do not, repeat not, need your support, this is something I face on my own.'

'Why should you face it on your own? Good heavens, we all need someone to be there for us.'

'I do not.'

He kept looking at the clock. Already he was fifteen minutes behind his usual time for leaving the house.

'You can't mean that?'

'I do mean it, try and get that into your head. Knowing you were in court would only distress me.'

'It shouldn't,' she said stubbornly. 'I'm your wife in case you have forgotten. If I am not there folk will think I have deserted you.'

'Let them think what they want. You should be thankful that I don't want you in court. Believe me, you are going to have enough to contend with. There will be plenty of talk though I am hopeful that it will merit no more than a small mention in the national newspapers. Not so the local press, this will be big news and they will make the most of it,' he said grimly. 'If you are to be living at home—'

'Where else would I be?'

'You could stay with Mother for as long as you wished.'

'No, I shall stay put, I have no intention of leaving here.'

'Then take my advice, lock the doors and take the phone off the hook.'

'You exaggerate.' But Felicity felt her throat tighten in alarm.

'Maybe I do, but it is as well to be prepared.' He frowned. 'As regards moving away from the district—'

'No, Tim, I don't think we should do that until we have some idea of what the future holds . . .'

'As you wish,' he said wearily.

'Since my presence is to be an embarrassment I shall stay away,' Felicity said through stiff lips. 'You can relax, I won't go back on my word.'

'Thank you. I can see you are hurt and angry, but believe me it is for the best. You will have to trust me.'

'You won't have anyone.'

She saw the small hesitation. 'Michael Lawson might put in an appearance. I don't think I mentioned it to you that Michael and I had a chat and I was to tell you that should you require help of any kind you only have to phone.'

'That was very kind of Michael,' she said quietly. Since he had taken all this time to tell her Felicity saw no reason to mention that she had been in Michael's company.

'He is a decent sort. By the way, he and Geraldine are divorcing. The news didn't come as a surprise to me.'

'I'm not surprised either. They seemed to be an ill-matched pair.'

He got up. 'Must get on my way now and thanks,' he said clearing his throat awkwardly.

'Thanks for what?'

'Just being you I suppose.'

She could only stare. 'I thought being me didn't please you one little bit.'

'I'm sorry, I haven't been easy to live with.'

'It isn't that, I hardly ever see you.' She forced him to look at her. 'This, for us, has been a long conversation yet at the end of it I am still no wiser. I don't know where you get to and if I wanted to get in touch I wouldn't know how.'

'Things will work out, Felicity, and I must go.' Before

he departed Tim popped his head round the door. 'I should be home by seven or maybe earlier.'

'I'm going to Broughty Ferry but I should be back long before then.' Hours before then. She and Adam Silver were having coffee together. At least she was telling him where she was going.

'Don't hurry for my sake.'

'I won't.'

Felicity heard the door close and got up hurriedly. Of all the days to be given that news it had to be today, she thought despairingly. Somehow she had to divorce it from her mind when she was with Mr Silver. Poor Tim wanting to go it alone. He had been putting on a brave face but now the cracks were showing. What must his feelings be – to have been known as a well-respected solicitor and shown up now as an embezzler. Such a horrible word and it shouldn't apply in Tim's case. Only who was going to believe that, folk were too ready to believe the worst. Until now she hadn't given her own position much thought but she would come in for her share of blame. A wife couldn't fail to see what was going on, someone was sure to say that. That was wrong, she hadn't. There had been nothing out of the usual in Tim's behaviour.

Felicity did the tidying up while thoughts chased through her head. She would like to think that it would be no more than a nine days' wonder but that was wishful thinking. In a busy town, yes, perhaps, but not in a small place like Hillhead where nothing much happened. The case would be the main topic of conversation in the shops. Especially the post office which was also the general store and in the hairdresser's. Why, she wondered, did tongues wag so freely while busy fingers coaxed hair into curls? The childish saying came back. Sticks and stones may break my bones but names will never harm me. That was worth remembering.

Tim had made mention of their finances, made a promise and she would hold him to that. They must sit down with pen and paper and he must explain exactly how she would be placed while he was – away from home. It was important. And for Felicity it was important that she put her talent to good use and begin to earn some serious money. Joanna's education must not suffer. If there was any danger of that Felicity knew that Maud would come to the rescue but she didn't want that. She wanted to earn enough to make her independent and that wouldn't happen unless she hid her troubles from Adam Silver. Someone with domestic worries was not a good investment, they couldn't be relied upon.

She had only left herself sufficient time to tidy the kitchen and make the beds, the rest would have to wait. Felicity flew through the chores then got herself washed and dressed. She spent a little more time than usual over her appearance. With the approach of autumn warmer clothes were called for and Felicity had decided to wear her light-weight tweed suit with a pale green blouse. She loved the feel of the material, it was pure silk. Maud had pressed money into her hand

and Felicity had tried to refuse to take it saying it wasn't her birthday.

'No matter,' Maud had said, 'I want you to buy something for yourself, something you wouldn't think of buying with your own money. Take it, Felicity, and don't spoil an old lady's pleasure.'

She had taken it and spent the lot on the blouse. Wearing it today might bring her luck. She could certainly do with a big slice. Mr Adam Silver would have no interest in her appearance, she could look a fright. His only interest would be in the work she produced. Felicity took a look at herself in the full-length mirror and decided she would pass. She thought she looked very smart. With a smile to herself she locked up then went to open the garage and drove the car out. It was a nuisance getting out to shut the garage but safer to do so. Then she was on her way. As she cleared the gate a neighbour waved from a doorway and she waved back. She wouldn't have to step on it, there was enough time to enjoy the journey. As she approached Broughty Ferry, Felicity caught glimpses of the sea and from that distance it looked very blue and smooth. The Parkside Hotel had a sea view and made the most of it in their brochure. It was a family run hotel and guests were warmly welcomed. Not everyone wanted that. Many businessmen and representatives favoured the larger and more impersonal hotels. Adam Silver, it seemed, didn't.

It had taken a determined effort but she was winning. Felicity was managing to distance herself from her troubles as fresh ideas for her little drawings kept popping into her head and as they did her confidence grew.

As she slowed down Felicity looked for and found the sign indicating the carpark could be reached by turning left into a narrow lane. The angle of the opening made it an awkward manoeuvre and she had three attempts before she was successful. Tim would have said that she should have sized up the situation and made a more intelligent approach. No one had been around to see her poor attempt so what of it. It wasn't much of a carpark, the ground was heavily pot-holed and there were no markings. Three cars were already there and Felicity parked near to them. She wondered why the owners had neglected to bring the carpark up to a reasonable standard. With so many people having their own transport it would have been a sensible move. Or at least they could have the pot-holes filled in, that wouldn't cost much. Her friend, Rachel, had been more far-seeing. She had inherited something similar when she bought the Cairn Hotel and the money spent on improving the carpark she looked on as money well spent.

Felicity didn't want to arrive too early, for all she knew Mr Silver might not be ready for her. She would take a few minutes to look around before going in. Picking up her handbag from the passenger seat she locked the car door and walked to an opening that led round to the front of the hotel. Many a time she had driven past the hotel, given it a glance and thought it attractive. She took time to study the building. There were several guest houses in the area but the Parkside was the only hotel. Most had been large family houses too big for the needs of today but ideal for guest houses. The Parkside Hotel was much bigger and had begun life as a mansion house. The owner of one of the largest jute mills in Dundee had had it built to specifications. With the huge profits to be made in jute there was a gradual move away from the smoke and grime of the city to the pleasant little seaside town.

She saw a gardener busy tidying the front garden and someone must have been watering the many hanging baskets judging by the pools of water at various places along the front of the building.

Her watch told her she could safely go in now. Opening the glass door Felicity walked over to the reception desk and stood. The young woman looked up and quickly removed the newspaper she had been reading.

'Sorry, I shouldn't be doing that but my friend has just had a baby and I wondered if the announcement was in the papers.'

'And is it?' Felicity smiled.

'No. I suppose her husband was too excited to remember to put it in. Can I help you?' she said quickly as an older woman came over to the desk, smiled to Felicity and went away with a handful of letters.

'Mr Adam Silver is expecting me.'

'You must be Mrs — Morrison,' she said after glancing at her notepad.

'Yes.'

'One moment and I'll go and tell Mr Silver you have arrived.'

She returned with a man who straightaway shot out his arm and gave Felicity a beaming smile.

'Mrs Morrison, delighted to meet you.'

'How do you do, Mr Silver.'

She liked his warm handshake. He wasn't tall, about average and of a slim build. His neatly cut hair was light brown. At a guess she would put him in his middle forties.

'We'll go into the lounge.' He turned to the young woman but she spoke before he could.

'Coffee? I'll have it brought to you in a few minutes, Mr Silver.'

'Thank you, Susan. The service is excellent at the Parkside, Mrs Morrison. My every wish is anticipated.' He touched her elbow and together they went through to the lounge. It was large and bright with a high ceiling. Around the walls were framed pictures of Scottish scenes and one of Highland cattle. The chairs and sofas were shabby and invitingly comfortable. One could relax here with a good book and a refreshment and be perfectly happy.

'Where would you like to sit?'

'I don't mind, anywhere will suit me.'

'Do you like beside the heat?' There was a log fire purring and hissing in the wide, old-fashioned fireplace. One of the logs moved its position and there was a shower of sparks that made them both smile.

'A safe distance from that,' Adam laughed. They took a window seat.

'This is a quiet time as you will have gathered. The other guests have gone about their business and it is quite possible that we shall have the lounge to ourselves.'

A young girl came in with the coffee and a plate of biscuits. The tray tilted alarmingly when she tried to hold it in one hand and Adam took it from her.

'I'm not very good at this,' she said shyly.

'It takes time and you are doing fine.'

'Shall I pour the coffee?'

'No, thank you, Linda, we shall look after ourselves.'

'That fire is sparking, I'll go and get the guard. It doesn't look nice but better to be safe.'

They watched her put the guard up then with a smile she hurried away.

'She only started last week apparently. A sweet child but I don't think she will last long. Things have a habit of falling out of her hand.'

'And breaking?'

'I'm afraid so.' Adam poured the coffee and left Felicity to help herself to sugar and cream. 'Will you excuse me for a few moments, Mrs Morrison, while I collect my belongings and bring them over. I dislike working in my bedroom and in any case it keeps the maids back. That is one of the reasons I come here, there is always a little corner I can make my own.'

'Does the hotel do well?' she asked for something to say.

'Like most hotels it has its good years and its not so good years. The weather plays its part. I try to avoid the Dundee holiday fortnight and the Glasgow holiday. These are the busiest times and the hotel can be full.'

'Broughty Ferry is popular with holidaymakers.'

'They even come from Dundee which is just a short bus ride away but then again as you know they don't have to go far from home to enjoy themselves. Give a child a bucket and spade and sand to play in and he will be as happy as Larry.' He opened his briefcase and took out a large brown envelope which he handed to her. She saw that her name was on it. 'Perhaps you would be good enough to read that, Mrs Morrison. Read it carefully and if everything is to your satisfaction sign it. I have marked the place with a cross. There is a copy for your own file. I'll leave you to tidy up my corner before *I* am summoned to do so.'

The contract was very clear and she had no hesitation about signing her name. In fact she got quite a thrill from it.

'All in order?' he smiled on his return.

'Yes, thank you, all satisfactory.'

'How is that coffee?'

'Very good.'

'Do help yourself to biscuits.'

She took one and put it on her plate.

'Before we get down to business and since we will be working so closely I think I should tell you something about myself. I'm married to Lilian my long-suffering wife—'

'Now, now! You are making that up.' She smiled.

'Perhaps I am but, joking apart, the kind of work I do and the amount of travelling involved means that Lilian is left a lot on her own with the two boys. She doesn't grumble, well she does but not too much. She accepts that if I didn't lead such a busy life the money wouldn't be coming in. You see, Mrs Morrison, it is in my own interests that you should be a success.'

She nodded and smiled. 'I can sympathise with your wife.'

'Meaning you are in the same boat?'

'No, not really. My husband isn't away overnight, but even so I see very little of him.'

'May I ask what your husband does?'

'Tim is a solicitor,' she said and felt her throat go tight. She picked up her cup and drank some of the coffee to stop the questions.

'Ah, a solicitor,' he smiled, 'your husband will want to know what you have signed and go through it with a fine-tooth comb.'

'I doubt it. To Tim this is just a hobby of mine.'

'Something to keep you out of mischief.'

'That is about it.'

'Then you must show him how wrong he is. Yours is a very real talent and when it comes to children's books the illustrations are as important as the story.'

'Did you say you have two boys?'

'Yes and rascals both of them. Duncan is twelve and

Neil is two years younger. No daughter but we haven't given up hope.'

'Our one and only is nineteen.'

'And at university I think you said. What is she studying?'

'English. We had thought Joanna would have gone in for teaching but she doesn't seem keen to do that.'

'Whatever she decides to do a good degree will stand her in good stead.'

'That is what Tim says. We'll have to wait and see, my daughter is very strong-willed.'

'Better that than being easily led.'

'You could be right, Mr Silver.'

'We need to get that sorted out. The name is Adam. In our business we use Christian names, that is if you have no objection?'

'None at all, I prefer it.'

'Felicity, isn't it?'

'Yes.'

'Unusual, I like it and it suits you if I may say so.'

'Cynthia Sutherland,' she said wanting to know about the author.

'You would like me to tell you about Cynthia?'

'If that is in order.'

'Of course it is and I am glad you asked. Where do I begin? If I tell you that Cynthia is eccentric it is in the nicest possible way. She is a joy to work with and I like her enormously. She can be funny and she can be exasperating but she is never dull.'

'Old, young or middle-aged?'

'Fiftyish.'

'Single or married or am I being too inquisitive?'

'No, you aren't. She doesn't wear a wedding ring but I think there might have been a husband once. Maybe he got in the way or maybe he went away. Not an easy life being married to someone who shuts herself away for hours on end. As to appearance, Cynthia is small and very slim with short-cropped iron grey hair and she has a rather endearing way of chuckling. As you will have gathered I am very fond of her.'

'A popular lady with children I imagine.'

'Strangely enough she is very shy with children and is reluctant to give talks. I mentioned that she is small yet she can stand out in a crowd simply by the clothes she wears. I'm no good at describing women's clothes, the best I can do is to say they are colourful and flowing. Lilian thinks she has gypsy blood.'

'I like the sound of her.'

'You will like the person too.' He paused. 'Are you houseproud, a tidy person?'

She looked surprised. 'No, I wouldn't say so.'

'I ask that because the lady's passion is collecting books. A lot of them are classics and others by favourite authors. I am not exaggerating when I say she has hundreds and hundreds taking up every available space in her house. She has them piled against the skirting board and the only two rooms to escape are the kitchen and bathroom. I've warned her she will break her neck if she isn't careful. There are books on the stairs, piled on every step.'

'What does she do about cleaning?'

'Not a lot. I gather there isn't much cleaning done.'

'When do I get a copy of the story?'

'The manuscript will be with you shortly and Cynthia will have made it very clear what she wants. Some pages she will leave blank, no instructions, and you will provide what you consider to be a suitable illustration.'

'She will leave that to me?'

'Don't sound so dismayed. She will want to discuss certain points with you either by letter or phone. Before you go I'll give you her address and telephone number. Remember I am there to deal with any problems and should I not be at home when you ring leave a message with Lilian. She acts as my secretary and I would be lost without her. Is there anything you want to ask?'

'No. My head is full of information. Thank you very much for all the trouble you have gone to. Perhaps I should be going now.'

'I must get on too,' he said when they were both on their feet.

He accompanied her to the car where they shook hands and Felicity had the feeling she had made a new friend.

Chapter Twelve

Three days had gone by since her meeting with Adam Silver and Felicity had said nothing to Tim about her visit to the Parkside Hotel. No one could blame her, she thought, Tim was lost in a world of his own and could barely rouse himself to answer her questions. Why did he have to be like this? Didn't he see what it was doing to her? She felt unwanted as though she had nothing to offer. True she couldn't take away his guilt or change what lay ahead, but her support in his hour of need should mean something. Apparently it didn't.

He was suffering, Felicity could see that and from choice he was suffering alone. Time was getting short and certain things had to be talked over. He had said so himself and when she reminded him of his promise to discuss their financial affairs his answer had been a dismissive wave of his hand and an irritable 'not now, maybe later'.

This evening they had eaten earlier than usual and by seven thirty the dining-room table was cleared, the dishes washed and Felicity was preparing to join him in the sitting-room. There was a small hope that he would sit with her for perhaps an hour before excusing himself and escaping to his study. Felicity was sure that was how he thought of it – an escape from the need to make conversation.

When the telephone rang she was folding up her apron and putting it away in the drawer. Felicity was about to hurry into the hall to answer it but Tim was there first. He must be expecting a call, it wasn't like her husband to rush to the phone to answer it, that was usually left to her.

Tim was frowning when he saw her. 'For you.'

'Who is it?' she asked.

'Someone calling himself Adam Silver and asking to speak to Mrs Felicity Morrison.'

'Oh,' Her face brightened.

'You know who it is?'

'Of course I do,' she said making to pass him. 'Adam happens to be my agent.'

'Your what?' His expression showed minor irritation.

'Tell you later.' She hurried to the hall table and lifted the phone. 'Adam, Felicity here.'

'Thank goodness. You know I was beginning to think I had got the wrong number. Twice I had to repeat my name and there doesn't appear to be anything wrong with the phone.'

'There isn't. My husband must have been lost in his own thoughts when he answered. I do apologise for him.'

'No need. I imagine solicitors have their worries too.'

If he but knew, she thought.

'The reason for the call is to let you know that a copy of the manuscript, *The Magic Shoe Box*—'

'Is that the title of the book?'

'Only until Cynthia can come up with something better or you can for that matter. She will be open to suggestions and as I was saying the manuscript is in the post and should be with you tomorrow or failing that the next day.'

'Good! I'm looking forward to reading it and getting started to my bit.'

'Rarin' to go, as they say?'

'Yes,' she laughed.

'Cynthia assures me that she has made everything clear but, as we all know, what is clear to one person is not necessarily so to another.'

'Very true but I'm sure I'll manage.'

'Of course you will but do remember if in doubt give me a shout. Better to come to me first without bothering Cynthia.'

'Is she kept very busy?'

'Not enough hours to the day is her complaint.'

They talked a little longer then hung up. Felicity stood for a moment smiling to herself.

Tim looked up when she came into the sitting-room and his eyes narrowed. He saw her heightened colour and shining eyes and was taken aback by the strength of his feelings. He felt both anger and outrage. Felicity had no right to look like that for someone else. Who was this person his wife had got involved with? Could he be jealous? Of course not, why should he be but curious, yes he was curious.

'Who was that you were talking to on the phone?'

'I told you who it was. That was Adam Silver and Adam is my agent.'

'Don't give me that damned nonsense. What on earth would you be doing with an agent?'

She sat down, some of the joy gone. 'What would I be doing with an agent? The same as anyone else I imagine. I am lucky to have someone like Adam representing me.' Felicity took a deep breath. 'This will be difficult for you to take in since you have always ridiculed my drawings.'

'I beg your pardon, I have never at any time ridiculed your sketches.'

'Perhaps ridiculed was the wrong word but you never thought much of them. Well for your information, Tim, there is a healthy interest in my illustrations. If you remember you told me to find myself a proper job—'

'Never mind that, why all the secrecy?'

'Coming from you that is rich,' she said with a strangled laugh.

'This is different and I ought to have been kept in the picture.'

'You would have been had you showed any interest. I am not secretive by nature and I did want to tell you. I wanted you to share in my success but I did not want a douche of cold water thrown in my face.

Better, I thought, to wait until I had something definite, something in writing.'

'And have you?'

'Yes.'

'Where did all this take place?' he said putting the fingers of both hands together like a steeple or in prayer. Solicitor with client, she thought.

'If you recall, Tim, I told you I was going to Broughty Ferry.'

'So you did and you left me to believe it was a shopping trip. That was probably deliberate.'

She swallowed and moistened her lips. 'You were meant to think what you wanted to think. Tim, I am trying very hard to control my temper and believe me it is not easy. You are impossible but I have to remember what you are going through and make allowances.'

'That is totally unnecessary,' he said stiffly.

She gave him a long look. 'I can never question you about anything but you reserve the right to question me. That surely cannot be fair but then as we all know life isn't fair.'

'Too damned right it isn't.' They both smiled.

'We will talk about this if you are genuinely pleased for me but not unless.'

'Why should I not be interested?'

'You are the one to answer that,' Felicity said quietly.

Tim settled more comfortably in the chair, stretched out his legs and gave the infuriating smile that said he was prepared to listen, to give her a little of his valuable time. 'I gather this didn't happen overnight?' He raised an eyebrow.

'No, it didn't. Thinking about it, Stuart, Joanna's boyfriend had something to do with it. He appeared to be very impressed with my sketches and that made me think that perhaps I should get another opinion.'

'You had already sold some.'

'Only to a very small concern. I thought I should try to aim higher.'

'That was ambitious of you.'

'It got results. Rachel suggested showing a few of them to her friend who has connections with the publishing world.'

'It pays to know the right people.'

'So I discovered. I also discovered that the right people are only interested in talent,' she said sarcastically. 'It would appear that I have what they are looking for. My illustrations found their way to Cynthia Sutherland—'

'And who might she be?'

'A very successful writer of children's stories. I'm thrilled to bits that she wants me to do the illustrations for her latest book.'

'Well! Well!'

She could see she was getting all his attention now.

'This is all very surprising, I have to say.'

'Is that the best you can do? Hardly the compliment I was waiting for. To express surprise is to be amazed that I of all people should have achieved any measure of success.'

'Your trouble, Felicity, is that you are too sensitive. I didn't intend you to take it that way. I am impressed.'

'Thank you.' She had misjudged him there. 'This could be my big chance, Tim, and if I make a success of it more work should come my way.'

'This is where this agent bloke comes in?'

'Adam takes charge of everything.'

'And gets paid sweetly for his trouble. A percentage of your earnings, is that it?'

'Yes and he will deserve every penny. Agents do a power of work.'

He was frowning. 'This contract you signed, I presume you have a copy?'

'I do.'

'May I see it?'

'No.'

'Pardon?'

'I said no, you may not see it.'

She saw his angry flush. 'I am a solicitor and you need me to safeguard your interests.'

'I do not, I am perfectly capable of doing that for myself.'

'That is where you are wrong. You wouldn't know what to look for, it needs an experienced eye for that.'

'With due respect, Tim, this is my business. I am not as easily taken in as you would like to believe. I read the contract over very carefully as I was requested to do and found it perfectly straightforward and satisfactory. I signed it.'

'More fool you. You were rushed into this.'

'I was nothing of the kind.' She began to laugh.

'I see nothing amusing.'

'You wouldn't. I do though. All of a sudden you have decided that your wife might have earning power and that has to be especially good in the circumstances.'

'Early days, don't count your chickens before they are hatched.'

'No danger of me doing that.'

'Since you are not prepared to take my advice I don't think there is any more for us to discuss,' he said coldly.

'Should I want it, your advice I mean, I'll seek it. Right now I don't need it. You know it all, I have held nothing back. You really do have a nerve, Tim. I have been open with you which is something you are not being with me.' She swallowed. 'How about you telling me what is going on? What do you get up to? You are gone from this house for a whole working day which makes me think you must be holding down a job. Is what you do so shameful that you don't want me to know what it is?'

'Am I gainfully employed you are asking and is what I do legal and above board?'

'Yes, Tim, that is what I am asking.'

'Let me put your mind at rest. I am not in employment, legal or otherwise. Which brings us very neatly to the subject you wished to discuss, namely our financial position.'

She nodded.

'The mortgage for the house is taken care of.'

'You mean you have arranged for the payments to be made?'

'Isn't that what I have just said?'

'You haven't said where the money is coming from.'

'That need not concern you.'

'That is where you are wrong. I am afraid it is very much my concern. Should I be left on my own I need to be in control. And to be in control I need the facts. You have to appreciate my difficulties.'

'I do, believe me I do.'

'Am I right in thinking that the money for the mortgage is coming out of—' she hesitated.

'Out of my inheritance was what you were about to say and the answer is yes.' He was frowning heavily. 'Why do you keep looking at me like that? Have I suddenly grown two heads?'

'Sorry. There is a mark on your shirt just below the collar. It looks like egg to me.' She got up to take a closer look. 'Definitely egg, what is it doing there, you don't like eggs.'

His hand went up to his collar and she saw that he was looking uncomfortable. 'You pick your moments, don't you? We were supposed to be having a serious talk about money.'

'So we were. Sorry again but that mark was annoying me.'

'It will come out in the wash won't it?'

'Yes, it should. I hope so, that is one of your best shirts. I'm relieved I don't have to worry about the mortgage.'

'Did you think you might lose the roof over your head?'

'Not exactly.' She smiled. 'I needed the reassurance.'

'The money won't last for ever, you will have to be careful.'

'I am used to being careful. My concern is for Joanna, I don't want her to go short.'

'She won't. There should be enough to keep you both until I am a free man.'

'And find yourself a job.'

They had slipped into accepting his loss of freedom. 'Yes.'

'I'm not too worried. With my qualifications and experience there is a very good chance I will be approached and offered a job. You see, getting a job won't be a problem, Felicity, finding one that suits me may take more time.'

'I'm sure things will work out for you.'

He made an exasperated sound. 'You keep saying that meaningless drivel. You cannot be sure when I am not sure myself.'

'Sorry,' she said shortly.

'You mean well and you say it to try and make me feel better, only it happens to have the opposite effect.'

'Sorry again and I'll try and remember that.' She got up. 'It's early dark tonight, I'll close the curtains and you can switch on the lamp beside you.'

He did that. 'By the way I saw Michael again and we had a drink.'

'Oh.' She waited.

'We were discussing my case, my impending case.'

'And?'

'And how long I am likely to be the guest of her Majesty's—'

She choked. 'I wish you wouldn't joke about it.'

'Be glad that I can.' He paused. 'Michael is always very concerned about you.' He looked amused. 'Could be he has a secret admiration for you, Felicity.'

'Don't be ridiculous,' she said and was annoyed to feel her colour rising.

'Oh, I don't know. My wife seems to have her admirers these days. First Michael then that fellow Adam something or other.'

'Adam Silver.' She laughed to hide her embarrassment. 'Michael is my husband's friend—'

'No, he isn't. He is a former colleague that is all.'

'There must be a degree of friendship when he is doing so much for you. Of course he is a friend and I would hope that he liked me. Adam is my agent, a happily married man with two sons. I would like to think we were friends.'

He nodded. 'Michael doesn't tend to look on the bright side.'

'Very sensible, he doesn't want to raise false hopes.'

'You could be right. In his carefully arrived at opinion he believes the maximum sentence I could expect would be four years—'

'What?' Felicity screeched.

'Four years reduced for good behaviour and as I am not likely to step out of line—'

'Reduced to what?' she said her heart in her mouth.

'Perhaps two and a half years. Eighteen months is, however, the more likely sentence with me serving no more than twelve.'

'A whole year,' she faltered. 'Oh, Tim.'

'I have warned you all along.'

'I know, but a whole year, it is such a long time.'

'The best I can hope for, Felicity. If I was to be given less than eighteen months for my crime there would be something far wrong with the system.'

'You are being very brave.' She blinked to hold back the tears.

'Putting a brave face on it which is not quite the same.' He gave a half smile. 'Things could be worse and with you likely to be earning real money you won't need so much from me.'

'No, Tim, ignore my money for the present. It would be better to allow me whatever amount you had decided. I am not extravagant and what is left over will go in the bank. Joanna's education must not suffer. I want to make very sure it doesn't. She needs to have money in her pocket to keep up with her friends.'

'You worry too much about Joanna.'

'I admit to worrying but you don't although you worry just as much. Did you read her letter? I left it for you on the dining-room table.'

'Yes, I read it. Not much in it apart from saying they are enjoying themselves.'

'Tim, that is what holidays are for, to enjoy. All the same,' Felicity said thoughtfully, 'I got the impression that much as she is enjoying the holiday she will be quite happy to be home.'

'To do some studying I would hope.'

'I wouldn't be so sure about that,' she smiled.

'High time that young lady was taking her studies seriously. You have to remember, Felicity, that Joanna is not brilliant, and if she wants a good degree she will have to work for it.'

'Tim, Joanna will know that herself.'

'I'm not so sure, I think studies take second place to her social life.'

Felicity didn't think that was true and felt annoyed. 'I don't think so, I don't think so at all,' she said shortly.

He gave a huge sigh. 'Just so long as she realises that she cannot go on depending on us.'

'We will see her through university.' She paused. 'Joanna may not be brilliant but she is bright and I see our daughter making a success of her life.'

'Time will tell. Incidentally, she doesn't mention when she is coming home.'

'She did in her previous letter. Not a definite date—'

'No, that would be asking too much. She wouldn't give that. She will just arrive, you wait and see. Typical of today's youngsters, no consideration for other people and certainly none for parents.'

'Heavens! That was quite a speech,' she said choking back the laughter.

'I see nothing funny in what I said. The young of today do what they damn well want.'

'I bet your parents said exactly the same about you. Each generation does, you know.'

'All right, maybe I was laying it on a bit thick but I don't recall getting anything like the freedom the young get today.'

She nodded. 'It is a different world we live in.'

'Whatever kind of world we live in I'm thirsty. It must be all that talking.'

'I'm not surprised. When did we last have so much to say to each other?'

He didn't answer. Instead he got up from his chair, stretched himself and yawned.

'Tired?'

'No, one doesn't have to be tired to yawn. What can I get you to drink, Felicity? I suppose you are going to say no.'

'Then you suppose wrong. We are going to drink to my success which is really our success,' she said generously.

'What will it be?'

'I don't mind. You can make me up one of your concoctions.'

'This is something I am going to miss. Pouring myself a drink I mean.'

Chapter Thirteen

The pencilled-in date of the twentieth of September was expected to be confirmed any day now. Felicity kept wondering if Joanna would be home before the case reached court or if it would be all over by the time she put in her appearance. Whichever it was the ordeal had to be faced. If she had only her worries to occupy her mind, Felicity thought she would have gone mad. What saved her was her work and she found it truly amazing that she could lose herself so completely in her sketches and be unaware of the passing of time. With such total concentration Felicity felt that she was bound to be giving of her best.

Housework took a back seat and had never seemed so unimportant. Felicity did only what was absolutely necessary and left the rest. Her mother would have called it a lick and a promise. Baking was something she enjoyed but hardly bothered with these days. She did no entertaining, her turn for the coffee morning was long past. She made excuse after excuse and eventually her non-appearance at various events had been accepted. Very occasionally there would be a phone call but mostly she was left alone.

Today Felicity had taken the trouble to bake and was busy rolling out the pastry when Tim came in. This was very early for Tim to be home and she glanced quickly at the clock before greeting her husband. One look at his face told her that the waiting was over and her heart began to hammer. For weeks he had been looking pale but now he was haggard and his skin had taken on an unhealthy pallor. That was bad enough but what alarmed her more was the panic-stricken look in his eyes. The air of bravado had gone and it was as though she were seeing Tim going to pieces before her eyes. He was making no attempt to hide it now, her husband was desperately afraid.

'Oh, God, Felicity,' he said brokenly, 'how am I going to get through this?' He sat down on one of the kitchen chairs and buried his face in his hands.

Felicity wasn't aware that she was still holding the rolling pin, looked at it stupidly, then put it down and gave her hands a quick wipe with a towel to take the flour away. Then she went to kneel down beside her husband. She wanted to cradle his head and take away the pain as she would a child. Her arms went round him and she pressed her cheek to his. For a few moments they remained that way and then Tim was easing himself away. He raised his head and she saw that his eyes were wet.

'Oh, Tim,' she said close to tears herself.

'No need to tell you, you will have guessed?'

'I think so.'

'I have to appear on the twentieth of September. I should be glad to get the whole thing over and a part of me is. The other part, the coward in me, can't face it.'

'You are not a coward, Tim,' she said fiercely.

'I try to imagine being locked up like a criminal for a year maybe longer. That shouldn't be, I am not a criminal. I made one mistake, a stupid mistake and yet for that one mistake I am going to be treated the same as the lowest of the low.'

'No, Tim, maybe long ago it was like that but not now. These are the sixties and everything will be much improved.'

He shook his head. 'That is what the public like to think and are encouraged to do so. The plain truth is that the public are not very concerned about the plight of the prisoner. If they had a hard time so what. It would make them less likely to reoffend.' He gave a lopsided smile. 'The matter wouldn't have given me a sleepless night.'

She didn't know what to say.

'A year, twelve whole months locked in a cell. It could even be longer, I am looking at the minimum. I'll go mad.'

'You will not, you will come through this.'

'And you, Felicity, what will it do to you?'

She looked at him in surprise. 'Me? Like you, dear, I will come through it. Life will never be the same, I

have accepted that, but there will be a future for us.
For the present I can cope with living here but once
you are free we will move away.'

'Where we go will depend on where I get a job, if
I get one. No. No, I will get one. Beggars can't be
choosers. I will take what I am offered.'

'This isn't very comfortable, come on through to the
sitting-room,' she said gently and was pleased when he
made no demur. He got up from his chair and went
with her. In the sitting-room he took his usual chair
and she went to the cabinet to pour him a whisky.
Neat whisky would have more effect but it wasn't the
way he usually took it. Felicity had been generous with
the measure and went back to the kitchen for water.
Returning with a small jug, she added some to the
whisky but only a very little.

'Here you are. Drink that, Tim.'

He took it gratefully and gulped down a mouthful.
Felicity brought over a small table and put it beside
him.

The whisky had helped and he looked more like
himself. He must have been feeling it too because he
was looking shame-faced and embarrassed.

'Sorry, not like me to give way like that.'

'You don't have to apologise to me. Giving way as
you put it could actually help.'

'The whisky did the trick.'

She smiled. 'Have it your way. There are times when
we all need help and perhaps a shoulder to cry on. The
pity is when pride gets in the way.'

'Mother was right when she said to me that you had hidden strength, which is just as well because you are going to need it.' He sighed. 'It was hopeless, of course, but I had hoped to keep my troubles separate from you and Mother. In your case and with it going to court, there was no way you were going to be spared.'

'A married couple should share their troubles. That is something you have never been able to do with me,' she said quietly.

'I know and you are not to blame.' He paused and looked at her. 'I can't say more.'

'All right I have to accept that and as regards your mother, you can put your mind at rest. She is separate from it. Last time I was over she was waiting for you to come home from school.'

'Poor Mother, how she would have hated that, to have her memory go. I can remember her once saying that the worst that can happen to someone is when the mind goes.'

'Her mind hasn't gone, just her memory.'

'She doesn't seem to be unhappy.'

'She isn't, your mother is very content and I know I am much more relaxed now that Mrs Haggarty is staying overnight. The woman is very good with your mother and she has our telephone number should she require to get in touch.'

'To hear you one would think I never went near my mother,' he said sounding very annoyed. 'I go regularly and much of what you were saying I already knew.'

'I know you visit,' Felicity said soothingly, 'Mrs Haggarty always tells me.'

'Just as well she does because the minute I am out the door Mother will have forgotten I was there.'

That was an exaggeration but she let it pass.

'Very sad but in the circumstances a blessing.'

Felicity nodded.

'Once my visits cease and were she to ask about me you can always tell a white lie and say I had called when she was asleep. She does take a lot of catnaps.'

'A lot of older people do.' She looked at him. 'You could do with a rest yourself, you look exhausted.'

'I am.'

'Lean back and close your eyes. I have a few things to do in the kitchen and when I'm finished I'll put the kettle on.'

'Tea being a cure for everything.'

'Not quite everything but a cup does wonders.' She left him and went into the kitchen. First she finished rolling out the pastry, then she covered the dish containing the meat which had been browned earlier on in the day. With a sharp knife she trimmed the pastry letting the scraps fall to the table. Usually she collected them together, rolled them out and cut out leaves to decorate the pie. Not today, there was no time for that and they went into the pedal bin. She quickly brushed the top of the pie with beaten egg and seeing the yellow reminded her of the mark on Tim's shirt. It was a silly little thing to remember. The stain had come out in the wash, but how had it got there in the first place? She would have liked to know. After checking that the oven was at the right temperature, Felicity popped the pie in the oven and noted the time when it should come out. The kettle reached the boil and she made the tea.

When she went back Tim hadn't moved. His eyes were open and he was staring at the wall opposite. If he heard her he made no sign and she quietly got the tea things ready.

'Oh!' He roused himself.

'That's the steak pie in the oven, don't let me forget.' She wondered if it would be eaten.

Tim drank his tea. Conversation had dried up and she waited for him to break the silence.

'You are remembering your promise, I hope?'

Felicity looked blank.

'The court. Do I have to spell it out?'

'I'm sorry, I wasn't thinking. The promise I gave you for me not to attend court?'

'Yes.'

'I won't break my promise.'

'Think about it this way, Felicity, you will be spared an ordeal. And while we are on the subject neither you nor Joanna is to visit me. I absolutely forbid it.'

'You are determined to keep us out of your life.'

'That is not the case and is not what I said. I would hope, indeed I am depending on it, that you will write to me and regularly. I shall look forward to those letters I can tell you.' He smiled. 'Make them long and newsy.'

'In which case it will be a lot of trivial stuff, that you wouldn't want to hear.'

'Very true,' he said with a laugh. 'It will be changed days indeed and anything you write will be welcome. I won't have much news to give you but I'll do my best.'

She swallowed the lump in her throat. 'You will be so alone, I do wish—'

'No,' he almost exploded, 'don't even think about it. God, what do I have to say to make you understand? Can you picture us desperately trying to think of something to say and feeling guilty for wishing the time to speed up and longing for the bell to ring.'

'It wouldn't be like that.'

'It would be exactly like that.'

'No visitors, you don't want anyone?'

'That is right. I do not want anyone.'

'Does this apply to Michael as well?'

'Michael is different.'

'Why should that be?'

'Michael understands the system and knows his way around. Actually he did a bit of court work.'

'I didn't know that.'

'I must try and remember that I will be a lot better than some.'

'Could you explain that?'

'My own company doesn't bore me. Some poor devils can't stand being alone. That steak pie—'

'I hadn't forgotten, another ten minutes before I need look.'

They were silent.

'You were thinking about Joanna?'

'Yes, I was. She is constantly in my thoughts,' Felicity said.

'I suppose nineteen is grown up.'

'Joanna would certainly think so. She is a young adult and we both have to remember that.'

'She might not want to write to me. If she doesn't don't put any pressure on her. In her position I probably wouldn't want to write either.'

'Give her time. She is bound to be devastated,' Felicity said quietly.

'It is going to be hard on you having to tell her.'

'Tim, she might be home before—'

'Before the case goes to court. True she hasn't given an exact date for her return but you should be prepared.'

Felicity shook her head. 'No, that would be less than useless. I'll have to hope the words come to me.' She sighed and got up. 'Time to check the oven.'

The day they had dreaded was here. In their separate rooms they had heard the clock chime each hour. Tim had made no move to return to their bedroom and Felicity didn't know whether she was relieved or disappointed. They might have been able to comfort each other or maybe not. The togetherness they had once shared was no longer there.

The weather had been changeable over the last few

days. This morning a weak sun peeped through the clouds but the rain wasn't far away.

Tim had spent a lot of the previous day with his mother. Felicity hadn't offered to accompany him believing he would prefer to be on his own. This was going to be very hard for him. His mother was frail and her heart wasn't strong and it must have been in his mind that this could be the last time he would see her.

It must have taken a tremendous effort but Tim was in control. He looked better, his skin wasn't so grey and the dark shadows below his eyes were less pronounced.

'How do you feel?' she said anxiously.

'How do I look?'

'More like your old self.'

'Arrogant and overbearing?'

'You said it, not me,' she smiled.

'Will I pass?' he said adjusting his tie.

'Oh, yes, Tim, you will pass,' she said her eyes brimming. 'Very smart and handsome I would say.' What would happen to his clothes, she wondered. Would he be allowed to wear his own? She couldn't ask questions like that but later she would ask Michael, he would know.

'Will smart and handsome help me?'

'It might.'

'Darling, take care, I hope things don't get too unpleasant for you.'

He hadn't called her darling in a very long time. 'Don't worry about me, I'll be fine.'

He looked at his watch and she looked at the clock. Then he held out his arms and she went into them. For a long time they embraced, then he took her face between his hands and kissed her.

'Stay there, don't come to the door.'

'I'll be thinking of you,' she said unsteadily.

'Do that and keep your fingers crossed.'

She nodded.

'I'm sorry, so very sorry. Tell Joanna that.'

Then he was gone.

Time crawled. She couldn't eat, couldn't keep still. She drank endless cups of tea. Her sketches were forgotten, everything was forgotten. All she could think of was Tim in that courtroom. She desperately hoped that he wouldn't break down. That, for Tim, would be the final humiliation.

This was torture. She was caught up in the suspense, waiting for the verdict. No, the verdict was guilty, that was already known. What was important was how they measured the guilt. Everyone wasn't treated alike. A betrayal of trust was always serious but when it involved a solicitor, it was seen to be so much worse.

There had been no sleep for her last night and precious little the previous nights. Occasionally her head would go back in the chair and she would drift off only to waken with a painful jerk and in a panic in case in those few minutes the phone had been ringing and she hadn't heard it.

When the phone did ring, Felicity ran to the hall and stood there hearing the ring going on and on and unable to bring herself to answer it. Then very slowly, like someone in a trance, her hand went to the phone and she brought the receiver to her ear.

'Yes,' she whispered. Not hello, just yes.

'Felicity, is it you?'

'Yes.'

'It's Michael.'

'I know. Is it over? Is that why you are phoning?'

'Yes. Felicity, it was what we expected. An eighteen months sentence.'

'Reduced to twelve for good behaviour – Tim told me that was likely.'

'Very probably he will only do a year.'

'Only?' She picked him up on it.

'Felicity, it could have been worse.'

'You mean we should be thankful for small mercies,' she said angrily.

'Are you all right?'

'How could I be all right?' she shouted and pressed a hand over her mouth. She had yelled at Michael.

'I'm coming over, Felicity, do you hear me?'

'I'm sorry, so sorry, Michael.' She was weeping. 'Forgive me.'

'Nothing to forgive. Listen, Felicity, and listen carefully. When I arrive I'll give three sharp knocks so that you will know it is me. I won't ring the bell. Don't under any circumstances answer to anyone else.'

'No one is likely to come here.'

'You cannot be sure about that.'

'Why not?'

'It will have been noticed that you were not in court.'

'Tim didn't want me to be there.' She paused to moisten her lips. 'Where are they sending Tim?'

'Newtonhill.'

'He thought it probably would be. Michael, why did you say it will have been noticed I wasn't in court?' she asked.

'Some reporter may decide since you didn't attend you could be at home. He wants a story and the public are always hungry for every detail.'

'What happened had nothing to do with me.'

'They don't know that.'

'How can they be so insensitive? Why should they want to add to my distress?'

'Felicity, you can't blame them. It is their job, what they are paid for, to get a story for their paper.'

'And the Morrisons are newsworthy at the moment? I suppose we are,' she said wearily. 'Michael thank you for phoning. I'm fine now, really I am. There is no need for you to come over.'

'I'm coming just the same. Expect me in half an hour or as soon after that as possible. And don't forget what I said,' he added.

'I won't. Three sharp knocks.' She put the phone down.

She felt on edge, the phone call had made her worse. She didn't think she could drink any more tea but

Michael might like a coffee. He didn't look after himself when it came to food. That would give her something to do. She would prepare a few sandwiches and if he wanted something stronger than coffee there was a selection of drink in the cabinet. The jar of instant coffee came into use when she was on her own but she would make proper coffee for Michael. Her mind kept leap-frogging and she had to check everything twice. Satisfied, she carried the tray through to the sitting-room and put it on the table. Then she sat down to wait. Answer to three sharp knocks but not to the bell ringing. Felicity wouldn't have described herself as the nervous type but here she was tensed up. Alone in the house everything was so eerily quiet.

The bell rang and she almost jumped out of her skin. She got up hastily and ran into the hall, then stopped dead. That had been the bell ringing not the three sharp knocks she was waiting for. It came again. A loud ringing then the letterbox rattled. 'Mrs Morrison, there is nothing to be afraid of, I only want a few words, five minutes of your time is all I ask.'

'Go away,' she mouthed. 'Just go away, please go away.'

There was something deeply disturbing about knowing that there was someone at the other side of the door wanting admittance while she stood there willing whoever it was to go away. The bell rang again and she pressed her back against the wall and felt her teeth biting into her lower lip. At last she could hear footsteps. The person was going away and she breathed a shaky sigh of relief. It was very tempting to go to the window and look out but she didn't. She might be seen and a movement of the curtain might bring him back. She was sure it was a man.

Maybe ten minutes later, it seemed a lot longer, the three sharp knocks she was waiting for sent her to the door. As a precaution she called out, 'Who is it?'

'Felicity, it's me, it's Michael.'

'Thank goodness.' She opened the door a fraction, just wide enough to see who it was. 'Come in, Michael.'

He stepped inside and she closed the door quickly. 'Felicity, you look scared out of your wits, what happened?'

'Nothing much, I'm scared of my own shadow,' she said trying to make light of her fear.

'Something or someone has scared you badly,' he said.

'Someone was here about ten minutes ago.' She was whispering.

'You didn't—'

'No. I didn't open the door. He spoke through the letterbox and he wasn't the least bit threatening.'

'He wouldn't be, all he would want was a story.'

'Michael, what Tim did wasn't so awful. It isn't as though he had murdered someone, for God's sake. If he had I could understand all this.'

'If he had you would have been whisked away somewhere where you wouldn't be troubled.'

'Why?'

'Because you are a well-respected family, the kind of people who do not make the headlines. Why did a comfortably-off solicitor do what he did? That is what they want to know and they think you have the answer.'

'If they only knew I am as much in the dark as they are.'

'If they knew that it would be an even bigger story. They would ferret out everything.'

She shivered.

'You are cold,' he said with concern.

'No, but we would be warmer in the sitting-room than standing in the hall.' She went ahead. 'Where did you leave your car?'

'At the gate.'

'You should have brought it in. Mine is in the garage and Tim's is away. He said something about selling it or letting someone have the use of it. I didn't pay much attention.'

He nodded.

The doorbell rang before they were properly seated and Felicity looked startled. It didn't have to be the same person it could be somebody else. When she made a move Michael shook his head and she sat down again. There was another ring and this time Michael got up to answer it. She heard the door opening and voices.

'Good evening, I would like a few words with Mrs Morrison.' It was a pleasant voice.

'Sorry, laddie, but you are out of luck. Mrs Morrison is away from home.'

'With due respect, sir, I don't think so. Her car is in the garage.'

'Very observant of you. The lady didn't feel like driving.'

'Sorry to have troubled you.'

The door shut and Felicity went back to her chair.

'You got rid of him?'

'For the time being. He didn't believe me and so may try again. I am not a very convincing liar.'

No, you aren't, she thought, you are too nice. She recalled an incident when Geraldine had told him to his face and in front of company, that he bored her to death. He hadn't answered. Those present were embarrassed but Michael seemed completely uncaring and his wife's victory was hollow.

Michael had a droll sense of humour that wasn't always appreciated. He was witty but there was never any malice. He could talk knowledgeably about any number of subjects without ever becoming boring. He was that rare thing, an interesting speaker who knew when to stop – and that was when the company would have welcomed more.

'Michael, I've made sandwiches but before we eat tell me about Tim. He didn't look nervous when he left but of course he must have been.'

'Tim did very well,' Michael said. 'He spoke quietly and clearly and answered the questions that were put to him. I felt there was a wave of sympathy for him. Most believed it was a gambling debt though that was never mentioned. Gambling does strange things to people and some in that courtroom saw him as a man driven by circumstances to do what was completely out of character.'

'There is no such thing as being a hundred percent sure but I am nearly sure it wasn't a gambling debt. I shouldn't feel guilty but I do. I should have been there — it was my place — but he was so adamant that I stay away.'

'Felicity, in his shoes I might have wanted that too.'

'You wouldn't have wanted Geraldine?'

'Oh, God, no. Perish the thought. She would have loved the role of playing tragedy queen and being dressed accordingly. That sounds unkind but I can assure you that is a fairly accurate picture. Now you—'

'Yes, me?'

'You are so very different. It isn't that you need to be protected, you are not weak, but one wants to shield you from any unpleasantness.'

She smiled, touched by the compliment.

The next little while was spent bringing through the coffee which had been percolating and setting the coffee table between them.

Once they were eating she said, 'Tim thought there was a chance I might receive a few unpleasant phone calls and he suggested I take the phone off the hook.'

Michael frowned. 'That way you would miss a genuine phone call that could be important. My advice would be to ring off as soon as you realise it is an unwanted phone call. Do that often enough and they will tire and stop.'

'Yes, I could do that.'

'Felicity, in a couple of days this will be old news. Tomorrow you might have a small problem but you can deal with that.'

'Pretend I am away from home?'

He nodded.

'I'll manage that, I'll get down to some work.'

'What about food?'

'I've plenty in,' she smiled. 'I don't need to step outside for a week.'

'You'll be fine and if you are worried at all don't hesitate to phone me.'

'I won't and I'll take your advice about not taking the phone off the hook. After all it could be Joanna trying to get in touch.'

'Do you know her arrangements? Has she said when to expect her?'

'She couldn't give an exact date. You know young people, Michael, they never want to be tied down to a time. She and Stuart are meeting up with friends on their way back and that will delay them. The first I will hear will be a call from Edinburgh to say which train she is catching and to meet her in Dundee.'

'You wouldn't be able to contact her even if you wanted to?'

'No. At least not very easily.' He was frowning and she didn't like that. Joanna didn't know what was going on. 'I could have phoned the farm where they were staying but I saw no point in that. What I have to tell her must be face-to-face.'

'I wish she was here to give you some support.'

'Well, she isn't,' Felicity said shortly. She moistened her lips. 'I know you didn't agree with her not being told and it could be that you were right. I'm no longer sure about anything. I blame Tim but some of that blame is mine. I let him dictate as though I didn't have a mind of my own. Now I find myself longing to see my daughter and at the same time dreading it. How does one go about breaking it to a nineteen-year-old girl that her father is in prison for embezzlement—'

'Tim is not an embezzler, not in my eyes. Many others will agree with me but that won't help. What he did was stupid and criminal, yes it was criminal. That money did not belong to him. It was a short-term loan and he must have decided there was a very small risk involved.'

'This won't be a nine days' wonder, Michael, not in this village. Not a lot happens and they will bleed it dry. Don't get me wrong, the folk hereabout are as nice as you could get anywhere but—' She shrugged.

'Being human they need to gossip?'

'That's about it.'

'Had it not been for Joanna you could have gone away.'

'No, why should I?'

'You will go out with your head held high.'

'I will not. I'll slip into the car and get my shopping where I am not known. I have been doing that for a while now. Oh, did I tell you that Tim does not want me or Joanna to visit him in prison? And should I feel like disobeying he will refuse to see me. A prisoner still has rights he informed me.'

'You are hurt and no wonder. Tim, to my certain knowledge, does not do anything without a good reason. You won't see it this way but it will be in your best interests. Remember, too, that however hard it is for you it is far worse for him.'

'I am being unreasonable.'

'You are being rather wonderful.'

'No tears. I have none left.'

In those moments Michael desperately wanted to take her in his arms but all he allowed himself were words of comfort. She thought he was doing this for Tim and it was true he wouldn't have deserted his former colleague but the real reason was to get closer to Felicity. She must never know that or it would be the end for him.

'Tim wants me to write so I suppose that is always something. He will want to know about his mother—'

'And if you are working on your sketches. He must be very proud of you.'

'How did you know?'

'A long time ago I did hear you went to art school and then Tim let drop that you are doing some serious work.'

She laughed. 'That makes a change. Until recently, very recently, my sketches were a bit of a joke with him.'

'Now the joke is on him and you are doing well. Tell me about your change of fortunes, Felicity.'

'A great deal of it was luck and the help of a friend. Through that friend an author of children's stories saw my sketches and liked them. She wants me to do the illustrations for her new book.'

'That is wonderful. Many, many congratulations.'

'Thank you. Amidst the gloom it is like a ray of sunshine.'

He got up and kissed her on the brow. 'You are going to be very successful, I feel it in my bones and now, Felicity, I have stayed longer than I intended.'

'You are worried about my reputation. A strange man leaving my house at this time of night. Tut-tut, what will the neighbours say?'

'Who knows?'

'Who cares?'

'I do, Felicity, I don't want anything to harm you.'

'Michael, you are a very dear friend and to be truthful I do not know what I would have done without you.'

'Tim cares very much about you and Joanna, that is why he asked me to keep an eye on you and see that all is well.'

'He did?' She looked so pleased and it was like a knife in a wound. There was no hope, never had been, Felicity was in love with her husband. Tim had called him the go-between and that was exactly what he was.

In bed that night Felicity lay wondering about Tim and where he was resting his head. Tim who liked his creature comforts and carelessly accepted them as his right. What about cleanliness, he was so particular, how high a priority was that in a prison? What kind of bedding? Who had used it before? She must stop thinking and worrying. It would do no good.

Chapter Fourteeen

The young couple, with eyes only for each other, looked tanned and happy as they collected their luggage from the overhead rack and waited their turn to get off. The train jerked and shuddered to a halt and they laughed, finding everything funny. It was not so amusing for those passengers thrown forward who were only saved from further mishap by the folk ahead who were lucky enough to have something to hang on to. Once on the platform, Joanna and Stuart struggled to put on their bulging shoulder bags and rearrange their hand luggage to make for easier carrying.

A few people coming into the station wore raincoats and several were carrying umbrellas.

'Here we are, back in Auld Reekie and surprise, surprise it is raining.'

'I bet it is cold too,' Joanna gave a mock shiver and looked to see what was taking Stuart's attention. His eyes were on the opposite railway line. There was a loud hoot as the train began to gather speed. He turned to her.

'Joanna, what do you say we leave all this and head back to France?'

'Leave all what?'

'Our studies, everything and take to the road.'

She giggled. 'Stuart you really are hopeless.'

'A nice thought you must agree,' he said wistfully, then more seriously, 'It needs a lot of guts to actually do a thing like that but if you could bring yourself to take a chance, it could be a wonderful experience. Something that would stay with you for the rest of your life.'

'Not for me, Stu, I couldn't do a thing like that. I think I must be a bit of a home bird. The holiday was marvellous and I wouldn't have missed it for the world. Yvette is a lovely person and she made me feel I was really welcome from the start and so did Robert.'

That pleased him she could see.

'They liked you, they must have when Yvette more or less told me that she thought we were right for each other. Not that I had to be told,' he smiled.

Her face went a rosy pink. 'Yvette, the romantic, she told me much the same.'

'Once we name the day,' he began.

'That won't be for ages, not until our studies are complete.'

'Nice to look ahead and think of our future. How about us spending our honeymoon in Provence?' he grinned.

'You are going too fast for me and I would have to

think about that. Italy would be wonderful. Florence would appeal to me and so would Venice.'

He made a face. Those are tourists' holiday destinations. Crowds and more crowds. Surely you don't want that?'

'Stuart this is not a serious conversation.'

'It could be.'

'Well, it isn't,' she said firmly then paused. 'You love Provence and the life there because you are their blue-eyed boy,' she teased. Joanna wondered if his love for the farm had something to do with getting the affection there that was missing at home. Joanna was greatly surprised that the friendship still existed between the charming French couple and the aloof Mr and Mrs Milton. Maybe the Miltons hadn't always been like that, in their younger days they might have been good company. It was years since they had seen each other and there was a strong possibility they would have lost touch had it not been for Stuart.

'They make a fuss of me—'

'Which you like.'

'Of course I do, I'm not used to it.'

'You take the place of the son they had hoped for.'

He looked at her quickly. 'What made you say that?'

'Yvette told me. She said they desperately wanted children but it wasn't to be.'

He nodded as they walked together out of the station. 'Yvette was all for a big family. A shame really when there are so many unwanted children in the world.'

'I know, it makes you wonder.'

'Wonder what?'

'Why they didn't decide to adopt and have a proper family.'

'They did give that some thought then they thought about fostering. With fostering they could give under-privileged children a taste of farm life.'

'Farm life wouldn't suit everybody.'

'So it turned out,' Stuart said. 'Some took to the life like a duck to water, Yvette told me, while others couldn't wait to get back to the town with its noise and its crowds, even its poverty. That was something they understood.'

'What was their main complaint?'

'The quietness of the country, that was what scared them.'

Joanna laughed. 'I found it anything but quiet, and as for that dawn chorus—'

'After a few nights you didn't even notice.'

'It was the mornings.'

'You got used to that too.' They were silent for a few moments. 'You are glad to be going home.' He sounded disappointed.

'Stuart, you are getting this all wrong. The holiday, us being together was terrific but I am longing to see my mum and dad and my grandmother. Stu, you must feel the same, you must miss your parents and your brother.'

'Not really. I'm fond of them, of course,' he said hastily, 'but I suppose I have grown away. There seems so little to say and once that little has been said I'm ready to leave. The parents wouldn't want to say it but it is probably a relief to them that I am no longer staying at home.'

'What about Nigel, he is fond of his big brother?'

'Nigel is a nice kid but that is all he is. There is too big a gap in our ages for us to have much in common. That will begin to even itself out as we grow older or I hope it does.' He laughed. 'A shocking thing to say I know, but what I would miss most of all, except for you, of course, would be my scruffy flat. That is the place I call home, a place where I can truly be myself and do as I please.'

Joanna thought with parents like Stuart's she might feel the same way and felt a rush of love for her own mum and dad. They could be exasperating at times, Dad especially, but she knew she had nothing to complain about. All of a sudden she wanted home. She wanted to phone her mother there and then and get on the next train for Dundee.

'Stuart, I've changed my mind,' she said, coming to a halt and forcing him to do likewise. 'I think I want to get the next train. I can phone my mum to come and meet me in Dundee.'

'No, you don't,' he said hurrying her along. 'I know what, we'll make straight for my flat, find out from whoever is around, what has been happening in our absence. Then we will dump my things and collect my car.'

'After all this time it probably won't start.'

'You are a ray of sunshine, aren't you? Actually it should be no trouble, Ralph was going to give it the occasional run so there is no danger of a flat battery or anything like that.'

'Had you told me that I would have known.'

'You should have more confidence in me, my sweet. I am very good at organising.' He paused. 'We'll nip over to see the parents, a very brief visit I promise and when we are there you can make your telephone call to your mother. OK?' He looked at her to see if his suggestion was meeting with her approval.

It wasn't what she wanted but it would seem churlish to say so. 'Yes, that's fine.' Her small sigh went unheard.

'Good. With that over I shall drive you to the station.'

'I want no last-minute dash remember, we get there in plenty of time,' Joanna said severely. 'I don't want to arrive at the station in time to see the tail end disappearing and my poor mother waiting for me in Dundee and having to cool her heels—'

'And her temper.'

'My mother doesn't have much of a temper and she would only lose it if something really got her goat.'

'Mine doesn't lose her temper either. Her deadly weapon is her look,' he grinned. 'Be on the receiving end of one of those and you will freeze.'

Joanna could well believe it. She wished it had been different. It wasn't like her to take an instant dislike to anyone. Perhaps it was the lack of warmth in their greeting. They had been perfectly polite but aloof and cold. Her parents had gone out of their way to make Stuart welcome and she had expected the same of his parents.

'Penny for them?'

'I wasn't thinking of anything.'

'Yes, you were wondering if I would get you to the station on time. Have no fear we will be there with time to spare.'

'Thanks.'

'It is going to be funny though, no not funny, strange.'

'What is?'

'Not having you with me. We've hardly been separated.'

'It won't be for long,' Joanna said gently, 'but I need to see everybody and sort out my clothes to take back to university. Mum, if I sweet-talk her, might be persuaded to buy me something new.'

'Ask your father for the money, he'll be a soft touch. I bet you can twist him round your little finger.' He frowned. 'Have I got that right?'

'I don't know.' She screwed up her face. 'I wouldn't call my dad a soft touch. That isn't to say he is mean, he isn't,' she said quickly, 'just careful.'

'Looks at both sides of the coin before spending it.' He smiled to show it was only in fun.

'That's the lawyer in him. Your father will be the same and you, my poor darling, are heading in the same direction.'

'Heaven forbid. There are times when I think law is not for me.'

'The holiday has made you unsettled but in a day or two you will be fine.'

When they left the station the blustery showers had given way to warm sunshine and already the pavements were drying.

'I do like Edinburgh and it is nice to see all this again,' Joanna said as they walked along Princes Street.

Stuart nodded. 'We take it for granted and it takes visitors to remind us that we have a lovely city steeped in history and endowed with memorable buildings. I should read it all up and sell myself as a guide. Good money can be made. What do you think of that idea?'

'The same as I think of most of your ideas,' she said laughing. 'Talking about them is as far as it gets.'

When the oncoming bus slowed down and proved to be going their way, Joanna and Stuart changed their mind about walking and jumped on baggage and all. Stuart got money out of his pocket to pay the fares and since they were only travelling three stops they didn't bother with a seat although several were vacant. They got off in an old part of Edinburgh in an area that boasted many listed buildings but it also had its share of slum dwellings. Many of the houses had a demolition order hanging over them. The order had been served and then forgotten. Glad of the unexpected reprieve, the landlords continued to make a killing from the money they got from students desperate for accommodation.

Stuart's mother had been horrified when she learned where her son was to live but less so when she discovered the cost of reasonable accommodation in Scotland's capital city. They weren't going to throw money away. Stuart could stay at home and travel and if he wasn't prepared to do that then he must make the best of it.

Only a very few of the original tenements remained. Most of the people had been rehoused. One elderly couple, who had spent most of their married life in the house had clung to their old home for as long as they could but eventually had given in to pressure from the family and agreed to move to a ground-floor flat that had been recently modernised and was in the same district.

Unlike those who had left before them the old couple had struck up a friendship with the students occupying the tenement block. They accepted that students were boisterous and that complaining would only make matters worse. Instead they befriended the young people, took in their parcels from the postman and gave advice when it was asked. In return the noise was reduced to an acceptable level and should there be a late-night party they were notified and even invited. The invitation was never taken up but it kept everybody happy.

Stuart had been lucky enough to get their flat when it became vacant. It was clean and had been well cared for. He had intended to keep the flat for his own use but had agreed that Ralph Robson, a fellow student, could remain there until he found a place of his own.

The two got on well together, so well that there was no further talk of Ralph finding another place to live.

One day, no one knew when, all these tenement buildings would be rubble. Stuart hoped it was far enough into the future to allow him to complete his studies. That hadn't seemed very likely at the beginning but there was definite hope now. The city fathers were busy elsewhere.

Joanna and Stuart left the bus to walk the few yards and Stuart beamed with pleasure and relief when he saw his car parked outside the entrance to the close. It wasn't hemmed in either which made for a change.

'Like meeting an old friend,' he said patting the bonnet of the car before they went up the stairs. Number sixteen, Stuart's flat, was on the first floor and had been furnished with the furniture collected from the back of the garage at his parents' house. The best of it had gone to the saleroom and what was left was considered to be junk and was due to be thrown out.

Stuart with the help of his friend, Ralph and his young brother Nigel, sorted through what was there then decided that nothing should be thrown out. What they didn't want for themselves would be gratefully accepted by other students who had little more than the bare necessities.

The close was very shabby and much in need of a coat of paint but that was the responsibility of the landlord. Even before the threat of demolition, nothing would have been done. Nobody complained or rather everybody complained, but not to the landlord. To do so might have meant them getting their marching orders. It was a roof over their head and if they lost it there was always someone else waiting. Someone who wouldn't complain.

Stuart had the key in his hand ready to open the door.

'Will Ralph be around?' Joanna asked. She liked Ralph.

'No. In his letter he mentioned something about a family wedding and an order to get himself there. Knowing Ralph he'll leave the minute he can.'

A slightly musty smell met them when the door was opened.

'Better open a window, Stu.'

'I'm going to.' Stuart struggled to open the window of the kitchen which was also the living-room. After a good deal of effort and a few choice words, he did manage to raise the window a couple of inches. Then he found it wasn't going to stay open without assistance.

'Joanna, see that bit of wood behind the door, give it here, would you?'

She bent down to get it and handed the bit of wood to Stuart.

'What are you going to do with it?'

'Use it as a wedge to keep this damned window open.'

'Must be something broken about it.'

'Clever girl. For your information this window needs a new cord.'

'Ralph is good with his hands.'

'Not all that good but better than me.'

'A new cord wouldn't cost much and would save all this bother.'

'You could be right and it wouldn't cost much. Paying someone to do the job might be pricey. It could be tricky and need an expert.'

'What rubbish. I bet it is perfectly straightforward and within the capabilities of most people.'

'Alas that may well be so. The more brilliant the mind – I can't remember the rest of that saying—'

'I don't recall there being one.'

'Maybe not but you get my drift.'

'Big head. You and Ralph are just a couple of scrooges not prepared to buy a miserable window cord.'

'My dear Joanna, you miss the point. It is not the money, it is the principle. The cord is not our responsibility and this piece of wood,' he said pushing it into place, will do the job very nicely. When the day of demolition finally catches up with this tenement building the new cord would be lost under piles of debris. Such a waste and an avoidable one.'

Joanna was shaking her head and laughing as she walked about the flat. It was the typical tenement building built in the early nineteen hundreds. The accommodation consisted of two good-sized rooms, one bedroom, scullery and bathroom: not all of them had a bathroom. The scullery was very small and every available inch was used. There was a cooker and the shelves held pots and pans and other equipment. Only one could work in the cramped area and Stuart and Ralph took week about doing the cooking. It was an unwritten rule that there would be no complaints. One ate what was put down and that was that. Fortunately they were both quite good at producing a meal. The old range had been removed from the living-room and a gas fire put in its place. Beside it was the meter known as the enemy. The gas fire gave out a good heat but ate up the coins at an alarming rate. Only when they were in danger of freezing to death did they light the fire. Instead they wore several sweaters and sometimes woollen mitts.

The bedroom had a single bed, a folding table, a cupboard used as a wardrobe and a chair. Ralph was well pleased with it and grateful to his friend. As well as a kitchen-cum-living-room there was the front room. The old couple, the previous tenants, had seldom used it. On Sundays they did and for special occasions like Christmas and the New Year. The minister was always shown to the front room – always being twice a year. They would sit uncomfortably and make polite conversation until the minister rose to go. Though there would be little dust – the front room was cleaned as regularly and as thoroughly as those in daily use.

Stuart slept and studied in the front room. He had it well furnished and the bookcases were filled to capacity. There was no desk but a small sturdy table did the purpose and for sitting on there was a swivel chair. The leather was badly torn and was why Stuart had fallen heir to it. Once it had graced his father's study.

Ralph's bedroom door was wide enough open for Joanna to see inside. Ralph had no bookcases but one wall had a shelf. Not a professional job, there was a definite slope but it was strong enough to take the weight of the small number of books he owned. Ralph did some of his studying in the university library. Joanna knew that Ralph's parents had had to make sacrifices to send their clever son to university. She also knew that Ralph felt guilty that he should be so privileged. This was a different world and one he couldn't share with his family. They were all proud of him especially Ralph's father who would boast in the pub about his son, the law student. The pity was that father and son got on better apart and each knew it. Ralph made every effort and probably the family did too but they were no longer comfortable. The law student no longer fitted in. One day, Ralph vowed, he would repay his parents for giving him his chance in life, only then would the guilt disappear.

True to his word Stuart did not spend much time in the flat. He had a few words with two of his friends who assured him that nothing of importance had happened in his absence.

'Come on, Joanna, we'll get on our way. That didn't take long, did it?'

'No.' She hoped the next call would be equally short or shorter, then was immediately ashamed. This was unfair of her. Maybe she wasn't blameless and they thought her standoffish. She would make a special effort.

The car started at the first attempt and Stuart gave a huge smile. Very soon they were free of the tenement buildings and heading for the leafy suburbs. Stuart seemed relaxed and happy: travelling didn't tire him whereas Joanna felt travel weary. To make matters worse she had a dull headache which she suffered in silence. Had she mentioned it to Stuart she would have had his sympathy but she didn't want that. She had told him she was a good traveller when she wasn't and her pride wouldn't let her confess.

'Are your parents expecting us?' she asked.

'I said we would probably look in.'

Stuart concentrated on his driving and Joanna closed her eyes. She wished now that she had insisted on getting that earlier train. Had she done so she would have been nearing Dundee.

'Here we are,' he said slowing down at the gate. There was a car in the drive. 'Dad must be home, that is his car.'

Why did she feel so apprehensive? It was stupid but she couldn't help it. Was it the surprise in Stuart's voice when he said that was his dad's car? What difference did it make to her? None at all. Their arrival must have been noted because Mrs Milton had the door open before they reached it.

'Hello, Mum,' Stuart said giving her a peck on the cheek.

'You are looking well.' She smiled to him.

'Feel great, we both do. All that sunshine and good food not to mention the hard work—' He stopped and laughed and when his mother opened the door wider they both went in.

Joanna had a fixed smile on her face. This was not her imagination, she was being ignored. Stuart must have noticed if his frown was anything to go by.

'We'll go into the lounge,' Mrs Milton said quietly. She was a good-looking woman who knew how to dress. The camel skirt and matching jumper looked expensive and no doubt they were. 'Sit down, Joanna.' A hand indicated where she should sit. Then she turned to her son. 'Stuart, we were expecting you to call and my instructions are to tell you that your father wishes to see you in his study as soon as you arrive.'

'What about and why the hurry?' It was clear he was annoyed.

'You will learn that when you go upstairs.'

'Why can't he come down? Has someone died?'

'Don't be silly.'

'Joanna, I'm sorry about all this but to keep the peace I had better go up. I'll make it short.' He smiled to her and she nodded.

At the door he turned back. 'This has to be a very short visit, Joanna has a train to catch.'

'All the more reason to get yourself upstairs quickly. You can be very difficult when you want, Stuart.'

'I could say the same about somebody else,' he muttered.

They heard his footsteps on the stairs, then a door closing.

'Yvette and Robert send their regards, Mrs Milton,' Joanna said quietly.

'Indeed. And are you at liberty to use their Christian names?'

'I am or I wouldn't be using them,' Joanna said coldly. All her good intentions were gone. The woman was plain nasty. 'They are a very charming couple and they made me so very welcome.' She put a lot of emphasis on the welcome.

'I thought, in the circumstances, that you would have gone straight home.'

What circumstances, she wondered. 'I did think about it but Stuart persuaded me to stay in Edinburgh ...' her voice trailed off.

'And now you are on your way home?'

'Yes.'

The woman got up to rearrange the already perfect display of flowers. The silence lengthened and there was no sign of Stuart reappearing. Joanna began to be alarmed. This wouldn't do, she wasn't going to miss her train.

'Mrs Milton, I have a train to catch.'

'So Stuart said.'

'I think he may have forgotten the time. Please, would you hurry him up?'

The woman looked taken aback at Joanna's abruptness and then after a small hesitation she got up and called from the bottom of the stairs.

'Stuart, are you remembering that Joanna has a train to catch?'

The door of the study opened as she spoke and Joanna heard Stuart's voice.

'Coming. I'm just coming.'

Joanna was on her feet, desperate to be gone, not only to catch her train but to be away from this house.

'We are going to be pushed for time, Stuart,' she said, not hiding her annoyance.

'We'll make it, come on,' he said abruptly. So abruptly that she looked at him in surprise.

There were no goodbyes. Stuart closed the door behind him and a glance at his face showed his expression to be grim.

'Stuart, is something the matter?'

'You should know the answer to that. I didn't need to hear it all, but surely you could have said something, prepared me. Heavens! I can't believe it.'

'Believe what?'

He didn't answer, just got behind the wheel and had the ignition turned before she was properly seated. He had been carrying a newspaper which he had put under the dashboard.

'I would like an answer, please. You can't believe what?'

Stuart was looking straight ahead. 'That you would keep it from me. Admittedly you couldn't have known the outcome but it will be much as was expected.'

Joanna heard the hurt and the condemnation in his

voice and turned to him in bewilderment. 'What are you talking about?'

He pulled out the newspaper and put it on her knee. 'Read it for yourself.'

She scanned the page wondering what she should be looking for. Nothing at first registered and then it did. The hairs on her neck seemed to rise and a cold hand gripped her heart. There was a buzzing in her ears and for a moment she thought she was going to pass out.

Stuart was becoming alarmed. His eyes kept going from her face to the road and back to her face. He saw the shock and disbelief written there and the terrible truth came to him, she hadn't known. He had broken it to her and he had been unspeakably cruel. No, he wouldn't accept that, she must have known, there was no way she couldn't have.

Joanna forced herself to look at the newspaper again. It stood out in bold, black print. Solicitor, found guilty of embezzlement, gets eighteen months. Timothy Morrison, her father, there was no question of a mistake.

'Joanna, you must have known.'

'I didn't,' she whispered and shook her head slowly.

'It can't have come as such a shock. You knew your father had been dismissed.'

Another shake of the head.

'You must have known,' he repeated. 'When I met your parents your father had already lost his job.'

She looked at him sharply. 'How did you know that? I didn't.'

'It is there in the newspaper, the date of his dismissal.'

'Oh.' She hadn't taken that in. 'Watch your driving,' she said automatically as an irate driver shook his head at what could have been an accident.

The near miss had unnerved him and he began to pay more attention to his driving.

'My father—'

'Would have made it his business to find out all he could. Not difficult for him since they share, or should that be shared, the same profession,' Joanna said bitterly.

'You can't blame him for that.'

In all honesty she couldn't but she couldn't bring herself to say so.

'He only made the connection —'

'I know, I know. I remember telling your parents that my father was a solicitor with Paton & Noble. And now, please, I don't want to hear another word. Just get me to the station and preferably in one piece,' she ended nastily.

She saw his mouth tighten and was sorry she had made that remark. It had been uncalled for. Stuart wasn't a careless driver.

When they arrived at the station there was the usual chaos. Stuart parked awkwardly knowing he would have to move on in a minute or two. Just enough time to get Joanna's luggage out of the back seat.

'You go ahead, Joanna, I'll find somewhere and be with you as soon as I can.'

'Don't bother,' she said picking up her bags.

'Don't be silly.'

'I do not want you on the platform,' she said very distinctly. 'In fact Stuart, I hope never to see you again and that goes for your hateful parents.' She didn't know she was crying.

'You can't park there,' an angry voice was saying.

Stuart got behind the wheel and drove away. There was no place to park, nothing he could see and for a moment he thought of abandoning the car and going after her. Then he thought it was futile and could make matters worse. What an end to their holiday.

Joanna checked the board for arrivals and departures. Her train was due in four minutes and it was only then that she realised she hadn't made that phone call to her mother. There would be no one meeting her. She would have to take the bus, an hourly service and with her luck she would just be in time to miss one and have almost an hour to wait for the next. And adding to her misery, with all the stops the bus made, it was a tedious journey. When she thought about it, did it matter, did anything matter?

Standing on the platform surrounded by her luggage Joanna cut a forlorn figure. Her head was pounding and she looked white and distraught. A few folk eyed her curiously, one woman made to stop and enquire if she was all right then changed her mind. Young girls could be steeped in misery one minute and laughing the next. This could be no more than a lovers' tiff, a misunderstanding that would be cleared up and once again the world would be a lovely place. The woman walked on remembering when she, too, had been young.

Stuart didn't know when he had felt so miserable and he had a horrible feeling that he had handled it all wrong. Yet he thought he had acted as anyone else would have done in similar circumstances. It was no use blaming his father. He would see it as protecting his son and making sure that no whiff of scandal touched his own practice.

After leaving the station Stuart drove to his own flat glad to be on his own. He needed to be alone to think. Once inside he flung himself into a chair, put his head in his hands and groaned aloud. Then slowly and painfully he relived the scene in his father's study.

'Sit down, Stuart.'

'What is all this about? Ordering me to your study as though I were a naughty schoolboy and where are your manners? Couldn't you have come down and said hello to Joanna.'

'I shall ignore that remark about my seeming lack of manners and I have no wish to see Joanna. I sincerely hope she never enters my house again. Read that and then you might understand.'

Stuart took the newspaper and his look of annoyance turned to shocked incredulity. His first thought had been that some solicitor known to his father had got himself into a mess but this was – only it couldn't be—

'That is Joanna's father, isn't it?'

'I – I—'

'Is it or is it not?'

'Yes, that is Joanna's father.' The words were forced out.

'She didn't tell you her father was in trouble?'

A shake of the head.

'She made no mention of it at all?'

'No.'

'Strange that, wouldn't you say?'

No answer.

'Unforgivable I would have said to keep you in the dark.' He paused and pressed his fingers together. Somewhere in Stuart's mind he made a note that when he became a solicitor he would refrain from doing that. If it irritated him, it must irritate a lot of people. His father was still talking. 'Perhaps she hoped we wouldn't make the connection and had forgotten that she had told us her father worked for Paton & Noble.'

'I don't know.'

'You have met him, this embezzler?' he said disdainfully.

Stuart nodded. 'I liked him, liked him very much and that is why I cannot make sense of this.'

'The worst scoundrels don't look the part. Don't spare the man any sympathy, Stuart, he got what he deserved. Some would say he got off lightly.'

'I wouldn't. I would have said a prison sentence was inappropriate.'

'Then you would be totally wrong.'

'The money has been repaid in full.'

'That doesn't alter the fact that the weakness is there. The man took for his own needs what did not belong to him.'

'I wonder how many others get away with it.'

'Don't be ridiculous. Thank God we only get the very occasional bad apple.' He leaned forward. 'This could be harmful to you, my boy, indeed harmful to us. Scandal is something we cannot afford and we must take steps to see that it doesn't touch us.'

'Why should it?'

'Your friendship with this girl—'

'This girl happens to be called Joanna,' he hissed, 'and I happen to be in love with her.'

'Stuff and nonsense.' The thin lips tightened. 'You cannot afford to be seen in her company, in the company of an embezzler's daughter. Have an ounce of sense and think for yourself. Put the girl right out of your life and do it now. There are other more suitable girls—'

'I know, like Eileen Blackford,' he said sarcastically. 'Don't you get tired trying to throw us together?'

'A charming girl.'

'She is, I quite agree. We are good friends and that is all and I may add that neither of us is interested in the other in the way you would wish it.'

'Love grows.'

'Does it? I wouldn't say there was much sign of it with you and mother.'

'That is enough,' he thundered. 'Your mother and

243

I have a very good relationship. An outward show of affection at our age is unseemly.'

At that moment Stuart thought he positively disliked his father and had some sympathy for his mother.

Thinking the interview as he thought of it, wasn't going as well as he had hoped, Mr Milton smiled. 'Hard on you, I know, but you must put her out of your life.'

'And if I don't?'

'That would be unfortunate for you.'

'Cast me off without the proverbial penny.'

'I would hate to do that but—'

'Not an idle threat?'

'No, not an idle threat. Don't disappoint me, Stuart, you are my son and I have high hopes for you. One day I expect you to take over from me. Nigel will never amount to much, your mother and I know that.'

'You could be very wrong. For those who are good enough there is a future in sport and Nigel is good.'

'Football,' his father said witheringly. Am I supposed to be proud of his ability to kick a ball?' He gave a deep sigh. 'We are talking about Joanna. Finish it off, son. In time you will realise it was the right thing to do – is that your mother shouting—'

Stuart came out of his trance. All the time he had been reliving the scene with his father, he hadn't moved. He got up and went over to the window. There was no view, just another row of tenement buildings. It should be depressing only it wasn't. This was home.

His father was to be pitied with his narrow outlook

on life. There was no sympathy for Joanna. She was her father's daughter and must suffer along with him. Guilty or not guilty, black or white, no shades of grey. How was Mrs Morrison coping with it? She had made a deep impression on Stuart. Joanna's mother was warm and friendly and he had envied the happy family atmosphere. All the more surprising when he knew now that they had that cloud hanging over them. She would stand by her husband, she was that kind. And her talent, she had been so modest. Stuart hoped that she would have a lot of success especially if money was to be tight. The loss of her husband's salary must make a big difference.

What about Joanna? Would her education suffer? Not very likely with a grandmother who, according to Joanna, was comfortably off. She would come to the rescue.

Chapter Fifteen

There was a lot of pushing and shoving with those in a hurry trying to get ahead of the slow movers. Joanna was thankful that she had managed to get a corner seat. She put her luggage on the rack then settled down to face the window rather than be drawn into conversation. There was a book in her bag she could have taken out. Not that she would have made any attempt to read it, but she could have pretended. Only she couldn't even be bothered to pretend.

The cold pane against her throbbing forehead gave welcome relief but after a few moments she drew away. That might draw attention to herself and that was the last thing she wanted. Someone might ask if she was all right. Joanna felt that she would never be all right again. Her whole world had collapsed.

The train began to move and, in a short time, the buildings rushed by giving way to green field after green field with glimpses of grazing cattle. The occasional church spire came into view along with tiny bridges over streams, then farms and farmhouses and outhouses. She took in nothing of what she was seeing. There was a strange numbness that made thinking difficult.

So many questions that needed answers. The same ones kept hammering away in her head. Why had it happened? What had made her father do such a terrible thing? What had come over him? Why had her mother kept it from her? — and that was the most bewildering of all. She wasn't a child. Surely a daughter, a grown-up daughter of nineteen years, should have been told and not left to find out, as had happened to her. Joanna's face burned with shame when she thought of Mr and Mrs Milton who had known all about it. They wouldn't believe she hadn't known, they must have thought she was brazen enough to carry it off. Stuart hadn't given her the benefit of the doubt, he had been quick to think the worst of her. How could you love a person and hate him in the same day? She wouldn't have believed it possible but now she knew better.

Most puzzling of all was why her father had required such a large sum of money. That question remained unanswered. Her father had refused to say and if that was how he wanted it no one could force him to tell. The newspapers would be unhappy, knowing the readers would feel cheated. Maybe her mother would be harassed and she was all alone.

She had heard of people doing quite dreadful things, acts that were completely out of character and the lapse being blamed on an illness, perhaps a nervous breakdown. That wouldn't apply to her father. On that last occasion when she had introduced Stuart, he had appeared absolutely normal and so had her mother. She had to hand it to them, they had put on a good show. A very, very good show. To Joanna it was inconceivable that they could have managed to hide all that from her. She who knew them so well. Yet it was all true. Her father had already been dismissed from Paton & Noble and an impending court case was hanging over his head.

She thought his one mistake and it was pathetic, was trying to lessen his guilt by making it out to be a short-term loan, no more than that. As a lawyer he should have known it wouldn't be well received. Taking what wasn't yours was theft no matter how you tried to dress it up. His unblemished record and the fact that the debt was repaid would be of little help since no reputable firm would employ someone with a prison record.

Joanna turned from the window and closed her eyes. The newspaper reported that Timothy Morrison had remained calm throughout the trial and only when the sentence was announced had he looked white and shaken. There was something else she had read in that newspaper and it had been about her mother. It was noted that his wife, Mrs Felicity Morrison, was not present in court. She had got a small mention herself. His daughter was away at university. There was no mention of which university. Joanna was glad about that.

Before the train drew into Taybridge Station, she was

reaching for her luggage. Luggage that held gifts for her mum and dad and her grandmother. A pretty chiffon scarf in different shades of blue for her mother and two lace-edged handkerchiefs for her gran. Her father's gift was a joke and had them, she and Stuart, laughing and the shop assistant smiling in bewilderment. Tim favoured sober ties as befitted a solicitor and Joanna declared that it was time he changed his image. The chosen one was gaudy in the extreme and she was going to dare him to wear it to the office. A sob almost escaped. Her father would have no use for a tie for a very long time. It made her wonder what he would be wearing. She shivered. Surely not prison garments, the thought of her father in those was too horrible to contemplate.

Thinking, thinking, thinking, she couldn't stop herself, painful though it was. What was this doing to her mother? She would come back to that. For now she would think about her poor gran. Such a wonderful, proud old lady and, forgetful or not, Joanna did not believe for a single moment that she did not have a very good idea of what was going on. Pretending otherwise was to make it easier on herself. The money to repay the debt must have come from her, no one else would have come to his rescue. Her mother had no money of her own or only a very little. Joanna knew from what she had picked up from conversations, that everything and that included the house, was in her father's name. Her mother had her housekeeping allowance which must have been adequate but gave her no measure of independence. How trusting and easygoing her mother had been. Joanna didn't think her generation would be so stupid. It would be equal shares or near enough. A thought suddenly struck her. What would they do for money with no salary coming in?

Walking along the station platform she felt conspicuous and imagined curious eyes watching her. It was awful to feel like a criminal, someone coming out of hiding. The sins of the father . . . She could see herself being pointed out as the daughter of that solicitor now in prison for embezzling the firm's money.

She thought about phoning her mother to say she was at Taybridge Station and would get the bus home only she didn't feel equal to it. She would just arrive. Keeping her head down Joanna hurried out of the station and along to the bus stance where a few people were already waiting. She checked that there was no one she knew. There wasn't.

After about fifteen minutes the bus drew up at the stop and they all got on. Joanna put her baggage on the other half of the seat. If the bus filled up she would have to remove it but it didn't seem likely. The next bus would be busy, all seats taken and probably one or two passengers hanging on to the straps.

The sky had darkened and there was a fine drizzle coming down as Joanna stepped off the bus. A ten-minute walk took her to the gate. How could everything look so normal when it was anything but? Desperate to be inside she hurried along the path, the key of the front door in her hand.

Felicity was upstairs working on her illustrations. This was to be her bread and butter and she was concentrating her whole mind on the work in hand. With clever strokes of the pen her little drawings were coming to life. She had the happy knack of seeing her work through the eyes of a child and could smile to herself as she worked. It was a welcome change not having to clear the kitchen table and a huge advantage to be able to spread the tools of her trade out on the desk and to leave them there. Taking possession of Tim's study and his desk had felt strange. It was as though she were intruding and that made her feel guilty. Then she thought how stupid could she get. Why shouldn't she make use of the study and Tim's desk? He wouldn't be requiring them for a long time. She began to wonder what it would be like when he was back home having served his sentence. She couldn't.

Sitting in the one position for so long had made her stiff and she got up to exercise her legs. A cup of tea and something to eat would be welcome. Earlier on she had thought vaguely about eating, except she couldn't be bothered. Adam had suggested she should make it a proper working day with regular breaks. It was good advice and maybe she should try to get into a routine and make herself proper meals. Once Joanna was home she would make time to cook and to bake. She felt slightly irritated that Joanna, in her last letter, hadn't given a definite date for their return. She knew they were hoping to meet up with friends and that could delay them. Joanna would phone when they reached Edinburgh.

That noise – she heard it again. Like a key turning in the lock. There were three keys to the front door. Her own. Tim had left his in the drawer in the sideboard and Joanna had the other key. Felicity had been cutting bread and dropped the knife to fly to the door.

'Darling, did you get a lift? I've been waiting and waiting for a phone call. Joanna—' she put her hand to her mouth and took a step back.

Joanna had dropped her luggage where she stood. There was no rushing into her mother's arms. Her face was a twisted, pained mask.

'How could you? How could you do that to me?' she stormed, her eyes filled with anger and anguish.

Felicity closed her eyes, her worst nightmare was coming true. Joanna knew, someone had told her.

'I'm so sorry, so terribly, terribly sorry.'

'A bit late for saying sorry,' she shouted. 'You can't even begin to know what I have come through. I wish I was dead.'

'Stop it, stop it this instant.' Felicity was shaking but forcing herself to keep control of the situation. She would try to act normally.

'You are wet, I saw the drizzle had started again, it has been off and on all day.'

Joanna stared at her mother then began to laugh hysterically. 'The weather, oh, my God, you can talk about the weather.'

'Yes, I can. Joanna, I am trying to be calm and I

suggest you try to be the same. Nothing is gained by a display of anger. This is awful for you, just as it is for me. Don't bother about your bags, leave them in the hall and we can deal with them later. Give me your coat and I'll hang it up to dry. Come on, do as I say,' she said when Joanna hesitated.

'There,' she said handing it over. The pent-up anger was spent but plenty smouldered below.

'Go upstairs, dear, and wash your face and your hair could do with a comb. Did you get the bus from the railway station?'

'Yes.'

'Why didn't you phone me?'

'No time,' she said abruptly.

'I don't know when you last ate but I was in the middle of making myself bacon and egg—'

'I don't want it.'

'Once it is in front of you you will enjoy it.' She smiled. 'More suitable for breakfast I know but it was something I fancied.'

Joanna turned wearily to go upstairs. Seeing what this was doing to her daughter Felicity felt a cold anger against her husband. For the first time she thought he was probably getting what he deserved. Not for what he had done but for the lives he was destroying. 'Darling, we can talk all night if necessary.'

It wasn't much of a smile but it was an attempt and Felicity was encouraged. That was the first hurdle over, the easy one admittedly but nevertheless a start. She went back to the kitchen, took an egg from the brown bowl and the remaining rashers from the packet. The oven was on to heat the plates and to keep her bacon and egg hot while she made fresh for Joanna. The kettle was beginning to sing.

How had Joanna found out? Who had told her? Someone who had seen it in the newspaper but who could that be? Why had she gone along with Tim? Because it had seemed best at the time. Why spoil Joanna's holiday? But a holiday spoiled or lost wasn't so terribly important. She should have listened to Michael Lawson, Michael who seldom took chances. Michael who looked at the possible consequences should something go wrong. Something had. A newspaper picked up and glanced at to pass the time or to read on the train. It could have been any of a number of things. The bacon sizzled and she turned it. She set another place at the kitchen table, made the tea.

Joanna had come downstairs and was in the sitting-room. She was sitting on the sofa clutching a cushion to her chest and crying silently. Felicity longed to take her in her arms and comfort her but knew this wasn't the time.

'Come on, dear, the bacon is crispy the way you like it.'

'How can you be like this, talk about ordinary things—'

'I have to, there is no other way.'

Joanna put the cushion aside and got up. 'You are trying to be brave but you are hurting inside?'

'Yes, I am, we both are but I am not having the food

go to waste. We are going to have this meal and we are going to enjoy it.'

'After we finish do you promise to answer my questions?'

'To the best of my ability. Sadly I do not have answers to everything.'

Joanna was hungry and ate all that was on her plate. She might be heartbroken, she was heartbroken but it hadn't affected her appetite. Felicity was relieved that she wasn't off her food. Her own appetite was poor but with Joanna at home she would have to make an effort.

'Never mind the dishes, we'll just go through.'

Joanna nodded and got up. Joanna went back to the sofa and Felicity pulled a chair forward so that they were almost facing.

'If I could understand, but I don't.'

'I know.'

'There are so many questions, Mum, and I don't know where to begin.' Her voice hardened. 'Yes, I do. I should have been told, why wasn't I?'

'For all the right reasons or so we thought. To begin with, Joanna, I thought that you should have been told.'

'Then it was Dad. I suppose he couldn't face me knowing about it though, of course, I had to know some time.'

Felicity winced at the bitterness in the young voice. 'It is true, he dreaded you knowing and wanted to put it off for as long as possible. His reasoning for not telling you was sound and he managed to persuade me to his way of thinking. You were to have your holiday in France and nothing was going to spoil that. When you came home would be the time to tell you.'

'You were preparing to tell me now?'

'Yes.'

'Were you dreading it?'

'I forced myself not to think about it. Your father thought I should have something prepared but that for me was impossible. I prayed that I would find the right words.'

'Not telling me was cruel. Not only that, I feel insulted. I am not a child to be protected. Had I known I would have made my own decision.'

'And what would that have been? To cancel your holiday and hide yourself away?'

'I don't know, but as I said the decision would have been mine.'

'It is no excuse to say we did it for the best, we were wrong.'

'Yes, you were, you were terribly wrong.' Her voice cracked. 'You can't know what it was like for me. It was the worst moment of my life.' Her voice trembled and she stopped for a moment. 'Even telling you about it makes me feel sick. This hankie is soaking wet,' she said looking at the sodden ball in her hand.

Felicity put her hand in her skirt pocket and brought out a handkerchief still in its fold. 'There you are.'

'Thanks.' She wiped her red-rimmed eyes, then blew her nose. Her head was going slowly from side to side as she spoke. 'It was so awful, Mum, the three of them—'

'Who might the three be?'

She swallowed. 'Stuart and his parents.'

'Oh.'

'The three of them knew and I didn't. Stuart had only just heard and he was mad at me for keeping it all from him and he wouldn't believe me when I told him I didn't know what he was talking about.'

'Oh, you poor darling but I'm not quite with you—'

'No. I have to tell you this bit. When we arrived in Edinburgh we went straight to Stuart's flat to leave his stuff, then we were to call in to see his parents for a brief visit.'

Felicity shut her eyes tight, she could guess what was coming.

'I was to phone you from the house and then Stuart was to drive me to the station, only when we got there Stuart was ordered, yes ordered, to see his father in his study. I thought he was going to refuse, I mean I could see how mad he was but maybe for the sake of peace he went up. I was left with his mother and she was – horrible.' The tears were streaming down her face.

Felicity felt a terrible anger that her daughter should have been treated in such a fashion.

'I could feel there was something wrong. I mean, Mum, it was the height of bad manners for Mr Milton not to come down and talk to us in the lounge.'

'It most certainly was.'

'I was angry and upset but I tried not to show it and the time was going on and I was worried about missing the train. That was when I told her to remind Stuart that I had a train to catch.'

'Good for you.'

Joanna smiled. 'She was a bit taken aback but she did go and call from the bottom of the stairs and Stuart came running down. I could see he was upset and I thought it was bad news, a tragedy in the family.'

'What made Stuart think you were holding something back?'

'Don't you see? Once Mr Milton made the connection and knew it was my dad he made it his business to find out all he could. Not all that difficult with both of them being solicitors.' She gave her mother a long look. 'That was a very convincing performance you both put on, you had me fooled. Everything seemed completely normal yet Dad had already lost his job and all this was hanging over his and your head.'

'You are talking about the time when Stuart came to visit us?'

'Yes.'

She nodded. 'I can understand Stuart thinking you must have known about your father being dismissed. That again was our mistake. We seem to have made a lot of mistakes.' She paused. 'You are angry with Stuart?'

'An understatement.'

'Don't be too hard on the lad.'

Joanna made a snorting sound. 'I never want to see him again and I told him so.'

'You don't mean that.'

'I mean it all right,' she said grimly.

'Joanna, my dear, we are all shocked, more than shocked and when we are like that we tend to say things we wish we hadn't. Stuart is probably feeling miserable.'

'Good, let him.'

Felicity hid a smile.

'Don't be making excuses for him, Mum, that relationship is dead. I mean it, Mum, so you needn't look like that.'

'I think I'll go and tidy the kitchen and wash the dishes.'

'I'll help.'

'No need. You can rest and we'll talk some more tomorrow.'

'Leave the dishes for now, I'm not tired.'

She nodded and sat down. Felicity was very tired but she wouldn't say so.

'I need more answers and I need them now.'

'Very well,' she said resignedly. 'And before I forget, put the clothes for washing straight into the machine.'

'Most of what I brought back is clean. Yvette let me do my own laundry when I wanted. She was great and so was her husband. I was made to feel like one of the family. Stuart is always treated that way. Why couldn't they have been Stuart's parents instead of the set he has?'

'Maybe it is a good thing we can't choose our

parents.' Felicity was wondering if Joanna was wishing she could exchange hers.

'Mum, your face is a giveaway and I think I know what was going on in your head. You couldn't be more wrong. You are the best and I am very lucky. Once I would have said that about dad but if I am honest I'm not so sure now. I don't think I'll ever be able to forgive him.'

'That is very harsh, Joanna. Please don't be bitter and remember your father is paying dearly for his mistake.'

'So are we, paying dearly for his mistake.'

'Your father wanted you to know that he is very, very sorry.'

'Is that supposed to make it all right?'

'No, nothing can do that.'

'I saw it, you know,' she said abruptly.

'Saw what?'

'The – the newspaper. Stuart got it from his father and he had it in his hand when he came downstairs. And you know what? He gave it to me to read in the car. That was when I found out.'

Felicity was chalk white. 'Oh, no, surely not. I can't believe Stuart would do that.'

'He did,' she said tonelessly.

'Then I am bitterly, bitterly disappointed. There was no need for him to be so cruel.'

Joanna felt she should be honest. 'No, it wasn't quite like that. You have to remember, Mum, that Stuart thought I must know about Dad being dismissed and the reason for it.'

'Even so.'

Joanna bit her lip. 'He shouldn't have jumped to conclusions. Why did Dad steal that money?'

'Borrow the money.'

'Borrow my foot,' Joanna said scornfully. 'He took what didn't belong to him, Mum, and that in anybody's book is stealing. What I want to know is where that money went. What kind of trouble was he in – or still is for that matter.'

'I don't know.'

'You must, you are his wife.'

'Joanna, aren't you doing exactly the same as Stuart? Presuming that because I am the wife I must of necessity know what my husband is doing.'

Joanna looked uncomfortable then shrugged. 'You noticed nothing different, he wasn't off his sleep or looking worried?'

Felicity shook her head. 'I wasn't looking for anything. With hindsight perhaps he was quieter than usual, but it hadn't been enough to have me remark about it.'

'You must have your own thoughts on what it might be.'

'Of course I have and sleepless nights. All that I could come up with was a venture that had gone wrong and pride kept him silent.'

'Which meant he couldn't clean out your bank account without confessing to you.'

Felicity smiled. 'We don't have a joint account. Had the money been there I am quite sure he would have taken it. Unfortunately for your father we had spent rather a lot on the house and the new garage and the balance was at an all-time low.'

'Gran then.'

'She did come to the rescue but too late to save him.' Felicity gave a deep, hopeless sigh. 'If he could have brought himself to confess to his mother none of this need have happened. Instead he decided to take a stupid risk.'

'He could have borrowed the money.'

'I think I said that, Joanna, and his reply was that he wasn't going to pay through the nose for a loan.'

'For a man who considers himself to be brilliant he has acted as the worst kind of fool.'

'I have to agree with that.'

'Will you – will you stand by him, be there when . . .'

'When he comes out? Yes, what else would you expect me to do?'

'Many wouldn't but you are the faithful kind.'

'He will need me when he gets out,' she said simply.

'Have you been to see him in – in . . .'

'Prison, we have to use the word. No, I haven't been to see your father for the very good reason that he does not want to see me, or you for that matter. It wasn't a request, it was an order.'

'He is in no position to order. If you want to go then go.'

'He doesn't have to see me. He can refuse. A prisoner has the right to do that.'

'I have no intention of visiting him now or ever so he is safe enough. Incidentally is this because he wants to cut himself off completely?'

'No. He wants me to write, letters would be appreciated. I shall write and I hope that you might bring yourself to do so as well.'

'Not a chance.'

'Bitterness that lasts too long is unhealthy. You have to come to terms with this, Joanna.'

'You appear to be coping pretty well and on your own too.' She said it grudgingly.

'Not quite on my own. I had Michael, Mr Lawson's support. Without him I don't know how I would have managed. He is to go in to see your father occasionally and let me know how he is. A sort of go-between,' Felicity smiled.

'Doesn't he think it strange that Dad doesn't want you to visit?'

'No, he can understand it. Prison visits can be an ordeal and I am to be spared that.'

'He has a point I suppose.' She paused and yawned. 'How about doing the dishes?'

'For once we could leave them until the morning?'

'No, you hate that. We'll do them, try to keep things normal.'

'Yes.' Felicity smiled gratefully. Then added, 'Thank you, dear.'

'I'm thirsty, we could have a cup of tea first.'

'Yes, a cup would be welcome.' They got up and went through to the kitchen.

Joanna went over to pick up the kettle and fill it from the cold tap.

'Mum, there's a drip, the water won't go off.'

'It will if you turn it hard enough. It needs a new washer.'

'That means the plumber?'

'Yes.'

'And you don't want anyone coming to the house?'

'Well . . .'

'Be honest, you don't.'

'I don't need you to tell me I am being pathetic.'

'You are not. I've only been home and in the house for a short time and I feel exactly the same way. On the bus I was dead scared that someone I knew would come on. Most of all I was ashamed, then it was anger and I felt so miserable and frightened.' The kettle boiled and neither of them noticed until the kettle lid began to rattle.

'You make it, dear, and I'll put out the cups.'

They stayed in the kitchen to drink their tea. Both nursed their cups as though for comfort.

'We both have to face facts and I am not showing a good example. The plumber is a question in point. Putting off phoning is just cowardice and I refuse to allow myself to become a coward.' She smiled. 'Remind me in the morning to phone the plumber.'

Joanna nodded. 'I'm sorry for that screaming and bawling when I arrived.'

'You had very good reason for acting the way you did.'

'I took it out on you and that was unforgivable. If only it hadn't been Stuart's father who found out. I mean it would still have been awful but that made it so much worse.' The tears were very close.

'I know,' Felicity said wretchedly. 'I was wrong, I should have insisted that you be told. My problem is I have become so used to obeying your father because it was easier to do so. Now when it is too late I can see the error of my ways.'

'Gran was at fault, she spoiled him rotten.'

'Joanna?'

'It's all right. I told Gran that to her face and she agreed. Her excuse was that he was such a lovable wee boy and a mother can't help doting on her son.' She made a face. 'Mum, we haven't talked about Gran.'

'I know. We are not going to talk about her tonight. We'll do that tomorrow and if you think you can face it we will go and see her.'

'It's too soon.' Felicity could see she was becoming agitated.

'That's all right, you don't have to go until you are ready.'

'I've got a gift for her from Provence and one for you and one for Dad. Dad's is a silly tie, it was to be a joke and I was to dare him to wear it to the office.' She choked. 'Mum, I'm talking quite naturally or near enough to natural?'

'You are doing very well.'

'Not inside. It is as though my father was split in two. One half is the dad I love, a pain at times but great for all that.' She swallowed and her voice hardened. 'The other half' – she paused – 'is a cheat and an embezzler.'

'That is unkind and untrue.'

'A court of law found him guilty.'

'He was guilty of a serious mistake and to his credit he never denied that. It has just occurred to me that perhaps he was shielding someone. The whole thing is so out of character.'

Joanna's eyes flashed angrily. 'He has got some nerve if he is shielding someone and he has put that someone before his own family.'

'You are right, of course you are, his own family would come first.'

'Is Mr Lawson the only colleague not to turn his back on Dad?'

'Michael is the only one to visit him where he is.'

'Dad and he were never close friends. He liked you though.'

'How would you know that?'

'When that scatterbrained wife of his began to act the fool and Dad left you to do his circulating as he called it, Mr Lawson always joined you.'

'That was because we were both without partners,' Felicity smiled.

'Could be I suppose, but from what I saw when I was dragged to these things, he enjoyed your company.'

'I hope so, I enjoyed his.'

'Mum, I'm tired.'

'I've gone beyond that.'

'We will leave the dishes until tomorrow.'

'Fine by me. There is no hurry for you in the morning, so lie as long as you want.'

'And you, you do that as well.'

'Yes.' Felicity thought she would be up early to wash the dishes before she got started on the breakfast. There was something awful about coming downstairs to dirty dishes. Like a bad start to the day but just this once she had a very good excuse.

Felicity wakened early and rather than risk falling asleep again she got up and dressed. In the kitchen she saw the dirty dishes beside the sink and decided they could wait until she made herself a cup of tea. She could wait her own breakfast until Joanna came down or she could take a tray up. No, perhaps not, she might be asleep. Better not to disturb her and leave her to come down when she was ready.

Felicity had just cleared up and set two places at the table when Joanna came in wearing her dressing-gown.

'Good morning, darling, I would have given you breakfast in bed—'

'No, I'm better up.'

Felicity looked at her anxiously. 'Did you manage to sleep?'

'Fitfully, I suppose. I heard the clock chiming two and then three.'

'I must have left the sitting-room door open. It has a lovely Westminster chime but I do find it a distraction booming out the hour especially when it is twelve and I find myself counting along.'

'Dad's not here, you don't have to wind it up.'

'Very true.' She smiled. 'For a bit of peace and quiet I'll remove it to the cupboard for the time being. There are plenty of clocks in the house and I'll find a replacement for the mantelpiece.'

Joanna sat down and watched her mother fill the toast rack and bring out another jar of marmalade. The cereal packets were on the table and Joanna stretched over to put some in her plate.

'In bed I was thinking—'

'That was why you couldn't sleep.'

'Did you believe I could stop thinking? Have you been able to do that?'

'No,' Felicity said quietly.

'Night is—'

'When worries get worse.'

'In my case when thoughts get clearer.'

Felicity nodded. 'You have managed to come to terms with this?'

'I will never be able to do that. All I can do is cope in my own way.'

Felicity wanted to ask what way that was but she didn't, perhaps she was afraid of what she might hear. She nodded.

'I got thinking about money. How are you managing without Dad's salary coming in? A proper answer if you please.'

'Very well, I shan't tell you not to worry about that.

I can tell you that we have no immediate problems regarding money.'

'I need to know more than that.'

'Your father got part of his inheritance, enough to pay off his debt and to pay the mortgage for the next twelve to eighteen months. I have no idea how much he got, indeed I know very little about our finances but your father assures me that I have nothing to worry about provided I am careful. Well, I am careful.'

'I'll say you are.' She was silently thoughtful. 'Gran must know.'

'She knows that your father has lost his job with Paton & Noble.'

'Poor Gran. She must be so disappointed.'

'Life is strange, Joanna, it can be very cruel but it can also be merciful. When you next go to Carnoustie you are going to see a big difference in your gran.'

'She's ill.'

'No, not ill. Her health is quite good but the forgetfulness has gone beyond that. She has become very confused.'

'Gran will never know about Dad being in prison?'

'No, that will be kept from her at all costs.' She smiled sadly. 'That last time I was over she was waiting for Tim to come home from school.'

'I don't think I can stand seeing her like that. Not my gran. She was so – so bright and intelligent,' she said unsteadily.

'Darling, don't upset yourself. Her mind is going but she is quite happy and content. We are very lucky to have Mrs Haggarty. She and your gran get on very well together and since the woman lives alone she was prepared to close up her house and stay with your grandmother. I can relax. The woman is trustworthy and she has our phone number should she need to get in touch.'

'This Mrs Haggarty, she has to know about Dad?'

'Yes, she knows.'

'Was she shocked?'

'If she was it didn't show. She did say that if Mrs Morrison ever found out it would not be through her.'

'That's good.'

'More tea?'

'No thanks, I've had enough.'

'You go up and dress.'

'Dad is in prison and I don't think I have taken that in. I'm trying to. They are allowed to wear their own clothes now, aren't they?'

'I think so, I don't know.'

'Can you imagine Dad sitting in a cell?'

'I try not to think of it and you must do the same. I haven't told you—'

'Something else you forgot or didn't want me to know?'

There was a flash of anger in Felicity's eyes. 'Not at all. I am having some success with my illustrations, that is all.'

'Sorry, that slipped out. That's great, how much success are we talking about?'

Felicity smiled. 'Quite a lot as it happens. I am doing the illustrations for a children's book and I have an agent, a very nice gentleman by the name of Adam Silver.'

'Wow! In amongst all the doom and gloom there is a ray of light.'

'Apart from the satisfaction this gives me I am earning money with the promise of more—'

'If you are successful, which you will be.' A shadow crossed her face. 'Stuart said he thought they were terrific and he wasn't just saying that.'

'Whatever success I do enjoy Stuart did play his part. It was his enthusiasm for my little drawings that made me think I should get a second opinion.'

'Which you did?'

'Which I did. The details will keep for another time but through your Aunt Rachel they reached the right person.'

'Dad never thought much of your drawings. Does he know?'

'Yes.'

'Pleased for you?'

'Yes.'

'Really pleased?' she persisted.

'Pleased and surprised and delighted that I shall be able to help out financially. Why don't you go up and dress? I'll clean up here and then we can talk or not as you wish.'

'Definitely more talk.'

After she dressed Joanna made her bed and looked

about. Her bags from the holiday lay unopened and she decided she should empty them and sort out what required attention. She would give her mother the scarf and some day, she didn't know when, Gran would get her two lace-edged handkerchiefs. The tie she would push into the bottom of a drawer out of sight. That done she went downstairs.

'Bed made, bags unpacked.'

'And those in your arms for washing?'

'Yes, please.'

'Leave them on the floor. I like to do the woollens separate.'

'Will Dad have to do the whole eighteen months?'

'Michael thinks twelve months.'

'A whole year is such a long time.'

'It will go by,' she said gently.

'You sound very resigned.'

'I suppose that is what I am. As for you, dear, you must try to live your life as you were doing.'

'That is quite impossible.'

'No, it isn't. You are not without courage. If you put your mind to it you will manage. Work hard and get your degree, that is very important.'

'Mum, I am not going back to university,' she said slowly and clearly.

'Oh, yes you are and I want no nonsense.'

'I don't want to go back.'

'It is not a case of what you want, it is what is best for you.'

'And you have decided for me that that is university.'

'Yes. It isn't often I put my foot down, but I am determined that you are not going to make a mess of your life. One in the family is enough surely.'

'That isn't fair.'

'What is fair? You will return for the new term and tomorrow we will go into Dundee and do some shopping. Don't dare suggest there isn't money. There is plenty for your needs.'

Joanna got up and walked about the room. 'Do you feel this is a prison?'

'No, it is my home just as it is yours. It is too early to decide what is to be done about the house.'

'What about the neighbours, what are they saying?'

'How should I know? I have no contact with anyone.'

Joanna looked at her mother curiously. 'You don't seem bothered or is it that you can hide what you are feeling?'

'What the neighbours think is not so very important. At the beginning it bothered me and you could say I prepared the ground. I made your grandmother the excuse and it wasn't a complete untruth because I do go to Carnoustie as often as I can. I opted out of the coffee mornings and I haven't shopped in the village since your father lost his job. A few invitations continued to come my way but these have stopped now.'

'Now they know the reason?'

'Yes. Remember, dear, it is just as embarrassing for them as it is for me. They will accept that I don't want to see anyone. People can be very understanding.'

'Not everyone, there will be those who will be loving this. Something to gossip about.'

'Let them,' Felicity said calmly.

'I don't want to go outside the door.'

'You needn't see anyone. We nip out of the back door and into the car. I do wave if I see anyone and I don't find that difficult.'

'Mum, you've changed and you know what?'

'No, but I'm sure you are going to tell me,' she smiled.

'All this with Dad is part of it but not all. Having this success with your illustrations has given you confidence in yourself.'

'And that was something I was lacking?'

'I think it was.'

Chapter Sixteen

Joanna had decided after all to accompany her mother to Carnoustie believing that putting the visit off for another day or two would make little difference and she did want to see her grandmother. Felicity heaved a sigh of relief that no persuasion had been necessary. She could have wished to see her daughter looking smarter but wisely remained silent. The girl wore her old, very short donkey-brown skirt and a loose-fitting green and brown striped sweater that looked as if it had gone to length in the wash. Felicity hadn't seen the sweater before. She thought it hideous and wondered if there was some sort of competition among the students to see who could look the sloppiest. In sharp contrast, Felicity looked smart yet casual in her tweed suit and hyacinth blue fine-knit jumper. Not the string of pearls though, that was associated with elderly matrons and twin-sets and therefore to be avoided.

Joanna had gone ahead to open the garage doors and Felicity was making sure that the back door was locked before crossing to the garage with the car keys in her hand. She smiled to see Joanna balancing on a large flat stone that at one time had been used to keep the garage door open. It was no longer necessary for that purpose but the stone belonged there and there it remained. Felicity reversed out well clear of the doors, then rolled down the window to hear what Joanna was saying.

'What was that? I didn't hear.'

'Do we leave the garage open?'

'No, better to close it. Not that there is anything worth stealing—'

'I don't know about that. My bike is there and some gardening tools.'

'With a flat tyre no one is going to get very far on your bicycle and as for the garden tools what is there is old and rusted. The shed, in case you haven't noticed, has a brand new lock, a strong one, and the lawnmower and everything of value is in it. Are you having difficulty?'

'It won't shut.'

'It will if you give it a sharp push. Shall I—'

'No, don't get out, that's it now. You know for an expensive garage it shouldn't have a badly fitting door,' Joanna said as she got into the passenger seat and pulled the door shut.

'I know. It was fine when we got it and your father blamed all that damp weather. He said it would come all right.'

'Only very obviously it hasn't.'

'That's right it hasn't,' Felicity said as she carefully

cleared the gate and turned into the road, 'and don't you dare suggest that I should do something about it because I neither have the time nor the inclination.'

'That's not like you.'

'A lot of things are not like me these days.'

'I can imagine,' Joanna said feelingly.

'Did you remember to bring your gran's gift?'

'Yes.'

'I love the chiffon scarf you brought me, I meant to bring it to show Gran.'

'You can do that another time.' She paused. 'Are we coming straight back from Carnoustie?'

'No, we'll take the chance to go into Dundee and get you some new clothes.'

'What for?'

'Joanna, what you have is shabby and you need something new to begin the term.'

Joanna was silent and Felicity stole a glance at the set face.

'Nothing need have changed and you must stop imagining things. Just be yourself and get involved in the usual activities.'

Joanna shrugged.

'Top priority is a warm coat so we'll get that first.'

'I don't want a coat, I don't need a coat.'

'Did I not hear you talking about a duffel coat?'

'Could be. I would quite like one of those.' She cheered up.

'We'll try Cairds first, that was where I saw them advertised.'

They drove in silence for a few minutes.

'Tell me about your agent. What did you call him again?'

'Adam Silver.'

'I like the name, it has a nice ring to it. I really am chuffed about my mother having an agent.'

'I'm rather chuffed myself.' Felicity smiled.

'You've met him?'

'Yes.'

'What does he look like?'

'I would put him in his middle forties and fairly average-looking, by average I mean pleasant-looking but ordinary.'

'As old as that?'

'Watch it, forties isn't that old, though I suppose it is to you.'

'Ancient,' she grinned.

'I liked him immensely. He has a warm friendly manner, and let me add that he is happily married with two young sons.' She laughed. 'Do I get the feeling that I am being interrogated?'

'No you are not, but I have to remember that you are not worldly-wise.'

'Meaning I need my daughter to keep an eye on me.'

'Maybe you do. You are an artist and artists do tend to go about with their head in the clouds.'

'Nonsense and not at all true.'

'Seriously, Mum, one day you could be famous.'

'I will settle for a moderate success. If I can just earn enough—'

'To give you independence,' Joanna finished for her. 'You are going to overtake that tractor?'

'I thought he might be disappearing down one of the farm roads.'

'He could be going straight on and he is a pest, look at him weaving all over the place. Give him a toot and pass.'

'That was what I was going to do. Oh, nice man he is waving me on.'

The road ahead was clear and Felicity increased her speed. 'What were we talking about?'

'Your wish to be independent.'

'I want it now but it wasn't always that way. What I had was enough and I wasn't looking for more.'

'Now it is different.'

'Yes, Joanna, it is very different.' She paused. 'I want to be able to stand on my own two feet.'

'I have that in mind too,' Joanna said quietly.

'That will come after you graduate.'

Joanna didn't answer and kept her eyes directly ahead.

'Oh, look, wretched roadworks, just my luck.' Felicity was frowning. 'I can never make out what they want me to do.'

'Follow the arrows, Mum, it is only a short diversion.'

'Why can't they make things clearer for people like me.'

'Mum, stop moaning it is perfectly clear.'

'To you, maybe, where do I go? Up there?'

'Of course, then turn left. Honestly, Mum.'

'Where does that get me?'

'Back on the usual road.'

'Thank goodness for that. Now I can relax and you can tell me what you were going to say.'

'Nothing. I wasn't going to say anything.'

'Yes, you were, so come on I want to hear it.'

'You've heard it before. I do not want to go back to university, repeat I do not want to go back.'

'Joanna, you must. Please, please do not throw away your chance to make a good life for yourself.'

'I do not require a university education to do that.'

Felicity thought she could do without this. 'Believe me, darling, I am not trying to make light of the difficulties. They are very real to you but you will come through this.'

'What if I am thoroughly miserable?'

'If you are determined to be miserable then you will be,' Felicity said, showing the first sign of impatience. 'You can come home at weekends if that would make it easier.'

'All that money for fares.'

'Money well spent if it would make you happier and as a matter of fact your father and I spoke about this.'

'He thought I might have a hard time.'

'Nothing of the kind, he wasn't thinking of you at the time, he was thinking of me. Of me being lonely and glad of your company.'

'You wouldn't be lonely, not now that you have your illustrations to think about.'

'It is true I can cope, but it would be lovely to have you at home at weekends.'

'When you are on your own do you eat properly?'

'I don't have regular meals, I eat when I am hungry and I don't think I will come to any harm.' She paused, worried about Joanna's very real reluctance to return to university. 'Don't do anything silly. A dead-end job would be such a waste and you would come to regret not staying on and working for your degree.'

Joanna gave an inaudible sigh. 'We are almost there.'

'Goodness, yes, so we are and I could so easily have missed the turn-off.'

'Not with me in the car.'

They turned into the cul-de-sac and in a few moments they had stopped in the drive close to the front of the house. Both of them opened the car doors at the same moment.

Mrs Haggarty was busy cleaning the brasses at the front door and smiled to them as she gave a final polish to the letterbox before putting the top on the Brasso tin and gathering together her cleaning cloths.

'Good morning, Mrs Haggarty, isn't this a lovely day?'

'It is, just one rainy day in five, that's not bad.' She looked at Joanna. 'Now there's a treat for the old lady, she'll be so pleased to see you. Oh, sorry, sorry, here I am blocking up the entrance and not letting you in.' She moved hastily to open the glass door. 'You'll find

Mrs Morrison in her usual chair in the morning room. She was dozing when I left her—'

'I was nothing of the kind,' came a querulous voice, 'I've only to close my eyes to be accused of sleeping.'

Joanna giggled. That sounded exactly like her gran and showed there wasn't much wrong with her hearing.

'Who is that, Rita, who are you talking to?'

'You are in for a lovely surprise.'

Felicity gave Joanna a gentle push. 'Go in first and I'll follow in a few minutes.'

Joanna stood in the doorway and felt a lump come into her throat. Maybe it was the shawl that did it but there was a difference in her gran. She looked so thin and frail as though a puff of wind would take her away. Joanna swallowed, forced a smile and went forward.

'Hello, Gran, it's the wanderer returned.'

'Bless my soul, it really is Joanna. Let me look at you child.' She was shaking her head. 'Doesn't your mother buy you any decent clothes?'

'She would if she got the chance and I don't see a thing wrong with what I've got on.' Joanna bent down to kiss the withered cheek and give her a hug.

'Careful, lass, I have to be treated like Dresden china in case I crack. Old age is a damned nuisance and one day you will know all about it. Maybe not, maybe by then they will have come up with a pill that restores all lost energy.'

'You are fine, aren't you?' Joanna asked fearfully.

'Of course I am. There are a few good years in

me yet unless I do something silly like falling down the stairs.'

'You can't do that now with your bed downstairs,' Felicity said, coming into the room and dropping a kiss on her mother-in-law's brow.

'I slept better when I was upstairs.'

'You'll get used to it.'

'I daresay.' She turned her attention back to her granddaughter. 'When did you get home from those foreign parts?'

'Yesterday.'

'It was really good of you coming so soon. You take after your mother, she is always so thoughtful. There are times when I think your father needs reminded of that. I'm not slow in telling him how lucky he is and next time he pops in I'll tell him again. Not that I see much of him, pressure of work and all the usual excuses but I don't complain, what would be the use. If I did it might put him off coming at all.' Her mouth began to work.

'You know that isn't true,' Felicity said gently. 'Tim is always very concerned for you.'

'He's a good son, I know that.' She sounded weary.

'Are we tiring you?'

'How could you do that, Felicity? I like it best when I have my own around me. Joanna, I didn't ask if you had a good holiday.'

'Super. It was super, Gran.'

'Such a silly word, why can't you just say that you enjoyed yourself?'

'Doesn't sound as good somehow.'

'You had me worried you know. Stars in your eyes you had when you were talking about that young man.'

Joanna made a face. 'Why were you worried?'

'I wondered if you would do something stupid like getting yourself engaged. Nineteen is far too young to settle down.'

'I'm halfway to twenty.'

'Still too young, don't you agree, Felicity?'

'Yes, I do.'

'Mum, you married young.'

'Your mother went into marriage too early. Tim was older but, even so, a longer engagement would have been better.'

'Gran, you have no need to worry about me. I never had any intention of getting myself engaged to anyone.'

'I'm not talking about anyone, I am talking about that boy you went off with.'

'Oh, him, he's history.'

'Ah, a tiff.'

'A lot more than that.'

'I'm old-fashioned I suppose, but I wasn't in favour of you and the boy going off on holiday together though now I can see it was maybe a good thing. You found out that he wasn't the right one for you.'

Joanna was beginning to look strained.

'Mrs Haggarty is preparing coffee,' Felicity said hastily.

'Yes, Felicity, Rita is very good. What is that, child?'

'A present from Provence for you.' She put the package on her gran's lap.

'Provence did you say? Now isn't that strange, I've been getting postcards from there.'

'Those were mine, I sent them.'

'How could you when you are here?' she said testily.

Joanna was looking uneasy.

'Open the gift, Joanna, your gran won't manage to undo the cord.'

'Maybe not, I'm all thumbs but I daresay there is a pair of scissors in the house. Unless that is, you want to save the cord. During the war we saved everything, had to, there were so many things we couldn't buy.'

Joanna had the knot undone and the paper removed.

'Hankies,' her gran said and sighed.

'I thought you would like them.'

'Who said I didn't. Of course I do. Much too good to use. I'll put them or rather the box in my dressing-table drawer and every time I go into it I'll see your gift. Thank you, my dear.'

'My pleasure.'

The eyebrows shot up. 'My, aren't we getting polite.'

Joanna, keyed up as she was, exploded into laughter and that started Felicity off. The old lady looked at them both then joined in. She stopped and wiped her eyes. 'That's what I like to hear, good hearty laughter, the best medicine of all.'

'Just what I was about to say myself,' Mrs Haggarty said as she came in with a tray. Joanna went over to help.

'I'll leave your mother to do the honours. If anyone needs me I'm upstairs doing out the rooms.'

'Rita, before you go—'

'Yes, Mrs Morrison,' she said, her hand on the door handle.

'What time did that laddie of mine say he would be home?'

'I don't think he did say,' she said with a straight face.

'Tut-tut, difficult to prepare a meal when you don't know what time they will be in. Still I shouldn't complain, Tim is a good lad. You are forever hearing about parents having problems with their family but I can honestly say that Tim has never given Edward or me a moment's worry.'

Felicity and Joanna shared a look. They had coffee and a piece of cake and halfway through her coffee the old lady nodded off.

'We should get away shortly, Joanna. You take the tray through to the kitchen and I'll pop upstairs to see Mrs Haggarty.'

The woman was dusting the top of the wardrobe with a feather duster.

'There you are, Mrs Morrison, was the coffee to your liking?'

'Very much so. How is everything?'

'Much the same. Tragic though it is to see someone

becoming so confused, it has to be a blessing too. She adores that son of hers.' She stopped. 'I'm sorry, I spoke out of turn. He is your husband.'

'I'm not offended and Tim sees it as a blessing too. His mother's good opinion means a great deal to him. We are just going. Joanna is practically in rags as you would see for yourself and I am dragging her to the shops in Dundee to get something decent for her back.'

'Students, you have to laugh at them or you would cry but I suppose it is all part of growing up. If there is anything at all to report I'll call you but remember no news is good news.'

'And don't you be working too hard. My mother wasn't particularly houseproud and she used to say the house would still be standing after we were long gone and what was the use of slaving.'

'She wouldn't be able to say that about some of the jerry-built houses they are throwing up these days.'

They left the house and approached the car.

'Mum, I was shocked, I see a big difference in Gran. Don't you?'

'I see a gradual change but you haven't seen her for a while which makes it all the more noticeable.' They got into the car and Felicity moved off.

'Does Gran know she gets confused?'

'I don't think so. She does admit to forgetfulness but no more than that and now, Joanna, we are going to forget Gran and everything else. This is going to be a shopping trip with lunch in between.'

'A duffel coat will do, I'll be happy with that.'

'It will do for a start and since you have set your heart on one we will make that our first buy. After that and no arguments if you please, we will look at skirts and blouses and shoes, we mustn't forget shoes. Come to think about it, I could do with a pair of good walking shoes.'

'You don't walk.'

'I don't do much of it it is true. A case of in the car and out, all very convenient but bad for me.'

'When you are at Gran's take a walk down to the beach.'

Felicity smiled. 'I might just do that, a good bracing walk.'

For all her lack of interest in clothes, Joanna appeared to be enjoying herself and was hugely delighted with her duffel coat which they got in Cairds in Reform Street. To please her mother she chose a skirt, a pinafore dress and two blouses. The final purchase was a pair of slip-on shoes for Joanna and medium-heeled lace-up shoes in pale brown leather for her mother.

'You didn't buy anything to wear for yourself,' Joanna said as they left the shoe shop.

'I don't need to. You see, Joanna, I buy good clothes that keep their shape and I don't choose anything too extreme which means they don't go out of date.'

'It also means you are never in fashion.' Joanna grinned.

'I shall let that pass,' her mother said.

'Seriously, Mum, I've hardly thought about Dad all day. Would you say that was a good sign or not?'

'I wouldn't call it a good sign or a bad one. Life has to go on and you are beginning to see that.'

'Maybe you reach a stage when you stop wondering why it happened and just accept that it has.'

'If you can do that I'm glad.'

'You can't do that yet?'

'I am accepting what has happened but not why it happened.'

'One day Dad might unburden himself.'

'Perhaps, but I am beginning to doubt that.'

'This is terrible for you yet you don't complain.'

'What would be the use?'

'Bottling it all up can't be good for you but you're coming through it.'

'Just as you are.'

'Mum, I know you don't like me talking about money but I have to ask you this. Where did the money come from for today's shopping?'

'If you must know it came out of my advance.'

'You get an advance? Jolly good.'

'I enjoyed spending that money, my money, in a way I found it—' She was searching for the word which Joanna supplied.

'Therapeutic. Sort of therapeutic was it?'

'Yes, that is it exactly.'

*　　*　　*

Joanna had gone back into her shell and for the last two days she was very quiet and withdrawn. Felicity noticed and worried but didn't remark or ask the reason. Perhaps she was thinking of Stuart, his name was never mentioned. Classes started on Monday but it was usual to be in residence a day or two before then. Joanna said she would leave on Friday morning.

'Which train do you want to catch? The nine thirty-two?'

'Yes. You don't have to bother, I'll get the bus.'

'Of course you won't. After I see you off at the station I'll go along to the art shop and get more supplies.'

The nine thirty-two was never very busy and it was no problem finding a corner seat. Joanna put her bags on the luggage rack and a magazine on the seat to show that it was taken. Her mother was watching her from the platform. Joanna smiled and went to the carriage door and let the window slide down.

'That is you all set?'

'Yes.'

'If there is anything you have forgotten I can send it on.'

Joanna nodded.

'Come home next weekend unless you are doing something special.'

'That isn't very likely but I'll see.'

Doors were being slammed up and down the train and Felicity stood back. There was a whistle and a green flag and then the train moved off, its final destination Edinburgh Waverley.

Chapter Seventeen

'Miss Reid—'

'Yes, Marion, what is it?' The woman sounded unusually sharp.

'There is a young lady at the desk who insists on seeing you.'

'It will be to do with the vacancy. Tell her she comes at the appointed hour or not at all. I'm much too busy to be bothered with this sort of thing.'

'It has nothing to do with the vacancy, Miss Reid. I thought it might be that and I asked.' Marion didn't want to be shown up as inefficient when she had done her best. 'I didn't catch the name and she had moved away before I could ask her to repeat it.'

'I'll come,' Rachel said resignedly. She gathered together the papers she had been working on and anchored them with a paperweight. There were times, she was thinking, when even the best receptionist fell short of requirements. Rachel left her office and walked quickly to the front desk and immediately noticed that the flowers in the tall vase were past their first freshness and should have been replaced. It added to her annoyance. 'Where is this person?' she demanded. There was no one waiting at the desk.

'Over there looking at the display case.'

The girl must have heard the voices and turned round. The woman gave a gasp when she saw who it was. Joanna hurried across.

'Aunt Rachel—' she began then stopped and bit her lip.

'My dear Joanna, this is a surprise I must say,' she said, giving her goddaughter a hug. 'Why didn't you phone to let me know you were coming?'

'I shouldn't have come. Mum is going to be furious.'

'She doesn't know?'

Joanna shook her head.

Rachel saw the strain on the young face and if she wasn't mistaken tears were very close. She didn't want the girl breaking down and the intense curiosity that would bring. Marion was looking busy but missing nothing.

'Here is the key,' she said taking it from her jacket pocket. 'You go along and make yourself at home. You remember the way?'

'Yes.'

'Of course you do. I'll be with you just as soon as I can.'

'Please don't hurry on my behalf.' Joanna felt she should say that since this, very obviously, was not a good time.

'I do have one or two things that require my attention then I am all yours,' she smiled.

'Thanks.' Joanna lifted her bag and put it over her shoulder. She felt conspicuous in the entrance hall and was glad to hurry along the corridor that led to the annexe and her godmother's apartment.

'Marion, have coffee and sandwiches sent to my apartment, will you?'

'Yes, right away.'

'Good girl.' Rachel was always fair. 'My apologies if I snapped your head off. Joanna is my goddaughter and goodness knows why she didn't phone me to expect her. You young people just don't think do you?'

Marion raised her beautifully shaped eyebrows then picked up the phone.

Rachel did what had to be done then turned her thoughts to her young visitor. This was no ordinary visit, the girl was deeply troubled and Rachel had a horrible suspicion that it had something to do with Tim Morrison. Had she learned the awful truth before Felicity had had a chance to tell her? She prayed it wasn't that.

Joanna had never been to Perth on her own, she had always been with her mother. She was feeling foolish now. It hadn't exactly been a spur of the moment decision, the idea had come to her earlier. Her mother was determined that she would take up university life and she was equally determined that she would not. Aunt Rachel would help her, that was what godmothers were for. Hotels were always looking for staff and she was prepared to turn her hand to anything. Joanna managed to smile when she thought of her mother seeing her off at the station. Very often she left before the train was due but this time she was there on the platform to see that her daughter was on that train.

She had money and her mother had given her extra. In fact she was in funds because her grandmother had pressed a five-pound note into her hand and touched her lips as though to say it was to be a secret. Without money she might have had to hitch a lift and her parents had always warned her against doing that.

Leuchars Station, she would get off there and she would ask someone about buses. There wouldn't be a direct service, that was too much to hope for, but she would find transport to get her to the Cairn Hotel. Here she was at the hotel – and now what?

Joanna took off her coat and put it over the back of a chair. The bulging shoulder bag was on the floor and she moved it to lean against the leg of the chair. She didn't sit down but wandered round the room examining it in some detail to keep her mind occupied. Joanna had been in it many times before but without paying much attention to the furnishings. She found that she liked the spaciousness, the comfortable chairs and matching sofa and the china cabinet that held only a few exquisite pieces. Any more would have detracted from the effect. Her mother had good taste too but in a more homely way. Aunt Rachel wasn't married, that made the difference. Joanna sat down and put her chin in her hands, then got to her feet quickly when she heard the door opening and shutting. Rachel came in.

'Here I am. Do sit down, Joanna.'

Joanna sat down in one of the easy chairs and Rachel took the other. 'Coffee and sandwiches will be arriving shortly. Are you all right?'

Joanna nodded but kept her eyes on the carpet and after a moment Rachel got up and put an arm round her shoulder.

'Poor you, life can be the very devil, can't it?' She looked at the bowed head and frowned. If, as she was all but sure had happened and Joanna had somehow found out about her father then the harm done could be immeasurable. Her heart went out to her goddaughter and to Felicity and she was even sparing some sympathy for Tim. There was a knock at the door and Rachel went to answer it. She came back with a tray which she put on the coffee table and straightaway began to pour the coffee. 'Darling, bring over one of the small tables for yourself and, yes, one for me too.'

Joanna did as she was asked and accepted the cup of coffee.

'Help yourself to sugar and cream. Maybe like your mother you prefer milk?'

'No, this is lovely.'

'Those sandwiches are for you. I can't afford to eat between meals but I will enjoy a coffee.'

'I have an awful nerve landing on you,' she whispered.

'If you are in some kind of trouble then this is exactly

where you should come. As your godmother I have a responsibility and I take that responsibility seriously.'

Joanna took a bite of her sandwich and when she had swallowed the mouthful raised her eyes to look at Rachel.

'Mum is going to have a fit. I'm supposed to be on my way to university.'

'I had come to that conclusion,' she said looking pointedly at the bag on the floor. 'What made you change your mind?'

'It wasn't a question of changing my mind, I had already made up my mind but Mum refused to listen. She said I had to go back and that was that.'

'Had to?'

'Yes. She was adamant. Mum thinks getting a degree is a passport to – to—'

'A good position, which it usually is, Joanna.'

'You didn't get a degree.'

'True.'

'And look at you, you've made a big success of your life.'

'Thank you, dear.'

'I mean it, you have.'

'Yes, I like to think I have. That aside your own prospects would be greatly improved should you gain a degree. With many employers these days it counts for a great deal and for some positions a degree is essential. You know all that.'

'I should. I have had it rammed down my throat often enough.'

'Now! Now!' Rachel laughed.

'I have to have a reason for not wanting to go back and you haven't asked what it is.'

'No, I am waiting for you to tell me.'

Joanna took a sip of her coffee. 'Mum said you knew,' she said very quietly.

'We are talking about your father,' Rachel said carefully.

'Yes.'

'I knew, yes.'

'You knew before me?'

'Yes I did and you are upset about that?'

'No, I'm not. If you think I am upset about that then you are wrong. You are Mum's best friend and if she had to tell someone it would be you.'

'You are angry and hurt because you weren't told.'

'Do you find that surprising?' Joanna said with a hint of sarcasm.

'No.'

'If you had been in my place wouldn't you have been upset?'

'Very probably.' She paused to take time to drink some of her coffee and perhaps to gather her thoughts. 'It wasn't as straightforward as that. Your mother went through agonies. She had great misgivings about letting you go off to France and not knowing about the trouble your father was in. Your father, on the other hand, thought you should be allowed to enjoy your holiday.'

'I know that, Mum told me.'

'I shared those worries with your mother and I came to the conclusion that Tim was right. Why spoil it all for you? Why not let you have a carefree holiday?'

'Maybe I wouldn't have gone.'

'Exactly. That occurred to us. We reasoned that it was time enough to break the news to you once you were back home.'

'It didn't work out that way.'

'So I gather and I am so sorry, so very sorry for the part I played.'

'I think I am only now beginning to appreciate what you were all trying to do.' She swallowed. 'You were doing it for the right reasons but I can't help feeling insulted. I am not a child and that is the way I was being treated.'

Rachel nodded. 'You are making me feel very guilty.'

'No, don't blame yourself, you did it for the best but it all went horribly wrong. Talking about it makes me go hot and cold.' Her voice trembled. 'Stuart's father is a solicitor and at one time I mentioned that my dad was a solicitor with Paton & Noble.'

'Ah.'

'He made it his business to find out all he could,' Joanna said shakily.

Rachel reached out to take Joanna's cold hand in hers. 'Do you want to go on, you don't need to. I think I know what is coming.'

'Some of it you might but not all. I want you to know so that you can understand how I feel. We – Stuart and I, called in to see his parents before he would drive me to the station. I have never liked Mr and Mrs Milton, they are so cold but for Stuart's sake I was trying to like them. The minute we arrived Stuart was told to see his father in his study.'

'That would be to tell Stuart about your father?'

'Yes. You have to remember, Aunt Rachel, that I knew nothing, I didn't know that my father had been dismissed from Paton & Noble whereas they knew everything.'

'Did the woman, Stuart's mother, say anything to you?'

'About that? No. She said as little as possible and I was trying to be polite and tell her about our holiday but she wasn't interested and I gave up. Stuart looked funny when he came downstairs and I thought there must have been a tragedy in the family. He had a newspaper in his hand.'

Rachel closed her eyes. She couldn't bear to see the pain in Joanna's.

'Stuart was angry with me.'

'Why should he be angry with you?'

'Because he thought I was bound to know what was going on and that I should have told him and saved that scene in his father's study. He knew I couldn't have known about the trial but that I couldn't fail to know that Dad had lost his job and was to be tried for embezzlement.'

'Don't tell me he let you see the newspaper—'

'He did. That was the first I knew.'

'How unspeakably cruel.'

'Then he saw my face and he knew — he tried to apologise but I wasn't having any. He couldn't get parked at the station and I was so glad. I took time to tell him that I never wanted to see him again then I ran for my train.'

'My poor, poor love, this has been a nightmare for you.'

'The worst possible. I hate Dad for what he has done to Mum and me.'

'That is very understandable. May I make one observation?'

'Yes.'

'You are being a little hard on Stuart I think.'

'I am not.'

'Do I get the impression that he is not very comfortable with his parents?'

'No one could be comfortable with those two.'

'My! My! You do have it in for that couple. Bear with me if you will. It can't have been very pleasant for the boy. He must have been thinking that forewarned is forearmed and you had failed him by keeping this from him.'

'He ought to have known I wouldn't do that.'

'We all make mistakes. I have a feeling he has disappointed himself.'

'Good.'

They were silent, each with their own thoughts.

'Aunt Rachel, you and Dad didn't always see eye to eye.'

'That is true.'

'You don't like him.'

'I don't dislike him. Liking has nothing to do with it. I happen to think that your father is too self-opinionated and he probably thinks the same about me.'

Rachel was glad to see a grin cross her face.

'Two bossy people and I am only joking.'

'You could be right. I am very sorry for your father and I can't imagine what this is doing to him.' She paused. 'In my opinion Tim should not have been given a custodial sentence and that opinion is shared by a lot of people. The money has been repaid in full, he has lost his job. He will never rise to the heights that were expected of him. That surely was sufficient of a punishment.

'Do you think someone had it in for Dad?'

'No, I don't think that for a single moment. Joanna, my dear, when a high-flyer like your father takes a tumble, there is a great sense of shock and anger. Why when someone has so much would he do such a thing? That is what they ask and they want to see that person shamed and punished.'

'Paton & Noble must have wanted that.'

'They felt their reputation had been damaged.'

'Had it?'

'No doubt they lost a few clients.'

'Serves them right for exacting such a price.'

'More coffee?'

'No, thank you. Gran came to the rescue but you would know that?'

'Yes.'

'She knew that Dad had lost his job and was in financial difficulties. She didn't want to know the details.'

'I believe your grandmother is a very intelligent person and it could be that she guessed but didn't want it confirmed. Her way of coping.'

Joanna looked at her admiringly. 'You could be absolutely right.'

'Dad doesn't want visitors or at least he doesn't want to see Mum and me.'

'Not altogether surprising. In his position I wouldn't want to see anyone close to me.'

'Most — most prisoners want to see their family.'

'The less imaginative. Tim would see it differently. He would believe that one would always remember visiting someone in prison, the experience would be stamped on one's memory and he wants you both spared that.'

'He wants Mum to write to him.'

'There you are then.'

'Mum will write but I won't.'

'I see.'

'No, you don't. I could write but I am not a hypocrite. This is all his fault, all this misery and the shame and he hasn't got the decency to tell Mum what he did with the money. If, and only if, he decides to come clean would I consider writing to him.'

'I see.'

'There you go again but you don't. I am not being unreasonable.'

'I never suggested you were.'

'Mum is being wonderful.'

'I know that.'

'She feels it though. I mean she never goes into the village so she doesn't come face-to-face with people. She just gets in the car and shops where she is not known. Dad should have done something about moving house but he didn't and Mum says she couldn't face it, all the upheaval and where would she go? In any case the house, like everything else, is in Dad's name.'

'Joanna, that will sort itself out and we can't do anything about it. I think we should concentrate on you. University is out?'

'Most definitely.'

'May I ask what your plans are? I presume you have made some.'

Joanna looked uncomfortable and studied her shoes. 'I've got a nerve I know but I sort of thought that I could stay with you for a while and make myself useful.'

'Useful in what way?' She was being hard on the girl but if she wanted to think of herself as grown-up then she would have to act accordingly.

'I'll do anything. I know how to clean out a room and make a bed.'

'To hotel standards?' She smiled. 'From what your mother tells me you are far from being domesticated.'

'That doesn't mean I am incapable of doing the work, it means it has never been necessary. You do have to train maids, don't you?'

'My maids get a thorough training. In a hotel guests

expect a high standard and I make sure they get it. I engage staff and I also fire them.'

'You give them a second chance I hope?'

'That depends.' She paused. 'Do not imagine for a single moment, Joanna, that you would be getting preferential treatment.'

Joanna held her head high. 'I wouldn't want that.' It didn't come out very convincingly.

'Fine.'

'I can stay?'

'Before I make any promises I am going to telephone your mother. If she were to learn that you had not arrived in Edinburgh I wouldn't like to imagine the state she would be in.'

'You do all the talking,' Joanna said anxiously.

'Young lady—'

'Please, Aunt Rachel, I'll talk to Mum tomorrow but I couldn't just now so don't try to make me.'

'Very well. I don't want you listening so make yourself scarce. Remove that clutter off the floor and take it through to the spare bedroom.'

'A maid's bedroom would do me.'

'Would you kindly do what you are told or I am going to be very cross. Once I am off the telephone I'll see about sheets and pillowcases and you can make your own bed. Use the wardrobe and there is plenty of drawer space.'

Joanna flung her arms round Rachel's neck. 'I'm so glad Mum asked you to be my godmother.' She picked up her belongings and went through to the bedroom. She had taken a big risk but it was going to be all right.

Rachel got up to shut the door, then sat down and reached for the phone. It was answered almost immediately.

'Good, I got you. I wondered if I would find you at home.'

'This isn't my day for Carnoustie. Joanna has gone back to Edinburgh. Sorry Rachel, we had hoped to get through to Perth but there just wasn't the time.'

'Felicity, are you sitting down?'

'As a matter of fact I am. Why, are you going to spring some awful surprise on me?'

'The awful surprise is here. I shouldn't have said awful surprise but this is going to come as a big shock.'

'Terence and you are naming the day.'

'Good God, no. Nothing like that. Felicity, I have Joanna here with me or rather at this very moment she is in the spare bedroom putting away her clothes.'

Rachel could almost feel the stunned silence and then there was a splutter.

'Just a minute, I'm not with you. You have to be joking, I went right into the station and waited until the train left.'

'Presumably she got out somewhere and made her way to Perth.'

'This isn't happening to me. Oh, my God—'

'Will you stay calm, please.'

'How can I? How could she do this to me on top of everything else?'

'She told you she didn't want to go back to university.'

'She must, she can't throw away everything she has worked for. Rachel, make her see sense.'

'I cannot. Felicity, the girl is nineteen. Think back to when we were that age and remember how problems got blown up out of all proportion. How do you think we would have coped with this? The poor girl is sick with worry. Her safe, comfortable life is no more and add to that the heartbreak of losing someone she loved and I am talking of Stuart. She has a lot of guilt feelings too because she cannot forgive her father. She still loves him but is deeply ashamed of him. The thought of people getting to know and talking behind her back is more than she can stand.'

'I know that, I am going through it but in Edinburgh she would be far enough away.'

'You cannot know that, particularly after what has happened.'

'That was just very bad luck.'

'There is a lot of that going around,' Rachel said drily.

'You don't have to tell me that. I don't know what to do for the best.'

'I can talk freely?'

'When have you ever not talked freely? Go on with what you want to say.'

'The truth as I see it, Felicity, is that Joanna is going to take a long time to get over this. Tim going to prison isn't the worst of it—'

'It is finding out the truth the way she did.'

'Yes.'

'I've made a mess of it. As usual,' she said bitterly, 'I let Tim talk me into it.'

'Stop blaming yourself. You thought it through and came to the same conclusion as Tim and so did I. You have nothing to reproach yourself for. You did what you thought best for your daughter and Joanna knows that.'

'I do want the best for her and to me it seems such a waste to have worked so hard for a place and then to give it up after a year. Tim is going to be angry and distressed when I write and tell him.'

Rachel frowned. 'Felicity, with due respect, you shouldn't worry too much about distressing your husband. He, alone, is responsible for what is happening and not Joanna.'

'Yes, I do know that, but what am I supposed to do for heaven's sake?'

'Keep calm and let me do the thinking for a minute. It could be that all is not lost and if I could make a suggestion—'

'Of course you can,' Felicity said impatiently.

'You could write to the university and explain that there is a family crisis and Joanna is badly affected by it. You don't need to tell them the truth, in fact I would advise against that. Letters are supposed to be confidential but remember they have to be typed and filed and no system is one hundred percent satisfactory. Whatever you decide to say make sure it is convincing and you may get a sympathy vote. They may agree to Joanna taking a year off her studies.'

'You really think that is possible?'

'It is no more than a suggestion, but well worth a try.'

'Too true it is. What would I do without you, Rachel?' The relief in Felicity's voice was very clear.

'Joanna might still refuse to return but she will have had a year to consider her own future.'

'This is quite wonderful, she could come home now and I promise not to mention the word university.'

'She could return home but I do not think that would be a good idea. Joanna needs a break from everything.'

'Me included?'

'You included, Felicity. Being at home would be a constant reminder and remember you don't need a disgruntled young woman moping about. You need to concentrate on your own work.' She paused. 'Not to do so would let others down.'

'I know and I certainly wouldn't want to do that.'

'Joanna will talk to you tomorrow. She is a bit scared.'

'No need to be, tell her I'm not angry and that's the truth. I should have been more understanding.'

'There you go blaming yourself.'

'I am partly to blame and you shouldn't be inconvenienced.'

'Who said I was? Joanna knows I lead a busy life and she is anxious to help – not just help, she wants to be fully employed.'

'Doing what?'

'We are short-staffed and I have been advertising for a maid.'

'A maid to do what?'

'The bedrooms.'

'You are not serious?'

'I am.'

'Rachel, that would be madness personified. I wish you saw the state of her bedroom here.' Her laugh was almost hysterical.

'I can imagine. Don't you worry. I have an excellent woman in charge of the domestics and by the time she is finished your daughter will know how to make a bed and have the bedroom ready for inspection or my name isn't Rachel Reid.'

Felicity giggled helplessly. 'I will want to see that day.'

'How long since I heard that giggle and how pleased I am to hear it. And now let me ask about Tim, how is he?'

'There isn't much in the way of news in his letters. I get more from Michael Lawson, you do know who I mean?'

'A former colleague of Tim's and someone you like.'

'He is being quite wonderful and in the middle of his own troubles.'

'What kind of trouble?'

'Michael is divorcing his wife.'

'Broken-hearted?'

'Relieved more like, but all divorces are supposed to be stressful.'

'Theirs wasn't a union made in heaven so having his freedom will be very welcome.' Rachel was laughing. 'I'm rather pleased with my single status.'

'Tim is quite happy to have Michael visit him occasionally and it is easy for him. He knows the system because he did some court work at one time.'

'Good. He is able to keep you informed.'

'Tim will be a model prisoner, that is what they say of those who cause no trouble.' There was a break in her voice.

'He'll make the best of it and time will pass.'

'Slowly. It can only pass slowly for Tim and I feel guilty that for me time passes too quickly.'

'The work is doing well?'

'Yes. Adam phoned to tell me that things are looking good and other work is already in the pipeline.'

'I couldn't be more pleased and before I go I had better tell you this. Joanna will be introduced as my goddaughter who is interested in learning the hotel business. That will save any misunderstanding or jealousy.'

'A thousand thank-yous for everything.'

'I have a feeling that I am going to come out of this rather well. Bye for now and Joanna will talk to you tomorrow.'

Felicity put down the phone and found that she was shaking. Joanna must have been in a state to do what she did. Mothers were supposed to understand and she hadn't. Not getting support at home Joanna had gone to her godmother and that had been a wise move. It was just possible the university would agree to Joanna having a year off her studies. She would get that letter written and post it off tomorrow.

The university had been swift to reply. They sympathised with the difficulties the family was experiencing and it might be possible for Joanna to take a year off her studies though it was something they were not keen to grant unless in exceptional circumstances. A decision would be made at a later date when she would be informed.

Felicity was overjoyed. It wasn't a firm yes but neither had it been dismissed out of hand. There was a reasonable chance and all she could do was wait and hope.

Chapter Eighteen

Joanna had been at the Cairn Hotel for three weeks and was beginning to despair of ever reaching the standard set by that awful Mrs Parker. The woman was impossible, she was a tyrant, the girls were all agreed about that. She was very, very thin and some wag had made the remark that to see her sideways was to hardly see her at all. She seldom smiled and her mouth was small and her lips appeared to be permanently pursed. Usually her pepper and salt hair was in neat stiff waves but at present it was frizzy which had done nothing to improve her temper. The frizzy hair was the result of a home perm which had gone badly wrong. The daughter of the neighbour who was still learning her trade had blamed it on hair out of condition. Not content with that, she had made matters worse by saying breezily that it would grow out and when it did Mrs Parker would get another perm but at half price. It was understood that the reply had severed relations. The neighbours were not on speaking terms.

The maids who tidied the bedrooms and did the general cleaning had giggled helplessly at Joanna's early attempts at bedmaking. It wasn't unkind and they were supportive. She was the boss's goddaughter who was learning the hotel business the hard way and therefore no threat to their own jobs. In a few weeks she would be moved to the dining-room and after that it would be reception. Joanna would shine there with her good appearance and natural charm.

A few of the guests were slow to vacate their rooms and the maids had to hang about waiting to get started.

'This is a bit of a waste of time,' Joanna said.

'Can't say anything or they might take the huff and not come back.'

'I suppose so.'

Melanie fingered the cigarette packet in her overall pocket. She could do with a puff but it would have to wait. 'You are doing all right, Joanna, if you don't mind me saying so.'

Joanna smiled. 'I must be. Parky actually gave me a word of praise.'

'The woman is going soft.' Joanna was popular with the staff and in particular with the maids. She didn't give herself airs and graces, she was one of them.

Joanna had surprised herself by finding that she was enjoying the work. The Cairn Hotel was a different world with a steady coming and going of guests. The initial shock to the system had come when she discovered her duties would begin at seven in the morning and if she wanted breakfast the kitchen was there and she could make it for herself. One thing was for sure, her godmother wasn't going to spoil her.

After careful thought Rachel had decided to throw Joanna in at the deep end. That way she would have no time to dwell on her troubles. For a girl who had been waited on hand and foot all her life it was a sharp awakening. Harsh perhaps but Joanna wasn't complaining. Rachel was very pleased.

It hadn't been easy but Joanna had gritted her teeth and got on with it. University life was a piece of cake compared with this and in future she would have a greater respect for maids. They did a power of work for a very small reward. Some guests were generous with tips but it usually went to the dining-room staff or the porters. The girls who made the beds and tidied the rooms were seldom remembered.

Rachel paid her goddaughter the going rate for the job. She didn't have to pay towards her upkeep although she had offered to do so.

'Don't be silly, Joanna,' Rachel had said crossly. 'You are a working girl during the day and my goddaughter in the evenings. I think it is all working out well, don't you?'

'For me it certainly is.' In the evenings she dined with Rachel. There was no social life but she wasn't looking for any. Because she had been so inexpert at the beginning everything had taken her twice as long and by the end of the working day she was exhausted. If Rachel noticed her goddaughter drooping she made no comment and Joanna was glad. She felt this was some kind of test and she wanted to come through with flying colours.

Once a week Felicity and Joanna talked on the phone. It was usually in the evening and if Rachel was around Joanna would hand the phone over so that they could have a chat. Not wanting to listen to their conversation Joanna would busy herself in the kitchen.

A letter had come from the university granting permission for Joanna to miss a year of her studies. Felicity had been overjoyed and had hoped Joanna would be the same or at least show some interest. She hadn't. Her mother didn't give in easily, that was for sure, but she had to be made to understand that nothing would make her change her mind.

'Mum, please don't take offence but this is my life and I want to live it my way. Going to all that bother was a waste of time and you should have asked me first.'

'You would have said no.'

'Exactly. You knew that yet you went ahead.'

'You might not know it yourself but you could change your mind.'

'Mum, I am not going to change my mind now or ever.'

'Very well I suppose I shall just have to accept that.'

Felicity was dismayed by Tim's reply to her letter. He had taken Joanna's side. She was old enough to make her own decisions – that hadn't been what he'd said before. Some folk had short memories. She read on. Placed as he was there was nothing he could do about it and if in later years she found that she had made a mistake then she had only herself to blame. In any case, he had ended by saying, it wasn't so important for a girl. Joanna would likely marry and then it would be somebody else's responsibility to keep her.

Felicity had fumed.

Felicity was upstairs in the study with several sheets of drawing paper requiring to be clipped together. She should have bought large paper-clips, added them to her list since her memory wasn't to be relied upon. All the time she had been working at the desk she had never opened a drawer. There had been no need until now. Tim must have had some loose ones if there wasn't a box. It was worth a look. There were drawers down each side of the desk and Felicity started with the top right. No luck there and the same went for the second and third drawers. How methodical he was, she thought. Everything neat and tidy and labelled. She pushed in the drawer and started on the bottom one which looked promising. There were several scribbling pads, elastic bands spilling out of a box, assorted pencils some with sharp points and some with none at all. She smiled. One or two had been chewed at the end. Not Tim surely? At the back were two bundles of letters, the top one had Tim's name and office address typed on it. She pushed them aside and smiled broadly when she saw a nearly full box of large-size paper-clips. Just the job. Some loose papers, badly crushed, had been pushed in by someone who must have been in a hurry. She could take a few moments to smooth them out. As she began something fell out from between the papers and landed on the floor. Felicity picked it up and saw that it was a snapshot of an attractive girl holding a baby in her arms and smiling into the camera. She put it aside and got on with what she was doing. Satisfied, she shut the drawer and got on with her own work.

She worked steadily, then much later raised her head and stretched her arms. She should move around more, sitting in the one position made one stiff. Food is what she should think about next. Getting up from the chair she caught sight of the snapshot and before going downstairs she went along to the bedroom. Once there she sat on the edge of the bed, switched on the bedside light and held the snapshot beside it. The face wasn't familiar and looking at the back she saw there was nothing written there. How on earth had it found its way into Tim's desk? Then she was remembering all those boxes brought from the office. It had been a rushed job and Tim must have gathered it up with other things. Felicity smiled, glad to have solved the puzzle. Someone would be sorry to have lost the photo and would be happy to have it returned. Next time she wrote to Tim she would ask him about it. Then she frowned. Maybe that wasn't such a good idea. He didn't know that she was making use of his desk. Surely he wouldn't mind, but then again he might. It was hard to tell. She wouldn't like him to think she had been rifling through his desk. The truth didn't always sound convincing especially in a letter. What would she say? I was searching for paper-clips and came across – no that wouldn't do. Far better that she put the snapshot back where she got it and say nothing about it.

Felicity had been out early to do her shopping. Michael was coming straight from the office and she was to have a meal ready for him.

'I don't want you going to any trouble, Felicity.'

'Michael, it is no trouble. I have to eat and cooking for two is easier than cooking for one. That apart, my goodness, you do so much for me, do let me do something in return.' She paused. 'Steak and fried onions, does that appeal?'

'I should just say it does.' She could imagine him smiling at the other end of the phone.

'You see I do pay attention. I remember you saying it was a favourite meal of yours but Geraldine—'

'Would never cook it for me because the smell of onions lingered for too long.'

'An open window would have taken care of that.'

'Geraldine is a hot-house plant and only in the height of summer would the windows be open. That said the only one regularly opened is the one in my study.'

She laughed. 'Now isn't that strange, it is – was the opposite in our house. Tim would not allow the study window to be opened, not even by a couple of inches. He said it would disturb the papers on his desk. And speaking of Tim I had a letter this morning. It tells so little.'

'I don't suppose much happens and Tim probably thinks what does isn't worth mentioning. He does write to you so that has to be something.'

'Yes, I have to remember that.'

After she put the phone down Felicity stood for a while deep in thought. Michael was becoming very important to her and that was a mistake. If Michael were to get even a hint of her feelings she could so easily lose his friendship. He wasn't the type to look at another man's wife and what was happening to her? Why was she having such thoughts? Because her husband was out of sight? No, not that at all, Tim was for ever in her thoughts and she just prayed that a spell of prison life wouldn't make him bitter. What would it be like, what kind of life would they have together once he had gained his freedom? She had no idea. Everlasting love, was there such a thing? Yes, some were blessed with that but somewhere along the way she and Tim had grown apart. She hardly dared to acknowledge it but in her heart of hearts she knew that she no longer loved Tim and she also knew that she would never leave him.

In the early afternoon the doorbell rang and after drying her hands on the kitchen towel she went to see who was there. Probably someone selling something she didn't need and she must harden her heart. She knew she was a soft touch but weren't we all meant to help each other and the poor soul would be only trying to make an honest living.

It wasn't a salesman who stood there.

'Stuart?'

'Hello, Mrs Morrison,' he said awkwardly.

She looked at him, he was as untidy as ever but there was a difference. The boy who had come to meet Joanna's parents had been happy and carefree. He didn't look happy or carefree today, he looked wretched and uneasy.

'You won't want to see me, I know but, please, may I come in?'

'Of course.' Felicity stood aside and when he was inside she shut the door and led the way to the sitting-room. The evenings could be chilly and she had the fire ready to put a match to before Michael was due to arrive.

'Sit down, Stuart.'

'Thank you.'

'I had better tell you straight away that if you have come to see Joanna you have had a wasted journey. She isn't here and I have no intention of telling you where she is.'

'I don't blame you. I let her down.'

'Yes, Stuart, you did.'

'She is all right, isn't she?'

'I find that difficult to answer. My daughter will cope in her own way. She is a survivor and she will get through this though it will take a long time. I am talking not only of her father—'

'I know, Mrs Morrison, instead of helping I made things so much worse.'

'You did.'

'Will she come back to Edinburgh?'

'I am not prepared to say.'

'Mrs Morrison, I am not trying to make excuses for myself but I have – I have to make an attempt to explain. If only Joanna had confided in me was what I thought then I wouldn't have been at such a disadvantage.'

'Your disadvantage as you call it was nothing to what Joanna went through. Your mother was very rude and my poor daughter didn't know where she had gone wrong. Even if Joanna had been in possession of the facts there was no excuse for what I can only describe as cruelty.'

'I can only apologise for my mother. She isn't the easiest person to get on with, but she wouldn't be deliberately cruel.'

Felicity admired him for that. The woman was his mother and he had to both apologise and rush to her defence.

Stuart was looking more wretched than ever. 'Honestly, Mrs Morrison, I didn't think it was possible for Joanna not to know about her father. Not the outcome of the trial, not that, but when I met you and your husband, Mr Morrison had already been dismissed.'

'Yes,' Felicity said heavily, 'I have to accept that you should be forgiven for believing that. We had decided to keep everything from Joanna, to let her have her holiday and tell her once she was home.'

He nodded. 'I can see how it was.'

'Do you? The way I see it is that you and Joanna

had been together long enough for you to know the kind of person she is. You chose not to believe her but rather what you were told.'

'By my father.' His mouth twisted. 'His word has always been law. I should be able to stand up to my father and I thought I was learning to, but rather obviously I haven't. My parents are good people but they have their own code of behaviour and obedience was one of the first lessons I learned. You can't know how much I envied Joanna the easy relationship she has with you and Mr Morrison.'

Felicity nodded sympathetically.

'I love Joanna and I am sick at heart because I know I have lost her and it was all my own stupid fault. It would be wrong of me to blame my parents. They truly believe that what they do is for my own good and that one day I shall see it and be grateful to them. What they do not realise is that they are in danger of losing both their sons. I haven't been to see them since – since this happened and my young brother is causing problems. He wants to leave school the minute he can.' Stuart smiled. 'Nigel wants to be a professional footballer and the word professional in that sense offends my father.' He grinned. 'My young brother is braver than I ever was and told Dad to his face that he was an intellectual snob. For his cheek he was kept indoors all weekend which was the worst possible punishment. I would have got by reading books but Nigel seldom opens one.' They were both laughing.

Then he was serious. 'I am so very sorry about everything.'

'So am I, Stuart. Life can be very hard.'

'In circumstances like this it is difficult to find the right words but I am going to try. I liked Joanna's father, I liked him a lot and I told her I thought you were both great. Maybe if I hadn't been so impressed it wouldn't have come as such a shock.' He got to his feet and took an envelope from his pocket which he placed on the coffee table.

Felicity looked at it then raised her eyes to look at Stuart. The envelope had the one word Joanna written on it.

'May I ask as a great favour to me, would you give that to Joanna? Maybe she won't read it. I hope she does. I have tried to explain as best I could and have asked for her forgiveness.'

'I'll see that she gets it, Stuart,' Felicity said quietly. 'I haven't offered you anything – tea or coffee?'

'No, thank you. I'll go now and thank you for being so kind.'

They walked to the door. Felicity opened it and found herself close to tears. She liked this boy, liked his honesty and his humility. He and his brother had what most would describe as a privileged upbringing. The best schools, a good home in ideal surroundings. All of these they had but what was in short supply was love, warmth and understanding. Impulsively she kissed him on the cheek.

'Goodbye, Stuart.'

'Goodbye, Mrs Morrison and thank you again.'

For a few moments she watched the long, loping stride then shut the door. She went back to the sitting-room and picked up the envelope. Should she send it to Perth or take it to Joanna herself? On reflection perhaps she should post it. Felicity wanted Joanna to read it and if it was just handed over Joanna might feel she should tear it up, that to open it would show weakness. Putting herself in Joanna's shoes she knew she wouldn't be able to resist opening the letter to find out what Stuart had written. That settled in her mind, Felicity scribbled a few lines to say that Stuart had called and left this for her. The scribbled note and Stuart's letter went into another envelope and Felicity addressed it to the Cairn Hotel, Perth. Once she would have popped out with a letter and posted it in the letterbox at the end of the road. Not now, she went further afield. All the same she was being ridiculous, this couldn't go on for ever. There was no need to stop and talk, she could be in a hurry, smile, pass the time of day and walk quickly away. That is what she would do. She went out, posted the letter and met no one.

Michael would be at Holmlea by seven or maybe sooner and should something urgent delay him he would telephone.

Felicity set the dining-room table and put out the crystal wine glasses. Michael was bringing a bottle and since it was steak he would make that red wine. It was a long time since she had taken such care with the setting of the table and it wasn't to impress Michael. He was the kind who would be pleased to dine anywhere and that could be the kitchen. She was doing it because she wanted to do it.

Michael arrived at a quarter to seven with the wine and a florist's paper. He handed both to Felicity.

'Michael, thank you very much but this is too much.'

He shook his head. 'I bought the flowers at lunch time and stuck them in the cloakroom. I gather I should have put them in water in the sink.'

'They are lovely but I shall go this minute and put them in water. Do help yourself to a drink.'

'What about you?'

'Oh, maybe a small sherry. You'll have to go into the cabinet for that.'

They sat down to their drink but by mutual consent there was no serious talk. That was going to wait until after the meal.

'I hope you are hungry,' she smiled, 'because I am.'

'You've been saving your appetite, starved all day?'

'I make do with a snack which is all wrong but it is so boring cooking for one.'

'And I imagine you forget the time when you are working?'

'I do and more so now. When I worked at the kitchen table it wasn't so easy to forget about meals. Now that I work upstairs in Tim's study I have everything spread out on the desk and the difference that makes.'

'I'm sure it does.'

'It didn't matter so much before because I was only doing the occasional drawings—'

'Whereas now you treat it like a full-time job.'

'It is a full-time job and I see it as a godsend. Not because of my success though that does count, but because it has given my life a purpose.'

'We all need that.'

'Michael, if you have finished we can go through to the sitting-room and have our coffee there and a comfortable seat.'

'That was a lovely meal,' he said getting up. 'I can't remember when I last enjoyed one so much.'

'You flatter me.'

'I speak the truth.'

Once the coffee was served and another log thrown on the fire they were silent for a few moments. There was no need to rush in and say something, the silence was comfortable.

'Tim,' she said looking at him. 'What kind of meal has he had?'

'Nothing like this, you can be sure.'

'I do get a description of the food and he is trying to make a joke about it. I imagine it to be disgusting.'

'No, it isn't,' he said firmly. 'The food will be of a reasonable standard and for some a lot better than they get at home.'

'You are not just saying that?'

'I'm not. The least attractive part will be how it is served. For someone like Tim used to china plates and decent cutlery the plastic plates and what passes for cutlery must be a bit off-putting, but then as they say if one is hungry enough one will eat anything and not notice how it is served.'

'I do try but I can't imagine Tim in those surroundings. I shouldn't be saying this but does he have to mix with all kinds, I mean thugs and hard men?'

He was smiling and for a moment she was angered.

'Forgive me I am not trying to make light of this. He tells me what he cannot put in a letter to you. You mention hard men and thugs and, yes, he does come into contact with them.'

'Will they try to harm him?' she said fearfully.

'Absolutely not. Your husband has to be the best protected prisoner. Tim has nothing to fear on that score. No one would dare to lay a finger on Tim, if they did they would come to regret it. They have their own grapevine and once they heard that they had a first-class lawyer in their midst they were highly delighted.'

'I would have thought that knowing he was a lawyer would be to Tim's disadvantage.'

'Quite the opposite. Here they have a sharp legal mind, a way of finding out, free of charge, how they stand. Some have marital problems that need sorting out and others have more complicated problems. They will listen to what he advises and Tim will come in for a lot of respect.'

'If it wasn't so serious I could find that funny.'

'Tim does find it funny and he is milking it for all he is worth. If there are any perks going Tim won't be forgotten whereas in other circumstances he would never have heard of them.'

'What about the warders, don't they see what is going on?'

'Some are very good at turning a blind eye.'

'That has to make me feel better. Tim isn't letting the place get him down.'

Michael didn't want Felicity worried but neither did he want her to get the wrong impression. Tim was coping but he had his bad days.

'Some days aren't too bad and other days are—'

'Very difficult?'

'Yes. It couldn't be otherwise, Felicity.'

'In the lonely hours what does he think about?'

'I can't tell you that but I should think he deeply regrets doing what he did and what this has done for those he loves.'

'Especially his mother.'

He looked at her curiously. 'Why do you say that?'

'It doesn't hurt me to say it. Tim and his mother are very close and let me add she is very good to Joanna and to me. I like my mother-in-law,' she smiled.

'How is the old lady?'

'She is becoming very confused I'm afraid, although we have to see this as a blessing in disguise. She will never know about Tim being in prison and if she wonders about his absence and she hasn't up to now, then she will be told that Tim has taken a job in England and that it will be some time before he can manage to get home for a few days. It is awful to tell untruths but I think it better than breaking an old lady's heart.'

'I couldn't agree more.'

'Oh, I should tell you I had a visitor this afternoon.'

'An unexpected visitor?'

'Very unexpected. Joanna's ex-boyfriend arrived at the door.'

'The boy she went on holiday with?'

'Yes. More coffee?'

'No thank you.'

'Oh, come on or I shall have to throw this out.'

'Too good to do that. Thank you, I will take another cup.'

She filled his cup then her own.

'Stuart was hoping to see Joanna. He knew that she hadn't returned to university. You know, Michael, I did feel sorry for the boy. He is just a boy and this has been terrible for him as well. Not that I let him off, I left him in no doubt as to what I thought of his and his parents' treatment of Joanna. But then again I can understand how it all came about.'

'He is young and we all make mistakes and you are hoping that Joanna will forgive him, not now but in time.'

'I don't see it happening but then again time is a great healer.' She paused and looked at him. 'I did tell you that Stuart's father is a solicitor and how it all came out?'

He nodded. 'We can never be completely sure

about anything. The chance of this happening was so improbable that it could have been dismissed, yet here we are.'

'No, Michael, you had your doubts, you were not very happy about it.'

'But that is me all over, I look for the little flaws.'

'I should have paid attention to you.'

'And I could so easily have been wrong. Before I go I must give you my bit of news.'

'I'm sorry, I've been so selfish and you haven't had a chance to talk about your life.'

'There is never a great deal to tell.'

'Until now,' she smiled.

'My divorce has come through.'

'What do I say? Do I congratulate you or is that in bad taste?'

'Tricky, isn't it? Divorce is failure. Failure to make a marriage work.'

'Divorce has to be better than an unhappy marriage.'

'I agree. Sadly it involves a third life. Children have to suffer for their parents' mistakes. Trudy shouldn't be too badly affected since we didn't see a great deal of each other.'

'That was a pity, but not your fault.'

'Some of it was my fault, I am not blameless.'

'You won't lose touch with Trudy?'

'I hope not. I did think I should see my daughter regularly and on her own so that we could build something. Now, Felicity, I am not so sure. Perhaps it would be a kindness to fade out of the picture and avoid Trudy being pulled two ways. Financially, of course, she would be my concern and I would always be there for her.'

'Of course you will. Don't lose your child, fight for her if you have to. The divorce is too fresh for you to think clearly. Trudy will make her own demands, children these days do quite a lot of demanding.' She laughed. 'Some of it we could do without. Seriously, Michael, a father is very important in a daughter's life and I am quite sure that Trudy does not want to lose you.'

'Felicity, you have the happy knack of always saying the right thing.'

'If only . . .'

Chapter Nineteen

'Adam, how nice to hear your voice,' Felicity said sounding surprised and delighted at the same time. She had lifted the phone expecting it to be Joanna calling from Perth.

'Did you think I had deserted you?'

'No, I didn't think that at all and it isn't so very long since we spoke.'

'Neither it is and I do know you have been working hard. I have been in touch with Cynthia Sutherland and she is very pleased with what you have produced so far.'

'Did she say that?' Felicity was smiling.

'She did. I rather thought she would have told you that herself.'

'Oh, she did,' Felicity said quickly. 'This is just me, I need to hear that you are both pleased.'

'Then rest assured that we are. The reason I am phoning, or one of the reasons, is to let you know that I have circulated samples of your work to those who

332

might be interested and I have had a very encouraging response.'

Felicity felt a flutter of excitement. She knew her work was good but she did need the feedback from others. All those years she had been content enough with her small success and now when bigger and better things were beckoning she had the feeling that she wasn't quite ready.

'Thank you, Adam, for all you do on my behalf.'

'My dear Felicity, you are paying me, remember.' He was laughing.

'I'm out of my depth, this takes a bit of getting used to.'

'Believe me in a little while you will be taking it all in your stride. However, that said, all work and no play isn't good for anyone. We all need to relax and enjoy ourselves.'

'Adam, I get a lot of enjoyment from what I am doing.'

'I know you do and it shows in your work.'

'Thank you.'

'Do you happen to have your diary beside you?'

'Yes.' She didn't but she had a notepad and pencil. Her diary was in her handbag with most of the pages blank. Her social life was non-existent. Felicity picked up the pencil and drew the notepad nearer. Why, all of a sudden, did she have this funny scared feeling?

'This could be a chance for you to meet up with writers of children's stories as well as illustrators like yourself. You creative people lead lonely lives. You need peace and quiet so it has to be that way.'

'I suppose that is true.' She nodded into the phone.

'Let me put it in a nutshell, Felicity, this is going to be an evening of interest and entertainment.'

'Adam, I don't think—' she began.

'I am not prepared to listen to any excuses, Felicity, this is something that you and your husband should make an effort to attend and let me say it does not take place until December.' He paused for a moment then went on. 'We have done this for several years but last year was the first time it was done on a large scale and it proved to be such a success that it was decided to keep to that and make it an annual event. As yet I do not have all the details but when I do I'll be in touch. This is to get in early and meantime I suggest you pencil in the eighteenth as the most likely date.'

She wished he would stop. For her to interrupt the flow of words would be nothing short of rudeness. She had to go on listening.

'As I have already said this is a get-together of authors, illustrators, representatives from the publishing houses and others. Felicity, look at it this way, you will be getting yourself known.'

Felicity was becoming ever more agitated and she could feel herself shaking which was ridiculous. For heaven's sake all she had to do was give her regrets and decline the invitation.

She took a deep breath. 'Adam, I really am terribly sorry but you will have to count me out.'

'Absolutely not. As yet I haven't told you where this is taking place.'

'I know that but it makes no—'

'Edinburgh we find is ideal. There is a good train service for those who don't drive and for those who prefer not to. I seem to recall you telling me that your daughter is studying at Edinburgh University so you probably know the city quite well.'

'Not really, just Princes Street and those streets nearby.'

'All you need. I don't as yet know which hotel but it will be central and it will be one with a reputation for good food and efficient service. As on previous occasions the wine will flow freely and the speeches will be short and witty. I think I can promise that a good time will be had by all.'

'How are you going to guarantee the speeches being witty?' she found herself asking.

'Because, dear lady, only those who have proved themselves entertaining in the past will be invited. No one wants to be bored out of their mind with a long, rambling talk and our committee members make as sure as they can that it doesn't happen.'

'Adam, I would love to be able to accept but it is out of the question. I'm sorry but I won't be attending.'

'You can't mean that?' He sounded put out.

'I do mean it,' she said firmly. She must leave no lingering doubts and hoped her tone of voice would show that this was final.

It was as though she hadn't spoken and Felicity put

her hand to her forehead and for a moment closed her eyes.

'This is going to be one very interesting evening, a fun evening as well and you, my dear Felicity, cannot afford to miss it. Please do not imagine for a single moment that you and your husband are going to be abandoned in a room full of strangers. I shall be there with my wife, Lilian, and it will be my pleasure to introduce you to those whom I think you should meet. Cynthia Sutherland is to make a special effort to be present. Poor thing she hurt her back not long ago and movement is painful.'

'I *am* sorry to hear that.'

'Cynthia is a very plucky lady and my bet is that she will be there.'

This was getting steadily worse and it must look as though she was making no effort whereas Cynthia Sutherland, bad back and all, was determined to put in an appearance. For a crazy moment she was tempted to blurt out the truth. I'm so sorry, Adam, but you see my husband is in prison – that would shock him into silence followed by acute embarrassment.

'Believe me I am not trying to make excuses, I know I would enjoy the evening but my husband wouldn't want—'

'How can you say that? Give the man a chance. You haven't asked him yet and this event doesn't take place until the middle of December. That gives you plenty of time to work on your husband.' Adam laughed good-humouredly. 'The invitations are going out early before you busy folk have your diaries filled. You owe it to yourself to be there and you must make your husband see that. For goodness sake the man must be proud of his wife.'

'Tim thinks of my little drawings as no more than a hobby, something to keep me occupied.'

'Surely not and if that should be the case then it is high time he was made aware of your very considerable talent.' She heard the first trace of irritation in his voice.

If only these were normal times and Tim living at home then the invitation might have received serious consideration or then again maybe not. That kind of evening when she rather than Tim, would be getting the attention, would not be to his liking. Tim wasn't used to taking a back seat.

Was that a sigh she heard? 'I've said my piece,' he continued, 'and I think we should leave it there but I warn you I am not giving up.'

'You can be very persistent.'

'Oh, I can and now let me go straight on to the next item of news. I am coming to your part of the country for a few days and will as usual be staying at the Parkside Hotel in Broughty Ferry. We have spoken at length just now but there are always things to discuss. If, however, you are pushed for time just forget it.'

'I would like to come,' she said quietly.

'Good. It will have to be either Wednesday or Thursday of next week. Which day would suit you?'

'Thursday. Wednesday is when I visit my mother-in-law in Carnoustie though that could easily be changed.'

'Don't do that, Thursday it is. How about making it lunch or is morning coffee better for you?'

'Yes it is. Could we make it the same arrangements as last time?'

'No problem, we'll keep it to that. I'll ring off now, Felicity, and look forward to seeing you at the Parkside Hotel.'

Felicity replaced the receiver and went thoughtfully through to the kitchen. She wanted quite desperately to go to this event in Edinburgh. There was so much she could learn and she would love to meet others with the same interests. And perhaps most of all she wanted to feel a part of what was going on.

Then it came to her, why not go on her own, what was to hinder her? Not everyone would have a partner and Adam wouldn't leave her stranded. It was very tempting but there was a danger. Adam, in all innocence, might mention that her husband was a solicitor and that could lead to questions. Where did they live? Which firm of solicitors employed her husband? Polite conversation, no one all that interested but by some trick of fate, and fate hadn't been kind to the Morrisons of late, a connection might be made. Unlikely but then again not impossible. She wouldn't risk it.

*   *   *

The postman had been to the Cairn Hotel and left a bundle of letters on the front desk which the receptionist had started to sort out.

'Is that the mail? I'll take mine, Marion,' Rachel said, stopping at the desk. The girl flicked through them.

'These are marked for your personal attention, Miss Reid, and there is one for Joanna.'

'Here she is. Joanna, a letter for you,' Rachel smiled to her goddaughter.

Joanna was wearing the regulation green overall which the maids wore while they did out the rooms.

'That's my mother's writing.'

'So it is,' Rachel said taking a look.

'Why take the bother to write when she could phone?'

'There is an easy way of finding out.'

'No time,' Joanna said putting the letter in her overall pocket. 'I'll read it during my break.'

Rachel was amused. 'My dear girl, read your letter if you wish. To hear you one would think we were slave-drivers.'

'Read it and make myself late, not on your life.'

'We are talking about a few minutes.'

'A few minutes and I'm for it,' Joanna grinned. 'You do have a slave-driver in the hotel. We are all scared to death of your Mrs Parker,' she said as they moved away from the desk. Joanna lowered her voice. 'What made you engage someone like that? Her face would crack if she tried to smile. Honestly, Aunt Rachel, there is no pleasing her.'

'Why did I employ her, you ask. The woman might be without charm, my dear, but to the Cairn Hotel she is worth her weight in gold. My domestics do a first-class job because they are trained from the start that nothing less is good enough for the Cairn Hotel. I could employ someone with excellent references and a pleasant manner but she wouldn't get the same out of the staff. In no time they would be cutting corners and giving me problems. Don't shake your head, Joanna, these are hard facts and you would be no better than the others. If you were pushed for time something would be neglected.'

'We wouldn't dare neglect anything with the dragon breathing down our neck.'

'Exactly my point and don't call the poor woman a dragon. She does have a nicer side.'

'Pity she didn't show it to us occasionally.' She glanced at her watch. 'With all that talking you've made me late and I am going to be in deep trouble.'

'Tell Mrs Parker I delayed you.'

'I will not. I do not take advantage just because the boss happens to be my godmother.' She made a face and turned to go.

'Joanna?'

She glanced back.

'You are doing very well and I am proud of you.'

'Thanks.'

Joanna was inordinately pleased about that. The position hadn't been made for her. She was doing a proper job and doing it well. Start at the bottom and work up. Once upon a time, she reminded herself, a very young Rachel had climbed the ladder starting on the lowest rung and working herself up. If she was to be serious about learning the hotel business, and she wasn't ruling it out altogether, then her next step would be learning to be a waitress. That could be tricky. She didn't have a steady hand. When she carried a cup and saucer there would be as much tea in the saucer as in the cup or so her mother made out. She couldn't imagine herself balancing plates on her arm. Joanna had said as much to Rachel who had replied that it would come with practice.

Joanna was not convinced. She knew she would be scared to death in case she dropped a plate of soup on the floor or horror of horrors, down someone's neck or in their lap. What did one do? Burst into tears or run a mile? Probably both. She had asked her godmother what to expect.

'Not instant dismissal, Joanna,' Rachel had smiled. 'Accidents do happen and the management accepts this. If it was put down to carelessness there would be a very severe reprimand for the offender with the threat of dismissal.'

'What about the poor diner with half a plateful of soup down his neck?'

'Sincere apologies and whatever was deemed necessary to compensate for the damage and pain if that was involved. Why? Are you about to offer your services?'

'Absolutely not, I wouldn't be any good.'

'You might with proper training.'

'No, I would be a total disaster. One is better to know one's limitations,' she said primly.

Rachel smiled and Joanna walked away. Her lateness would have been noticed so there was little point in hurrying.

'Cutting it a bit fine, aren't you, Joanna?' Mrs Parker said looking pointedly at her watch.

'I'm sorry.'

'I doubt that. You weren't even hurrying yourself.' The thin lips pursed disapprovingly. 'In a dream world of your own it looked like.'

'I'm sorry,' Joanna repeated and suddenly felt weary. 'I have a lot on my mind, Mrs Parker.'

'Don't we all. That is no excuse. Most of us can manage to get ourselves to work on time and you have the advantage of living on the premises.' She waited for Joanna to speak.

'It won't happen again,' she mumbled.

'I should hope not. I will say no more about it this time, Joanna, but should it happen again I might consider it necessary to report the matter to Miss Reid.'

Joanna was in danger of losing her temper. All this carry on because she was a few minutes late. The angry retort died on her lips. The other maids wouldn't dare cheek back and neither would she.

'Did you say something?'

'No.'

'I am aware of your relationship to Miss Reid and it was her wish that you should be treated exactly the same as the other maids.'

'That is the way I want it too and I don't recall getting any special treatment,' she said spiritedly.

There was the ghost of a smile. 'You didn't and you didn't look for it which is to your credit. On you go, enough time has been wasted.'

Joanna hurried away. One of the maids winked, she must have heard most of the exchange. Joanna opened the bedroom door and grimaced. How one solitary male could be responsible for such a mess was unbelievable. She picked the bedclothes off the floor and stripped the bed of its crumpled sheets. The wet towels had found their way from the bathroom to the bedroom floor and cigarette ash was spilled over the dressing-table. Thank goodness he was only staying for two nights.

The letter had been completely forgotten until now and she touched it in her overall pocket. Why was she delaying opening it? Because that is what she was doing. No one was around to see what she was doing. It niggled why her mother hadn't telephoned and it made her uneasy.

Once the room was put to rights Joanna took the letter from her pocket and slipping her finger into the space in the flap she tore it open. Inside was another envelope together with a scrawled note from her mother. Joanna was written on the envelope and seeing it her mouth went dry. She knew who the sender was and her heart began to pound painfully. How dare he. He had no right to try and make contact, no right to invade her newly found privacy. And the nerve of him arriving on her mother's doorstep after the damage he had done. Did he imagine for one moment that she would have anything to do with him? Hadn't she made it clear enough that she never wanted to see him again? Apparently not.

Stuart couldn't have been confident of finding her at home or he wouldn't have had a letter with him. Her mother hadn't said much in her note — just that Stuart had called and was anxious that she should get his letter. She pushed the lot into her pocket thinking she would deal with it later.

Her work was only getting part of her attention as her mind kept straying to the letter. The question she kept asking herself was whether she should tear it up unopened and never know what Stuart had written. That would be the sensible thing to do since she wanted nothing more to do with him. The nothing more to do with him could still apply if she read it and she would have the satisfaction of knowing what he had written whereas he would never know whether or not she had read his letter.

The benefit of an early start was to be finished work by four thirty. Sometimes Joanna went along to Rachel's office and gave some assistance but today she didn't. She took off her overall and hung it up in the maid's cupboard, then went straight to the apartment. She had her own key to let herself in. Joanna went through to the bedroom, sat down on the bed and kicked off her shoes. After all those hours on her feet it was heaven to wiggle her toes and ease the pressure. Narrow shoes suited her foot but were not ideal for her present employment.

The letter was in her hand and for a long moment she looked at it and then losing patience with herself she slit the envelope open. Taking out the sheet of paper and seeing that cramped writing Joanna wasn't prepared for the rush of feeling. She only got as far as My dear Joanna, when the floodgates opened. There was no one to witness her distress and she let herself go. Not all of it was for Stuart, it was for everything that had gone wrong in her life. After the storm of weeping she felt better. She dried her eyes, blew her nose, tucked the handkerchief up her sleeve and began to read Stuart's letter.

My dearest Joanna,

I can't tell you how many attempts I have made and all of them screwed up and thrown into the w.p.b. What happened on that dreadful day and my own part in it was unforgivable. I am writing that in my letter yet I am seeking, no I am pleading, for your forgiveness.

Our holiday together was so marvellous and I like to think that we were both blissfully happy. I know I was. How could it have gone so wrong? The days without you are empty and dull. My work is suffering and I couldn't care less. Though, of course, I shall have to get down to some hard work or throw it up altogether. That is a possibility and should give you some idea of the state I am in.

It came as a great shock as well as a bitter

disappointment to learn that you were not returning to university. One of your friends told me.
The girl with the curly brown hair and freckles.
I wouldn't be very popular if she was to hear of
the description. I should remember her name but
I don't. She also said that you might be taking a
year off or that was the rumour going around.

I just wish that all of this was a bad dream
and you and I could be back together visiting our
usual haunts.

To hear from you would be wonderful, to
know that I am forgiven would make life bearable.
Wherever you are, whatever you are doing, I wish
you well.

Yours,

Stuart

When she finished reading the letter her face was
sad then very slowly and deliberately she tore up the
letter. There was no wastepaper basket to hand so she
gathered the pieces of paper together and put them in
the envelope to be disposed of later. It was wrong to
think she could put all that had happened behind her.
Her kind of trouble would never go away, the shame
was always there and all she could do was deal with
it the best way she could. There was pretending. She
could pretend to herself that her father had changed
his job and it was too far away for him to be living at
home. Anything was better than visualising her father
in prison. She just couldn't and maybe that was why

he had made the decision that his wife and daughter were not to visit him. Or maybe the humiliation was too much for him.

Joanna didn't want to go anywhere near. She knew that the memory of the inside of a prison would have haunted her for the rest of her life. By her refusal even to write, her father might think that she was disowning him and maybe she was. She was grateful that he hadn't written to her. Had he done so she might have felt obliged to reply. He was leaving it to her.

Joanna had only been sitting in her bedroom for twenty minutes though it seemed a lot longer. The need to get outside and into the fresh air was strong and so was the need to be alone with her thoughts. If she went now she could slip out without being noticed. Joanna washed her face in the bathroom and dried herself with one of the fluffy white towels hanging over the towel rail. The mirror above the wash-hand basin showed that the redness around the eyes had almost gone. A dab of powder and a trace of lipstick would do. She put on a change of footwear and slipped the warm jacket off its coat hanger. This one was kept for the cold weather since it buttoned up to the neck. November was just around the corner.

Chapter Twenty

Like Edinburgh, Perth was a city steeped in history and like Edinburgh it drew the visitors. Perth was neither large nor small but fell somewhere in between. It was a lovely city lying between two parklands, the South Inch and the North Inch. The wide open spaces were ideal for family picnics and could accommodate all kinds of sport. Children could play in safety and shout and scream to their heart's content. It didn't appear to bother the adults and if it did they could move away to a quieter spot.

Joanna was beginning to know a little of the city's history. There were books in the hotel lounge and many of those were very old. She went through them half-heartedly. They didn't look all that interesting but she would borrow one for her bedside table. A chapter or two might send her to sleep. It didn't. Joanna was finding it fascinating reading and mentioned the fact to her godmother.

'I'm glad you've found something to interest you.'

'Have you read any of them?'

'No time I'm afraid but one day I will get round to it.'

'Did you buy them at a sale?'

'I didn't buy them, Joanna, or not directly, they came with the hotel.'

Joanna smiled. 'You could have some valuable books among that lot.'

'I very much doubt it. Someone would have gone through them to make sure there were no first editions. Seriously, my dear, while you are here you must try and see as much of Perth as you can.'

'I intend to. Some of your staff, born and bred in Perth, know nothing about their own city.'

'That doesn't surprise me in the least, I can well believe it. People do not bother about what is on their doorstep but let those same people go to another town or city and they will make every effort to see as much as possible.'

Not so long ago taking a walk on her own would never have occurred to Joanna yet here in Perth she was doing that and enjoying it. She had purchased a guidebook and had been to visit the house of the Fair Maid of Perth. Another time she had wandered around St John's Kirk and promised herself that next time she would go inside to see the priceless collection of old pewter and silver sacramental dishes she had read about. Her father had a copy of *The Thirty-Nine Steps* and after reading it and enjoying it she and a friend had gone to Dundee to see the film. To stand outside John Buchan's birthplace gave Joanna quite a thrill. Had John Buchan been appreciated in his lifetime, she wondered, or had fame come too late for him to enjoy it?

Today her thoughts were not of John Buchan, she was thinking of Stuart. She could picture him writing and rewriting the letter to her and the abortive attempts falling short of the wastepaper basket. He had always been a poor shot. In the end he had got it right. Sincerity leapt off the page and so did the pain. He was hurting and she wouldn't have been human if she had not been secretly pleased. She who had suffered so much and would go on suffering should not be made to suffer alone.

Joanna got herself back to the hotel in plenty of time to change before going down to dinner. To begin with she had rebelled about eating in the dining-room. It made a mockery of her working as a maid during the day, she had said, and she would find it embarrassing. There was a perfectly good kitchen in the apartment and she would make something for herself.

'That you will not do, my dear girl. You will dine with me in the evenings and kindly do not try to make yourself out to be what you are not. You are not a maid.'

'Yes, I am.'

Rachel sighed. There were times, like now, when the girl could be difficult. 'For want of a better word you are a trainee.'

Joanna smiled. 'I am nothing of the kind. I am doing the work of a maid and being paid accordingly.'

Rachel had become impatient. It had been a difficult day and it hadn't left her in the best of humours. A bag of laundry had gone astray, a cupboard door had stuck and an over-enthusiastic helper had used enough force to wrench the knob off necessitating sending for the joiner who had taken his time about coming. And as if that wasn't enough some fool had left a tap running in the cloakroom with the stopper in place and the basin overflowing.

Rachel had won the day as had been expected and the evening meal for both of them became a time when they could relax and enjoy each other's company.

Tonight the dining-room was quiet, it was only a quarter to seven and most of the guests, including non-residents, were having a drink in the cocktail bar and studying the menu.

Rachel always dressed well. She was wearing an emerald green jersey suit and with her bright auburn hair, Joanna thought she looked stunning and said so.

'How very kind of you to say so. The older one gets the fewer compliments come our way,' she smiled.

'I bet Terence pays you compliments.'

'Of course he does and I expect them. Have you chosen?'

'Yes.'

The order was taken and after a few minutes a glass of white wine arrived on a tray for Rachel and a jug of water in which there were ice cubes was put on the table for Joanna to help herself.

'Might I return the compliment and say how well you suit that pinafore dress.'

'You've seen it before.'

'I know but not with that blouse.'

Joanna looked pleased. 'My dress sense must be improving. This I will have you know I bought myself in Perth and it cost me most of my first week's wages.'

'Not all that expensive if your wages covered it.'

'You said it, not me,' Joanna grinned.

'The rate for the job, young lady.'

'Mum sent me money for clothes or to buy anything I needed. I don't need anything so I am sending the money back.'

The food had arrived and Rachel's fork stopped halfway to her mouth.

'You are going to do what?'

'Aunt Rachel, Mum hasn't much money, she can't have and I can keep myself. You don't take money from me for food and lodgings and what I earn is found money.'

'Joanna, I want you to listen to me and listen very carefully. You are not going to send that money back. That would be a dreadful thing to do and so hurtful. Tact, my girl, does not seem to be your strong point.'

Joanna was taken aback. 'That isn't fair,' she said indignantly. 'I would never do anything to hurt my mother. You are the one who doesn't understand,' she almost hissed.

They had both stopped eating. 'What do I not understand?'

'Mum doesn't have Dad's salary coming in or rather she doesn't get the same housekeeping allowance as she used to.'

'Of course I know that. I also know that your mother is not in financial difficulties. We go back a long way, your mother and I, and we have always shared our worries. Don't be upset if on this subject I should be better informed than you.'

'I'm not.'

'Good. That's a relief. The mortgage on the house is being paid—'

'With Gran's money, I know that.'

'Yes, thanks to your grandmother there is no danger of falling into arrears and perhaps having the house repossessed.'

'Does that happen?'

'All too often. For some people the future looks rosy when it isn't.' She paused. 'This success your mother is having with her illustrations could not have come at a better time. As she said herself she is earning real money and hopefully that will go on. I'm sure it will. Your mother is very talented and she richly deserves any success that comes her way.'

Joanna was thoughtful. 'I am beginning to see what you mean about Mum being hurt. She wants to do this, she wants to give me something.'

'Of course she does, it would give her a lot of pleasure.'

'OK. I'll buy clothes and if you have the time perhaps you would come with me and help me choose.'

353

'I'll make the time.'

They had reached the dessert stage and were studying the sweets on the trolley which had been brought to their table. After a minute or two of indecision Joanna decided on the pavlova and fresh cream. Rachel took the fresh fruit salad but declined the cream.

Joanna gave a sigh of satisfaction. 'That was simply delicious, I love it when the meringue melts in your mouth.'

'Too sweet for me. I think we should make our own coffee tonight and have it in the sitting-room. No coffee, thank you, Polly,' she said to the waitress who had come to take away the sweet plates.

They got up and left the dining-room which was beginning to fill up. Once inside the apartment, Rachel went to the kitchen to make the coffee, leaving Joanna to set the cups on the coffee table. She did that, then closed the curtains and switched on the two lamps. The centre light which had been on she turned off since Rachel preferred subdued lighting.

'Joanna,' Rachel called from the kitchen, 'go through to my bedroom and you'll see a box of chocolates on the dressing-table. Bring it and we'll have them instead of a biscuit.'

'Black Magic,' Joanna said putting the box on the table. 'Somebody loves you.'

'From Terence, he knows my weakness for chocolates,' Rachel said, coming through with the coffee. 'We are going to ration ourselves to two each then the box is to be closed and removed out of sight in case we are tempted to make beasts of ourselves.'

'They are for you, not for me.'

'They are for both of us.'

'I do like your Terence and not just because he brings chocolates,' she grinned. It was true. She liked the tall, broad-shouldered man who had been a part of her Aunt Rachel's life for a long time. Once she had asked her mother why they didn't get married and had been told that she must not ask questions like that. Her Aunt Rachel was happy with the situation as it was and her personal life was her own affair.

'I'm very glad to hear that. Terence has a lovely nature, Joanna, and when things get on top of me, which occasionally they do, he is the one person who can calm me. I call him my lifeline.'

'I always think of you as unflappable.'

'Not true, though I like to give that impression. Incidentally it is not all one-sided, there are times when Terence needs me but not so often as I need him.'

They had their coffee and chocolates and Joanna insisted that Rachel remained seated while she carried the coffee things through to the kitchen and put the small table back in its place. She rinsed out the cups, then decided to wash them properly and put them away. That done she returned to the sitting-room and sat down in one of the comfortable chairs. In a few minutes she was leaning back with her eyes closed.

'Tired, dear?'

Her eyes flew open. 'No, I'm not.' She smiled but

it was a forced smile and Rachel saw it.

'My dear, something is wrong.'

'Nothing is wrong.'

'There is and you should tell me what it is.'

'I'm feeling a bit sad that is all. That letter from Mum—'

'Yes,' she said encouragingly.

'She was sending on a letter from Stuart.'

'Oh.'

'It was a very nice letter.'

'Then why should it make you sad?'

'Because, Aunt Rachel, he shouldn't have written, it just makes it all the worse,' she said wretchedly.

'You would rather that your mother hadn't sent it on?'

'I don't know.'

'Your mother must have been in two minds as to whether to send it or not.'

'She likes Stuart.'

'That would influence her?'

'I would think so, wouldn't you?'

'Possibly.'

'I wanted to tear up the letter without reading it.'

'Only you couldn't bring yourself to do that?'

She opened her eyes wide. 'I did do it, I tore it up.'

'After you had read it?'

She nodded. 'That sounds weak.'

'Not at all. Most people, myself included, would have done the same.'

'You are saying that to make me feel better.'

'No, I am not.'

'Say what you like, he had a nerve calling on my mother.'

'I would have said it was rather brave. Poor lad, he can't have known what kind of reception he would receive or there again he had met your mother so he would have known he wouldn't get the door slammed in his face.'

'Maybe I would have done that, shut the door in his face.'

'I should hope not, a well-brought-up girl like you.'

'After what he did I had every right.'

'What he did was completely out of character and I can't help having some sympathy for Stuart. You have to make allowances. The boy was totally unprepared for what took place in that study. You should try putting yourself in his place, Joanna.'

'It was far worse for me.'

'I am not disputing that, but for the moment we are talking about Stuart not you. In the circumstances he could be forgiven for feeling resentful and hurt.'

'Because he thought I should have told him what I didn't know myself,' she said scornfully.

'Yes, because of that. He would expect you to know that your father had been dismissed from his job and the reason for his dismissal.'

'Where are your sympathies?'

'Mostly with you, but I do spare some for Stuart. None of us is perfect.'

Joanna remained silent.

'You have been very open with me, my dear, and I appreciate that.'

'I've told you everything, Aunt Rachel.'

'I know,' she said quietly, 'but there is something I don't understand.'

'What?'

'That first time when Stuart took you to meet his parents – they should have been pleased with his choice of girl. You are blessed with good appearance, you have a pleasant manner and you are intelligent. Added to those, you come from a good home and your father—'

'Was a respected solicitor. Yes, all of that went down all right and I have to be honest. Mr and Mrs Milton weren't exactly welcoming, just – well the nearest I could describe it would be coldly polite. I wasn't being singled out and I believe any other girl would have received the same treatment.'

'Would I be right in thinking they had someone else in mind for their son?'

'Yes. The daughter of a very close friend. Stuart said it was absolutely crazy, that Eileen and he had never been—'

'Sweethearts.'

'Just good pals thrown together a lot and they did like each other.'

Rachel shook her head at the stupidity of some parents.

'Actually I have met her—'

'And found you had nothing to fear?'

'I liked her and she and Stuart carried on you know like brother and sister, trading insults but all in good fun. Most certainly she didn't act as though I had stolen her boyfriend.'

'One day it is all going to sort itself out.'

'Not with me it won't.'

'If you can't find it in your heart to forgive then I am afraid it will be your loss.'

Joanna's fingers were nervously pleating and unpleating her skirt.

'Whether I forgive him or not doesn't come into it. I love Stuart, I am not going to deny that, but I won't marry him. It would only be storing up unhappiness.'

'Forgive me, but I am not following.'

'It isn't going to go away, you know, the stigma of having a father who has spent time in prison. Nothing can alter that.'

'Sadly I have to agree with you there.'

'It is far worse for me, I am the one to suffer most.'

'How do you arrive at that?'

Her eyes met Rachel's. 'This isn't self-pity though it sounds like it. These are facts.' She took a deep breath. 'My father will serve his sentence,' she said slowly, 'then he will be free to move away and make a new life for himself.'

'And what of your mother?'

'Mum will go with him. She might not want to, but she will because she will see it as her duty.'

Rachel nodded in agreement.

'None of us will ever be free of the stigma. Dad didn't receive an eighteen months' sentence, Aunt Rachel, he was given a life sentence.'

'Surely—'

Joanna ignored the interruption and went on. 'I do know what I am talking about, I should, I've gone over it in my mind often enough. I'll be brief. Dad will be an ex-convict, my mother an ex-convict's wife and I – I will be the daughter of an embezzler who spent time in prison for his crime. None of it is my fault yet I am the one who will suffer most. What I have to carry with me is far worse than a prison sentence.'

'Joanna, you are being slightly ridiculous.'

'No, I'm not. Can't you see, I thought you might. My life is just beginning but as far as I am concerned it could be finishing. My parents have experienced the joy of falling in love, becoming engaged then getting married. Then they had me. In other words they have had a good and a full life until now. They had all those years before this happened.'

She had Rachel's full attention and she was nodding slowly.

'Everything you say is true and I wish I could make it easier for you.'

'You can't. No one can. It is a cross I have to bear.'

'In time it will get easier, it has to.'

'Of course and I know that. I can't go through life in black despair,' she said with a brave smile. 'I have to make the best of it.'

Rachel felt like weeping for this poor tormented child and murderous towards Timothy Morrison.

'Stuart isn't close to his parents?'

'No and I think he still wants to marry me.'

'His parents would come round in time especially if there was to be a grandchild.'

'Not even then. They would never accept me and up to a point I can understand that. No one wants to be associated with scandal. For myself I could live with his parents not accepting me. What I couldn't live with—' Her voice broke and she swallowed painfully.

'Stop now, don't say any more this is upsetting you too much.'

'No, I'm all right, really I am and I want it all said.' Her voice was wobbling and she gave herself a few moments before going on. 'I've spent hours and hours thinking about this and what kind of future we would have if we were together. If we had children they could learn the truth about their maternal grandfather and I would rather die than that.'

'What your father did wasn't so very terrible.'

'I am inclined to agree that it wasn't so terrible, maybe that is what makes it worse. It isn't the crime, it is the fact he was sent to prison for it. Don't shake your head as though it could never happen. It could happen so very easily. Things get said that shouldn't and children ask questions. They don't ask for answers they demand them and if they consider the answers less than satisfactory that makes them all the more curious. There is no such thing as a safe secret, Aunt Rachel.

All one needs to provide is an approximate date and it is easy enough to get old newspapers from the reference library.'

'Anything is possible we know that but I can't help thinking that you are painting an unnecessarily gloomy picture. People have short memories and others have come through this and worse.'

'I don't doubt it but I don't find that particularly helpful.'

Rachel thought this had gone far enough. 'No, I can see that. You prefer to wallow in misery and make everyone else miserable. I'm sorry if you think that harsh but it needs to be said.'

'I deserved that.' The voice was very flat. 'You should have shut me up before this.'

'No, talking something through always helps. You have said yourself that you cannot change what has happened, so accept that and don't waste your energies on wishing what might have been.' The phone rang startling them both.

'Terence, probably, I'll take it in the bedroom.'

'Just as I thought, it was Terence, she said returning fifteen minutes later and smiling. 'He was asking for you and I said we had started on his chocolates.'

Joanna felt a little embarrassed but relieved to have got it all off her chest. She couldn't have said all that to her mother because they were too close. It was a different kind of closeness she shared with her godmother, one where it was easier to talk without hurt feelings.

'You will think this a funny thing to say but I feel safe with you here in Perth.'

'That's fine.'

'At home I wouldn't have gone outside the door in case someone I knew wanted to stop and talk. Mum is the same, she goes everywhere in the car.'

'Joanna, my dear, you are more than welcome to stay here for as long as you wish. I am enjoying having you here and I think your days as a maid should end. Waitressing is not for you, I think you would agree, but a spell in reception should suit you.'

'There isn't a vacancy. Marion isn't leaving.'

'I hope not. Marion will take you in hand and show you what is wanted. You will pick it up in no time, then you can assist when necessary and at other times you can help me in the office. How does that sound to you?'

'It sounds perfect. Thank you very much.'

'The pay is better,' Rachel smiled.

'Great.'

Chapter Twenty-One

'Felicity,' Rachel said into the phone, 'you have missed Joanna by a few minutes. She's gone out for her daily exercise, as she calls it.'

'Alone?'

'Yes, Felicity, alone.'

'Actually, Rachel, it was you I wanted to talk to. Is Joanna fine, she isn't upset I mean?'

'She's fine, why should she be upset?'

'I'm not sure if I did the right thing sending on Stuart's letter. You do know about it?'

'Yes, or I should say I know she got one and she did say it was a nice letter,' Rachel said carefully.

'I was sure it would be.'

'You don't need to worry about Joanna, she is coping well.'

'She can't be coping all that well when she goes out walking alone,' Felicity said tartly. 'At her age she should be having some sort of social life.'

'She isn't ready for that yet.'

'I feel so wretched, Rachel, and I feel I have let everyone down.'

'What nonsense. How can you say that?'

'Because it happens to be the truth. I'm a failure.'

'You are depressed.'

'Yes, I am depressed and you would be too if you were in my shoes.'

'Has this got anything to do with your own work?'

'Absolutely not. That part of my life is fine. I wish everything was as good.'

'Come on then, tell me what has brought this on?'

'Nothing has brought it on, it's there and it never goes away.' She paused. 'Rachel, my husband doesn't want to see me, and my daughter, rather than be with her own mother, is staying with you, my best friend. What does that make me except a failure?'

'You are not a failure but you are feeling very sorry for yourself. Tell me, are you sitting down?'

'What has that got to do with it? I'm not as it happens. I'm standing on my own two feet and I am not about to collapse in a heap if that is what you are thinking.' There was an exasperated edge to her voice.

'Felicity, I mean it, get yourself a chair.'

There was the sound of the phone going down, then in a few moments it was lifted.

'Why do I let everyone boss me around?' she said childishly.

'This is not bossing but it could have something to do with you being the kind of person who needs protecting.'

'Thanks very much, that makes me feel a whole lot better I don't think. Well, here I am sitting down and waiting to hear what you have to say.'

'The only reason I wanted you seated is because this could take a while.'

'What about your busy schedule? Aren't you usually rushed off your feet?'

'To hell with my busy schedule. When my best and oldest friend is depressed and feeling sorry for herself then my schedule can go out of the window. Pardon my French if my language is upsetting you.'

'If that was all—'

'Felicity, will you be quiet and listen. Tim, for reasons of his own, and they may be good reasons, does not want his wife to visit him. He does, however, want a regular supply of letters from her and he is answering them. That does not strike me as being someone who does not care about you. He cares enough to want to save you from what could only be an ordeal. Am I making myself clear?'

'I suppose so.' It was said grudgingly.

'Good. We have disposed of – sorry wrong word – we have dealt with your supposed failure regarding your husband and now we come to my goddaughter who loves her mother very dearly but does not want to be in Hillhead. You cannot blame her for that. Joanna wouldn't want to come face-to-face with those who had been her friends at school or anyone else she knew. Stands to reason, you are doing the same yourself.'

'I go out.'

'In the car.'

'Joanna could be with me.'

'That would work for some of the time. What about the other hours in the day, how would she occupy herself? You have to remember, Felicity, that your drawings can take up a large part of your day. And as I have heard you say you do not like to be disturbed while you are working. That being the case having Joanna moping around would be bad for her and bad for you.'

There was the sound of a deep sigh. 'You are making me feel guilty.'

'That is not my intention, far from it. Like most mothers you want what is best for your daughter—'

'Of course I do.'

'What you want for her and what she wants for herself—'

'I know – I know – don't go on about it. We don't see eye to eye but I am looking to the future and she is only dealing with the present.'

'Maybe that is all she can do at this moment. The young don't think ahead.'

'Exactly and that was what I was trying to hammer home. If she decided to ignore Stuart's letter I do not see him pestering her, he isn't the type. She could have gone back to university and if she wished returned home at the weekends. I was bending over backwards to make things easier for her.'

'Felicity, face the truth. You were doing everything in your power to get Joanna back to Edinburgh. You weren't listening to her.'

'Oh I see, that is the way of it, you listen but I don't,' she said in a rising note of anger.

'Calm down, please. Adopting that attitude isn't going to help.'

'I'm sorry, I shouldn't have said that, and after all you have done.'

'Forget it, I do understand.'

'Rachel, I can't help worrying about what is to happen and I don't just mean Joanna's future. Everything is horrible but you are quite right about Joanna being a prisoner in her own home. She is better with you.'

'She is fine, she really is. Joanna will work things out in her own way and in her own time.'

'I go hot and cold thinking about it. Rachel, she must have been desperate to do what she did. I mean pretending to be going back to Edinburgh – she must have changed stations, had it all planned.'

'Maybe it wasn't planned, just a spur-of-the-moment decision.'

'I don't think so.'

Rachel didn't either.

'I have this to say to you, I am very impressed. Your daughter is doing a good day's work for me. She gets paid the rate for the job and she is quite chuffed to know that she has earned it.'

'Are you sure she has?' Felicity said doubtfully. 'When she left home she certainly wasn't domesticated and only the very minimum would be done at university.'

'True it wasn't a very promising start but sheer

determination got her up to the standard required. She passed the test and Mrs Parker—'

'The dragon lady.'

'I must put a stop to the maids calling her that, it could come to her ears. Mrs Parker does a power of work for me and the girls should be grateful for the excellent training they get.' She paused. 'I was going to say that Mrs Parker was satisfied. I know your trouble.'

'Do you?'

'You resent Joanna doing the work of a maid.'

'I just think it is a waste of a good education.'

'Education is never wasted. This is experience. Every day is a school, isn't that what they say?'

'I wouldn't know.'

'Lots of students do hotel work during the holidays and are prepared to take whatever job is available. If you find it more acceptable think of this as Joanna doing a holiday job.'

'You make me sound awful but I have to say what I think. I would much prefer to think of this as a year off her studies.'

'Safer not to do that. Joanna may have different plans for her future.'

'Like in the hotel business?'

'She could do worse.'

'If she did as well as you I would be very proud, but in the meantime she goes on making beds and tidying rooms?'

'We were talking about that, Joanna and I. A few weeks in the dining-room was mentioned.'

'As a waitress,' Felicity said in a scandalised voice. 'Don't even think about it. Now that would be one huge worry. Joanna is not clumsy, I mean she doesn't break things but she seems incapable of carrying a cup of tea without some of it spilling into the saucer.'

'I have noticed and Joanna and I both agree that the dining-room should get a miss. I'm rather sorry about Joanna not having a steady hand. She is such a lovely girl with a friendly manner and she would have been an asset in the cocktail lounge.'

'What are you going to do with her?'

'Give her a while at reception.'

'Now that would meet with my approval. She would be meeting people and you never know—'

'Know what?' Rachel asked though she thought she knew what was coming.

'She might meet a nice young man who would help to take her mind off her troubles.'

'One never knows. Let us give Joanna a rest and tell me about your mother-in-law. Is she still as confused?'

'At times she is but there are other occasions when she can be alarmingly alert.'

'Asking awkward questions.'

'Mrs Haggarty, that's the housekeeper and I are rather good at changing the subject when it gets on dangerous ground. Let me give you an instance. Last week she asked me why I was on my own again and why that son of hers couldn't come with me since now that he isn't working he must have plenty of time on his hands.'

'She knows.'

'About Tim being dismissed from his job, yes she knows that, but no more or as far as we know. Mrs Haggarty and I have to be on our toes because that same lady can be very nippy when she chooses to be. She does admit to taking short naps during the day and finds it an amazing coincidence that Tim should always choose those times for his visits. We now have her permission to prod her awake.'

Rachel was laughing. 'She sounds a wonderful old dear and maybe not so confused as she gives out to be.'

'It isn't put on, she does get confused.'

'For some of the time. It could be that she prefers not to know.'

'I have always said that.'

'Why didn't you say that Tim was working down south and arrange for her to get the occasional letter. That shouldn't have been too difficult.'

'I hinted at something similar but Tim for some unknown reason wouldn't go along with it. He depends on me to keep his mother happy which brings me to my next moan. I'm full of them.'

'No, you aren't but hurry up I haven't all day. Tell me quickly what this is about.'

'Why do troubles never come singly? Tim is suggesting that I make my home with his mother and save all the travelling to Carnoustie.'

'Sell your home?'

'He didn't actually say that in the letter but he must be considering it.'

'Would you be prepared to live in Carnoustie?'

'No, Rachel, I would not. I would do a lot for Tim's mother but I draw the line at that.'

'Has she asked you herself?'

'No. And I let Tim know that there was nothing doing. Heavens, Rachel, you should see the house, nothing has been done for years and to bring it up to a reasonable standard would cost a great deal of money.'

'When the old lady passes on it isn't going to be worth a lot?'

'Tim says it should fetch a good price. Structurally it is sound and slates are replaced when necessary. The inside is where it needs money spent.'

'What does it have in its favour?'

'The house is ideally situated and has a pleasing frontage. The garden is quite big but without being sprawling. A gardener comes regularly to keep it tidy and free of weeds.'

'Added to which Carnoustie is a popular place to live.'

'Yes. Good-sized family houses don't come on to the market all that often. Whoever decided to buy could do the house up gradually and if he took my advice he would put in a modern kitchen and a new bathroom. What is there is antiquated.'

'Don't weaken, hang on to your own house.'

'I haven't much say, the house is in Tim's name.'

'You do have rights but we'll go into that another time. And now I must ring off.'

'Cheerio, Rachel, and thanks for everything.'

A little later Joanna popped her head in the door.

'A short walk, you're early back.'

'It's starting to rain.'

'Your mother phoned a short time ago.'

'Have I to ring back?'

'Not unless you want to.'

'Not especially. What was Mum saying?'

'We were just chatting but she is worried about you.'

Joanna sighed. 'Mum is always worried about me. What is it this time?'

'That letter from Stuart. She wondered if she had done the right thing by sending it on.'

Joanna shrugged. 'Doesn't much matter since she did send it on.'

'Phone tomorrow and tell her it was a nice letter and thank her for sending it on.'

'Maybe I don't think she should have sent it on.'

'And maybe you should try and make things less difficult for your mother. Tell a whopper if you need to. Like most of us you've told plenty in the past so don't baulk at this one.'

'You are very protective of my mother.'

'I always was or tried to be. She is very easily hurt.'

'OK, I'll phone tomorrow and I'll keep it short.'

'Why should you do that?'

'Because Mum says I am not to take advantage.'

'You don't. You are to use the phone when you

want to and you do not have to ask my permission.
You didn't ask permission at home, did you?'

'Of course not, but that is different.'

'It is not different. This is your home for the present
and I would want you to treat it as your home.'

'Thanks, you are really great. Dad was a bit mean
with the phone, not calls from the house,' Joanna said
hastily, 'but he took a dim view of it when I wanted
to reverse the charges from Edinburgh.'

'I should think so too. That is a horribly expensive
service and should only be used in an emergency.'

'That is exactly what Dad said. The only thing was
we couldn't agree on what was an emergency. 'Having
no money to make a call was surely one but he didn't
think so.'

'Neither would I. Poor budgeting was your problem
I would have said. And now, please, I have done nothing
but talk and I must get on. There are masses of things
requiring my attention.'

'Let me help.'

'You have done your day's work.'

'I'm a glutton for punishment.'

'Very well. I could do with some assistance. You
could check the invoices and head off phone calls. I
am not available to anyone.'

Chapter Twenty-Two

Two women were sitting having coffee at a table in the Parkside Hotel in Broughty Ferry. One of them was craning her neck to see through the greenery.

'I can't see properly for those wretched palm leaves, but I think that is Felicity Morrison.'

'A friend of yours?' her companion asked.

'No, not really. At one time we lived not far from the Morrisons, then we moved. Ah, here comes our coffee and I'm ready for it.' She beamed to the waitress and then frowned. 'Not biscuits, dear, it was shortbread we ordered.'

'Sorry, I thought you said biscuits. I'll take these back and bring shortbread.'

'You don't mind?'

'Not at all.' The waitress left the pot of coffee beside the jug of cream and pushed the bowl of brown sugar nearer. Then she picked up the plate of biscuits and walked away. She went through the swing doors muttering to herself.

'What are you muttering about?' One of the kitchen staff asked, 'or is that you swearing under your breath?'

'I could be excused. Honestly, some folk would swear black was white. She said she asked for shortbread when she most definitely asked for biscuits. The woman with her didn't say anything, scared to disagree with her pal I suppose. Shove some shortbread fingers on that plate, would you?'

'Thank you, dear, how very kind.' They waited until the waitress had gone.

'What a very charming girl and so obliging. Nothing is ever too much trouble and you can't say that about some places. Oh, dear me, no, barely civil some of them.'

The head nodded in agreement. 'They seem to forget that it is the likes of us who keep them in a job. They would do well to remember that.'

'Oh, Madge, the man moved and I got a good look. It is Felicity Morrison. I wonder who that is with her?'

'Not her husband I gather?'

'Most definitely not her husband. I'll tell you about him later.'

'Could be a salesman with all that stuff on the table.'

'I don't think so.'

'Obviously know each other well, they seem to have plenty to say.' She took a bite of her shortbread. 'Lovely, you can taste the butter.'

'Made on the premises, you can always tell the difference.'

'You were going to tell me about the husband.'

'So I was.' Her voice dropped to just above a whisper. 'He is in prison.'

'Never.'

'Such a shock to everyone. Didn't you read about the case? You must have, it got plenty of coverage.'

'Remind me.'

'Her husband is Tim Morrison, you know he was a solicitor with Paton & Noble.'

'Now that does ring a bell.'

'Embezzling a client's money.'

'Of course I remember now. Enjoying a lifestyle beyond his means and thought he would get away with it.'

'I do feel sorry for the woman, such a disgrace.'

'Save your sympathy, my dear. If your husband was living beyond his means, don't you think you would have noticed? I know I would.'

'Yes, I suppose so,' Madge said and drank some of her coffee.

'He got eighteen months. My husband thought he should have got more. I mean if you cannot trust a solicitor who can you trust?'

'Indeed as you say, who can you trust.'

'His wife didn't go to the trial. There was a lot of talk about that.'

'Too ashamed I expect.'

'Poor soul, what must her thoughts be.'

'She looks happy enough at the moment. Look at them, they are having a good laugh.'

'Who could blame her if she has taken up with someone else.'

Madge sniffed. She didn't like the turn the conversation had taken. She was a regular churchgoer, a member of the Women's Guild and a visitor to the housebound. Not all appreciated the visits.

'She is a married woman and she ought to remember that.'

'A man and woman can have a perfectly innocent friendship or do you think that is impossible?'

'I have never given the matter much thought, but since you ask I'll answer it by saying that it might well be possible but it is a mistake to encourage gossips.'

'My curiosity is getting the better of me I have to confess,' Stella said as she helped herself to more coffee. 'Susan at the desk would tell me if she knew. What do you think, should I ask?'

'It would do no harm.'

'I'll make it sound casual.'

'There's your chance, someone is taking over from Susan. Try and catch her eye.'

'I would if she would turn this way.'

'Good, she has seen us.'

'Give a wave and beckon her over.'

The very tall brunette came over to the table. 'Hello, ladies, haven't seen you for a while.'

'We've been here but you must have been off duty. Susan, dear, we are going to be a little bit naughty.'

Susan raised her eyebrows.

Stella nodded her head in the direction of the palm

leaves and then dropped her voice. 'The lady at that table reminds me of someone who used to live near us. A Mrs Felicity Morrison.'

'That is Mrs Morrison.'

'I was almost sure I was right. The gentleman with her, would you know who he is?'

'One of our regulars. That is Mr Silver. I've seen them together before. Mr Silver is very nice, I've got to know him quite well. The lady is very charming but I don't know her.'

'Poor woman, it is a tragedy.'

'What is?'

'Her husband—'

'Did he die?'

'Oh, no. The man is in prison.'

'I'll sit down beside you for a few minutes. This is my official break, so don't worry you are not getting me into trouble.'

'We wouldn't want that. All this was in the newspapers not so very long ago but you young girls don't read the news do you?'

'No time.' She looked at both women. 'You've gone this far, you had better tell me the rest.'

'Very well, but let us keep our voices down. Susan, this is in confidence.'

'Of course. What is the man supposed to have done?'

'Not supposed to have done, he was found guilty. Guilty of embezzlement, Susan.'

'Oh.'

'Taking money that didn't belong to him,' Madge said thinking the girl didn't understand.

'I know what embezzling means. Is he going to pay it back?'

'He already has.'

'How long did he get?'

'Eighteen months.'

'That's stiff, isn't it? I mean he paid it back, so no one is losing out.'

'Dishonesty has to be punished.'

'So does bashing people about and all they get is a rap over the knuckles.'

'I think they get a little more than that,' Madge said.

'The point is, Susan, that Mr Morrison is a solicitor and that makes it so much worse.'

'Tough on his wife.'

'Yes, the whole family has to suffer.'

'Is there a family?'

'One daughter at university the newspaper said.'

'Worst of all for her, she would get my sympathy and now ladies I must love you and leave you.'

Stella put her fingers to her lips.

'Not a word I promise.'

'They are not making a move and they were in before us.'

'I know, Madge, but I think we should get our bill. I still have some shopping to do.'

'I haven't, but it is time I was on my way home.'

*　　*　　*

The hotel was quiet. Felicity had gone and Adam went over to chat to the girl behind the desk.

'How is the love life, Susan?' he smiled.

'At the moment non-existent.'

'I can't believe that.'

'It's the hours, Mr Silver, shifts are hopeless. I think I'll have to look out for a nine-to-five job though I would probably find it dead boring after this. I mean this is cheerful. Incidentally, the two ladies having coffee—'

'What two ladies? I didn't see anyone.'

'Behind the plants, you wouldn't have seen them or not very easily. One of the ladies recognised Mrs Morrison, an old neighbour I think she said.'

'Why didn't she come over?'

'She wouldn't have wanted to do that.' She paused. 'Might have been embarrassing.'

Adam looked at her sharply. 'In what way would it have been embarrassing?'

'Not what you are thinking. I wasn't going to tell you because this was told to me in confidence.'

'Susan, what are you talking about? You have me utterly confused.'

'I suppose I'll have to tell you now. You do know that Mrs Morrison's husband is a solicitor?'

'Yes, I do know that.'

'He might not be one now. Don't they get struck off or something?'

'Susan, I have no idea what you are talking about.'

'I thought you didn't. Mrs Morrison's husband is in prison.'

He was too shocked to say anything and Susan felt a quiver of excitement that she should be the one with the startling news.

'I didn't read it in the newspaper but the ladies said it got a big splash. I suppose it would, he would be well known.' Adam still hadn't spoken. 'Apparently he got eighteen months for embezzling the firm's money.' She looked at him for a long moment. 'You didn't know?'

'No, I didn't.'

Adam was beginning to recover from the shock and he didn't want this spread.

'Susan, will you promise me something and I am being very serious?'

'Promise you what?'

'That you won't mention what you have just told me to anyone else?'

'I won't. No reason why I should. It isn't as though I knew the people concerned. I thought I should tell you since you are friendly with the lady.'

'I appreciate that. She is a very nice lady, Susan, and we shouldn't add to her suffering.'

Susan was a kind-hearted girl. 'No, we shouldn't,' she said and meant it.

Someone came over to the desk and he walked away. He wanted to be on his own, he needed to think and the best place to be left undisturbed was his bedroom. This was awful. Poor Felicity. He closed the bedroom door, sat on the side of the bed and groaned aloud. He had nearly mentioned that function again and how relieved he was that he hadn't. What a clumsy brute not to have realised that she wasn't making excuses. Why couldn't he have accepted that she wasn't going and that was that? But no, he had gone on and on refusing to take no for an answer.

There would be no mention of the function in Edinburgh. Further to that, Felicity would never know that he knew about her husband being in prison. He would make very sure about that. The Parkside Hotel had been convenient in every way but he would not be returning. There were other small hotels that might suit him equally well and it was a small price to pay for guarding Felicity's secret.

Chapter Twenty-Three

Felicity was at home when Michael phoned in the afternoon. He always rang beforehand to see if it was convenient to come.

'Yes, Michael, it is and don't go home. Come straight here from the office.'

'No, that is kind of you, but I won't do that.'

'Yes, I insist. We can eat at eight or thereabout and don't worry I know how you can get held up so I shall expect you when I see you.'

'I feel guilty putting you to all that trouble.'

'And what about the trouble you go to for me? Please come, Michael, and don't picture me standing over a hot stove. The meal will be simple, something I can prepare beforehand. You could safely describe me as a good plain cook.'

'An excellent cook as I already know.'

'Actually I do enjoy cooking but I can't be bothered when it is just for one.'

'I almost said I know the feeling, but I'm afraid

I am a rotten cook. Maybe I should make enquiries about those classes they advertise. You know the ones I mean, simple instructions on how to cook a tasty meal for one. Or perhaps more suited to me, the idiot's guide to home cooking.'

She was laughing. 'Do they really have classes like that, Michael?' she said in mock seriousness.

'If they don't they should.'

'Sorry, I'm keeping you talking when you have work to do.'

'That can safely be left for a few minutes. I took the opportunity to phone you when I am in the office on my own. My secretary is taking time off for a hairdressing appointment for some special occasion.'

'A very understanding boss.'

'Not at all, there is method in my madness. Jennifer will work all the harder when she gets back. And when I need her to stay late she is always obliging.'

'Works both ways.'

'That's it. Felicity?'

'Yes?'

'Next time may I take you out for a meal or' – she heard the hesitation – 'would you rather not?' He was thinking that Felicity might not like to be seen in his company in case it gave rise to talk and there had been enough of that already.

She was quick to reassure him. 'Thank you, Michael, I would enjoy that very much.' And so she would, she couldn't remember the last time she had been out for dinner.

'You would? I'm so glad. You see I was afraid—'

'Of wagging tongues? Michael, I have gone beyond that. I no longer care and that is the truth. It could be different for you.'

'It isn't. Gossip is something we should all ignore and I would refuse to let it bother me.'

'Which is just as well because I think our reputations may already be in tatters. Your car at my gate won't have gone unnoticed.'

'I did think of parking some distance away.'

'I'm glad you didn't. That way it would look as though we had something to hide. Michael, I am going to ring off now and let you get on with your work.'

She replaced the receiver and for a moment or two stood beside the phone smiling to herself. She always felt comfortable with Michael.

Felicity had done her shopping earlier with the thought that she might be cooking for a guest. It would be what she promised, a simple well-cooked meal. She wasn't out to impress. Leek and potato soup would make a good starter and to follow she would grill loin chops and have them with small potatoes and a selection of vegetables. In the butcher's window the loin chops had looked particularly nice. As for the pudding she thought her apple pie would go down well. She was supposed to have a light hand with pastry. With that decided she could go upstairs to the study to do some work. She was getting as much of that as she could cope with.

Shortly before half past seven the door bell rang.

Felicity had been arranging the loin chops on the grill pan and stopped what she was doing to answer the door. In her hurry she forgot to remove her apron.

'Hello, Michael, come in,' she smiled.

'Not too early am I?' he said stepping inside.

'Of course not, I did say to come when you were ready.' She went ahead to open the sitting-room door. 'Have you had a busy day?'

'Much as usual.'

'Which means it was busy but not run off your feet. Pour yourself a drink and relax and the evening paper is there if you want to glance at it.'

'How lovely to be looked after like this.'

'Tim would have called it fussing.'

'I wouldn't. By the way, I do like the pinny if you don't mind me saying so,' he said mischievously.

'Oh dear!' She looked down at her apron with its bold butcher's stripes. 'How awful of me. I'm not exactly the perfect hostess going to the door with a pinny on to greet my guest.'

'On the contrary I think it looks very welcoming.'

'Certainly striking,' she smiled. 'Joanna bought it for me ages ago, when she was still at school. I can't recall what the joke was but I do remember hearing about the enormous amount of trouble she went to to find this. There was a lot of whispering going on between her and Tim.'

'You knew there was a surprise in store.'

'Yes.'

'Happy times?'

'Yes, Michael, they were happy times and I should remember that when I am feeling down. And now you must excuse me while I get back to the kitchen.'

With the soup piping hot and everything organised Felicity returned to the sitting-room to find Michael looking very much at home with his long legs stretched out before him and reading the newspaper. He put it down and smiled. 'You see I took you at your word and made myself at home.'

'I'm glad you did. The meal is ready so we'll go through to the dining-room. I hope you are hungry.'

'I am.'

They went through. Felicity had removed the apron. She wore a light grey skirt with a patterned blouse in a wool and cotton mixture that was both attractive and warm. Michael's admiration showed in his eyes and seeing the table set for two he felt a glow of pleasure. He had never known this cosiness with Geraldine and he had no right to these feelings for another man's wife. And yet, was it just wishful thinking or had he glimpsed in Felicity's face something that was more than friendship? Imagination was all it had been, she was just being her usual charming self.

'Sit down, Michael, and I'll bring the soup.'

He sat down and unfolded the stiffly starched napkin. Felicity had taken two out of the drawer. She didn't think she would be bothering about starching napkins in the future. That was all very well for a dinner party but hardly necessary otherwise. Tim hadn't agreed when he had been handed a limp napkin. It had been the small things he had always been particular about. She wondered how changed he would be when he came out. Poor Tim, he wouldn't be seeing starched napkins for a very long time.

Felicity carried through the soup and they both took a warmed roll from the basket.

'Michael, I don't think we should get into a serious conversation until we reach the coffee stage.'

'I quite agree. Good food should be appreciated and one cannot do that while carrying on a serious conversation.' They exchanged a warm smile across the table. How easy she was to be with and how anxious she was to bring her husband and daughter into the conversation. He had drawn attention to her apron and that had made her think of happier times.

He couldn't recall many. In his failed marriage the happy times had been few and far between. They had made a mistake and there was no use trying to apportion blame. The trouble had stemmed from the fact that he and Geraldine had been totally unsuited and it hadn't taken them long to discover that. Had it not been for the arrival of Trudy the separation would have come a lot sooner. He supposed they had done what countless other couples had. Tried to make a go of it for the sake of the children. Sometimes it worked and sometimes it didn't. In their case it hadn't. They hadn't quarrelled, he would never answer back which infuriated her. He had kept silent and they had been like strangers sharing a house. It had been no life at all.

Everlasting love – how many shared that? But those

who did were truly blessed. When Michael thought of his ideal woman it was always Felicity who came to mind. To him she was everything a woman should be – warm and loving and understanding. So many qualities yet she hadn't been appreciated. Michael could never understand Tim. Why had he flirted, harmless though it was, it had to be hurtful to his wife.

'Penny for them, Michael, you were miles away.'

'Sorry. If I was thinking at all it was of how very nice this is.'

'Isn't it? I'm enjoying it too.'

'I talk not only of the food,' he grinned, 'excellent though it is. The company has a lot to do with it.'

'Yes, Michael, I think it has a great deal to do with it. I know I never find much pleasure in eating alone so you see you are doing me a favour. For once I am eating a proper meal instead of being lazy and making do with a snack.'

'You should eat, Felicity, it doesn't do to neglect yourself.'

'I know and I am quick enough to tell other people that.'

'Tell me about Joanna, how is she?'

'She seems to be content.' Felicity gave a deep sigh.

'You aren't?'

'How could I be? My daughter should be at university, instead of which she is content to be working as a chambermaid. I know I have to accept the situation, it is her life, but I do find it hard.'

'Of course you do.'

'I feel it is such a waste and she was doing well. It wasn't as though she was struggling.'

'She won't go back to university?'

'Absolutely not. She is adamant about it.'

'Then I am afraid you will have to force yourself to accept that.'

'I know, I said I was accepting the situation since there was nothing I can do about it.'

'I could tell you to stop worrying but I would be wasting my breath.'

She nodded and tried to smile.

'The way I see it – if you want to hear?'

'I do.'

'The last thing Joanna wants at the present time is to be told what to do. Leave her alone would be my advice, Felicity.'

'On no account should I mention the word university.'

He nodded. 'Joanna will like you for that. She will believe that you are leaving it to her to make her own decisions. In the end that could pay dividends and she will be seeking your advice.'

'If only,' she sighed.

'Give it a chance.'

'I will. Rachel would go along with that.'

'Rachel being your friend who owns the hotel where Joanna is working?'

'Yes. She is also Joanna's godmother. At the time I was terribly hurt about Joanna going to Rachel.'

'It was natural enough to feel hurt. Any mother would.'

'Joanna's explanation was that she went to her godmother because I wouldn't listen and she was right about that. I refused to listen. All I could think about was getting Joanna on that train and back to the university. I felt once she was with her friends she would pick up her life again. She saw that as being impossible.'

'Things seldom work out as we would wish but sometimes in the end it comes right and in a most unexpected way,' he said gently.

'Then I must go on hoping. Tim knows all about it but he was no help. He said to leave her to make her own mistakes and she would learn from them. I felt so angry, so let down.'

'Hardly helpful I have to agree.'

'Michael, I am neglecting you. There is more apple pie if you would like some.'

'No, thank you, Felicity, you gave me a generous helping and I thoroughly enjoyed it.'

She got up. 'Then I think we should go through to the sitting-room, and have coffee in front of the fire.'

Michael was on his feet. 'Before that could I perhaps make myself useful and carry these dishes through to the kitchen?'

'No, Michael, no thank you, I'll do that while I am waiting for the coffee. What you could do if you don't mind, is add a log to the fire and bring over the coffee table. Don't put it too near the fire in case of sparks. I do love a log fire but it has its disadvantages.'

Some time later Felicity was nursing her cup and watching the log settle with a small shower of sparks but none that travelled far.

'Michael, I keep thinking of Tim in that awful place and I weep inside for him.'

He nodded.

'Is it very depressing? What a stupid question, how could it not be, of course it is.'

'Felicity, there are lighter moments and some humour as well,' he said.

'I wouldn't have thought there was much to laugh about.'

'Nor would I, but there are always those who can find something to smile about.'

'Tim won't.'

'Maybe not but on the other hand he does have a sense of humour and he might appreciate the joke.'

'Or pretend to.'

'Not all of them are hardened criminals, not by a long way, but even the hardened types have a soft side. You know, Felicity, I would suggest to anyone wanting to make a study of human behaviour that they go along to the prison at visiting time or just before it. Whole families arrive as though it was a pleasure jaunt, a day out. Little ones are clutching toys and the older ones carrying games to help keep them amused. The noise is incredible and there is a lot of light-hearted banter, though I have to add there is also some very foul language.'

'Which the children can do no other than pick up.'

'No doubt as their parents did before them,' he smiled.

'How does one break the pattern?'

'I don't know, Felicity, but I am glad it is not our problem.'

She nodded. 'It is not the kind of place where you are likely to bump into someone you know.'

He raised his eyebrows. 'How very strange that you should say that.'

'Why? Have you seen someone you know?'

'Not exactly.'

She waited for him to go on.

'I did see a woman I knew by sight, but for the life of me I can't place her.'

'Was she visiting someone?'

'It looked like it.'

'Did she recognise you?'

'No. She wasn't looking my way. She was hurrying out and I was going in.'

'Annoying isn't it when you can't remember?'

'Very. I find that trying to prise something out of the sub-conscious only drives it deeper. If I leave it then at some unexpected moment it will drift to the surface.'

'I've known that to happen to me.' She looked over at his cup. 'More coffee?'

'Yes, please.'

Felicity filled Michael's cup and then her own. Neither of them spoke for a few moments.

'I do appreciate what you are doing for Tim and I

know he is grateful. You must be his only visitor—' She broke off, swallowed the lump in her throat and went on. 'There are times when I feel I should ignore what Tim said about visiting and just go. I am his wife and I should be there for him. Maybe he is secretly hoping that I will do that.'

'Maybe or it might upset him.'

'I wouldn't want to do that. Heaven knows he has enough to put up with without me making it worse. I won't do anything not just yet.'

Michael thought he should change the subject. 'Tell me what you have been doing with yourself this last week.'

'Wise to change the subject,' she smiled. 'What have I been doing? Not a great deal. Two visits to see my mother-in-law and the rest of my time is spent working.'

'How is that doing?'

'Very well. To be honest I don't know how I would have survived without it. Oh, I almost forgot, I did have another outing. My agent wanted to see me and we met in the Parkside Hotel in Broughty Ferry for morning coffee. Adam, his name is Adam Silver, is such a nice man, I am very fond of him and he is so helpful.' She looked over at him. 'I am so lucky to have him as my agent.'

Michael felt a stab of pure jealousy and was immediately ashamed. Surely he shouldn't grudge Felicity her friends. The more she had the better.

'This Adam will be looking after your interests?'

'Yes, he does. Adam is very good at explaining and I understand him perfectly.'

'Why shouldn't you?'

'Because Tim always made me out to be hopeless. Anyone with any artistic talent must have their head in the clouds.'

'Not in your case.'

'Thank you. I used to think I was pretty useless about money matters because if you are told that often enough you start to believe it.'

'Not you?' He was laughing.

'Yes, me. That has all changed. I feel a lot more worldly now that I am doing some serious work or it may have something to do with what has happened.' She paused. 'Adam doesn't know about Tim.'

'No reason why he should, is there?'

'It can be a little awkward and I do have to watch what I am saying. I mean, he asked me to bring my husband along to a function and he was a bit put out when I said it was out of the question and qualified that with saying it wouldn't interest him or words to that effect.'

'Making it worse.'

'Yes. He hasn't said anything more about it.'

'So you can relax,' he smiled.

'I hope so.'

He leaned forward to touch her hand. 'Do you find it easier now?'

'Michael, it has to be. There is a limit to what one can stand and after that point is reached it starts to get a little better. I keep telling myself that the worst is over and nothing could be as bad again.'

'I wondered if you would move away from the district, but I am glad you stuck it out.'

'I'm not sure that I had a choice. Apart from going to Carnoustie and living with my mother-in-law which I wasn't prepared to do, there was no place for me to go. At one point Tim did make mention about selling the house but it all seemed too much for me at the time and the matter wasn't raised again.'

He nodded and looked at the clock. 'Felicity, I think I should go now and thank you for a lovely meal.'

They both got up.

'Once again my thanks to you for all you do.'

He shook his head as though to dismiss it. 'We haven't arranged an evening. Could we do that now?'

'Michael, I don't have to go hunting for my diary and I see no point in pretence. All my evenings are free.'

'What an amazing woman you are, not many would be as honest as that.'

'Not many would have as many blank pages.' That set them both off laughing. Michael picked up his briefcase, he never left it behind in the car. 'Shall we say Tuesday of next week?'

'Yes, thank you, and I shall be delighted to make that an entry in my diary.'

'Where shall we go? Have you a preference?'

'No, Michael, you choose.'

'When it comes to evenings out my diary is similar

to yours. I'll ask around and see which are the places recommended.'

They had reached the door. 'I'm looking forward to a night out, Michael.'

'So am I.' He kissed her cheek. 'Goodbye, Felicity.

'Goodbye, Michael.'

'Remember to lock the door.'

'I won't forget.' After he had gone she double-locked it and for a moment leaned against it. She was looking forward to an evening with Michael. It was a very long time since she had had to think about what to wear for a dinner engagement.

Chapter Twenty-Four

Since she did her best work in the morning, Felicity got up at six feeling refreshed and ready to begin on her illustrations once she had the house in order. When the phone rang she was sitting in the kitchen having tea and toast. The shrill ring so early gave her a start but it wasn't nearly so alarming as it would have been during the night when every kind of disaster would have flashed before her eyes. Even so alarm bells did ring when a glance at the clock reminded her of the early hour.

'Hello,' she said hesitantly.

'Mrs Morrison, it's Rita Haggarty.'

Felicity's heart missed a beat and her mouth went dry. 'My mother-in-law, something has happened.' She pulled over a chair and sat down. Her legs had gone weak.

'I'm afraid it is bad news. Mrs Morrison died during the night.'

'But — but she was fine yesterday,' Felicity stammered.

'Seemed that way to me too. She went to bed at her usual time and made no complaint.'

'When did you—' She couldn't go on.

'Find her? You know how I always go into her bedroom before I get dressed just to check that she is ready for her early-morning cup' – a tremor reached her voice – 'at first I thought she was asleep and then when I went nearer I knew she wasn't. I phoned the doctor right away and then I phoned you.'

'How awful for you, Mrs Haggarty.'

'It was a shock. I've seen death before but it still gives you a queer feeling. Did the phone waken you?'

'No, I'm up and dressed. Mrs Haggarty, I'll be with you just as soon as I possibly can.'

'Don't you be rushing and coming to grief. I've been looking out at the weather and that mist doesn't look like lifting. Remember, lass, she's gone and rushing here isn't going to alter that. Mind that isn't to say I won't be glad to see you but I am perfectly capable of seeing to things until you arrive. The doctor hasn't far to come – oh, that's the doorbell, it'll be him. I'll have to go.' The phone clattered down.

Felicity knew she was in shock and for the moment incapable of clear thought and that rushing about in the state she was in was pointless. She would be better to sit down and try to finish her tea and toast and then decide what had to be done and in what order. Picking up the cup she drank some of the lukewarm tea but found she couldn't face the toast. It went in the bin. Next she cleared the table and left the dirty dishes on the draining board. An overnight bag, she would need that. Better to be prepared. Should it be expected of her to stay longer, and it very well might, then she could come back to Hillhead for a change of clothes. Thank goodness she had been to the bank and there was money in her purse. She stopped suddenly. How awful, for a few minutes she had actually forgotten about Tim. Tim who should by right have been the first to be informed of his mother's death. Somehow she had to get that news to him and it shouldn't be a problem. She could phone the prison and ask to be put through to the governor. Only she might not be put through to him and have to give the information to someone else. That someone might be sympathetic or there again he might not. Poor Tim, he was going to be devastated when he heard. What should she do? What would be best? She could go and see Tim herself and break it to him gently. No, she didn't think she was up to that. Michael would know what to do. Michael her saviour. The poor man must wish he had never got himself involved.

So much to think about and she was dithering. That wouldn't do, she had to concentrate. First she would pack her bag and get herself ready then she would check the windows. There was no milkman to worry about, she had stopped the delivery and bought only what she needed. The newspapers would continue to come but that didn't matter, they would go through the letterbox and land on the floor. She wouldn't be gone all that long.

Mrs Haggarty had warned her about the mist and it was bad here. Felicity reversed the car out of the garage then got out to close the doors. The cold dampness went right through her, warm coat and all, and she shivered. This was the kind of weather she hated, the sky overcast and the clouds heavy, as if ready to unleash a downpour. Felicity disliked driving with the windscreen wipers going and hearing that irritating whirring noise they made. She sat well forward in her seat and peered into the patchy mist that hung over the fields drifting in and out of the wet hedges. Being so early in the morning traffic was light which made for easier driving.

The journey seemed to take for ever and she gave a sob of relief when she turned the car into the cul-de-sac and then through the gate and up to the house. Mrs Haggarty must have been watching for her arrival and had the door open. They were both unable to speak for a few moments and clasped hands in sympathy.

Mrs Haggarty was the first to recover. Her face was white.

'I'm that glad to see you. I was fine, then I suppose it was the reaction setting in.'

'I got here as quickly as I could.'

'I know. I know. I didn't want you hurrying.'

'The doctor—'

'That was his ring at the door when we were talking on the phone. He was very kind. Her heart wasn't strong and it just gave out. He did say that Mrs Morrison wouldn't have suffered.'

'We have to be thankful for that.'

'Come into the kitchen—'

'I must make some phone calls.'

'Another few minutes won't make any difference. The kettle is on the boil and I am sure you could do with a cup of tea or maybe you would prefer something stronger?'

'No. No, thank you. A cup of tea would be welcome.' Felicity couldn't control the shiver.

'I've the heating on but it still feels cold.'

Felicity knew what she meant. It had been the same when her own mother had died. When death was in the house there was a chill that no amount of heating removed.

There was a telephone in the hall and one in the morning room.

'Don't be doing your phoning from the hall, even with that sausage thing at the door it doesn't keep the draught out.'

'I know they don't do much good. I'll use the morning room.' After a cup of tea and a biscuit Felicity went along the hall and opened the door of the room where her mother-in-law had spent so many hours of her day. The sight of the empty chair brought a lump to her throat. Only now did she begin to feel her own personal loss. There would be a blank in her life that would be difficult to fill.

Felicity phoned Paton & Noble and gave the extension number of Michael's office. She was prepared to speak to Michael's secretary but it was he who took the call.

'Michael, I do apologise for troubling you during office hours and I hope this isn't too inconvenient.'

'Do stop apologising, Felicity. Knowing you this is important or you wouldn't be calling.'

'Tim's mother died in her sleep.'

'I am sorry to hear that.'

'Her housekeeper phoned to tell me—'

'Felicity, where are you speaking from?'

'Carnoustie. I've just arrived.'

'You are not going to be there on your own?'

'No. Mrs Haggarty is a live-in housekeeper. As usual I need your advice. Should I phone the prison governor or go there myself and tell Tim. Michael, he is going to be so terribly upset and I can't bear the thought of him hearing the news from someone who – who—'

'Felicity,' he interrupted gently, 'it won't be like that. The prison padre will break the news to Tim.'

'Do I phone the governor?'

'You could do that but I suggest that I phone on your behalf.'

'I can't ask you to do that,' she said protestingly.

'You haven't asked, I offered.'

'It would be enormously helpful if you would but I am already so much in your debt.'

'There is no debt just a helping hand from a friend and as to my work don't worry about that. It is important, it is my living, but it is not all important. What I can't do today will hopefully be done tomorrow.'

'Michael, you are always so calm, you never get into a flap.'

'I try not to since it is so much energy wasted. I have a notepad here and you can give me your Carnoustie address and telephone number.'

She did that.

'Once we are through talking I will get in touch with the governor who in turn will contact the padre. They do occasionally have to deal with this kind of thing and the correct procedure is laid down. It could be that Tim would want to see you and if so I shall take you there myself and then leave you. On second thoughts it would be better if you took your own car and followed me.'

'Michael, I do know how to get there. It is the next bit that worries me.'

'Perfectly simple. There are people on hand to help you.'

'Of course. I've only got to ask.'

'That's right.'

'I think I should go, don't you?'

'That has to be your decision, Felicity.'

'I know and it is a difficult one. When Tim gives orders he expects them to be obeyed.'

'Was it an order?'

'Most definitely it was.'

'Then don't go would be my advice.'

'There are the funeral arangements, so much to see about.' For a moment a surge of panic overwhelmed her.

'Tim cannot be of much help to you where he is. He will expect you to take charge.'

'Will Tim be allowed out for the funeral?'

'Yes, almost certainly he will.'

'The press – will they make the connection?'

'That is always possible but highly improbable I would have thought. Still you can't be too careful. My advice for what it is worth.'

'Please, it is important to me.'

'Unless you consider it necessary I would suggest you did not put the death in the newspaper until after the funeral. The fewer people who know about the death the better and the less chance there is of a photographer appearing on the scene.'

'I hadn't thought of that – surely they wouldn't – at a time like that.'

'Tim being out for his mother's funeral would be news. After the funeral you could put a small notice in the deaths column on the lines that the funeral took place of the late—'

'Maud Morrison,' Felicity supplied. 'Thank you, Michael, that is very helpful.'

'Is there family to notify?'

'No. There are several cousins scattered around the country but no one she kept up with.'

'That certainly makes it easier. Felicity, I had better ring off now and get in touch with the governor. When I have something to report I'll be in touch.'

'Thank you, Michael, thank you very much.'

She replaced the receiver, and felt as though a load had been taken off her shoulders. She pressed her fingers to her brow. Joanna was next. She would phone Perth and ask to speak to Rachel first.

Rachel sounded breezy. 'Felicity, is this to say we can expect a visit from you?'

'I wish it were that but sadly it will have to be postponed. Tim's mother is dead, Rachel. She died very suddenly.'

'Oh, I am sorry to hear that and you must be very upset.'

'I am. You know I was talking to her yesterday,' she said brokenly. 'I can still hardly believe it.'

'Where are you? At home?'

'No, in Carnoustie. Mrs Haggarty is here with me. I thought I should tell you before I broke it to Joanna.'

'Poor lass, this on top of everything else.'

'I know and this is going to upset her terribly. She got on very well with her grandmother.'

'Before I go and find her how would it be if I drove Joanna to Carnoustie and left her there with you?'

'I appreciate the thought, Rachel, but to be honest I think Joanna is better where she is. Mrs Haggarty is very capable and she will help me.'

'You could be right and since you are not alone. I'm reluctant to ask this but what about Tim?'

'Michael is arranging for him to be told. The padre does that.'

'Good. It needs someone with training to handle it.'

'I wish I could be with Tim at a time like this

but I am reluctant to go and maybe upset him further.'

'Stay away. If he wants to see you he knows he has only to say so. Hang on, I see Joanna.'

Joanna was handed the phone. 'Mum, great to hear your voice. When are you coming?'

'Joanna, I have bad news.'

'What is it?' she faltered.

'Darling, your gran died very suddenly.'

'No.' There was a wail of distress. 'Not Gran, please, not Gran.'

'Joanna, she didn't suffer, she just slipped away in her sleep. It was a peaceful end.'

'I'll never see her again.' She was weeping.

'We are going to miss her terribly but she would be the first to say that mourning has its place but life must go on.'

'That doesn't make it any easier,' she sniffed.

'You have to be brave.'

'Where are you? At home or in Gran's house?'

'I'm in Carnoustie. Mrs Haggarty phoned to tell me and I went there or rather I came here right away.'

'What about – what about Dad?'

'The padre will break the news to your father.'

'Will he be allowed out to see to everything?'

'He will be allowed out to attend the funeral. Michael – Mr Lawson said there would be no problem about that. I imagine I will be seeing to the arrangements.'

'You'll go and see him?'

'I don't know so much about that.'

'In your place I would just go.'

'You aren't in my place so you can't possibly know,' she said letting annoyance creep into her voice.

'Sorry — it's just that I feel strange—'

'Joanna, if there is something worrying you tell me.'

'I've never been to a funeral and I suppose I'm a bit scared.' That wasn't strictly true. She was uncomfortable at the thought of seeing and having to talk to her father. If she could get out of going to the funeral she would, but there again if she didn't attend her mother would be upset. She would be looking for some support from her daughter.

'There is nothing to be scared about, believe me it isn't the ordeal you imagine, Joanna. I can't say for sure but I think your father would want a short service in the house and that would be all.'

'Will neighbours and friends come to the house?'

'I don't think so.'

'Because of Dad?'

'They will think it better to stay away. I know that is what I would do.'

'Poor Gran, it just makes everything awful.'

'You are not to say that, Joanna,' Felicity said sharply. 'It is not going to be awful at all.'

'For Dad it has to be.'

'All the more reason for us to be supportive.'

'Will someone be with him?'

Surely she didn't think her father would be in handcuffs.

'He can be trusted, your father isn't likely to make a run for it,' she said more sharply than she intended.

'I didn't mean that.'

'No, you didn't and I'm sorry. These are difficult times and I don't think I am coping very well.'

'You are, Mum. You are. I'm the one being impossible but I don't seem able to help it.'

'It's all right, dear, we'll get over this just as we have got over everything else.' She didn't think they had. How could they? Their lives had been turned upside down.

'How long will you be staying in Carnoustie?'

'I don't know, I'll have to go home for some clothes but I'll keep you informed. Joanna, I should ring off now.'

'Before you do, was Mrs Haggarty the one to find Gran?'

'Yes.'

'That must have been awful for her but worse if it had been you. I mean Mrs Haggarty isn't family.'

'That is true but I am very glad of her I can tell you.'

'I should be with you.'

'No, darling, you are better where you are.'

'You will phone or shall I?'

'Leave it to me and now I must go.'

'Goodbye, Mum, I'll be thinking of you.'

'You should be thinking of your dad too.'

'I'll try.'

Felicity put the phone down and went in search of Mrs Haggarty. She was in the kitchen.

'That's Joanna told.'

'Took it badly did she?'

'Yes, they were very close.' She paused. 'I'm at a loss. I don't know what I should be doing.'

'The undertaker sees to everything, Mrs Morrison, and if he is unsure of anything he will ask. As regards the catering—'

'Catering,' she said faintly.

'In a small way. Once the funeral is arranged if you could give me some idea about numbers – not everyone comes back to the house from the cemetery but it is as well to be prepared. I'll arrange for tea and sandwiches and I'll be there to do the serving if that is what you want.'

'Yes, please. The funeral is to be private and I don't expect many to attend.'

'Have you notified the newspaper?'

She really should have told Mrs Haggarty before this. 'No, I am not going to. There will be something after the funeral,' she said vaguely.

'I see.'

'We think it best,' she said by way of explanation.

'I'm sure that is the sensible thing to do, Mrs Morrison. Have you done all your phoning?'

'One more and I think that should do.'

'You are getting there, just take it easy.'

'Yes. Things are clearer, my brain is beginning to function,' she said wanly.

'I'll go upstairs and see about the bed in the guest room. It will need fresh sheets and pillowcases and I don't know about you but I like a bit of weight with the bedclothes. Two blankets and a quilt should do you but there will be an extra blanket on top of the wardrobe should you need it.'

'I don't think so, but thank you.'

The woman bustled away and Felicity picked up the phone. She had almost forgotten about Adam and he might want to get in touch. If he wasn't available she would leave a message with his wife. The number was ringing out.

'Hello.'

'Mrs Silver?'

'Yes, speaking.'

'Felicity Morrison here.'

'Hello, Mrs Morrison, you are in luck. The man himself is around, I'll go and give him a shout.'

Felicity smiled. For her that conjured up a couple completely at ease with each other and a happy home. She heard voices, the thud of heavy, hurrying feet on the stairs then the phone was lifted.

'Felicity?'

'Hello, Adam, I'm phoning to let you know I'll be away from home for a few days.'

'A short holiday and a much deserved rest?'

'No, Adam, a family bereavement. My mother-in-law died very suddenly.'

'How sad, I'm sorry to hear that.'

'She was a lovely lady, Adam, and I am going to miss her so much.'

'Are you in your own house?'

'No, I'm in Carnoustie, that is where she lived.'

'I seem to remember you mentioning that.'

'As yet there are no definite arrangements but I would expect to be here until after the funeral.'

'This has got to be a strain so do look after yourself, Felicity.' She heard the concern in his voice and the familiar lump was back in her throat. People were kind and it showed at times like this.

'My mother-in-law's housekeeper is a very capable person and she has more or less taken control for which I am deeply grateful. Adam, as regards my illustrations—'

'As regards work, my dear Felicity, you will not give it a thought. Heavens, you have been working like a Trojan and you richly deserve to take a rest from it.'

'Thank you. Everyone is being so kind,' she said unsteadily.

'People care about you, that is why. I wish there was something I could do but all I can do is look after your interests at this end.'

'Which is a huge help believe me.' And it was, she thought, it could be her livelihood. 'Once I'm home I'll ring you.'

'I'll look forward to that.'

Adam replaced the phone and stood for a moment looking thoughtful. Not once had Felicity mentioned her husband and it was his mother who had died. But was that so surprising with her husband in prison. Poor Felicity, it was a crying shame. Why was it that the nicest people were made to suffer? Where was the fairness in life? How many others had asked the same question knowing there was no answer.

'Is everything all right, Adam?' his wife said curiously.

'Yes, dear, everything is fine. I was just thinking.' He smiled. 'Felicity is having a few days off, that is what she was phoning about.'

'Is that all? You had me worried for a moment.'

He would never say a word about Felicity's husband being in prison. The secret would be safe with Lilian but, even so, that knowledge was better kept to himself. Felicity had to be protected.

Chapter Twenty-Five

On the morning of the funeral a car drew up at Grange House and a tall man wearing a dark suit got out. He was very pale and for a few moments he stood quite still and looked about him. Then he squared his shoulders and walked up to the front door which was open. Before he stepped inside the man looked back and hid a smile as he watched the driver of the car having to make several attempts at the difficult turning before driving out of the cul-de-sac. Tim had his hand on the knob of the glass door when it opened and Felicity stood there.

It was a difficult moment, neither knowing quite what was expected.

'Tim?' How pale he looked, she thought, was that what they meant when they talked of prison pallor?

'Felicity.'

They each took a step forward and embraced awkwardly. Like a couple out of practice which, she supposed, was what they were.

'How are you, Tim?' she said quietly.

He shrugged dismissing the question. 'I can't believe she has gone, I can't take it in.'

'Nor me. It was the suddenness.' Felicity closed the glass door. 'You could do with a cup of tea.'

'I could do with something stronger which I shall get for myself.' The master taking charge on his return, she couldn't help thinking. 'I take it that everything is in its usual place?' He raised his eyebrows waiting for an answer.

'Nothing has been changed,' Felicity said quietly.

'Good.' He went ahead and she followed.

This was awful. She had expected it to be difficult but not like this. Complete strangers would have been more at ease.

Tim was wearing the dark business suit he had worn on the morning he left home. The white shirt had been freshly laundered and the tie was quiet. When Felicity had returned to the house for clothes for herself she had packed a case for Tim. She put in one of his dark suits together with a white shirt, gold cuff links, black tie and black shoes. On the point of closing the case she suddenly remembered underwear and socks. The black socks took a bit of finding, they were at the back of the drawer.

Felicity watched Tim take out the whisky bottle and saw his hand shake as he poured the amber liquid into a glass. He took a drink.

'I needed that,' he said, sitting down and then getting up again as though he couldn't settle.

'Yes, I'm sure you did. This is an ordeal for us all but especially for you.'

He nodded.

She had to go so carefully, think before she spoke, in case she said the wrong thing.

'This isn't important, dear, but I brought a black tie—'

'Thank you.' He fingered the one he was wearing. 'I'll change this.'

'I brought a suit and underwear from the house—'

'No, I won't bother. The tie though, I'm glad you thought of a black tie.'

So was she. 'Shall we go into the sitting-room?'

'Is there anyone there?'

'No.'

'What about Joanna – isn't she here?'

'Yes, I think she might be upstairs.'

'Avoiding me, I suppose.'

'No, not at all. Joanna is very upset about her gran and when she feels weepy she goes upstairs.'

He nodded, accepting the explanation or appearing to do so. Picking up his whisky glass they left the dining-room. The furniture had been rearranged in the sitting-room with the chairs over against the wall. There was a table at the far end of the room covered with a stiffly starched white tablecloth. That for some reason seemed to unnerve him.

'Why all this?' he said harshly.

'Just ourselves, Tim,' she said soothingly. 'No one is expected. It will only be the minister, your mother's solicitor and ourselves. Mrs Haggarty offered to take charge of the refreshments and I left it to her. She said it was always safer to provide extra food in case it should be required. If people come we can't turn them away.'

'No one should just turn up. Michael said there would be nothing in the newspaper until after the funeral.'

'I know and I went along with that.'

'Some of the neighbours will know but hopefully they will do the decent thing and not turn up,' he said bitterly.

She swallowed hard. Tim sat down and she took a chair half facing him.

'Tim, I wanted to break the news to you myself. I loved your mother and we could have shared our grief. It is so hurtful of you not to want me especially at a time like this.'

'Let me put the record straight. I have never at any time said that I didn't want you. All I said and I thought I had made it perfectly clear, was that I didn't want you or Joanna visiting me in prison. Visiting someone in prison is a shameful experience. You should be thanking me.'

'Should I?'

'This is a part of my life I want to keep separate, can't you understand that?'

'I am beginning to.'

'Joanna has never written to me,' he said accusingly as though Felicity were to blame for that.

'No, she hasn't but then neither have you written to her.'

'That was because I didn't want to put Joanna in a position where she would feel obliged to reply.'

'I can't help thinking that you are going out of your way to make this harder for yourself.'

'If I am that is my business.' He suddenly sounded very weary and drew a hand over his brow. 'Better get it over. Tell Joanna to come down, that I want to see her. And, Felicity, on our own if you don't mind.'

'I don't mind in the least.' Felicity got up and left the room. Joanna wasn't in the bedroom and neither was she in the bathroom, the door was wide open. She hurried downstairs and along to the kitchen. 'Mrs Haggarty, have you seen Joanna?'

'She's out. I thought we might be short of milk and Joanna offered to go to the shops. My fault, I should have asked the milkman to leave extra but it completely escaped my memory.'

'That's all right, the walk in the fresh air will do her good.' Felicity's eyes filled with tears and she turned away but not quickly enough.

'Lass, I've upset you. Joanna won't be long – I could have gone myself.'

'No. No. You have enough to do. That isn't what is upsetting me. Sometimes I'm crying and I don't know it.' She did know what she was crying about. No matter how hard she tried she didn't seem able to please Tim.

'The build-up of the last few days, that's what it

is. Once today is over you will feel different. Your husband . . .' she said uncertainly.

'He is bearing up wonderfully, Mrs Haggarty,' she said coming in quickly. She had no idea what Mrs Haggarty was about to say but she didn't want to hear it.

The back door opened. 'Here she is.'

Joanna handed over the milk. Then she took off her coat and with a smile for her mother went ahead to hang it up on the hallstand. Felicity followed her.

'Your dad is in the sitting-room, he wants to see you.'

Joanna's face went suddenly white. 'No, not yet, I'm not ready.'

'Don't be silly. He is your father and he hasn't changed.'

'Maybe I have though.'

'It will be all right.'

'Will you come?'

'I'll give you a few minutes on your own, then I'll come in. We will have to think about a bite to eat. I'll go and give Mrs Haggarty a hand.'

Felicity watched her daughter take a deep breath then walk to the sitting-room. When the door was shut she walked away.

Tim was on his feet as soon as his daughter came in. She wasn't smiling, she looked apprehensive.

'I won't bite,' he said with a half smile.

Her expression didn't change. If her father was

expecting a hug and a kiss he was disappointed. She sat down and a moment later he did too.

'How – how are you?' she said.

'Bearing up, I suppose you could say. And you, Joanna, how are you?'

'OK.'

'It hasn't been that long but you look more grown-up.'

'Is that so surprising?' she said harshly.

'You sound very bitter.'

'That is because I am bitter.' She paused. 'You look thinner.'

'Do I?'

'Probably the food is so awful that you don't take much of it.'

'The food, as it happens, is passable which is more than can be said for the serving up. When I gain my freedom I hope never to see a plastic dish again.' He laughed and it had a strange sound in that house of sadness.

'Poor Dad. If you hadn't been so well brought up it wouldn't have been so bad for you.' She gulped. 'I keep thinking of her – of my gran. I wish I had gone to see her more often. I wish—' she choked and stopped.

'Your regrets are nothing compared to mine.'

Her handkerchief was in a ball in her hands. 'Why did you do something so awful?' she blurted. 'You've spoiled Mum's life and you've ruined mine.'

He flinched.

'Nothing is ever what it seems.'

'A useless statement,' she said scornfully. 'A husband and wife are not supposed to have secrets from one another.'

'Everyone has secrets.'

'Not that kind.'

'Perhaps not,' he said wearily. 'Do you hate me, Joanna?'

Could she hurt him more than he already was? He was suffering, she could see that, but then they all were. No, she had no sympathy to spare, it was a time for the truth and the question had come from him.

'What I feel is something very close to hatred.'

'I find that harsh, hurtful and sad.'

'Do you now? Well that's too bad. I am not going to apologise for telling the truth.' She swallowed painfully. 'We – we shouldn't be having this kind of conversation, not today of all days.' She shivered. It was as though she could feel her grandmother's presence.

'No, you are quite right we shouldn't be talking like this.' He paused and moved restlessly in the chair. 'You disappointed me by not going back to university.'

'Not according to Mum.'

'That was because I didn't want to appear to be taking sides. I said to leave you to make your own mistakes.'

'It doesn't matter, university was never all that important to me. I let you and Mum talk me into it.'

'Is What's-his-name, Stuart, still a part of your life?'

'No,' she said shortly.

'My fault? If so, I'm sorry.'

She stared at him. 'You have the nerve to ask if it is your fault. Yes, it is. You have ruined my life. And don't get it all wrong, Stuart did not walk out on me, I did it to him as a favour. His parents, if I am any judge of character, would disown him if he were to continue to see me. I couldn't do that to him.'

Felicity came in then and seeing their set faces thought that Joanna must be giving him a hard time. There was a lot of her grandmother in Joanna.

'Sorry to interrupt but I think we should have a bite to eat and then it will be time to get ready.'

'Of course.' Tim was on his feet and made for the door. Joanna followed but slowly.

The minister, a tall thin man with a scholarly stoop and kind eyes came to the house and gave a short but moving service. Tim sat between Felicity and Joanna. Felicity saw her husband fighting for control and reached for his hand. He squeezed her fingers. It was the nearest they had come to comforting one another. Joanna was weeping into her handkerchief. The solicitor sat alone and Mrs Haggarty, the only one in deep mourning, occupied a chair near to the door. Maud, Felicity remembered, had never been in favour of black, not everybody suited it she had said and navy or grey were perfectly acceptable. Felicity wore dark grey and Joanna wore the black skirt she wore in reception with a white blouse.

As was the custom, only the men went to the cemetery. At the graveside they were joined by Maud Morrison's gardener. The man was invited back to the house for a refreshment but he declined.

At Grange House the ladies waited for the return of the men. When they arrived looking cold they sat down to tea and sandwiches served by Mrs Haggarty. There was a decanter of whisky and glasses on a side table for those who desired a stronger drink. The minister would have liked a dram. He had no quarrel with alcohol but he had a church meeting to attend and sadly he had no peppermints in his pocket. The solicitor did not approve of strong drink.

The minister was the first to depart and when he did Mrs Haggarty, quickly and carefully cleared the food from the table and Maud's best china. Tim watched until she had completed the task and closed the door behind her, then he took charge.

'I think we should go through to the dining-room and use the table there,' he said, looking at the elderly man who for many years had been his mother's solicitor.

Mr Gerald Hamilton nodded his agreement and lifted his briefcase from the floor at his feet. Joanna looked bewildered and Felicity took her arm and led her from the room.

The solicitor sat on a high-backed dining-room chair behind a handsome mahogany table. Tim, Felicity and Joanna sat facing him. In the silence he opened his briefcase and took out some papers. After adjusting his spectacles Mr Hamilton began to read the Last Will and Testament of the late Maud Beatrice Morrison. He began with the bequests, there were three. Maud had remembered the church, her gardener, Henry Holmes and Mrs Rita Haggarty.

'Should I ask Mrs Haggarty to come in?'

Tim shook his head and the solicitor said hastily, 'No, Mrs Morrison, that won't be necessary. Mr Holmes and Mrs Haggarty will be informed by letter.'

Felicity felt foolish. She had been under the impression that those mentioned in a Will were entitled to be present and were then required to remove themselves before the rest of the Will was read. Maybe there was no set rule about these things.

Mr Hamilton cleared his throat. 'The Will is perfectly straightforward.' Again he cleared his throat and Felicity was beginning to wonder if she should offer to bring a glass of water but no, he was fine, he had started to read.

'To my son Timothy, I bequeath two thirds of my estate and the remaining one third to be shared equally between my daughter-in-law Felicity and my granddaughter, Joanna.'

Felicity drew in her breath sharply. She hadn't expected anything like that. Perhaps a piece of jewellery but no more. As for Joanna, she thought there would be a small legacy from her grandmother.

The documents went back into the briefcase and the solicitor was on his feet. He shook hands with Felicity and then Joanna. Tim walked with him to the door and after a few minutes' chat they shook hands and the solicitor took his leave.

Mrs Haggarty had been busy. The sitting-room furniture was back in its usual place apart from the table which she couldn't manage to move on her own.

Tim's eyes kept moving to the clock. She heard his sigh. 'One more hour of freedom.' He gave a rueful smile. 'I could make a run for it but I won't. All the same I can understand why some are tempted and take a chance.'

'Oh, Tim,' Felicity said wretchedly.

'Mum, don't look so worried. Dad wouldn't be so daft.'

'What you really mean is your father wouldn't have the guts and you would be right.' He got up. 'I'll go and freshen up.' When he came down he handed Felicity the black tie. 'About Grange House, Felicity – it will have to go on the market some time but I would want to—'

'Decide what you want to keep?'

'Yes. A lot of what is here is junk which can go out.'

'Tim, I don't want the responsibility. It isn't for me to decide what should be kept. Why not leave things as they are until you are available?'

He frowned. 'Who would look after the house?'

'I'm fairly sure that Mrs Haggarty would be agreeable to coming in one day a week to give a dust and see that all is well.'

'And the gardener could carry on as before?'

'Yes. Once in a while I would pop over.'

'That seems satisfactory.'

When there was the sound of a car stopping Tim went quickly to the window.

'That is my transport more or less up to time.' He kissed Felicity and she saw that there was a film of moisture on his brow. 'Take care,' he said.

'You too.'

He waited for Joanna to make the move and she did. Her arms went round his neck. 'Maybe I'll manage to write a few lines. If I do, do I take it that you will reply?'

'I can promise that. Don't come to the door, I'll see myself out. Then he was gone.

Joanna looked anguished. 'Mum, I was horrid to him.'

'If you were he has forgiven you. Are you serious about writing?'

'Yes, I think I am.'

Felicity left it there. Shortly after ten o'clock mother and daughter retired to the guest room with its twin beds. Joanna talked well into the night, it was as though she couldn't stop herself. Felicity longed for her to be quiet so that she could get some sleep but forced herself to stay awake.

'Mum, were you surprised that Gran didn't leave everything to Dad?'

'I felt sure she would remember you.'

'Didn't you expect anything at all?'

'A keepsake, a piece of jewellery, something like that.'

427

'Dad was a bit shocked, I could see that, but he hid it well.'

'I didn't notice.'

'He is going to need money. Dad isn't going to get another job in a hurry. I mean who would want to employ someone with a prison record?'

'You can be very outspoken.'

'Only to you. If he gets something, say down south, will you go with him?'

'Of course.'

'Sell the house and just go.'

'The house will be sold.'

'Once you have somewhere to go.'

'I suppose so.' She yawned.

'You are lucky, Mum.'

'I hadn't noticed.'

'I mean with the work you do. Your job goes with you, so it doesn't matter where you live. You know what I think?'

'No, but you are going to tell me.'

'I think Gran was worried with Dad being sacked from his job that he might do something else foolish and lose his money.'

'Perhaps.'

'She liked you and she would want to know that you were taken care of. Not that you are in any great need, not the way your illustrations are taking off.'

'That may not last.'

'Of course it will. Good illustrators are always in demand.'

'You seem to know a lot about it.'

'With an about-to-be famous mother I made it my business to find out,' she said smugly.

'Good night, dear, I really would like to get to sleep.'

'Poor Dad, I bet he isn't sleeping. I bet he is lying wide awake and thinking.'

'Joanna, please.'

'OK. I'm snuggling down. Good night, Mum.'

'Good night, dear.'

Chapter Twenty-Six

The day's work was over and Joanna and Rachel were relaxing in the sitting-room. Joanna was sitting on the white sheepskin rug and Rachel was lounging on the sofa. An open box of chocolates was an arm's length away on the low table.

'Joanna, go on have another, you don't have to watch your weight.'

'I shouldn't but I think I will.' Joanna licked her lips and took her time before selecting one. Then after taking a tiny bite she looked to see what was in it. 'Strawberry cream — yum, yum.' She closed her eyes in ecstasy.

'Must you?' Rachel said in a pained voice.

'Just checking to see how strong-willed you are.'

'What a little monster I have here.' Rachel snatched the box, put the lid on and pushed it well back on the table. She was smiling and thinking how she would miss these evenings with Joanna when the girl decided it was time to go.

'Aunt Rachel, I've been thinking.'

'Have you?'

'I've been doing a lot of it.'

'Then it has to be serious.'

'It's about Stuart.'

'I thought it might be.'

'I have to remember that he did write and he went to no end of bother to get the letter to me.'

'That is so.'

'And I was wondering—' She stopped.

'You were wondering if you should reply. You can't make up your mind.'

'I'm scared it would seem like a climb-down?'

'It needn't. You are merely acknowledging his letter.'

'He'll think I haven't been in a hurry.'

'Neither you have, but that isn't a bad thing. You weren't going to rush.'

'What do you really think I should do? I would value your advice.'

'Follow your heart.'

Joanna smiled. 'I like the sound of that. What made you say it?'

'Because it is what you should do. I can still remember what it was like to be young and in love and how awful everything seemed when things went wrong.'

'Did something like this happen to you? No, it couldn't.'

'No, not like that.'

'Something happened though?'

'Yes.'

'I shouldn't be asking you this, Mum would be furious.'

'Furious with you if you asked me what?'

'Asked you about Terence. Are you in love with him?'

'Am I in love with Terence?' Rachel seemed to be giving the matter some consideration. 'No, I don't think so but he is very important in my life.'

'You do like him a lot?'

'I adore the man,' she smiled.

'He loves you.'

'How would you know that?'

'Because of the way he looks at you when you are not aware of it.'

'What a very observant goddaughter I have. Thank you, dear, that is rather nice to know.'

'That time you were speaking of . . .'

'You mean when something went wrong in my love life,' she laughed.

'Yes and I bet it wasn't funny. How old were you?'

'About the age you are now which is why I brought the matter up.'

'What happened? Was it just a silly quarrel and both of you too proud to apologise and make up?'

'No, it wasn't a silly quarrel. It was a small matter about not telling me he was married.'

Joanna looked shocked. 'How terrible for you, Aunt Rachel.'

'It was.'

'Were you heartbroken when you discovered he had been deceiving you?'

'Darling child, I was devastated. It was like my whole world was collapsing about me.' She paused to take up a more comfortable position on the sofa. 'Philip was a lot older than me which was a big attraction. He was a real man about town and I was thrilled to bits to think he was interested in me.'

'Tell me what he looked like?'

'Tall, good-looking, very polished and utterly charming.'

Joanna made a face. 'I would have run a mile from someone like that. Stuart isn't in the least bit handsome.' She made it sound as though that was a feather in his cap.

'How did you get to know he was married?'

'He gave me that information himself. He could see I was getting serious and that had him worried. Men like Philip, and there are quite a few, enjoy a fling with a wide-eyed innocent. To them it is just a bit of fun and if someone should take it seriously then that someone is dropped like a hot brick. They are not going to risk their marriage.'

'They don't care about leaving the poor girl heartbroken?'

'Philip was full of apologies which didn't mean a thing.'

'Did it take you long to get over him?'

'For a couple of weeks I wept into my pillow, then anger took over. Anger at myself for being such an idiot. The humiliation, that was the bad part, I felt such a fool and I hated people feeling sorry for me or at least pretending to be. More than likely they thought I should have known better. Their sympathy would be with the man's poor wife and rightly so.'

Joanna nodded.

'A lesson if nothing else. It made me wary about future relationships.'

'I'm glad it didn't put you off completely,' she grinned.

'Cheeky girl. What I had mistaken for love was infatuation with an older man experienced in flattering gullible young girls.'

'You wouldn't make the same mistake twice.'

'No and I wasn't looking for a serious attachment because by then my sights were set on making a success of my life and a husband would have been in the way.'

Joanna was curious. 'Have you any regrets?'

'No, I can honestly say I haven't. The life I chose suits me. That said I do enjoy male company and let me tell you there are many occasions when to have a presentable escort is a great advantage. Better service, better everything.'

Joanna was enjoying this. 'Enter Terence.'

'Yes, enter Terence. There are no disapproving glances when Terence and I are seen together. He is a widower as I may have mentioned and I am a single woman.'

'You want it kept to friendship whereas Terence—'

'Is perfectly happy with things as they are. He has a family, Joanna. Two sons and a daughter. One son works in London and the other is abroad. Neither of them would have any objections to their father remarrying. Not so Morag. She would go to pieces.'

'Surely not.'

'Where her father is concerned, Morag is very possessive. He is her whole world.'

'Something wrong there, she sounds a bit barmy to me.'

'She isn't barmy I assure you and up to a point I can understand and sympathise with her. You see, Joanna, Morag had just finished school when her mother died. There was no question about her going on to university, she wasn't in the least academic. She is clever with her hands and she was very keen to stay at home and look after the house. Needless to say someone would come in to do the heavy work.'

'Terence went along with it?'

'On the face of it yes. The poor man didn't know what to do for the best. He was mourning the loss of a wife and the family was heartbroken at losing their mother. Terence was advised to let Morag stay at home, that if it didn't work out he could make other arrangements.'

'She was coping,' Joanna said not without admiration.

'Morag was doing very well indeed.'

'How old is she now?'

'Late twenties. Not over the hill by any means but

I don't recall a boyfriend in her life. There is an old school chum she keeps up with.'

'Not much of a social life.'

'Her choice and she is very content with her life.'

'What does she look like?'

'I think I would have to describe her as ordinary. You wouldn't pick her out in a crowd. Pleasant-looking but ordinary. She has a very good pair of hands and does a first-class job of looking after the house.'

'And her father?'

'Absolutely.'

'She makes a first-class job of looking after him,' Joanna laughed.

'He wouldn't do so well with me I can tell you. Possibly he knows that too.'

'Seriously, Aunt Rachel, I can see how awkward it would be for Terence to announce that he was considering marrying again. His daughter has given up a lot for him and he owes her something in return.'

'Terence sees it that way, I don't. Morag did herself a favour. She didn't want to go out in the world to make her living. She wanted to stay at home and be safe. Some females are like that, they have no confidence in themselves.'

'Keeping everything as it is suits the three of you.'

'Exactly and now not another word about me. I am going to ask the questions.'

'Fair enough.'

'Do you want Stuart back in your life? A straight answer, yes or no.'

'Yes, but—'

'No buts. You don't want to lose Stuart?'

'No.'

'In which case you must reply to his letter.'

'I see that now,' she said slowly.

'You've had time to consider.'

'I know Stuart so well. If I ignore that letter it will be the end. He won't pester me.'

'By replying you are in no way committing yourself. You are doing the polite thing and, of course, leaving the door open.'

Joanna brightened. 'That is all I am doing, leaving the door open.'

Rachel was frowning. 'Boys, young men, can be very easily hurt so don't give him false hope. That would be very cruel.'

'I'll tell him I value his friendship.'

'You could do that.'

'Then what?'

'Heavens, I don't know. If you love each other enough there will be a way through this.'

'Not if his parents have anything to do with it.'

'Stuart might not consider being estranged from his parents too high a price to pay.'

'Maybe not, but it would make me feel awful. I don't like them, I can't stand them, but I wouldn't like to be responsible for the split. And another thing, there might come a day when Stuart might regret—'

'Might. Might. Might. There might not be a tomorrow. One has to make decisions.'

'I shouldn't have to make this kind of decision,' Joanna said mutinously. 'It is all Dad's fault.'

Chapter Twenty-Seven

Michael Lawson felt he had enough on his plate without making time to visit Tim Morrison. The last few days had been hectic, added to which he had been saddled with a particularly difficult case. In the end Michael decided to go but not at his usual time.

The same young woman whose face he couldn't place was leaving the prison when he arrived and as before she was hurrying. That was the moment when it came to him where he had seen her. His mouth tightened.

When he went in was it his imagination or did Tim look uncomfortable? Sitting down he faced Tim across the table.

'Nearly didn't make it, this has been one of those awful weeks.'

'Much as I enjoy your visits you could have given it a miss. I don't want you putting yourself out.'

Michael was looking at him closely. 'You've had a visitor, haven't you?'

The eyes widened. 'Have I?'

'Come off it, Tim. I saw that young woman once before coming out of the building but couldn't place her.'

Tim was shaking his head. 'Don't know what you are talking about.'

'Then let me refresh your memory. It came to me in a flash who she is. The agency sent her, must have been that time Jean was off ill.' He frowned. 'It will come – Hilary – Hilary something.'

'Henderson,' Tim said reluctantly.

'That's it, Hilary Henderson. What is going on, Tim?' he said quietly.

'Nothing.'

'Why does she come to visit you? You are not going to deny she has been here?'

Tim shrugged. 'What if she has? If she wants to visit me, then she is at liberty to do so.'

'But not your wife and daughter – they are not at liberty to visit you.'

'That is totally different and if I may say so it is none of your damned business,' he said through clenched teeth.

'That is where you are wrong. If you recall you were quite keen that I should be the go-between and Felicity has come to depend on me for news of you.'

'We correspond. That should be enough.'

'Felicity doesn't find it very satisfactory. You don't say much in your letters.'

'There isn't much to say.'

'You are hiding something. Better to tell me what this is about.'

Tim looked utterly weary. 'You would never understand.'

'Try me.' When there was no response Michael spoke again. 'There was a lot of talk about you and Hilary Henderson.'

'I thought you were above that. I thought you didn't listen to office gossip.'

'I don't, but I am neither deaf nor blind.'

'A little harmless flirtation, that was all.'

'Is that the way Hilary saw it?'

'I thought so.'

'Only you were wrong.'

'No, I wasn't wrong. Hilary knew that I had a good marriage and she accepted that.'

'You went on seeing each other?'

'Very occasionally. I had made up my mind to end it and Hilary agreed that it would be best.'

'It didn't end?'

'It did and that is why it came as such a bombshell—' Tim was nervously gnawing at his thumb.

'She broke her word?'

'No. Hilary found that she was pregnant with my child.'

'Oh, my God!' He looked at Tim quickly. 'Could she have been trying to trick you?'

'Hilary would be incapable of doing something like that. No, she was carrying my child.'

'Are you in love with her?'

'I don't know, I might be.' He swallowed and then spoke slowly and carefully. 'She isn't what you would like to think.'

'I never suggested—'

'No, but it was in your mind. Hilary and Felicity have this in common, they are both honest, sometimes painfully honest but that aside let me go on. Hilary had a pretty rotten start in life and she is alone in the world. Her father died and her mother married someone a lot younger and the last thing she wanted was an attractive daughter hanging around.'

'The little I saw of her in the office she struck me as a very capable young woman well able to look after herself.'

'She has had to be. The trouble started when she had to leave the place where she was living. Strict rules. No children. That got her in a panic and possibly she thought I wasn't doing enough to help.'

'Were you?'

'I was half out of my mind with worry. I didn't know what to do, so I was doing nothing.' He half smiled. 'It was Hilary who brought me to my senses. She put the plain facts before me. I was to buy a house for her and the baby and, if I did that, she would make no further demands.'

'Did you believe her?'

'I did. She would keep her word, I knew that.' Tim passed a hand over his face. 'You know the Bingham Estate, those new houses going up?'

Michael nodded.

'She wanted one of those. The smallest, the two-bedroom and living-room would do her nicely.'

'Did she ask if you could afford it?'

'Hilary decided I could. She had taken the trouble to go and see where I lived and felt her demand was modest.'

'You can see her point.'

'Don't get me wrong, I didn't have a problem about paying for accommodation. What I had in mind was a rented house but she wasn't having that. It had to be the new house, bought outright and in her name. That and a few sticks of furniture. She had it all worked out.'

'And if you refused?'

A shadow crossed his face. 'She said she would have no hesitation about going to Paton & Noble and telling them she was pregnant with my child.' He paused. 'Hilary didn't expect me to lose my job but she was fairly sure that it would put paid to any hope of advancement.'

'Blackmail. Would she have gone through with it?'

'I wasn't prepared to risk it.'

'In the event, you could have let her do her worst and you would have been better off than you are now.'

'Don't I know it,' Tim said ruefully. 'As luck would have it money was a bit tight at the time. Felicity and I had spent a lot on the house and there wasn't much left in the bank.'

'Did you consider a second mortgage?'

'Michael, I considered everything. Felicity doesn't

take much interest in financial matters but a second mortgage would have taken a bit of explaining.'

'Did Hilary threaten to tell Felicity?'

'Never. She said she would never willingly break up a marriage but she knew how to hold out for what she wanted. Come to think about it Hilary would have made a good lawyer. She very badly wanted her own house, paid for and in her name.'

'That to her spelt security.'

'Yes,' Tim said heavily, 'somehow I had to find the money. Borrowing was out, it would have been too expensive, ridiculously so. My mother would have come to the rescue but she would have required an explanation and a good one.'

'Not a lady easy to hoodwink.'

'No, very shrewd and she would have insisted on Felicity knowing all about it. My wife and my mother always got on well.' He let his hands fall on to the table. 'That is the whole unhappy tale. That is how it happened, Mike, a loan until I could organise something. It was never theft.'

'If this had been out in the open—'

'I could have made it easier for myself? Possibly, but then it would have dragged in Felicity and Joanna. My mother's memory had started to go so she wasn't the big problem she might have been.'

'Don't you think if you had been honest with Felicity that she would have stood by you?'

'Yes, I think there was a good chance she would but I didn't want her to know.'

444

'Tim, that is crazy. You can't keep this hidden for all time.'

'Some manage it and up to now I have.'

'The baby?'

'Peter is a super little lad,' he said proudly.

Michael was looking at him strangely. 'How can you go on living two lives?'

'Hilary has her house, she won't make any trouble.'

'Everything is Hilary, isn't it? What about Felicity?'

'What about her?' he said impatiently.

'You have to remember that she doesn't know why you took that money and she is going to keep on wondering until she finds out for herself.'

'You are meddling in what doesn't concern you. Leave it, Mike, and I'll deal with it in my own way.'

'That isn't good enough.' He leaned forward. 'Tim, I am telling you this, if you don't tell Felicity about the baby then I will.'

Tim's face went a shade paler. 'You wouldn't do that.'

'I would, though I hope it won't come to that.'

Tim gave him a sharp look. 'I suppose I've had my suspicions about you and my wife and this goes to confirm them. You are in love with Felicity and maybe you two—'

'Watch it, Tim,' Michael said in a cold hard voice. Don't judge other people's standards by yours. You might cheat on Felicity but she would never cheat on you.'

445

'You had better go, Michael, that is time up anyway. Don't come back, you are no longer welcome.'

Michael was on his feet. 'Write and make a clean breast of it to Felicity.'

'Or you will tell her? I haven't much choice have I?'

'None at all.' He turned and walked out.

After a few minutes Tim got up slowly and walked to his cell where he did a lot of thinking. That Michael would carry out his threat he was in no doubt. And did it matter, did he really care? In a way it would be a relief to get everything out in the open. Always having to be on one's guard was very wearing. And there was another reason he hadn't reckoned on. There was Peter, his son. He couldn't just walk away, he didn't want to walk away, he wanted to see his son growing up. And that could only happen if he openly declared Peter to be his son.

Should he send for Felicity and tell her face to face? No, he couldn't do that. He would take the coward's way out and send a letter, a very carefully written letter. With his lawyer's training he would first make out a draft, get everything in its correct order before putting it in letter form.

Michael felt drained and wretched as he left the grey, forbidding building that housed the wrongdoers and walked to where he had parked his car. Had he overstepped the mark and taken too much on himself? Would Felicity thank him or would she resent his interference? Wasn't it an unwritten law that one should not interfere in a domestic dispute? Better to leave the parties to sort it out themselves. The police were always reluctant to get involved unless tempers boiled over and it became violent.

Maybe he should stay away from Felicity until he had had time to think. She would be expecting a visit from him tonight but he would wait until tomorrow or even the day after.

It was the next day when he arrived at Holmlea and parked his car at the gate. Careful thought had convinced him that he had no right to interfere. Tim had probably expected that and there would be no letter.

Felicity was her usual welcoming self. 'Michael, how nice to see you.'

'Sorry I didn't manage before but there was a bit of a panic at work and I got held up.'

'No need to apologise, it is very good of you to come and I am very grateful.'

'Coming to see you is a pleasure and it is I who should be grateful.'

'Sit down, Michael, you look so tired. I am going to get you a drink, I know how you like it and to keep you company I'll pour myself a sherry.' She put both glasses on the table then sat down.

'I haven't seen you since before the funeral,' Felicity said quietly. 'Everything went according to plan, as you said it would. Tim was remarkably composed. Joanna thought he was thinner, I didn't see much difference in him apart from him being pale. He was in conversation with the minister for a while and thanked him for the service.' She smiled. 'The solicitor did his duty and he too got his thanks.'

Michael nodded.

'My biggest worry was how Joanna would behave. She was so unforgiving and bitter. She thought the world of her father and he disappointed her.' She paused. 'You could say Tim disappointed a lot of people.'

Michael nodded again. 'Felicity, I think my visits to Tim have come to an end.'

'I understand.' Felicity tried to hide her shock and dismay. Michael's visits had become a very important part of her life. 'Although you won't be visiting Tim please don't make yourself a stranger, you will always be welcome.'

'Thank you but I think it better that I don't.'

She thought he meant gossip. 'That's all right, Michael, I understand.'

After finishing his drink he got up. 'I'll go now and thank you for the drink. I'll see myself out but be sure to lock up after I've gone.'

'I'll do that. Good night, Michael.'

He raised his hand. 'Good night, Felicity.' The door shut and it was a very final sound. After a moment or two Felicity went to lock it then she slowly walked back to the sitting-room and sat down. A wave of sadness swept over her. She shouldn't have allowed Michael to become so important in her life when she knew it had to end. It was the suddenness that disturbed her. Had he guessed her feelings and been embarrassed? That it might be that made her face burn with shame.

Had it something to do with the night he had taken her out to dinner? She had gone to a lot of trouble to look her best and the admiration in his eyes had been reward enough. She had blushed with pleasure when he said that the deep blue of her dress was the exact blue of her eyes. That evening had been all she could have wished and she had thought it had been the same for him. Before they parted his lips had brushed her cheek and then somehow it had turned into a real kiss, a lingering kiss as he held her close in his arms.

Michael was divorced, he was single again but she wasn't. Had she forgotten or just chosen to forget that she was a married woman?

It was three days after Michael's visit that the letter arrived. She recognised Tim's writing but wondered at the bulkiness. Maybe he was enclosing something but what? She could open it and find out. Before slitting the envelope she filled her cup. She liked two cups at breakfast time, the second one with the morning paper if it had arrived. It had but she would read Tim's letter first.

No enclosures, just three pages written on both sides. She began to read. The tea, untouched, was stone cold and she was shivering though the kitchen was warm. This wasn't happening to her, it was some kind of living nightmare. Felicity forced herself to read it all again and felt sick, physically sick. Upstairs she dragged herself to the bedroom and lay on the bed staring up at the ceiling. She must have slept and when she awoke it had taken a few minutes for it all to come rushing back. The shock of discovery, that first dreadful shock was over and she found herself remarkably calm. It was as though someone had taken charge of her and she was happy to obey. She got a notepad and a pen from the study and went downstairs. She could have done this in the study but the study reminded her too much of Tim. The kitchen table would do for the purpose. First she skimmed the letter for the information she required. There was a name, Hilary Henderson, and an address of sorts. She thought it might be enough to find the person she was looking for. She wondered what would be the best time, other than the evening, to find a young mother at home. She thought back to when Joanna had been a baby. There was no right time, one just took a chance. She would go tomorrow and make it the forenoon. If the young woman was not at home she would return in the early afternoon when the baby might be having his nap.

What did she look like, this woman who had done so much damage? A sudden thought struck her and she stood stock-still. Then with a funny little noise coming from her throat she flew upstairs. There was an angry throbbing at her temples and she put her hand to her head. She knew exactly where she could put her hand on it. The drawer in the desk and it was below a pile of papers. It was there, she picked it up triumphantly, the photograph of a smiling girl with a baby in her arms.

Tim's baby, it had to be. Tim's son, she was sure of it. Much as he had loved his daughter he had longed for a son. Felicity closed her eyes against the pain.

There was work to be done but somehow she couldn't face it. It was impossible to concentrate. This couldn't go on, but there was an excuse for today. Adam Silver was a very understanding man but he might be less so if she was going to neglect the work she was paid to do. One way or another this business had to be settled and quickly. In his cell Tim was protected and away from it all. She saw him as viewing the situation from a safe distance. His part was over, his confession made.

The day dragged on as she knew it would but by evening she had everything settled in her mind. She knew what she was going to do. God gave one strength when it was needed and Felicity felt she had been given extra to deal with this. She wouldn't be able to think clearly until it was behind her. There was no reason to seek advice from anyone since she had no intention of taking it. She would make the decisions, decisions that suited her.

Chapter Twenty-Eight

Felicity felt that she had barely slept and on opening her eyes remembered the reason for the troubled night. The letter — Tim's letter. After the disbelief and then the anger had come a calmness that had surprised her. She had found herself capable of clear thinking and of making plans. She was going to make it her business to come face-to-face with this woman who had destroyed her family. What she would say when she got there, Felicity had no idea, but she was sure the words would come when they were needed. That was yesterday's plans made for today and here she was nervously seeking to postpone the ordeal.

Her head ached, she felt listless and depressed and even wondered if it was worth getting out of bed but, of course, she had to. After five minutes of lying on her back and gazing at the ceiling, good sense prevailed and she got up and dressed.

It was at times like this that one was advised to keep as much as possible to the usual routine. Good advice no doubt and she would take it. First she had to get rid of the headache and two aspirins washed down with water should give early relief. She had her usual breakfast after which she cleared the table, washed and dried the dishes and put them away. Next she went upstairs to make the bed and give the bathroom a quick clean. The rest could be left for another day. One person didn't make much work and really a once-a-week clean was enough.

The car was left in the drive on the odd occasion when she had forgotten to put it in the garage or couldn't be bothered to do so. Felicity was glad that last night hadn't been one of those occasions. There had been overnight frost and the car windows would have had to be scraped.

The Bingham Estate had been much advertised in the press and was easy to find. It was little more than a half-hour's drive from Hillhead. As she approached the site Felicity wondered if she could go through with it and what, if anything, would be gained. Why was she punishing hereself? And what if she broke down and made a complete fool of herself? On the other hand if she were to take cold feet and drive home she might forever regret the lost opportunity. No one knew she was doing this, no one could stop her and since she had come this far she would go through with it.

Felicity stopped at the entrance to the estate. It was still a building site. Some of the houses were no further on than the foundation but one area of the estate was complete with most of the houses occupied. Felicity decided to leave the car where it was and do the rest on foot. The ground was muddy and she had to be careful where she put her feet. Further on she came to an unmade road with a sign that said Laburnum Place. She wondered if the other roads would be given the names of trees. The houses in Laburnum Place looked to be quite small. A few energetic souls had made a start on the garden but most new owners appeared to be content to wait for the spring and the better weather. One of these houses, she thought, could be the one for which she was looking.

Felicity walked slowly trying to decide which door to knock on and enquire if they knew of a Hilary Henderson, a young woman with a baby, who was living on this estate. A few yards on and she knew she had arrived. She needed to look no further. It had given her quite a jolt to see Tim's car in the drive. She had thought it had been sold.

Her stomach was churning with nerves and she jumped when she heard the voice. It came from a woman looking over the fence and holding several small toys in her hand.

'Are you looking for Hilary?'

'Yes.'

'You've just missed her. I saw her from the window pushing the pram, she's probably gone to the shops.' Her hand indicated the direction.

'Thank you, I'll come back later.'

'I'll give her a message if you like.'

'No, thank you.'

The woman gave a small shrug as though she was

slightly offended then turned her back and went into the house shutting the door.

Felicity felt a flood of relief at the small reprieve. It could help her to be more relaxed. Her hands were freezing and she had left her gloves in the car. She would go and get them. Back at the car she wondered about sitting in the car but decided she was better being active. She would take a smart walk to the shops and perhaps have a coffee to put off more time.

There were quite a number of shops and she found herself spending a long time at the babywear. The display was very attractive and on an impulse she went in.

'Can I help you?' The woman was middle-aged with a pleasant smile.

'I was looking for a gift for a baby. A baby boy,' she added.

'A new baby?'

'No, not a new baby, something to suit a one-year-old.'

'Eighteen months to two years I would suggest. Something to grow into.'

'I quite like the woollen suit in the window, the pale blue with little white bunnies.'

'Sweet, isn't it? That is for a two-year-old. I'll get it out of the window and meantime look around.'

'Thank you, I will.' Felicity was enjoying looking at the baby clothes.

'Here we are,' the woman said putting the little suit on the counter. 'Has anything else taken your eye?'

'You have a lot of lovely things but the pale blue is my choice. I'll take it.'

'Would you like it gift wrapped?'

'No, no thank you.'

Felicity was outside with her package and next door was the coffee shop. A quick coffee would be welcome.

Back in Laburnum Place, Felicity knocked on the door of number 6. It was opened almost immediately and Felicity got her first look at Hilary Henderson. She would have recognised her from the photograph. Felicity thought her attractive rather than pretty. She had thick auburn hair inclined to be bushy and a creamy white skin and she was giving Felicity a hesitant smile.

'Miss Henderson?'

'Yes, I'm Hilary Henderson.'

'I am Felicity Morrison, Tim's wife.'

'Oh!' She looked startled then recovered. 'Do you want to come in?'

'Yes, I would if you don't mind.'

She didn't answer, just opened the door wider and Felicity stepped in. There was a tiny vestibule and a glass door leading into the hall. In the hall there was a half-moon table with a glass vase in the middle. The walls were painted cream and the colour was continued into the living-room. Felicity thought it would be the same colour scheme for the whole house. A neutral colour was safe. There was a pram against one wall.

'Is the baby asleep?'

'I'm afraid so,' she smiled. 'Peter is wide awake when other people are asleep.'

'Not much rest for you?'

'No.'

'Will it disturb him if we talk?'

'No, he's sound. You can say what you have come to say, Mrs Morrison.'

Felicity talked. 'I knew nothing about the baby until yesterday. Tim told me in a letter, a long letter full of explanations and apologies.'

'That surprises me. His intention, as far as I knew, was to keep it from you.'

'For how long? How can you keep something like this a secret?'

'Tim thought it possible.' She paused. 'Mrs Morrison, can we get one thing clear,' she said very quietly.

'By all means.'

'Believe me I never set out to wreck your marriage, that was never my intention. What happened should never have happened, but it did.'

'You knew he was a married man.'

'Yes, though he didn't always act as though he were.'

'Tim could be silly, I know that. What you did, Miss Henderson, was nothing short of blackmail.'

Her eyes flashed angrily. 'That is not true.'

'Tim has told me everything.'

'What I did I did for Peter. I threatened Tim about telling the firm because I was desperate and it was to bring him to his senses. All he could do was bite his nails and look worried.'

Felicity hid a smile, she could well imagine.

'Maybe you don't agree, it doesn't matter but I thought Tim's son should have a decent start in life. This is what I demanded, a modest house. That was all. I was going to bring up my son myself. With a roof over our head I could manage the rest. I can hold down a good job, I am very capable.'

'I imagine you are.'

'I have to be with no family to support me.'

'With such a young baby you can't find it easy to work.'

'Not easy but I manage. The agency I work for has been very good to me. They are giving me work to do at home for the time being. I have my own typewriter and I am qualified to do book-keeping or any kind of clerical work.'

Felicity felt a reluctant admiration for this young woman. She wasn't feeling sorry for herself. She had made her demands known and they had been met. Now it was up to her and she was prepared to go it alone and bring up her child.

'Don't you feel responsible for Tim being where he is?'

'No, why should I?'

'You threatened him.'

'What he did was stupid and he knows it.'

'You were asking rather a lot.'

'No more than he could afford.'

'You don't know what he could afford. We have a mortgage on our home.'

The girl shrugged.

'Where did you imagine Tim was going to get that kind of money and why couldn't you have been content with a rented house?'

Hilary crossed her legs and leaned back in the chair. 'The second part of your question I will answer first. No, I was not prepared to live in a rented house. I had to feel secure and I would only be that if the house was fully paid and in my name. That was my one and only demand. Where was Tim going to get the money you ask? Mrs Morrison, you must know the answer to that. Your husband is a lawyer, he was in a well-paid profession. Maybe he didn't have that amount of money in his bank account but he could have borrowed it as others do. But no, not Tim, he wouldn't do that, and forgive me for this Mrs Morrison, but there is a mean streak in Tim. Rather than be charged for borrowing he preferred to—'

'Make use of the firm's money. He was extremely foolish, criminally foolish I have to say, and I can only think that was because he was too worried to think straight.'

'I go along with that, he was sick with worry about you and your daughter.'

'This might be hard for you to believe, Miss Henderson, but had Tim been open with me from the very beginning I could in time have forgiven him. It wouldn't have been easy but we all make mistakes.'

At that moment the baby gave a cry of distress and immediately Hilary was over at the pram with soothing words until the steady breathing began again. Felicity had got up from her chair to look at the infant. Her face softened as she looked at the petal smooth skin.

'He's lovely,' she whispered.

'Can you blame me for wanting the best for him?'

Felicity shook her head. 'No, I can't.' They went back to their chairs. 'You visit Tim in prison?'

'Because he asked me to.'

'That I find very hurtful. He wanted to see you but not me or Joanna.'

'You should see it as a compliment.'

'How do you arrive at that?'

'You and your daughter are too refined. The disgrace of visiting such a place would have been too much whereas I, I'm the tough one, I can take most things in my stride.'

'So can I if given the chance. Oh, perhaps you could answer this. When Tim lost his job he continued to leave home at his usual time and didn't return until the evening. At a guess I would say he was here with you. Am I right?'

'Yes, he was babysitting. My neighbour, for a small charge, would have kept Peter while I got on with some work but that seemed unnecessary when Tim was idle.'

'Tim looking after a baby, I don't believe it. He wouldn't have a clue.'

Hilary smiled. 'Nothing drastic was asked of him. Tim could read the newspapers while Peter slept and if I was very busy he could manage to boil an egg. Peter likes a finger of bread dipped in egg yolk. Why are you smiling? Don't you believe me?'

'I do as a matter of fact and it gives me the answer to a puzzle. I did wonder how Tim had managed to get an egg yolk stain on his shirt when he never eats eggs.'

'Oh dear, I slipped up there, I should have noticed.'

Felicity got up, she hadn't expected to stay this long. 'Thank you, Miss Henderson, for agreeing to see me and for being so honest.'

Hilary got up too. 'Please don't call me Miss Henderson, I hate it.'

Felicity smiled and handed over her package. 'A little gift for Peter, I saw it in the shop window and couldn't resist buying it.'

Hilary looked on the verge of tears, she was obviously very taken aback.

'You – you brought a gift for Peter, I don't know what to say except thank you very much. May I open it now?'

'If you wish. It will be too big but he'll grow into it. Babies get so many gifts of small sizes and so little wear out of them.'

Hilary didn't answer, there had been very few gifts for Peter. Instead she opened the package and exclaimed in delight.

'It's lovely.'

'You like it?'

'How could I not? It's perfect and so very kind of you. Mrs Morrison, you are a very nice lady and I just wish it hadn't been you who had to be hurt.'

'We've all suffered, Hilary, but life has to go on. It is unlikely that we will meet again so let me wish you well. I won't tell you to look after little Peter because it is obvious to me that you are a good mother.'

They were at the door and Hilary opened it.

'Goodbye, Mrs Morrison.'

Felicity nodded and smiled and walked away. This hadn't been at all what she had expected although she couldn't have said what she expected. Certainly not as it had turned out. She liked the girl, even admired her for her strength of character. No one would walk over Hilary Henderson and she had been quick to disclaim responsibility. Tim, she said, had brought his troubles on himself by his criminal stupidity. No one had forced him to do what he did. And that, Felicity agreed, was very true.

Chapter Twenty-Nine

No one knew of her decision to visit Tim and that was the way Felicity wanted it. Had she told Michael the likelihood was that he would have tried to dissuade her. Why, she wondered, did everyone confuse gentleness with weakness? One could be gentle but strong-willed, as she was about to prove or so she hoped. She just wished the weather was better. The winter had started very early which was depressing and this was a particularly cold spell. Not a dry cold spell which could be invigorating but with a swirling mist that hung about and clung to everything.

When she got out of the car, Felicity shivered and not just from the cold. It was at the sight of the grey, harsh building. Folk were entering it with the confidence that came from regular visits. She knew from Michael what the procedure was and how only to approach someone in uniform for directions. Once inside the building Felicity crossed over to a pleasant-faced man in prison warder's uniform. Halfway through he changed his mind about giving directions and instead escorted her to the visitors' room.

Felicity was grateful. 'Thank you, that was very kind of you,' she smiled.

He returned the smile and went quickly back to his duty point. Felicity took a deep breath and went in. Tim was near the door and raised his eyes from the newspaper. Seeing his wife he got awkwardly to his feet. They didn't touch.

'Funny, you know, I had a feeling you would turn up. Sit down, Felicity, it's a hard chair I'm afraid,' he said apologetically.

'This is fine.' She sat down and he did too. 'I didn't bring you anything, I'm sorry, I never thought.'

'No need, my wants are taken care of.' He folded the newspaper and put it neatly to the side. His nails once so well cared for were bitten and ragged. His mother had told her that as a young boy she had had a hard time curing him of the nervous habit. She looked away but he had noticed. 'Nasty habit, I must stop myself doing it.'

She nodded.

'The letter brought you?'

'Yes.'

'I can only repeat what I said in the letter. I am truly sorry for all the distress I have caused you.'

'Why couldn't you have been honest from the start? That is what troubles me most.'

'I couldn't bring myself to do that.'

'You must have known it was bound to come out some time.'

464

'No, not necessarily. Others have got away with it.'

Her lips curled. 'Others have got away with it,' she repeated.

'An unfortunate slip of the tongue, it wasn't what I meant to say.'

'What did you mean to say?'

'Felicity, I wanted to say that I hoped, when I get out of this hell hole, that we could move away to a different part of the country and start afresh. Easier now when I don't have Mother to worry about and Joanna seems to be managing her life.'

Felicity looked at him and remained silent.

'Financially we are going to be just fine. It might take a little while for me to get fixed up with a job but I'll get something, and together with what you are earning from your illustrations there is the money Mother left you. I thought it very generous of her, didn't you?'

'Yes, very generous.'

'Came as a complete surprise, did it?'

She looked at him coldly. 'I had no idea your mother was including me in her Will.'

'Nor me, she didn't mention it.' He moved restlessly in the chair. 'I have to admit to thinking it strange, I mean husband and wife share.'

'Not always.'

'Don't get me wrong,' he said hastily, 'I'm pleased about it, just surprised that's all.'

'Joanna—'

'Joanna has come off all right. What is she complaining about?'

'She isn't, she is pleased and grateful. I was about to say that Joanna suggested her gran had left the money that way so that I wouldn't miss out.'

'How could that happen?'

'Very easily if we don't have a life together.'

'For God's sake, what are you talking about?'

'I am talking about your baby son and his mother.'

'That is all taken care of. Hilary got what she wanted and she won't make any more demands.'

'What are your feelings for Hilary Henderson?'

'I like her but I love you.'

'I went to see Miss Henderson.'

His mouth fell open making him look like a fish, she thought.

'How on earth did you manage that?'

'A little detective work,' she smiled. 'You left enough clues in your letter. As I was saying I paid a surprise visit to 6 Laburnum Place and saw your son and his mother. I went there expecting to hate the young woman but instead I found that I liked her. She has courage and she is honest which is more than can be said for you.'

'Just a minute,' he said angrily. 'You and your holier-than-thou — what about you and Michael Lawson?'

'What about Michael?' she said quietly.

'He's fancied you for a long time, I'm not stupid, Felicity. The only reason Mike came to visit me was to have an excuse to see you.'

She shook her head. 'Michael has been a good friend to you.'

'We were never friends, just colleagues.' Tim leaned

over the table and took her hand in his. 'Why are we saying these hurtful things to each other? I wish I could turn the clock back but I can't and surely we are all allowed to make one mistake.'

'We all make mistakes but sometimes there is no—'

'Don't say it. If we both try we can recapture what we had.'

'No, Tim, and I am not prepared to try because I am no longer in love with you.'

'Because I'll have a prison record, you wouldn't be able to forget that.'

'No, you are quite wrong. If I loved you I could live with that.'

'It is Michael sobersides, well all I can say is that you are well matched,' he sneered.

'I won't answer that, but I will say one more thing before I leave.'

'Go ahead, it might be interesting.'

'I think you more than like Hilary and she is very fond of you.'

'So?'

'So I am divorcing you, Tim, that is definite. All little boys need a daddy and I believe you and Hilary would make a good match.'

'Could be you are right, I promise to give it my careful consideration and in case you haven't noticed visiting time is up.'

'Goodbye, Tim, and good luck.'

He heard the tap-tap of her high heels and then she was gone.

Felicity hurried to her car and felt an overwhelming sense of relief, she was almost light-headed with it. The dark clouds were lifting and giving a clearer view of the way ahead. Was Tim right? Dare she hope that Michael was in love with her? Sometimes she had thought he might be, then put it down to wishful thinking. There was no doubt of her own feelings. When it had happened, when she had known it was love, she couldn't have said, only that it seemed like for ever.

When she arrived home Felicity went straight to the kitchen to fill the kettle. She was very thirsty and she was shaking. That had come on suddenly and she could only suppose it to be delayed reaction. Thank goodness it hadn't happened when she was driving.

The cup of tea helped and so did the fifteen minutes' rest in the chair which she forced herself to take. She wanted to be absolutely calm before she made the telephone call.

Adam answered the phone.

'Felicity, how nice to hear your voice. How are you?'

'I'm fine, Adam, thank you and my reason for the phone call is to ask if I may still take advantage of the invitation to the event in Edinburgh.'

'Of course, this is great news.'

'I'll be coming on my own.'

'Don't worry about that, you will be well looked after, I'll see to that. One lady I know is going to be very happy about this. Cynthia Sutherland was so disappointed when I told her it was unlikely you would manage to come.'

'How is she?'

'Improving by the day or so she says.'

'Adam, I'll need overnight accommodation.'

'Quite a few will be staying and the hotel is offering a special rate.'

'Good. May I leave that with you, Adam?'

'You may, I'll see to it.'

'And' – she hesitated a moment – 'I think to avoid any awkwardness I should tell you—'

'No need, I assure you.'

She frowned, wondering what he meant, then carried on. 'Tim and I have separated, an amicable parting I may add.'

Adam closed his eyes knowing how near he had been to putting his foot in it. 'These things happen, Felicity, but you are all right?'

'I'm fine.'

'That's good. Leave everything with me and I'll get back to you.'

'Thank you, Adam.'

The next morning Felicity was up bright and early. The house got a reasonably good clean and after her coffee break she phoned Rachel to tell her that she would shortly be on her way to Perth.'

'Should I tell Joanna or do you want it to be a surprise?'

'I'll leave it to you.'

'A surprise I think. Drive carefully won't you?'

'I always do.'

Felicity took it easy and enjoyed the run. She parked the car behind the hotel then walked to the front and up the steps. Joanna was behind the reception desk and she held back for a few moments to watch her daughter. She looked very much the efficient receptionist and Felicity felt a glow of pride. This was a far cry from her student year when looking smart was to be ridiculed and not many students thought it worth the risk. Better to go with the crowd. The guest with whom she was dealing was a stout country gentleman wearing plus-fours and a tweed jacket. He was smiling his thanks and only when he moved away did Joanna catch sight of her mother. With a screech of surprise and delight she came rushing from behind the counter to give Felicity a hug.

'Why didn't you phone?'

'I did and we, Rachel and I, agreed to make it a surprise for you.'

'A super surprise,' she laughed as Rachel came over to greet her friend.

'You must be dying for a coffee.'

'I had one before I left.'

'That was a while ago, have another with Joanna.'

'No, I am not going to take her away from her work, we can talk later.'

'Nonsense. On you go, Joanna.'

'Are you sure?'

'Don't argue with the boss. I'll take over, it is good for me to keep my hand in.'

Felicity was grateful. 'We'll talk later, Rachel.'

Rachel nodded. 'I'll phone to have coffee sent over.'

Mother and daughter went along to Rachel's sitting-room and in a very short time the coffee arrived. Joanna poured and they sat with a low table between them.

'Anything new to report, Mum?'

'Yes, quite a lot.'

'Would you mind listening to mine first?' she said sounding bubbly.

'No, go ahead, I'm all ears.' Felicity smiled, pleased at the change in Joanna. The girl looked happier than she had been in a long time.

'It concerns Stuart.'

'I thought it might.'

'We phone and exchange letters and he came to see me here. Aunt Rachel liked him.'

'I'm sure she did, Stuart is a very likeable lad.'

'He's cheesed off with university.'

'Joanna!' Felicity remonstrated.

'All right, fed up with it then. He doesn't see why he should do something his heart isn't in. Just because it is a family law firm,' she added.

Felicity was looking thoughtful. 'Joanna, you will have to go very carefully here. Stuart might be doing this for you and it would be a great pity—'

'If he found that he had made a mistake and blamed me? Don't think I haven't thought of that, I have, and I'm putting no pressure on him. It will be his decision.'

'It might not look like pressure,' Felicity said gently, 'but Stuart might feel he has to do this.' She hesitated. 'What would he do, what kind of job?'

'Farming, something he has always wanted to do.'

'Not easy to get a foot in unless you are from a farming family.'

'His friends in Provence would welcome him.'

'And what about you?' she smiled. 'How would you spend your days?'

'Mum, we have given this a lot of thought and maybe this was all meant, me coming to live with Aunt Rachel. Provence, my dear Maman, and its farms are a magnet for tourists. Thanks to my excellent training I could take in paying guests.'

'I don't know, I really don't.'

'Don't start worrying, nothing is going to be rushed.'

'I'm glad to hear it and my advice would be to encourage Stuart to get his law degree. Whether he uses it or not, he will have it. Should farming turn out to be less than he hoped he has something to turn back to.'

Joanna was frowning at the way the conversation was going.

'We all have to make sacrifices, dear. Don't ask too much of Stuart. He may not be close to his parents but he won't want to lose touch completely. Can't you find it in your heart to forgive Mr and Mrs Milton?'

'No.'

'I can't think that is your final word, I hope it isn't.'

'Leave it, Mum,' she said shortly.

'Yes, it is your life, and now perhaps you will listen to my news.'

'OK.'

'What you are about to learn is going to be a big shock.'

'I'm getting used to those.'

'Rather than tell you about it and I am sure to miss bits out, I want you to read this letter,' she said handing it over.

'No, that is a private letter.'

'It concerns both of us so please read it and take your time, it is quite long.'

Joanna fingered the pages. 'Heavens!' She began to read.

Felicity watched the changing expressions. They went from shocked incredulity to a head-shaking disbelief. Joanna looked up.

'How could he? How could he do that to you?' she said hoarsely.

'None of this was meant to happen, Joanna.'

'He was having an affair—'

'No, I don't believe it was ever that. Your father liked to flirt, he liked to think of it as a harmless bit of fun, only this time things went too far.'

'She tricked him—'

'No, I don't believe that.'

'Mum, get into the real world. It is all very well to think the best of people but you have to face facts. There are some folk out for all they can get.

You can't know that that female didn't get pregnant on purpose.'

'I am reasonably sure she didn't.' Felicity paused. 'What I have yet to tell you is that I went to see the girl.'

'You did? How did you know where to find her?'

'Not too difficult. I had a name and not too many houses in that estate were occupied.'

'What is she like?'

'Young, attractive, slim figure and auburn hair. I went expecting to hate her but I didn't.'

'She is sitting pretty in her own house and at least we know now about the money. Not surprising he couldn't tell us.'

'A very modest house, Joanna. She stuck out for her own home to bring up her baby son and who would blame her for that. In similar circumstances I might have done the same.'

'Not you but never mind, go on.'

'The baby was sleeping. The pram was in the sitting-room and I had a peep.' She smiled. 'Joanna, he is lovely and Hilary will be a good mother.'

'How can you tell?'

'One can, it is in the look. Mother love is very special. Hilary loves that baby just as I loved you. Peter is the baby's name – Peter Timothy.'

'Mum, it has only just dawned on me,' she said with awe in her voice, 'that baby is my half-brother.'

'Yes.'

'That gives me a funny feeling as if – as if – I don't

know how to put it. I have a sort of duty to him because we are related.'

'Yes, he is your half-brother. Peter is the innocent in all this.' She paused. 'I bought a gift before I went and I was glad that I did. Hilary showed such pleasant surprise.'

'Maybe I should send something. What do you think?' She looked at her mother.

'I think you should do exactly what you want.'

'I will then.'

'That isn't all I have to tell you. After seeing Hilary and the baby I went the very next day to see your father.'

'In prison?'

'Where else?'

'You went against his wishes, good for you.'

'I had ceased to consider his wishes and, as it turned out, he half expected to see me.'

'I'm puzzled, Mum, about how this all came about. What made Dad write and confess?'

'Michael Lawson had something to do with it. He is no longer visiting your father and I think they must have had words. Maybe Michael knew and forced his hand.'

'Could be, I suppose. What are you going to do, try and forgive him?'

'I have forgiven him,' Felicity said quietly.

'You will wait for Dad and then take up your life together.'

'No, I won't do that. Had I still been in love

475

with your father I imagine that would have happened.'

'What is Dad saying?'

'He fully expected me to wait for him. The house would be sold and we would make a new life somewhere else.'

'Was he devastated when you said it wasn't on?'

'Not quite devastated but definitely surprised.'

'What are you going to do?'

'Divorce your father and lead my own life.'

'Does he know?'

'Yes. I suggested to him that he should think seriously about making his future life with Hilary and being there for his baby son.'

'How did he take that?'

Felicity smiled. 'Your father was never good at taking advice but I have a feeling he might this time.'

'Would Hilary have him?'

'I think so. In fact I think they might suit each other. He won't walk all over Hilary.'

'The way he walked over you.'

'That was partly my fault. I was too soft.'

'Thanks for coming to tell me all this, Mum,' Joanna said, getting to her feet. 'I should get back to the desk now. Are you going to show Aunt Rachel the letter?'

'No, I wouldn't do that. The letter was for our eyes only. I'll tell Rachel enough for her to know what is happening.'

Chapter Thirty

When Felicity arrived home from Perth in the early evening she felt completely drained but satisfied that the day had gone so much better than she had dared hope.

After putting her coat over a chair to be taken upstairs later, she kicked off her shoes, wriggled her toes and stretched out on the sofa with a cushion for her head. She might as well be comfortable she decided as she gathered her thoughts together. It was frightening to think how much her life had changed in a few short months. She shook her head in perplexity. How could she ever have believed that the day would come when she would want to end her marriage? At the beginning there had been so much love, where had it gone? She did recall when love had cooled a little. It was when she became aware of her husband's flirtatious ways. She had felt humiliated and hurt but she had not taken him to task. Had she done so she knew what he would have said. He would not have denied anything, just laughed about it and assured her that it was only a harmless bit of fun and she had nothing to worry about. Perhaps that was true but it had continued to annoy if not exactly worry her.

Marriage was for ever was what she had been taught and one had to accept the bad with the good. If she were to be completely honest with herself Felicity couldn't recall a time, if one excluded the present day, when she had been really unhappy in her marriage. Tim wasn't a bad person just shallow, and she knew that he had never wanted this to happen. As he had tried to explain in that letter, he had been caught up in events that had spiralled out of control and his usual clear thinking had deserted him. Felicity could spare some sympathy for Tim but she could never bring herself to live with him again. That was why she had gone to the prison, to tell him that to his face. A letter would not have sufficed, he had to be made to understand that she meant what she said and there was no possibility whatsoever of her changing her mind. That would be difficult for Tim to grasp since she had always been in his shadow. He had always made the decisions and she had always gone along with what he decided.

Those days were over and not before time. The new Felicity was someone who could look after herself. She was doing it now and making a reasonably good job of it. Her success with her illustrations had given Felicity confidence in herself. There was a great deal of satisfaction in doing something one loved and being fortunate enough to get paid for it. Her job was rewarding in every way. She no longer had to worry about money and the legacy from her mother-in-law was her little nest egg.

Maybe she should get herself up now and make a cup of tea. She felt rested and the small activity would do her good. The kettle was filled and put to boil and the tea made. Felicity carried it through to the sitting-room, put the cup and saucer on the low table and sat in a nearby chair. She took a few sips then turned her thoughts to her daughter. Felicity felt she no longer knew Joanna as she once did and she had been apprehensive about how she would cope with this latest blow. How to tell her, what would be best. She had thought long and hard about the wisdom of giving Joanna her father's letter to read, knowing how strongly he would have objected to that. In the end she was glad that she had.

Tim must have taken a lot of time and care to get it right and the letter was a masterpiece in detail. He had pleaded his own case with a great deal of skill while at the same time managing to show sufficient remorse and regret for his mistakes.

Joanna had shown a surprising maturity and she had been remarkably calm. Not that she was letting her father off, far from it, she had made it clear to Felicity that she abhorred what her father had done but there were no visible signs of distress. This was regrettable behaviour but it was nothing compared to the disgrace she felt in having a father in prison. The break-up of a marriage was commonplace and surely it was better to part company than stick with a marriage that had failed. Felicity found herself nodding. The young had different values from their parents but who was to say who was right and who was wrong. She was remembering it all and felt a smile tug at her mouth. That had been a nice moment when Joanna had acknowledged the baby. And then the show of delighted surprise when it suddenly struck her that this tiny babe, given the name Peter Timothy, was her half-brother. He was family, they shared the same father and rather than pushing him away, ignoring his existence, she had mentioned buying a gift. The girl's heart was in the right place.

Felicity thought that Joanna's apparent ease in accepting the situation between her father and Hilary Henderson could be explained by her own troubles. She had enough of them. She and Stuart had some important decisions to make. And talking of decisions Felicity had an important one to make. She desperately wanted to see Michael and to hear his voice. Should she wait until tomorrow or phone him right now? If she waited until tomorrow the call would be taken by his secretary and she would want to know who was calling. Michael might not mind that but she couldn't be sure. She had to remember his abrupt departure from her house and no proper explanation. Before she could talk herself out of it Felicity got to her feet, went into the hall and made the call. It rang and rang and she was on the point of putting the phone down when it was answered.

'Michael Lawson speaking.'

'Michael, it's Felicity. I was just about to ring off.'

'Sorry, I was called to the door, a woman collecting for some charity. I'm glad you didn't ring off.'

'Michael, if you can spare the time and if you are agreeable I would very much like to see you.' Maybe she shouldn't have said, very much, that could be too much and scare him off.

'Why should I be anything but delighted?'

'Well, that last time—'

'Ah, my abrupt departure, that was unforgivable. I need to explain that to you.'

'Maybe you could do it tomorrow evening unless that is inconvenient?'

'I do have a meeting I must attend and it will likely go on until about eight. Is that too late?'

'Not at all. Eight or thereabout would be fine.'

'How are you, Felicity? I should have asked that first.'

She laughed. 'I'm not sure, I think I'm all right which has to be surprising in the circumstances. Michael, I am going to ring off and I'll see you tomorrow evening.'

'Looking forward to it. Goodbye, Felicity.'

She had expected an overactive brain to keep her awake but instead she went out like a light and awoke feeling refreshed and ready to face the new day. She washed and dressed and went downstairs to prepare her breakfast. Michael would have eaten so she wouldn't have an evening meal to prepare. There was enough in the house for her own needs and shopping could wait until another day. The hours stretched ahead and she would use the time to get ahead with her illustrations.

It was almost nine o'clock before Michael showed up and Felicity was chewing her thumbnail nervously and trying to decide whether the meeting had gone on longer than expected or, dreadful thought, he was having second thoughts about coming to Holmlea. When the ring did come she almost flew to the door.

'Felicity, I do apologise,' he said stepping inside. 'Is this too late? Shall I go away and come back another evening?'

She was smiling. 'Of course it isn't too late.' She closed the door and went ahead to the sitting-room. The soft light came from the two table lamps and there was a cheerful fire.

'This is cosy,' he said rubbing his hands.

'Sit down beside the fire and get yourself warm.'

He waited until she was seated before taking the chair she had indicated.

'Honestly there are some folk who talk for talking's sake. The business could have been completed a good hour earlier. To tell you the truth I was very nearly walking out.'

'I'm glad you didn't, I would have felt responsible.' She got up. 'Michael, help yourself to a drink and I am going to see about coffee.'

'What about a drink for you?'

'I don't think so.'

'Come on, I don't like drinking alone.'

'All right a small sherry and I do mean small.'

Felicity was glad of the few minutes in the kitchen to get a grip on herself. She wanted to appear cool and calm which she wasn't. There was no reason to feel nervous but she did. She busied herself and when everything was on the tray she carried it through and put it on the table. She poured the coffee and put the milk and sugar beside Michael for him to help himself.

Felicity sat down and took a few sips of her coffee. 'You must be wondering why I asked you to come.'

'I was very pleased to get the invitation.'

'Were you, Michael?' She paused. 'I was almost afraid to ask you after—'

'My abrupt departure on the last occasion I was here. I can't blame you. All I can do is apologise and try to explain.'

'No, don't. An explanation isn't necessary, I assure you. There is a lot I have to tell you – I want to tell you. Is that coffee to your liking? The shop was out of my usual blend.'

'Very much to my liking, thank you.'

'Tim sent me a long letter.'

'Oh.' He closed his eyes for a moment.

'What he had to tell me came as a total shock to me.'

Michael was looking wretched. 'Felicity, I am the one to blame. I forced his hand. I'm afraid I gave Tim an ultimatum, either he came clean about Hilary and the baby or I would tell you myself.'

She nodded. 'I know, it was all in the letter.'

'All I can say is how very sorry I am. I had no right, no right at all, to take that on myself. It was none of my business as Tim was quick to tell me.'

'Don't apologise, Michael, I am very glad you made it your business.'

'Is this you being generous to make me feel better?'

'No, it is not. This is something I had to know and I'm thankful it is all out in the open.'

'You had no idea?' he said, sympathetically.

'Absolutely not. I never dreamt of anything like this and finding out was simply dreadful.' She shook her head. 'Can you imagine the kind of strain Tim must have been under to keep this to himself? It must have been—'

'Hell, sheer hell, I don't doubt, but I am more concerned about you. Tim after all has only himself to blame.'

'We all make mistakes and I can feel sorry for Tim. Having me know about it must be a huge relief. He couldn't bring himself to tell me. Mind you, looking back, there were clues but I was too blind or too stupid to see them.'

'Or too trusting.'

'Whatever.' She took another drink of her coffee. 'The kitchen table was where I used to do my sketches until I decided to make use of Tim's study and his desk. There was no reason to open the drawers but this particular day I was on the hunt for paper-clips and to cut a long story short a snapshot fell out of a bundle of papers. It was of a young woman and a baby.'

Michael was watching her.

'I had a good look but the girl was unknown to me.'

'I gather it was Hilary.'

'Yes.'

'Surely you must have wondered what it was doing in Tim's desk?'

'I was mildly curious until I remembered the time when Tim had to clear his desk in such a rush. I supposed it had got there by mistake. I do recall thinking someone would be sorry to have lost it. Actually it was a good likeness and don't look so startled. I felt a visit was called for.'

He said nothing just looked at her admiringly.

'I am very glad I did go.' She paused. 'Had you met her Michael?'

'I had seen her around the office but she never worked for me.'

'I both liked and admired her. She has a lot of pluck and was not at all the awful creature I was expecting to see. That baby will be well looked after, she will see to that. She got the house and she would work to keep them both was what she said. There was no false modesty either. She is efficient and can just about state her own terms.'

'Which is just about true,' he laughed. 'We've had a few temps to help out and Hilary by all accounts was by far the best.'

Felicity's face softened. 'The baby is lovely. He was in the pram in the living-room and slept all the time I was there apart from a few moments when he whimpered and opened his eyes. Lovely blue eyes and I think I saw a likeness to Tim.'

'You are an amazing woman, Felicity.'

'Far from it but I am stronger than I used to be,' she smiled. 'Strong enough to do what I should have done before. I went to see Tim and to have it out with him.'

'On your own,' he said incredulously.

'Of course and it was very easy. A very nice warder took me along to the visiting room.'

'Not many come in for that kind of treatment. Directions are all they get.'

'Maybe I didn't look bright enough.'

'Maybe he wanted to be in the company of an attractive woman.'

'How kind. Seriously, after I had said my piece I felt sorry for Tim. He didn't mean any of this to happen and I'm sure not a day passes when he doesn't regret what he did.'

'Can you forgive him?'

'I already have. As I told him I just wish he had been honest from the beginning.'

'He wouldn't want to lose you, he wasn't prepared to take the risk.'

'That is what he said.'

'Once he got over the shock of seeing you he must have been overjoyed.'

'He said he half expected me to turn up, that the letter would bring me.'

'Which it did.'

'Which it did, Michael. I am coping very well and I find that living alone holds no terrors for me,' she said feeling she should explain that.

'You've had a little practice.'

'Yes I have and as I say I'm doing all right. Mind you, the fact that I have no real financial worries helps. What I earn keeps me, and Tim's mother remembered me in her Will which was marvellous of her. That is my little nest egg.' She paused. 'Michael, this has been all about me, I want to hear about you and what is happening in your life.'

'Perhaps something is about to happen.'

She looked at him sharply.

'Paton & Noble don't know it yet, but I would be expecting to work out my notice before long.'

She mustn't let him see her shock and disappointment and managed a smile.

'That is a surprise. Where are you going if you are at liberty to tell me?'

'Of course I can tell you. I have finally decided to go into partnership with a friend of mine, we were students together.'

'Oh, you spoke of that before. Isn't it somewhere in Border country?'

'Yes.'

'What made you decide? Was it the divorce and a need to make a new start somewhere else?'

No, my darling, he said silently. You are the reason. I had hoped you would leave Tim and there might be hope for me but I should have known better. Tim, no matter what he has done, holds your heart.

'Something like that.' He was silent for a few moments. 'What are your plans once Tim is free?'

'I don't know. This house will have to go on the market. Tim will have two houses to sell, this and his mother's.'

'Tim is bound to get a job and, of course, you will go where the job is.'

She was looking at him strangely. 'I imagine he will, but Tim and I have no future together. Haven't I made that clear?'

'Not to me you haven't.'

'Then let me put that right. I am divorcing Tim and I shall go my own way. Where I shall end up I have no idea which is rather nice. I can choose. As for Tim I hope that he and Hilary will make a life together and give that little boy a proper start with a mummy and daddy.'

'Tim must be devastated.'

'At losing me, no he won't be. We were drifting apart long before any of this happened. Sorry, Michael, I am neglecting you. More coffee?'

'No thank you.'

'Then excuse me while I take these through to the kitchen,' she said stacking them on to the tray.

'The table I shall see to, I know where it goes.'

When she got back Michael had moved to the sofa and indicated that she should join him.

'In a minute,' she said, doing some unnecessary tidying up.

'This is not you putting a brave face on it, is it?'

'Am I broken-hearted that my marriage is ending? No. I suppose, like you, there is a feeling of failure.'

'You didn't fail, far from it. Tim had a very loyal wife.' His arm had been on the back of the sofa but now it was round her shoulder and he had drawn her close to him. 'About living on your own, is that what you really want?'

'That would depend. I mean if the right person were to . . .'

'Propose?' he suggested.

'Then I might accept for some time in the future when my freedom comes through.'

'I didn't dare hope, I thought you saw me only as a friend.'

'That was all we could be, just good friends.'

'And now,' he said softly, 'I can tell you how much I love you. From the very first moment we met you were special to me and you will never know how much I envied Tim.'

Felicity's eyes were shining as she turned to face him. There was a future. The idea of spending the rest of her life with Michael was sheer bliss. She had dreamed of it but never imagined it would happen. Now that it had she felt almost bereft of speech. When she could she asked him about the job in the Borders.

'I will only take it if you would be happy there.'

'I could be happy anywhere with you,' she said softly.

'We could take a trip to the Borders one day soon and have a look around.'

'Look at houses?'

'Yes. We shall need a fairly large house, I mean two of the rooms will be made into studies, one for you and one for me and a guest room, perhaps two, for Joanna and Trudy should they want to come and spend time with us and, speaking of Joanna, how is all this affecting her?'

'To be honest she is wonderfully relaxed. This is so much less awful than having a father in prison. She is all right, Michael. Stuart is back on the scene and they have their own problems to sort out.'

'Felicity, once you find the house of your dreams.'

'Once we find the house of our dreams,' she corrected him.

'You must live there.'

'Where will you be?'

'Until we can be married I shall make do with furnished accommodation.'

'Won't you mind?'

'Of course I'll mind, but I would expect to spend a great deal of time with you.'

'I should hope so.'

'Look at the time,' he whispered, 'it is almost midnight. What are the neighbours going to think?'

'I don't give a damn, they can think what they like.' And that was the truth she thought.

'Good girl,' he said, as she snuggled in and midnight struck.